THE SPARK OF RESISTANCE

WOMEN SPIES IN WWII

KIT SERGEANT

CONTENTS

ALSO BY KIT SERGEANT

Historical Fiction:

355: The Women of Washington's Spy Ring

Underground: Traitors and Spies in the Civil War

L'Agent Double: Spies and Martyrs in the Great War

Be sure to join my mailing list at www.kitsergeant.com to be the first to know when my newest Women Spies book is available!

Contemporary Women's Fiction:

Thrown for a Curve

What It Is

This book is dedicated to all of the women who lived during the Second World War and whose talents and sacrifices are known or unknown, but especially to the real-life women upon whom these characters are based.

And to Norman Fanter, Sr, Harvey Feeley, Charles "Chuck" Pfeifer, and Marin Sergeant: thank you for helping keep the world free, especially for your great-grandchildren, my beloved Thompson and Belle.

GLOSSARY OF TERMS

Abwehr: German Military Intelligence

Boches: a derogatory term for Germans

FANY: First Aid Nursing Yeomanry; members of the all-female charity often worked for the SOE

Feldwebel: a German military rank, approximately equivalent to a sergeant

F Section of the SOE: the French Section of the British Special Operations Executive

Gestapo: Nazi Secret Police

Halifax: a bomber, mostly used for dropping supplies and parachuting agents

Hudson: a Lockheed light bomber, used for reconnaissance and agent pick-ups

Huns: another derogatory term for Germans

Lysander: another bomber, also used for reconnaissance and agent pick-ups

MI6: British Secret Intelligence Service

Wehrmacht: the German armed forces

Whitley: another bomber, also used for reconnaissance and agent pick-ups

PROLOGUE

MAY 1945

era Atkins barely recognized the woman standing alone on a platform at Euston railway station. She was clad in a bedraggled coat, unusually thick for this time of year, that hung too loosely on her frail figure. "Yvonne?"

The woman turned. At only eighteen, she had been one of the youngest hired, and still bore the look of a child, though now a starved one with dark circles around her eyes and matted blonde hair.

Miss Atkins had the mind to hug her, but was afraid she'd either break the girl's bones or Yvonne would collapse under the weight of her former boss's arms.

"I'm sorry to keep you waiting," Miss Atkins said instead. "Was your journey all right?"

Yvonne attempted a smile. "As good as could be expected."

Pleased as Miss Atkins was to see Yvonne, her thoughts were eclipsed by one, niggling inquiry. She voiced it after they had settled into the car, Miss Atkins sitting as straight as always, Yvonne's head leaning against the seat. "What do you know of the other girls?"

Yvonne's eyes flew open. "The other girls?"

"Yes. Who else was with you?"

Yvonne closed her eyes again, scrunching her face in recollection. "I saw Alice at Ravensbrück, and they said there was another British woman there, Lise, but she was in solitary confinement and I never got a good look at her face. And I encountered Louise, Nadine, and Ambroise at Saarbrücken when I was taken there, temporarily. I remember going into a prison hut and seeing them, and thinking, 'The whole women's branch of F Section is here.'"

Miss Atkins mentally matched the code names with the real identities of her girls: *Didi Nearne, Odette Sansom, Violette Szabo, Lilian Rolfe, and Denise Bloch*. Nearly forty women had gone into the line of fire, and most of them, except Yvonne, were still missing in action. "I've been looking into it, but I was notified that there had been no British females held at any concentration camp."

Yvonne turned to her. "I never told them I was a British agent. I thought I would have a lighter punishment if they believed I was French. But I knew that Louise, Nadine, and Ambroise felt differently." She shook her head sadly. "They were moved out of Torgau the night before I was."

"And what do you think became of them?"

"I don't know," was Yvonne's terse reply. "I'd heard they were brought back to Ravensbrück, same as me, but I never saw them again."

They arrived at Yvonne's father's house. Miss Atkins reached out, as though to touch her former employee's tangled curls, but thought better of it. She folded her hands across her lap. "Don't worry," she told Yvonne as the driver helped her out of the car. "I will find them."

CHAPTER 1

MATHILDE

*H*e moved through the crowded restaurant with the lithe limbs of a Gypsy. Indeed, his eyes were as black as a Roma, though his hair was styled like a Frenchman's.

Those dark eyes now focused on Mathilde. "Do you mind if I sit here?" He did a good imitation of a Parisian accent, but she could detect a hint of something else.

"Not at all." Jeanne leaned forward, the décolletage of her velvet top dipping low. She patted her impeccably coiffed hair. "And you are?"

"Armand Borni." He glanced over at Mathilde, as if to weigh whether or not his perfectly French name fooled her.

Mathilde stretched her lips into a thin smile. It was one of those dull evenings at La Frégate, the kind when she questioned just what she was doing there. Jeanne had requested their usual seat near the entrance, the better to watch the comings and goings of wealthy Parisians attempting to escape the gloom of their lives under the Occupation.

The undoubtedly fictitious Armand arranged his napkin on his lap. He met Mathilde's eyes for a split second before hers dropped, focusing on his teeth, which, like his accent, were obviously fake. She tucked a strand of her own unruly dark hair back behind her ear as she caught sight of a pair of German officers entering the restaurant.

The crowd immediately fell into a palpable hush, the way

Mathilde's classmates used to at boarding school whenever the subject of their gossip came into earshot.

"Feldwebel Müller," Monsieur Durand, the owner, rushed over to the newcomers. "How good of you to come." He reached out to pump the German officer's hand a few times before turning to his companion and repeating the gesture.

Armand's face showed the tiniest frown before it returned to its carefully staged neutral expression.

Jeanne looked up. "It's Feldwebel Müller and Leutnant Fischer again. They come here every Friday night."

Mathilde, still unversed in the Wehrmacht ranking system, glowered as Monsieur Durand led the men to his best table, where an older couple was already seated. The restaurant owner gestured for a passing waiter to assist in moving the couple. "Those Nazis must be pretty important for Durand to oust the Bergers from their table."

"Of course they're important," Jeanne responded pointedly. "Even though they are low-ranking officers, if La Frégate becomes part of the *Gaststätten für Reichsdeutsche*, Monsieur Durand will probably get a pay raise."

"What is the *Gaststätten für Reichsdeutsche*?" Mathilde's tongue stumbled over the unfamiliar German words.

"It means 'restaurants for the German Reich.' My husband's printing house was told to make pamphlets for the visiting German soldiers. They have lists of all the vendors promising accommodations for them, even..." Jeanne leaned forward to whisper, "brothels." She sat back and took a sip of wine. "Any business in the pamphlet gets special treatment and won't be subject to rationing." Her voice dropped once more. "Not to mention Durand's mother-in-law is half-Jewish. He probably hopes to work his connections so she doesn't get deported."

Mathilde, never the type to conceal her emotions, shuddered. It wasn't enough to see the grayish-green suited soldiers marching around her beloved city. The notion of watching them ravage a meal in her favorite restaurant made her sick to her stomach. "I don't understand how we let them into Paris so easily in the first place, and now here we are, catering to their every whim."

"What do you mean?" Jeanne asked. "You are not wishing that we were still fighting them, are you?"

Mathilde sighed. "No. What was to be done was done. But I still hate that they are here. I cannot stand to see the swastika flying over the Eiffel Tower."

Throughout the women's conversation, their new guest had remained silent, but chose that moment to speak up. "You cannot just hate the Germans."

"What do you mean?" Mathilde asked, turning toward him.

He laughed. "I've only known you for a few minutes, but even I can see that you deal in absolutes. You cannot simply hate them, you must despise them with every thread of your veins."

She put a manicured finger to her lips as she glanced at the oblivious Germans across the room, indulging in a steak meal even though today had been declared a meatless day. "Why leave anything half-finished? If one is to hate, one must do it fully."

Armand's expression deepened for a brief moment before he dug into his salad, stabbing at a piece of lettuce with more force than necessary.

"There are ways, you know," Armand's statement as they left the restaurant was carefully casual.

"Ways to what?" Mathilde asked, her eyes on Jeanne, who was several steps away, trying to wave down a cab.

"Defeat the Nazis."

"I'm not sure if you know this, but our soldiers refused to fight them here." Mathilde spoke deliberately slowly, as though Armand were half-deaf, not concealing the fact she recognized he was a foreigner. "We signed a peace treaty that resulted in our soldiers being captured as prisoners of war. And now they've taken over our city and shame us every way they can." She nodded toward a nearby placard that had been printed in German above the old street sign. Because of the blackout, the streetlights remained unlit and the French sign was barely visible, but the black-lettered words on the German one were quite legible, though unpronounceable. *As bulky and awkward as a swastika*, Mathilde thought. *As unwelcome as the Germans themselves.*

"I am well aware of Paris's plight," Armand replied. He leaned in closer, his voice low. "What would you think if I told you we could establish communication with London to pass on our own propaganda? To encourage our compatriots to challenge the Germans any way they can?"

Mathilde's mouth dropped open.

Armand glanced at Jeanne's back. "I cannot say anything else here. There are spies everywhere. But not the right kind."

Jeanne finally succeeded in her task and turned to Mathilde as the cab stopped.

"Aren't you coming?" Jeanne demanded. "Curfew is in half an hour." They all looked at their watches. Mathilde had once thought time was beyond being owned, but the Germans had even taken control of the city's clocks and turned them all to Berlin time, two hours ahead of Paris. As a result it seemed even the sun was reluctant to confront Hitler; with winter looming, it set earlier and earlier in the evening, shrouding the already-dispirited city in even more darkness.

Armand shut his pocket watch with an audible click as Mathilde waved her friend along.

"Come to my apartment," Mathilde said once Jeanne's cab had pulled away. She wrapped her thin fingers around Armand's and led him down the street.

"I know nothing of espionage," she told him when he was comfortably seated on her couch.

"But you know France... much more than an exiled Pole."

Mathilde nodded to herself as she fixed them chicory coffee. "You're Polish. What happened to make you hate the Germans so much?"

He laughed. "Besides being from Poland?" His tone dropped as Mathilde sat beside him. "I was a fighter pilot before I was taken prisoner by the Nazis. They sent me to a POW camp."

Mathilde's eyes widened. "Did they torture you?"

"I managed to escape before they could do their worst. A widow hid me in her house and then gave me her husband's papers." His voice grew hoarse. "But my brother is somewhere in one of those camps. And my parents are still in Poland." He put his hand over hers. "You have to help me. I will not accept that Poland is defeated."

She squeezed his hand. "I think the same of France. And now that the occupiers refuse to hire me as a nurse, I have more time on my hands."

His face hardened. "I should warn you that this work will be extremely dangerous—"

6

"I don't mind the risk," Mathilde interrupted. "As you said, I do know people in most parts of the country, especially in the Free Zone." This included her husband, but she of course made no mention of him.

He took on a dreamy look. "Can you imagine you and I plotting against the Germans? You'd become the Mata Hari of the Second World War."

"Mata Hari? Didn't she betray her own country?"

He laughed and Mathilde couldn't help but smile. She paused to mull over what Armand was proposing. In what he would probably claim was her characteristic, all-in way, she decided to be the best spy the Allies had. "If we are to be working together, I suppose I should know your real name." She said it both out of curiosity and as a test, to see if he trusted her fully.

He did not hesitate. "Roman Czerniawski."

It was her turn to laugh. "That's quite a mouthful. I shall call you 'Toto.'"

"Toto? As in the dog in the *Wizard of Oz?*"

"Yes." She touched his arm. "As in my dependable sidekick."

"Oh, so now I'm your sidekick? It was my idea in the first place."

She shrugged. "You're cute, with big brown eyes just like Toto."

"What's your full name?"

"Mathilde Lily Carré."

He put his hand on her knee. "I think Lily suits you better than Mathilde. I'm going to call you Lily from now on."

She bestowed her most seductive smile on him, thinking he wouldn't be the first man to refer to her by that particular name.

CHAPTER 2

ODETTE

The gray-haired gentleman took a sip from his teacup before asking, "Tell me, Mrs. Sansom, how did you come to have those pictures of Calais's beaches?"

"Were they helpful? I've been wanting so badly to do something for the war effort, so when I heard that the Royal Navy was requesting pictures of the French coast, I sent them in right away." Odette frowned. "I know they were just panoramics of my brother and I when we were growing up, but—"

"Oh, they will work quite well. I take it you were born in France?"

"Yes. I moved to England when I got married, but I grew up in Amiens, and my mother is still there, suffering under German rule. My father was a banker, but he died at Verdun in the Great War."

Major Guthrie cleared his throat. "As did many. At that time, we thought it would be the war to end all wars, but now, with the Nazis…" He trailed off, appearing at a loss for words, the way Englishmen often were when the subject of Hitler was brought up.

"If it would help, I could draw you a picture of the Amiens village square."

He seemed relieved at the digression. "I think we probably have one in our files." He set his teacup down before clearing his throat again. "Mrs. Sansom, I believe that your French background might be quite useful to the War Office."

She sat back. "The War Office? What would the War Office want with me?"

"We need people who are familiar with France, and who speak the language, of course."

After a moment's thought, she replied, "I do want to help as much as I can, but I have three young girls, and my husband, Roy, is fighting on the continent." Major Guthrie's face fell, so she continued, "Perhaps I could do some translating for you? Or house soldiers?"

"Yes." He attempted a wan smile. "Raising three children on your own is quite a large undertaking. But I would like to pass your name on. As you said, we might have some part-time work for you."

"Of course."

It wasn't until she got back to Somerset that she realized Major Guthrie had neglected to return her photographs.

A few weeks later, Odette was sitting in a lounge chair, taking in the pleasant country sun when her youngest daughter, Marianne, dumped a packet on her lap. "Here's the mail, Mummy." Marianne waved an opened envelope in the air.

As it fluttered, Odette caught sight of a red cross printed at the top. "What's that?" she asked, her heart beginning to race. *What if Roy was hurt?* The prospect of losing her husband didn't fill her with as much fear as one might expect. Their relationship had been strained long before he went off to war, and she had more than proven herself capable of being the sole provider of care for her children. Still, she'd hate to have to tell her daughters that their father had been wounded... or, worse yet, killed.

"It's Uncle Louis," Françoise, her oldest daughter said sadly, sounding much older than ten. She sat at her mother's feet. "He's in a hospital in Paris."

Odette snatched the letter from Marianne and scanned it, but there was not much more information about her brother than what Françoise had already stated.

"But you can't go and visit him, can you?" Marianne's voice had taken on the little girl's whine it often did when she was upset.

"Even if you could go, you can't stop Grandma's house from getting overrun by Nazis." At eight, Lily, the middle child, was ever the realist.

"No," Odette refolded the note. "No, I cannot go to France. I wish I could."

"What's this?" Françoise's deft fingers lifted another official-looking envelope. "Who is Captain Selwyn Jepson?"

"I don't know," Odette answered wearily, longing for a moment of peace, away from prying young girls.

"He's asking you to visit him in Whitehall next week."

Odette gathered up the rest of the letters, the one from Jepson falling to the bottom of the pile. "It probably has something to do with that part-time job Major Guthrie mentioned."

"Are you going to work for the war?" Françoise demanded.

"If I can fit it in, I'd like to do some little thing," Odette replied.

"But you aren't going to leave us, are you, Mummy?" Marianne's voice grew even higher as her eyes reddened. They'd already been forced to evacuate their London home for the safety of the Somerset countryside, away from the Luftwaffe bombers that had been terrorizing the city for the past year. It had been enough uprooting for the six-year-old. For all three girls, and Odette herself, for that matter.

Odette reached out to pat Marianne's hand. "Of course not, *chérie*."

CHAPTER 3

DIDI

*D*idi tossed yet another rejection letter onto the floor. "The Women's Royal Naval Services only wanted drivers."

Her sister Jackie, older by four years, nodded at the paper on the ground. "I must have gotten twice as many as you. The WRNS sent me that exact same letter. I probably shouldn't have told them I can't drive in complete darkness with all of these black-outs."

"Do you think…" Didi cleared her throat. "Did it ever occur to you that we shouldn't have come here?" It hadn't been easy getting out of Occupied France, even though they were British citizens, but they'd eventually managed to escape via Spain. The entire journey had taken nearly six months, and now that they were finally free, relatively speaking, they were having difficulty securing jobs.

Jackie raised a thin eyebrow. "What would you have done, stayed in France? You know the Germans regarded us as nothing but foreigners."

"We lived in France almost our whole lives. Britain feels more foreign to me."

"Well," Jackie bent down and picked up the letter. "If you want to go back and be subject to the will of the Nazis, then do it. I'm going to stay here and do what I can to fight the Germans." She crumpled the paper. "If only they would let me."

· · ·

A few days later, Jackie received a note from a Captain Selwyn Jepson of the War Office asking for an interview.

"I told you my time would come," Jackie told Didi.

Didi snatched the notice from her sister. "He says you 'possess qualifications which may be of value in the war effort.' What does that even mean?"

"Why, I suppose it could mean nothing at all," Jackie replied loftily, clearly not believing her own proclamation.

Everything had always come easy to her beautiful older sister and Didi felt the need to take Jackie down a peg. "Especially if they find out you can't drive during the blackout."

The words hit their mark and Jackie's smile drooped into a frown.

The pangs of guilt were too much for Didi. "On the other hand, maybe this Selwyn Jepson is an important man and needs you for a task no one else can do," she added. "The return address is the War Office, after all."

Jackie nodded. "I'm sure you'll get a similar letter soon."

But she didn't, and, as the date for Jackie's interview came closer, Didi grew even more anxious.

"Be sure to tell them about me," Didi called after Jackie as she left for the War Office wearing her nicest dress, a smart blue one sprinkled with white polka-dots.

Jackie turned back and waved a gloved-hand. "I will."

"And good luck!"

Jackie straightened her straw hat before continuing down the street.

Didi spent a few tense hours waiting for Jackie to return. She meant to clean the small room they shared in the boarding house, but found it hard to concentrate on any one task.

"Well?" Didi asked by way of greeting once her sister came home.

"Well what?"

"What did Captain Jepson want?"

"It was a job as a driver for FANY—the First Aid Nursing Yeomanry."

"A driver? Did you tell him you can speak fluent French?"

"Yes."

Something about Jackie's behavior wasn't sitting right with Didi. "And the driving at night thing? He didn't mind about that?"

"No."

Now Didi knew Jackie was hiding something—it wasn't like her sister to give one-word answers. "Why would they hire you for a job any English girl could do?"

Jackie cast her eyes around the empty room. "Okay, as it turns out, I'll be working with a brand-new organization. The SOE."

"What does that stand for?"

"Special Operations Executive." The pride was obvious in Jackie's voice. "The French section. They wanted me because I grew up in France and can speak the language fluently. The FANY driver thing is just a cover."

"A cover for what? What work will you be doing?" Her eyes widened as a thought occurred to her. "Are they sending you back to France to be a spy?"

"Listen," Jackie put a hand on Didi's arm. "I've already told you too much. I promised Captain Jepson I wouldn't say anything about this to anyone."

"What about me?" Didi asked. "Did you tell them you had a sister who also speaks French?"

"Of course," Jackie replied distractedly. "Now I have to figure out what I'm going to wear to my first training session."

Finally, a month after Jackie's interview, Didi received her own meeting request from Captain Jepson. She too put on her best dress and, after placing her gas mask in her purse, set off for the address given in the letter, which turned out to be a sparse room in the Victoria Hotel.

With his beautifully-cut gray suit and groomed salt-and-pepper hair, Captain Jepson looked nothing like a military recruiter. After asking Didi to sit in the lone chair opposite his desk, he started by telling her his task was to recruit women for the SOE.

"Why women?" Didi asked.

"In my opinion, women are much more suited for this type of position than men. Women have a far greater capacity for a cool and lonely courage."

It didn't take Didi long to realize her suspicions about her sister working for an espionage unit had been correct. "I would like to be considered for the same sort of thing that Jackie is doing."

His gaze traveled from her jaunty hat to her sensible-heeled shoes. "I think you might be a bit young to be an agent."

"I'm nearly twenty-two, and only four years younger than Jackie."

He nodded before picking up a paper. "Your full name is Eileen Mary. Where did Didi come from?"

She shrugged. "The family legend is that Jackie had a hard time saying 'Eileen.' Didi rolled off the tongue easier, so Didi I became."

"And are there other Nearne children?"

"I have two brothers. My middle brother, Frederick, is in the Royal Air Force."

"You are the baby of the family." Jepson made a mark on the paper in front of him. "Your father is a doctor, so the family is obviously well-off, and you were educated in a Catholic school."

The finality in his voice, as if he'd already rejected her, made Didi's heart beat faster. "When the Nazis came, we were forced from our home. They told us we were 'enemies of the state,' even my mother, who was born in France, because she married an Englishman. They confiscated most of our possessions, so we are no longer considered, as you put it, 'well-off.' Jackie and I had to learn to chop firewood, cook, and clean."

"Why do you want to go back to France now so soon after leaving?"

"Both Jackie and I want to do something to fight Germany. That's why we came here to England in the first place." Didi could tell she was losing the battle. She spread her arms out. "Look, I can keep my own company. Should the need arise, I can work all alone. I can do anything you ask. I just want to be able to do something for the war. Even a little thing."

"Some little thing." Jepson made another mark on the paper with his pen before settling his gaze back to her. "You seem to be a bright young woman, though you've also led a sheltered life. I'm not sure you are ready to be a field agent, but perhaps we can start you as a wireless operator or a decoder."

She folded her arms across her chest. While she was disappointed that she wouldn't be heading back to France as an SOE operative any time soon, Jepson hadn't completely refused her. "I'd prefer to learn how to work a wireless." She figured the training for that line of work would be the most beneficial when she finally convinced Jepson to put her in the field.

CHAPTER 4

MATHILDE

*M*athilde accompanied Armand to the Free Zone in central France. Since the French government had been pushed out of Paris in the Armistice, the town of Vichy had become its temporary seat. Vichy was a world away from the Occupied Zone, and even maintained the old French time. To Mathilde, it seemed the light was brighter, the autumn leaves more colorful, the fall weather more pleasant.

Armand and Mathilde took separate hotel rooms at the Hôtel des Ambassadeurs and she spent the first few days wandering about the town, not exactly sure why she was there. Armand was never around; she would occasionally catch him deep in conversation with other men in the lobby, but that was the extent of their companionship.

That is until she heard a knock on her door a few evenings after their arrival in Vichy.

"Where have you been?" Mathilde asked him by way of greeting. "Why did you invite me here if you insist on ignoring me?"

"I am sorry, Lily."

She wanted to continue her tirade, but he held up his hand. "Wait until you hear what I have to say." She took the seat across from him at the little table as he went on, "I've been tasked with an important mission by our mutual governments in exile. They have given me permission to create a network of agents in the Occupied Zone."

Her eyes widened with appreciation. "Toto, that's fabulous!"

"Yes," he agreed, his voice rising in excitement. "And I want you to help me run the network."

"Me?"

"Yes. You are the only person I know who possesses the necessary qualities for this kind of work. You are intelligent, brave, and, I suspect, ruthless. Not to mention I trust you implicitly."

"Oh, Toto!" She clapped her hands. "This is exactly what I've been wishing for!"

He stood up, inviting her into his arms. "Just think, I will be the general, and you will become my chief of staff." He led her across the room in a waltz.

She quit dancing, regretfully letting his strong arms drop from their embrace as a thought occurred to her. "General Borni, what shall we call this network of ours?"

His eyebrows lowered in thought. "Well, we will be working in the French underground to provide London with information on how to stop the Germans. What about the International Allies?"

She shook her head. "Too long. What about Interallié?"

He reached for her again, pulling her even closer. "That's perfect," he stated before his lips met hers in a long, lingering kiss.

Armand spent that night in Mathilde's room. The next day he gave up his room to move into hers and they fell into a pleasant routine. In the mornings, she helped him learn to read French and tried to coach the Polish out of his accent. In the afternoons, Armand attended meetings while she went out for walks around the town or took in the waters at the Vichy spa. Each night before they made love, Armand would fill her in on everything he'd discussed with his contacts, Mathilde occasionally interrupting with what she considered intelligent questions.

Once the business of the day was concluded, the burgeoning couple often turned to small talk, with Armand carrying on most of the conversation. He told her of the time he'd been walking by a Paris train station, passing stretcher after stretcher of wounded French and British soldiers. "I could just see their faces drop once they caught sight of all those Germans surrounding them on the platform."

Mathilde nodded, remembering how she felt the first time those grayish-green uniforms came marching through her city.

"But those men refused to give in. One of them propped himself up on his stretcher and sang the opening lines of 'It's a Long Way to Tipperary.'"

"It's a long way to go," she added, quoting the unofficial anthem of the British army.

He gave her a sad smile. "Nothing can defeat guys like that." After a moment of silence, he added, "My fellow men in the Polish Air Force were cut from the same cloth. I hate to think of them now, suffering at the hands of Hitler. If the Widow Borni hadn't given me her husband's passport, I might never have gotten out of that region. They would have captured me and put me back in the POW camp."

Mathilde heard the tears in his voice and marveled at how someone so intelligent and proud could sometimes seem so vulnerable. She decided to change the subject. "Was she pretty, this Widow Borni?"

Armand rubbed his eyes before giving her a curious look. "Not nearly as pretty as you. Nor as quick-witted," he added, reaching out to twirl a strand of her black hair. "After I escaped, I vowed I would do everything I could to help the Allies win." His sensual lips eased into a slow grin. "Just think of all we can accomplish once we get Interallié up and running."

Mathilde lifted her chin. "We will rid Paris of those Boches once and for all."

"Once and for all," Armand repeated before leaning in for a kiss.

The next evening Armand was late getting back to the room and Mathilde went downstairs, knowing he was conferencing in a small room near the hotel lobby. She kicked off her shoes before sitting down in a large leather armchair to wait for him.

With each passing hour, Mathilde grew more bored, wishing she'd brought a magazine to read. She hadn't realized that she'd been anxiously scratching at the arm of her chair until a couple of American journalists paused to gawk at her. "What are you, a cat?" one of them asked.

"Excusez-moi?"

An amused grin on his face, he nodded at her curled hand and light scratches on the leather.

"Of course she's a cat!" Armand's voice boomed. "She is *ma petite chatte*," he added in poorly accented French, extending his arm to her.

THE SPARK OF RESISTANCE

Later that night, after they'd once again made love, Armand declared that from then on, her Interallié code name would be 'The Cat.'

Armand left for Paris again a few days later, leaving Mathilde to learn the game of spying. On his direction, she went to the Deuxième Bureau, France's military intelligence agency, which, like the government, had been relocated to Vichy.

Armand had given her the address on the Boulevard des Etats-Unis but when she arrived it looked nothing like the spy lair she'd pictured. From the outside, the nondescript building resembled a warehouse, and the threadbare carpeting and concrete walls of the entryway did nothing to dispel that impression.

She was greeted by a man in full military dress. "Can I help you?" His voice was more growl than anything else.

"I'm looking for the man in charge."

His scowl momentarily disappeared. "I suppose that would be me." He stuck out a gruff hand. One eye was hidden by the glare of light underneath a monocle; the other never left her face. "Captain Sardanapalus."

Mathilde refrained from commenting on his tongue-twister of a last name. "I'm here to discuss your efforts with assisting the Parisian objective in ridding the country of Germans."

His visible eye became steely. "I have no idea what you are talking about."

Mathilde refused to become flustered. "I have been sent here by Armand Borni."

No sign of recognition flashed in the Captain's face. "Under the Armistice, we are tasked with protecting Marshal Pétain's government."

This must be a test, she concluded. "We both know that Pétain is a puppet for Hitler."

Sardanapalus sighed. "Follow me," he told her before opening a door off the rear of the lobby. He led her up the stairs to a small, bare room.

"So you wish to join Armand Borni's network." Sardanapalus sat down in a rickety wooden chair behind an equally rickety desk.

Mathilde balked at the word *join*. "For your information, I am helping him run Interallié."

"You? A woman?" He gave her a dismissive look. "If that's so, then what do you need from me? I imagine you know all about intelligence gathering: recruiting agents, running networks, and using secret inks."

"Well," Mathilde spread out her hands. "Not really. That is probably why Armand sent me to you."

"What exactly will be your contribution to this network, then?"

Clearly being on the defensive isn't going to work with this ornery captain. Mathilde decided to switch tactics. "I realize that collaborating with Marshal Pétain, and therefore being in bed with Hitler, was not your idea. You want to help the Allies, but," she cast a pointed look at his threadbare shirt, "you need gainful employment to keep a roof over your family's head."

Sardanapalus rubbed his forehead. "So be it. If Armand wants to have a woman as his second-in-command, I suppose he could do worse than hire the likes of you."

Mathilde refrained from pointing out that she was actually on equal footing with Armand as head of the network. She leaned forward. "Now, about these secret inks.

For the next week, Mathilde met every day with Sardanapalus. He taught her the ins and outs of espionage, including the fundamentals of Morse code and the importance of pseudonyms.

"Mine will be 'The Cat,'" Mathilde said without hesitation.

Sardanapalus nodded. "Very fitting." He picked up an onion and handed it to her. "Peel this while I juice an orange."

"This seems like the makings of an extraordinarily distasteful lunch," she replied.

He gave her a scornful glance. *If I were to give him a new code name, it would be Sardonic-palus, simply from the looks he gives me,* Mathilde thought.

He mixed the onion peel into the orange juice with a paintbrush before handing her the brush and a sheet of paper. "Write something down on this."

She did as he bid as he continued, "Instruct your contacts to run an iron over this seemingly blank piece of paper, and voila, everything you've written will be revealed."

Mathilde stared in wonder at the bare sheet. It was true: her painted words had disappeared.

Later that night she tried ironing the paper, and it was just as Sardanapalus had said. "Interallié" appeared in her own flowery handwriting, and underneath that, "The Cat + Toto."

On her last day of training, before Mathilde was to return to Paris, Sardanapalus cautioned her to never let Armand out of her sight. "One never knows what goes on in the heads of foreigners," he stated dryly.

"Oh, I trust Toto—Armand—implicitly."

He frowned. "Have you learned nothing? Never trust anyone implicitly, especially not a hot headed Pole."

Her lips curled into a fake smile. "You're right, of course, Captain. I regret that I am leaving, for I'm sure you have much more knowledge to impart."

He waved his hand. "I've taught you as much as I can. The rest you will learn on your feet."

She practically floated back to the hotel, her steps lightened by the prospect of seeing Armand again in only a few days' time, and officially beginning their collaboration.

"Ah, Madame Carré," the desk clerk proclaimed when she entered the lobby. "You have a visitor."

"Is it Monsieur Borni?" she asked, the hope obvious in her voice.

"No. Monsieur Carré has come to call. Your husband, I believe," he added unnecessarily.

In the corner of the lobby, a man, much leaner and harder than she remembered, arose from her favorite chair.

"Maurice." Mathilde's voice was barely above a whisper. "How did you find me?"

"Your father, of course. You know he always keeps tabs on you."

She silently cursed Papa and his old-fashioned sense of chivalry. "I take it you have been given leave."

"I have." Maurice glanced nervously around the lobby. "Shall we adjourn to your private accommodation?"

The last thing Mathilde wanted was to be alone in a room with her husband, but she acquiesced anyway.

"France is lost," Maurice declared once his wife had handed him a whiskey. He sank onto the bed. "You must come back with me to North Africa. We will take up our lives as we did before the war."

"You cannot be serious." She poured herself a generous helping of sherry before seating herself primly in an armchair. "Great Britain will aid us in our fight. France must not give in fully to the Nazis."

"No, Lily, you are wrong. The Nazis are the new world-order and Britain will eventually lose. If they were smart, they would conform to Hitler's regime just the way France has."

For the second time that day, Mathilde resorted to her fakest, widest smile. Her husband had never been one to fight, always wanting to take the easy, cowardly way out. So different from Toto. "If you want me to go with you, I must collect my things from Paris."

"Of course." He patted the space beside him on the bed. "I've been waiting so long for you."

She considered telling him she'd mentally ended their relationship when he went off to war. They had been living in scorching Oran at the time, and as she stood on the pier of the North African port, the sea seemed as infinitely blue as the sky above. She'd hated North Africa —as she'd told Maurice, she was always 'bored, bored, bored'—and almost even welcomed the thought of war when Hitler began his relentless annexation of Europe. Maurice had been given the choice between shipping off to Syria or the Western Front. The fact that he had chosen Syria, where he would most likely never see any action, made him seem even more spineless in her eyes. She herself had always lived for adventure and unpredictable situations. Maurice had not known it, but Mathilde had decided right then on the pier that she would declare her husband dead and join the fight on the Western Front as a nurse.

In her mind, their marriage had been over for nearly two years, but there was no sense in getting into it now. "I'm sorry, Maurice, but it is my time of the month. We cannot lay together as husband and wife right now."

His face sank, his underdeveloped chin tucking even more into his neck. Mathilde resisted the urge to slap him. "Actually, I suppose I might as well go back to Paris as soon as possible," she stated casually. "Tonight would be as good as time as any."

Maurice choked on his drink. "Now? You know how difficult it is to move past the demarcation line."

"I have papers. Remember, I used to work as a nurse." She forced her voice to take on a soothing tone. "And you should stay here. Relax. Take in the waters tomorrow, and the next day, while you wait for me to return."

Maurice nodded, his eyes heavy from exhaustion. "Yes, and then we will continue our lives the way we did before the war."

After she'd hastily packed her bag, Mathilde left her sleeping husband for the last time. She planned to contact a lawyer to draw up divorce papers as soon as she returned to Paris.

CHAPTER 5

ODETTE

Odette hurried through the London streets, late as usual, wishing she had more time to enjoy the bustle of the city, which was so different from quiet Somerset. The skyline was familiar enough, after all, she'd lived there for almost five years, but she was unaccustomed to the multiple bombed-out basements and scarcely-standing buildings still bearing their Blitz scars.

The address she was given was the Victoria Hotel, a once opulent building which had clearly been requisitioned for the Ministry of War; its intricately tiled floors were now scuffed and the brocade wallpaper faded.

The man behind the desk in Room 238 looked to be in his early 40s, with graying hair and soft brown eyes. His impeccably-cut suit contrasted with the surroundings: a small dusty room, empty apart from his desk and chair and another hard-backed chair placed across from him.

He gestured for her to sit and, after introducing himself as Captain Selwyn Jepson, stated in French, "At Major Guthrie's request, we've made some inquiries into your past, and we are quite sure that you will make a good fit for our new program."

"Inquiries?" Odette plopped into the rickety chair. "What do you mean? I wanted to help out, so I sent some photographs to the War

Office, and here you are, digging into my deepest secrets." She meant the comment to come off lightly but Jepson bristled anyway.

His face was stern as he replied, "I assure you, we've only uncovered enough information to establish that you are exactly what we need."

"Captain," Odette's eyes traveled around the sparse room but there was nothing on the bare walls to indicate what she was getting into. She settled her gaze back on Jepson. "Who do you think I am? It sounds as though you are recruiting me to be some kind of secret agent. I can do no such thing: I'm a war wife and a mother of three."

He lifted a pen out of an inkwell only to set it back down. "Our biggest obstacle thus far has been the language barrier. There are not many Britons that can speak fluent French—and those that attempt to go over without a proper accent often don't come back. What we really need is someone who was born in France, who knows the territory, the customs, all the little subtleties that only a native would."

She took a deep breath to calm her racing heart. "I'm sure there are plenty of French men who found themselves in England before the invasion happened."

"Yes, that is so. But women can move about France far more freely than men at this point in time."

"You mean with the Nazis occupying Paris, I take it?"

He nodded. "How do you feel about Nazis?"

"I hate them. Doesn't everyone?"

He steepled his hands. "Do you hate all Germans?"

"I suppose not. Just those that sympathize with Hitler. The other Germans are to be pitied."

"But some of those very same Germans killed your father."

She paused before answering in a quiet voice, "You've done your research quite well, Captain. Yes, my father was killed at Verdun." She pinched the palm of her hand, trying to suppress the tears that were threatening.

Jepson must have sensed that a change in subject was needed. He picked up a sheet of paper. "I have your files from the convent school you attended. The nuns said you were intelligent and respectful, with the exception of occasionally demonstrating a rebellious spirit."

Odette couldn't figure Jepson out. Was this an official interview or not? At any rate, it was a simple enough task to provide him with the information he seemed to be seeking. "I had polio at seven, where I temporarily lost both the use of my legs and my eyesight. When I finally was whole again, I promised myself I would live life to the fullest." She nodded at the file. "Occasionally that meant disobeying the nuns."

"How long were you blind?"

"Almost three years. The doctors told Mother I would never see again, but she refused to give in to that diagnosis. She took me to what our neighbors in provincial France would call a 'witch doctor,' but, sure enough, he eventually cured me."

"You must have developed incredible senses to compensate for your lack of eyesight during that time."

"If you say so." She gave him a hesitant smile. "What exactly would you have me do, Captain Jepson?"

"How would you like to go to France and take on the Nazis?"

"You cannot be serious. I can't just jump on a boat and travel across the Channel."

"No, but we have other ways of inserting our agents into occupied zones. If such a thought interests you."

"It does not interest me at all, Captain. As I've mentioned and as you've probably read, I have three young daughters."

"Françoise, Lily, and…" he picked up the file. "Marianne."

"Yes. And, seeing as their father has already gone off to fight the Nazis, they need me more than ever." He did not reply, so she continued, "It's not that I don't love France—I do—but my home is here now."

He ran a hand through his salt-and-pepper hair. "So you are content to just stand by and watch your native country succumb to terrorists?"

"I am more than willing to do my part, as long as that does not include marching straight into enemy territory, and leaving my girls without a mother. Despite what that might say," she gestured toward the file, "I am not the right person for that type of work."

Jepson sat back in his chair. "I think you are. And before we send you 'marching into enemy territory,' we would have you undergo a rigorous training, where we would certainly determine whether I am right… or you are."

She stood. "Thank you for your confidence, but I am afraid I have to decline your offer."

Jepson escorted her to the door before handing her a piece of paper. "That's my direct number, should you change your mind. And God help the Nazis if you do."

His final statement echoed in Odette's head as she walked toward the train station. How could Jepson think a woman like her could do anything to the Nazis? She didn't possess any extraordinary abilities; she wasn't an athlete or a genius, and she was definitely not capable of the brute strength it would take to do the sort of things he suggested.

Travel to France, Odette thought, an amused smile forming. *Me.* But the smile faded as quickly as it had appeared. What if everyone thought as she did? What if Churchill or de Gaulle decided they couldn't defeat Germany and let Hitler roll over the rest of Europe as Marshal Petain did in France? The train arrived, cutting off her thoughts, and she stepped aboard.

She stared out the window as the train passed her favorite park. It was barely recognizable: the ornate iron fence had been removed, probably in order to forge more Allied weapons, and most of the green lawn had been turned into vegetable gardens to grow food for the soldiers. She forced away all of the questions that were dancing through her mind, determined to only focus on what she would make her girls for dinner that night.

For the next few weeks, the mail brought more bad news: the Nazis had officially confiscated her mother's home, her wounded brother had developed an infection, and her husband Roy had been shipped to the North African front. When Mother phoned to tell her that some of Odette's childhood friends had been captured and sent to internment camps, it was the last straw.

As Odette hung up the phone, tears formed in her eyes. She went to the kitchen window to watch her girls play tag underneath the large willow tree in the front yard. Here she was, cowering in the safety of Somerset while the Allies were fighting to keep her children—and the rest of the world—free. Could she really be content with watching other people sacrifice everything while she herself did not even lift a pinky for the war?

But I'm not that courageous. Not like my father. Her mind flashed to another willow tree, this one in France, next to where Father was buried. Her grandfather used to take Odette and her brother to visit their unknown father's grave every Sunday and tell them stories about how he was as a child. One day Odette finally worked up the courage to ask how he had died.

"He survived the Battle of Verdun, unlike most," Papi replied in his strong voice. "But after your father had returned to camp, he found out that two men in his squadron were missing. He went back to the front line to search for them, only to be slain by a German machine gun."

Louis had begun whimpering and Odette's face crumpled as she stared at the dirt beneath Father's gravestone.

"Don't you cry. That was the type of man your father was... willing to sacrifice himself to save others." He dug out a medal from his pocket. "Look here. This is the *Croix de Guerre*. They gave it to me after he died. Only France's bravest receive medals like this."

Louis, his tears forgotten, reached out to touch the medal.

Papi hung it around Louis's neck. "Someday there will be another world war, an even bigger one, and it will be your duty, and yours too, Odette," he paused until she met his eyes, "to be as fearless as your father was."

Papi's words echoed through her head now as she walked to the telephone. She knew what she had to do: contact Jepson and let him know she was willing to do the training. In her mind, failure was inevitable. Once they realized she was no spy, she could return home satisfied that she had at least tried.

A few days later Odette left the girls with family before once again boarding a train to London. Jepson had instructed her to meet with the head of SOE's French section, Major Maurice Buckmaster.

This time she made her way to 6 Orchard Court in the West End. The large limestone building with Greek columns was just off Baker Street, behind Selfridges, and looked nothing like what she had pictured.

A tall man in a dark gray suit answered the door. He stepped aside and gestured for Odette to come in, though he never asked for her name. He led her down the art deco style hallway, the sweeping ferns nearly touching the parquet floors, to an equally ornate apartment door. After unlocking it, he ushered her inside. "Please wait here," he told her in a deep voice.

"In the bathroom?"

He nodded as he shut the door, locking her in. Odette walked across the plush pink carpeting and sat gingerly on the side of the bathtub, an enormous onyx one, in the most unusual waiting room she'd ever encountered.

A few minutes the butler returned and guided her to the office, where a trim, clean-shaven man was seated. He rose as the butler left and came over to pump her hand as though she were his mate about to engage in a game of squash. "Mrs. Sansom, I'm delighted you've come."

Odette tried not to show how taken aback she was at his casual manner. "Thank you, Major Buckmaster."

"You can call me Buck." Introductions concluded, he sat on the corner of the large desk, his thin legs dangling in front of her. "Tell me about yourself."

"I'm sure you've been informed that I have three children."

"Children? My God, you do not look old enough to have children."

Odette smiled sheepishly. "I may appear young, but in my thirty years on this Earth, I've been through a lot." She told him of overcoming polio and rheumatic fever as a child.

"There are even more risks as an agent of the SOE," Buckmaster cautioned her. "It takes a toll on both your body and your mind. You will have to live a double life, lying to the majority of people you will meet. And if you get caught, there is not much we can do to save you, for doing so could compromise the entire operation."

"Save me from what?"

"Whatever the Gestapo have the mind to do to you: prison, forced labor camps, death by firing squad or hanging."

Odette couldn't help from swallowing audibly.

He looked over at her. "Did you want to reconsider?"

"No." *I'm only committing to the training*, she reminded herself. Surely the Gestapo couldn't do anything to trainees.

"And your husband, does he approve of this?"

Odette leaned forward, her feathers unexpectedly ruffled by this energetic man. "My husband is stationed in North Africa. I didn't have time to ask his permission, but, once he receives my letter, he will be made aware of my decision."

"Well, if you say so." He jumped down from the desk and dug through a drawer. "You are going to need an alias." He pulled out a file and flipped through it. "What about Céline? We like to give our agents at least a semblance of familiarity about their codename, and seeing as how it's your middle name…"

"Céline will do just fine."

He nodded before shutting her file. "Then I believe it's time for you to meet Miss Atkins."

"Miss Atkins?"

"She's in charge of the ladies of F Section." He motioned for her to follow him down the hallway. His walk was predictably jaunty. "You'll like her," he called over his shoulder. "All her girls do." He paused at yet another door, knocking twice before opening it.

Miss Atkins was tall and slim, of a seemingly indeterminate age, though her hair held only a hint of gray. She carried herself across the room with great dignity, her grayish-brown eyes warm as Buckmaster introduced her to Odette.

"Please have a seat," Miss Atkins told her, gesturing toward a sage-green armchair. Her accent was so perfectly English that it almost sounded foreign.

Odette nearly sank into the overstuffed chair.

"She'll take good care of you," Buckmaster said. He gave a little wave before shutting the door.

Miss Atkins lit a cigarette before turning to Odette. "So you grew up in France?"

"Yes. In…"

"Amiens." Miss Atkins blew out a ring of smoke. "I know all about your background."

"Oh," Odette replied. Unlike Jepson and Buckmaster, Miss Atkins had no need for a file folder to remind herself of the facts of Odette's life.

"And your girls, have you made arrangements for their care while you will be away?"

"Yes, I've enrolled them in boarding school. Should the training extend to their school breaks, they will stay with family."

"Your husband Roy's I presume, since your mother is still in France and your father is deceased."

It was not a question, but Odette answered in the affirmative anyway. "With Roy's aunt and uncle."

"Good." Miss Atkins put out her cigarette, her rings flashing in the dim light. "If you need any help finding suitable schools or childcare,

I'd be happy to assist. I've also arranged lodging for you in London before you leave for training."

"If you'll pardon me, Miss Atkins," Odette leaned forward. "I was wondering how I would explain…"

"How you will explain your new position to your daughters?" She let out a tinkling laugh after Odette gave an astonished nod. "Yes, you cannot disclose to them that you are working for the Special Operations Executive." She got up and opened the closet door. Her voice was slightly muffled as she continued, "You can tell them you are employed by the First Aid Nursing Yeomanry, or FANY." She reappeared holding a khaki-colored dress. "The higher-ups love creating acronyms for anything having to do with the war. There's the SOE, the FANY, the RAF, and their counterparts, the WAAF."

Odette accepted the proffered dress. "The WAAF?"

"The Women's Auxiliary Air Force. A few other women have been recruited from there, as well as the real FANY." She handed a red beret and black belt to Odette. "I suppose Buck told you that the FANY is a civilian unit. Since that is your cover, if you are caught as a civilian engaged in sabotage behind enemy lines, you will be punished as such. Not that those Nazi fools pay much attention to the Geneva Convention, anyway."

"I understand." Odette fingered the cloth of the beret. "Miss Atkins, do you mind explaining to me exactly what the F Section and the SOE for that matter does? No one really told me what it is I'm actually expected to do in France."

Miss Atkins lit another cigarette. "They never do. They're full of secrets, Jepson and Buckmaster. My lips are also supposed to be as tight as a clam but," she opened her mouth wide and let out a wreath of smoke, "I can clarify the essential information."

She sat in the armchair across from Odette, her legs primly folded in front of her and showing not a hint of ankle. "Prime Minister Churchill saw the need to build a network of insurgents in German-occupied territories to sabotage the Nazis, to—as he put it—'Set Europe ablaze.' This type of guerilla fighting was not something the British military was willing to commit to, so the SOE was established as a sort of clandestine army to create secret soldiers." She leaned over to ash her cigarette. "The Resistance is young, but it's thriving. Our network of agents has thus far recruited hundreds of members, blown up communication towers, and bombed munitions factories."

"I'm not sure I'm capable of any of those things."

She laughed. "The women of the F section are usually used for couriers or wireless operators. Besides, none of us are exactly military, except for Buckmaster, of course, who was on one of the last boats out of Dunkirk. Jepson was a mystery writer, I was a secretary, and many of our male operatives were lawyers, doctors, even scientists."

"And I'm just a mother," Odette replied with a shrug of her shoulders.

"No, don't say that." Miss Atkins gave her a searching gaze. "Jepson is a master at judging people in the first minute he meets them. He thinks you have great potential, and so do I, by the way. In the assessment he gave me after your interview, Jepson stated, 'God help the Germans if we can ever get her near the Nazis.'"

"He said something similar to me." Odette didn't feel the need to explain she'd never actually be going to France. She was certain that Buckmaster and his ilk, including the hospitable Miss Atkins, would soon realize that Odette wasn't F Section material and would release her from training as quickly as they had hired her.

That night in her hotel room, Odette stood in front of the mirror, outfitted in her new uniform. Even to herself she looked different, older, more severe somehow. The cut of her cheekbones stood out in her normally round face and there was a tenacious look in her eyes she'd never seen before. Gone was Mrs. Sansom, the wife and mother. In her place was Céline, the FANY recruit. She looked like the person Miss Atkins and Captain Jepson claimed would be a threat to Germany.

What if I really could do it? Odette put her hands together and pointed her fingers like a gun before aiming at the mirror. Once she'd regained her eyesight, she'd been a crack shot with a pistol as a girl. Surely that could be useful. Maybe Captain Jepson was right about her senses being more keen because of her blindness. And of course she was familiar with the French countryside and could speak the language fluently.

She straightened the red beret and then tightened the belt at her waist. *God help the Nazis… I will be going to France.* Her reflection grinned back at her, making her cheeks round once again.

CHAPTER 6

MATHILDE

In no time, Mathilde managed to find a spacious apartment in Paris's Étoile district that was perfect for their new line of work. She showed her French Red Cross papers to the landlady, explaining that she and her "cousin" would be renting it. It had two bedrooms, but Armand installed himself in the main one, along with Mathilde. He did not have many belongings save for the same bag he'd brought to Vichy, and a seemingly endless supply of maps, which he hung on every available wall space.

Mathilde did her best to make the apartment look cozy, though Armand would have been content for it to resemble an office at Army headquarters. The first night after they moved in, she went out to buy a bouquet of dried roses. She wasn't usually the type to appreciate flowers, but for the first time since she'd stopped being a nurse, she felt as if she had a purpose, that she was contributing to the war effort. And she wanted to celebrate. Armand had yet to mention the fact they were trying to erect an espionage network to cover the whole of Occupied France with practically no money, and, on Mathilde's part, very little experience. He was full of enthusiasm and ideas and Mathilde squashed her doubts, refusing to make him forfeit either in the face of their enormous undertaking.

When she returned, Armand was sitting at the wobbly table he'd rescued from the garbage and now used as his desk. A blank pad of paper sat in front of him. He dipped his pen in ink thoughtfully as Mathilde asked what their first task would be.

"To recruit agents, of course," he said, scribbling something on the paper. "That will be your mission."

"Mine? How will I know they are friendly to our side? And why would they listen to a woman, for that matter?"

Armand's pen paused. "They'd probably rather listen to a woman than a Pole. Not to mention you speak French much better than I." He resumed writing. "There is a man I was told to contact by the name of Maître Brault, a prominent lawyer. We will pay a visit to him tomorrow. But, *ma petite chatte*, we are going to need a lot more people. Do you know of anyone else?"

Mathilde thought fast. "René Aubertin. He's a childhood friend, and I believe he's back in Paris."

Once again, Armand stopped writing. "Do you trust him?"

She nodded. She had run into René on the street in Orleans just after it had been rumored that the Germans were pushing toward Paris, when the city had been filled with French troops and refugees. Mathilde had been ordered to help establish a new hospital there and René was a lieutenant in a tank battalion. They'd found time to meet for a drink, where they had, of course, discussed the war and the threat of an armistice between France and Germany. René had stated that he believed what Churchill promised: that the Allies would conquer Hitler in the end.

A niggling concern now popped into Mathilde's head and she voiced it aloud: "How do you know this Maître Brault will listen to us?"

Armand reached into his briefcase to display a white envelope before tucking it back inside. "He will."

Maître Brault had a friendly, wide face and graying hair. He admitted them into his office without hesitation, but frowned when Armand announced their business. "That sounds awfully dangerous. If the Nazis get wind of what you are doing, they won't hesitate to imprison or even murder you."

Armand remained unconcerned. "That's only if they catch us."

Maître Brault's lips turned up in an amused smile. "I can see that you are determined to establish this so-called network of yours. What is your ultimate goal?"

"Why, to overthrow Hitler of course," Mathilde replied. "To see our respective countries liberated."

Maître Brault's smile faded, and Mathilde felt as though she had said the wrong thing.

Armand must have sensed it too. "Don't you see?" He spread out his arms. "The Nazis might be winning right now, but it won't always be so. The SOE has been tasked by Winston Churchill to 'Set Europe Ablaze.' Interallié will be that spark, the one that will light the fire of Resistance. Eventually we will have enough flames to consume Germany and set France free."

Maître Brault leaned forward. "How do I know that you aren't a Nazi yourself, trying to recruit me so that you can arrest me?"

Mathilde awarded him a mental point. How can you be sure anyone is who they say they are these days?

Armand pulled out the white envelope he'd shown Mathilde the night before and handed it to Maître Brault. "You can trust me."

Maître Brault opened the envelope and scanned the letter inside. "This is from my nephew."

"I met him in Vichy," Armand replied. He pushed forward a small picture which had fallen out. "As you can see, this photograph is of his wife and new baby."

Maître Brault's face softened. After he'd examined the photo, he tucked it and the letter back into the envelope. "All right. I will help you. I am going to Bordeaux in a few days. I know some contacts there who will be of use to your network."

"Thank you, Maître Brault," Mathilde replied. "You will not regret this."

He carefully placed the envelope in his desk drawer. "I hope not."

That night Armand took out a marker and divided his map of France into seven sections, labeling them A-G. "We will need to find leaders for all of these sectors as well as agents to work under them."

Mathilde frowned. "You're talking at least fifty men, or women."

Armand put the cap on his marker. "It won't be that difficult. Like Maître Brault, each man will have his own contacts, and they will know of some more, who will know of some more. It will grow organically." He reached out to help her up from the couch. "You'll see."

He led her into the bedroom. His lovemaking had changed since

Vichy; it had always been passionate, but now it seemed even more energetic and intense.

Afterward she lay on his chest, listening to his heartbeat, wondering if she could sync hers to his. Soon he was snoring, and Mathilde sat up to light a cigarette. Maurice, her husband, had always wanted to cuddle for hours after sex, and it was usually she who went to sleep, if only to get him to stop talking.

Mathilde ashed her cigarette, thinking that, for all Armand claimed to trust her, and she him, there was something he was keeping from her. *Maybe he has a secret spouse somewhere as well.* She glanced lovingly at his sleeping form. With the exception of his guttural snoring, he reminded her of a helpless little boy. *As long as he is sharing my bed, I guess I can't fault him for whatever his secret is.* With that, she stubbed out her cigarette and then turned off the light.

The next day Mathilde telephoned her friend René Aubertin, who agreed to meet her on a street bench near his place of work as a civil engineer.

René was waiting for her when she arrived. After a warm embrace he sat down and patted the spot beside him. "What's this all about?"

Mathilde was too excited to sit. "Remember when we met in Orleans and talked about getting back at the Germans?" He gave her a blank look as she continued, "Well, I know how we can do that now."

"Mathilde," René looked up and down the abandoned street. "What are you talking about?"

She perched next to him. "I'm helping to launch a network of saboteurs."

He gave her a mocking smile. "Are you now?"

She grabbed his arm. "René, I'm serious. Toto and I—"

"Toto? As in the dog in the *Wizard of Oz*?"

She dropped her hand. "No. As in a man. His real name is Armand Borni."

"Armand Borni," René repeated. "Such a French name. Is he the man who is responsible for that glow I see now? Or is it this supposed network?"

"Glow? Now it's my turn to ask what you are talking about."

"I've known you since you were a girl, and while you've always been wildly enthusiastic, or even—" he gave her a knowing glance, "just wild, I've never seen you so confident before. It's as if you're ready to set the world on fire."

"No, just Europe."

He sighed. "Okay, Mathilde, tell me what you've got planned."

After she'd filled him in on her and Toto's plans for Interallié, he gave yet another sigh. "While it certainly sounds unbelievable, I have no reason to doubt what you say is true. And I don't think I could consciously pass up a chance to get back at the Boches."

"So you will join us?"

He pointed a finger at her. "I'll do even better than that. I know of a man," he glanced around again. They were still alone, but he lowered his voice anyway. "A man by the name of Marc Marchal, a chemist, who has started something similar. I'll bet he'd be willing to merge his men with your network."

"Oh René!" Mathilde couldn't help clapping her hands like a little girl. "That's wonderful!" She planted a kiss on her old friend's cheek.

He stood up. "I'll get in contact with Marchal as soon as possible and meet you in two days' time."

"I knew I could count on you!" Mathilde called before racing off to share the good news with Armand.

True to his word, René contacted Marchal, who promptly became known as Uncle Marco, and who, in turn introduced Mathilde to his contacts, including a railway engineer with information on German troop movements and a high-ranking officer in the Explosives Service. Mathilde congratulated herself on the new recruits, but didn't let herself rest until she had more.

Procuring men off the street proved a much more difficult task. She never knew if the people she approached would be pro-Allies, pro-Vichy, or even pro-Nazi. For this, she relied on her training from Sardanapalus in Vichy. She'd bestow her customary smile on them and ply them with compliments and alcohol until she got them to confess their loyalties. If they declared themselves as "a de Gaulliste," Mathilde would explain that Interallié worked directly with de Gaulle from his exile in London. If they said they were a pro-Briton, she would emphasize Interallié's SOE contacts on Baker Street. And if at any time they hinted at sympathy with either the Vichy Government or the Germans, Mathilde would stretch her arms in a yawn, claim to be exhausted, and then take her leave. She never used her real name in case of just that scenario, telling her new acquaintances to refer to her as "The Cat" instead.

Among the people Mathilde drafted by other means was Mireille Lejeune, who worked as a concierge on the Avenue Lamarck, and her police officer husband, Boby Roland, who was willing to supply them with blank identity cards to help ease the movement of their agents throughout the countryside. Perhaps their most unusual volunteer was a former officer of the French Air Force nicknamed Kiki. His source of income was not readily apparent, but Mathilde asked no questions when he offered to donate a large sum of money to Interallié. After that, he seemed to only have one idea in his head: to capture a German plane and fly it.

Once the agents had been recruited, it was also Mathilde's job to explain to them what kind of information Interallié was expecting. As Armand put it, "To defeat the enemy, you have to know where he is." This was more complicated than it sounded, so Mathilde devised a detailed questionnaire, which asked how many troops they'd seen and requested descriptions of their uniform insignias, and any identifying marks on their vehicles. It was enough for their operatives to document these markings and up to Mathilde to determine their significance. She bought a book at a bookstore on the boulevard Saint-Michel which helped to identify each section of the German army. In this way, she could follow the movements of German troops throughout Paris.

Since telephone calls could be recorded and the mail censored, there had to be another way of exchanging information. Mathilde came up with the idea of placing letter boxes in the homes and businesses of Resistance-sympathizers throughout the city.

That evening was like so many others, with Mathilde pouring through the agents' reports retrieved from the letter boxes while Armand repositioned the marker pins he used to represent the German positions.

"Where is the signal battalion which left Niort now?" Armand asked.

Mathilde, quite proudly, replied with the correct information.

"*Ma petite chatte,*" he said as he ruffled her hair. "She can accomplish anything she wishes."

CHAPTER 7

DIDI

*D*idi joined Bingham's Unit, a section of SOE's women decoders and wireless operators named after its founder, Phyllis Bingham. It was an arm of the SOE, but, like Jackie, Didi told everyone she worked for the First Aid Nursing Yeomanry, or FANY.

The best part about using FANY as a cover was the uniform: a khaki jacket and skirt complete with a shiny brown leather belt, wide enough to flatter any figure. When Didi was handed her kit at Lilywhites Department Store in Piccadilly Circus, she was told to keep her shoes and belt polished at all times as well as to make sure the lines of her linen-colored stockings were always straight.

As she left the store in full dress, she encountered two men in officer's uniforms, who promptly saluted her. Didi mimicked them, touching her fingers to her right eyebrow, unsure if she was doing it properly. One of the men shot her a leering look as she passed, and Didi felt her face heat up. Was she ready for the attention her new attire was bound to attract?

Didi's wireless training took place in STS 54, otherwise known as Fawley Court, a beautiful red-bricked mansion in Buckinghamshire. She and a group of other girls were installed in the attic of the house.

Other than the attic being stifling hot at night, even in September, the whole place had a college-dormitory atmosphere about it. Though the FANYs were cautioned to conduct themselves like ladies at all times during the day, after lights-out, they told each other coarse jokes about their instructors and giggled late into the night.

Didi didn't socialize much with the other girls. She was determined to be the best wireless operator the SOE had ever seen, and dedicated herself to memorizing all the nuances and dots and dashes of Morse code.

The lessons also included map reading and first aid, which, while recognizing the necessity of the drilling, Didi found somewhat boring. Though she was able to master the required Morse rate of twenty-two words per minute relatively quickly—it reminded her of taking piano lessons when she was younger—she ached for something more exciting.

She got her chance when she was informed by the head instructor, Mr. S. H. Gray, that she was being posted to Hut 6 to learn how to send and receive messages.

Hut 6 was one of many half-cylindrical Nissen huts set on the back lawn of the mansion. The concrete floor, combined with the iron siding, meant that, like the attic, the hut was a furnace in the summer.

When Didi entered the cavernous shed for the first time, the door banged shut behind her, but the women hunched over their desks did not seem to hear it through their headsets.

"Ah, you must be Miss Nearne," the aging officer in a too-tight uniform greeted her.

"Yes, sir, Didi Nearne, reporting for duty." As it often did lately, a Morse equivalent flashed through her mind. D-i-d-i: Dash-dot-dot, dot-dot, Dash-dot-dot, dot-dot.

"Captain Charles Smith. I've been told you are quite the sharp one," he turned and started marching across the floor, Didi following him, "but I'm sure you'll find that coding agent messages is a different field from learning Morse."

"Yes, sir."

He paused in front of an empty chair. "This will be your station."

Didi nodded as she pulled out the hard-backed chair.

"The wireless is the best link we have to our agents on the ground in France. Obviously we can't send straightforward messages out: the

Germans are always listening. We use a special coding system here that is impossible for the Boches to break. Your first job will be to learn the codes, and then, if you're good enough, we'll eventually get you on a regular sked."

She quickly surmised that 'sked' was a shortening of schedule.

Captain Smith tried, unsuccessfully, to pull his jacket over his protruding belly. "Are you any good at crosswords?"

"Pardon?"

"The ability to complete crosswords often results in exceptional coders." He gave her a sidelong glance. "But not always." He leaned over the desk, placing a pencil and square pad of grid paper in front of Didi. "Okay, the first thing you need to understand is that the field agents use poem codes."

Didi had no idea what a poem code was, but was too afraid to ask.

Her instructor seemed unaware of her ignorance. "Or Bible verses, or famous quotations, something they can easily remember."

She finally caught on. The agents used poems as the basis for their ciphers. "So it doesn't have to be written down in case they are ever searched," she finished aloud.

He started scribbling on the top sheet of paper. "Exactly. To encode his information, an agent chooses five words from his poem. You will know which five words he chose because the first thing he will send will be what's called 'an indicator group.'" He turned the paper so Didi could read what he'd written: *My name is Ozymandias, king of kings. Look on my works, ye Mighty, and despair!*

Captain Smith drew a line after the first 'king.' "Now let's say he uses the words 'my-name-is-Ozymandias-king.' You will put a number 1 under the first 'A', then a 2 under the second 'A', and a 3 under the third 'A,' then the next letter in alphabetical order is 'D', so that will get a 4, and so on." He handed her the pencil and Didi finished writing numbers underneath the phrase so that it looked like this:

M Y N A M E I S O Z Y M A N D I A S K I N G
11 20 13 1 12 5 7 18 17 22 21 14 2 15 4 8 3 19 10 9 16 6

"Good," Captain Smith told her. "That's your transposition key. Now let's say you wanted to send a message for a Lysander pick-up in

Le Mons at 9 pm Thursday." Captain Smith started writing underneath all of the numbers.

11	20	13	1	12	5	7	18	17	22	21	14	2	15	4	8	3	19	10	9	16	6
L	Y	S	A	N	D	E	R	P	I	C	K	U	P	A	R	R	A	N	G	E	D
L	E	M	O	N	S	T	H	U	R	S	D	A	Y	A	T	9	P	M	X	X	X

"Just fill in the extra spots with Xs. Now using the transposition key, the letters under 1 are a, o and the numbers under 2 are u, a..." He continued writing. At long last he showed her the new version:

aouar9aadsdxetrtgxnmllnnsmkdpyexpurhapyecsir

It looked like gibberish to Didi, but Captain Smith wasn't done yet. "Your job is actually to decode the messages coming in from the field, and usually they are much longer, at least 200 letters. But if you have the transposition key, you can easily go backwards." He then went on to show her how to interpret the message by relining the letters in numerical order under the words from the poem.

Didi peered at the columns he was making on the square paper. It seemed ridiculously easy now that she knew how to do it. *Maybe too easy.* "Let's say the Germans managed to crack one message and get an agent's poem code. Couldn't they then know exactly what the message was every time he sent one after that?"

Captain Smith paused his writing. "I suppose that's possible, but it hasn't happened thus far."

"But how can you know?"

He put his pencil down with a sigh. "Our duty is not to question why. I do as I'm told. And so should you, especially as a FANY with no experience in the field."

No experience yet, she thought resentfully.

"Now for the security checks," Captain Smith continued.

Didi sat straighter, hoping these security checks would be more impressive than the poem codes.

"They are different for each agent, but usually consist of three 'dummy' letters inserted throughout the message, such as **KIO** in the first sentence and **HRP** in another. In some cases, the field operator is instructed to purposefully misspell certain words. The absence of these 'mistakes' may indicate that the agent is in trouble."

"So I should always make sure they've inserted their security checks."

"Well," he scratched at his chin. "Don't be too vigilant—sometimes the agents just forget to use them."

"Forget to use them?" Now Didi was completely exasperated. "If these security checks are the difference between the SOE knowing their men are safe or possibly sending messages with the nozzle of a Luger to their temple, how could someone 'just forget?'"

"They might not be typing with a gun pointed at their head, little girl," he spat out, "but they're under pressure enough as it is. We can afford them a little leeway in forgetting minor details."

Didi didn't consider them 'minor details,' but she kept her tone deferentially neutral as she recited his instructions back to him. It wouldn't do her any good to get kicked out of wireless training. "So be aware of occasional security checks, but don't assume their absence means the agent has been compromised."

"Exactly." He appeared mollified. "And be mindful of Morse mutilation." Taking note of Didi's confused look, he clarified. "That could be from the agent typing the Morse in wrong, or it could be from atmospheric interference in the transmission." A FANY at another station motioned frantically at Captain Smith. "You'll get the hang of it," he told Didi as he walked away.

Her head spinning with all she had just learned, Didi's eyes roamed around the room. On the wall opposite her desk was a poster with the words, "Remember, the enemy is listening." Next to that was a green chalkboard with a list of each of the agents' code names and scheduled time. She peered at it, wondering which agent was to be Jackie's wireless operator when she left for France.

When Didi returned to the attic, one of her roommates, Yvonne Baseden, informed her that the girls were going to sneak out to a nearby officer's club.

"Sneak out?" Didi replied incredulously. "How can you do that? We work for the SOE. It's their job to know everything."

"Shh." Yvonne held a finger to her lips. "You and I know we work for the SOE, but most of the others don't."

"What do you mean?" Didi lowered her voice slightly. "We had to sign that document promising we would never speak of anything confidential to anyone. It's pretty clear that we're employed by an underground government agency."

"Most of the other women think we are actual FANYs and, since no one else has ever bothered to correct them, I didn't think it was my place." Yvonne paused to catch her breath and looked reluctant to continue, but did so anyway. "You might have noticed yourself if you'd ever deigned to talk to anyone else."

"It's not my job to make friends here." Yvonne was even younger than Didi, but somehow made it seem like she was eons older.

"Still… it wouldn't kill you to get out and have some fun." Yvonne shed her jacket and shook out her hair.

"What are you doing? You're never supposed to be out of uniform." Even Didi could hear the goody-two-shoes whine in her own voice.

Yvonne, clad only in her slip, started filling the sink with water. "Have you any bleach?"

"No."

She found some in a cabinet and dumped almost the whole bottle on top of her uniform. Didi, not wanting to reprimand her any further, watched with red eyes and burning nostrils as the khaki fabric faded into a dull pink. Yvonne pulled the plug and then began to rinse off her newly-lightened jacket. "Much better," she said aloud.

Didi just shook her head.

Didi caved and accompanied Yvonne and a few other girls to the Spread-Eagle Pub. Didi knew she had made a mistake the minute she entered the brick-walled, dimly lit pub swarming with men both in plain-clothes and various uniforms. Though some of the men were quite handsome, they just seemed all the more potential interferences to her work.

"My, oh, my," Yvonne whispered, her eyes widening. "Jackpot."

"Fannies!" a dark-haired, clean-shaven man exclaimed.

"That's FANY," Didi said pointedly.

He lurched toward her. "Care for a drink?"

"No," she replied as Yvonne stated, "Yes."

He elbowed Didi out of the way to speak to her roommate. "Are you working for F Section too?"

Before Yvonne could reply, Didi steered her clear of him. "He could be an SOE mole, seeing if we'll confess our secrets." She repeated something their instructors had hammered into them from Day 1: "Careless talk costs lives."

"I know." Yvonne waved her hand. "I'm not interested in doing anything to get me fired. I just want to have a little fun, for once." She began swaying to the Glenn Miller song playing on the gramophone in the corner.

A glass of sherry was thrust toward Didi. Though she was tempted to shove it away, she didn't want to spill it and make a scene. She reluctantly accepted it.

"Your uniform seems darker than theirs."

Didi looked up at the fair-haired man who nodded toward Yvonne and a few other girls doing the swing on the dance floor.

Unsure how to respond, Didi just shrugged.

The blonde man took a gulp of beer. "Are you posted at Fawley Court?"

This time she sipped at her sherry in lieu of a reply.

"It's okay, we're all SOE here."

"I'm not—"

He leaned against the wall, his large hand spanning multiple bricks. "We're training to be field operators. What about you?"

"I don't know what you're talking about." Didi recalled what Yvonne said regarding some of the girls not knowing who they were working for. "I'm just here to learn Morse code."

"So you're wireless." He attempted a smile. "Maybe you'll be my interpreter. I'll send you a personal message when I get to France. What's your middle name?"

"You don't even know my first name and now you want to know my middle name?"

He shot her an apologetic grin. "I'm sorry I didn't bother to ask for your real identity. We're all using code names anyway."

"I haven't been given a code name." She said the first thing that came to her mind. "Dash-dot-dot, dot-dot, Dash-dot-dot, dot-dot."

"Didi." His blue eyes flashed. "And your middle name, Didi?"

She took another sip of sherry before giving him the Morse equivalent of 'Mary.'

"Well, Didi Mary, I'll be sure to send you a hello one day."

"I'll keep my eyes out." It could have been a good line to bid him adieu, but she wasn't ready to leave yet. She suddenly realized how lonely she'd been these past weeks, with Jackie gone and no one to talk to except perhaps Yvonne. And Captain Smith. "When do you think you'll be going into the field?"

Another grin. "You know I can't tell you that. We've probably already said too much." He tried to make his face serious as he glanced around the room. "There are spies everywhere."

"Not here in England."

"I don't mean the Boches. I'm talking about Buck and Vera's informants."

"Who are Buck and Vera?"

His eyebrows furrowed. "You never met Maurice Buckmaster or Vera Atkins?"

She set her drink down on a table. "I told you, I'm just here to learn Morse."

He took a sip of beer, his eyes never leaving her face. "Your job is more important than that. You're the lifeline of the operators in the field —you keep us alive. Do you know that the average time a wireless operator can be on the ground is only a month before the gonios find them?"

"Gonios?"

"The Gestapo's radio-detection vans. They can home in on signals, and they if they catch you…" he made a slicing motion across his neck. "I might not be long for this world."

His imploring, puppy-dog expression made Didi change the subject. "I wish I could go to France and give Hitler a piece of my mind."

He nearly dropped his drink. "The SOE doesn't employ women as agents."

Didi folded her arms across her chest. "Shows how much you know. I happen to have inside information that they're training a group of women right now."

One of his eyebrows lifted. "How did you find that out?"

She didn't mean to reveal so much, but it was too late now. "My sister is in that group. Maybe you'll work with her someday."

"Is she as pretty as you are?"

Didi felt the familiar twinge of jealousy whenever Jackie was brought up, but she squelched it down with another sip of sherry. "Prettier."

Her face grew hot under his gaze, which seemed to penetrate right into her innermost thoughts. "I doubt that." He extended his hand. "Care to dance?"

"You haven't told me *your* name." Clearly the sherry had gone to Didi's head.

"My code name is Archambault. It's an old French surname."

"I know. But what is your real name?"

"Tsk-tsk." He held a finger up to Didi's mouth. "We don't want these lips to sink any ships."

She took a step back. "I shall call you Archie, then."

He didn't appear to hear her, so intent was he on staring at the spot where his finger had just been.

She'd never kissed a man before, but for whatever reason, she didn't feel shy when Archie leaned in. His lips touched hers for just a second before he pulled away. "I couldn't help myself," he said softly. His eyes held an inquisitive look as he waited for her reaction.

She stepped closer and reached up to entangle her fingers in his hair.

They kissed again, longer this time, until a loud voice said, "What do we have here?"

Didi broke from Archie's embrace to see Yvonne standing next to them, her hair darkened with sweat from dancing.

"We were just getting to know each other a little better," Archie stated casually, his hand back on the wall.

"Is that so?" Yvonne's voice was full of amusement as she turned to her roommate. "I never knew you had it in you."

"She was just indulging me in one last kiss before I come face to face with Hitler," Archie said, shooting Didi a conspiring grin.

Yvonne grabbed Didi's arm. "C'mon, we've got to get back before curfew."

"Bye, D.M. it was nice meeting you. Keep your eyes out for that message!" Archie called at their retreating backs. Didi wanted to run back to him and demand his real name, or at least ask for more than the promise of a personal dispatch that would never be aired, but she knew that both were impossible. She settled for giving him a sad little wave before Yvonne pulled her out of the pub.

"Who's D.M.?" Yvonne asked once they were outside, the cool night air a relief after the humid bar. "And who was that guy, anyway?"

Archie—obviously not wanting to let on that Didi had told him her real name—had shortened Didi Mary to D.M. "I don't know who he was," she replied honestly. *But I hope to meet him again, someday.* She took one last peek at the Spread-Eagle Pub before they turned the corner and headed back toward Fawley Court.

CHAPTER 8

ODETTE

Odette's training took place at a country house near Guilford called Wanborough Manor, a grandiose, Elizabethan-style house mansion on a hilly ridge known as 'the Hog's Back.'

Odette was greeted at the door by a beanpole of a man with dark hair and a wiry moustache, who introduced himself as Major Roger de Wesselow. He led her into the oak-paneled ballroom, where lemonade and sandwiches were being served.

She sat on a threadbare loveseat and took a bite of sandwich before casting her eyes around the room. The black-out curtains had been pulled aside to let the daylight in, the sun casting dusty rectangles onto the brick-red carpet.

"Hallo," a bright voice called. Odette looked up to see a tall woman extending her hand. "Name's... er, I suppose you're supposed to call me Claudine." She spoke with a thick Irish accent and appeared to be in her late 30s or early 40s. "That's Adele," she gestured to a dark-haired woman with gray streaks in her hair sitting in a nearby chair. "She escaped from France in the nick of time, before Hitler's jackboot squashed every hope of getting out of there."

The woman named Adele waved at Odette, who couldn't help noticing how shrewd her blue eyes were.

"And now here we are, trying to get back in," Claudine chuckled.

"Pardon?" Odette asked.

"That's what we're here for, ain't it? So the SOE can send us back to France to stir up trouble?"

"All right now, ladies." Major de Wesselow held up his hands. "It's time to get down to business." He began pacing across the floor in front of the fireplace, and Odette marveled how his spindly little legs could manage to hold up the rest of his body. "From now on, I only want to hear French out of you. No English is allowed—if you wake up screaming from a nightmare, I want to hear only French curses."

"*Merde*," Claudine helpfully provided.

"*Exactement*," Major de Wesselow said, pointing at her. He resumed his pacing and began to ramble in poorly accented French. "You happen to be the first women's training group. From here on out, your class will be known as 27-OB-6. There will also be several male classes here. You will refer to all of your instructors by their proper military titles and afford them their due respect. They are here to challenge you, work you out to the limits of your prowess, and then some. You will be watched throughout your month-long stay, and then a report will be made to help the SOE decide how best to employ you going forward." He paused as Miss Atkins and another woman, a fragile, doll-like creature with porcelain skin, entered the room.

"Forgive our lateness," Miss Atkins stated. "This is Jacqueline Nearne."

"Code-name?" Major de Wesselow barked.

"Jacqueline," Miss Atkins' companion unexpectedly replied, meeting the major's steely eyes. Odette was impressed that the young woman could be so bold.

A muscle played out in de Wesselow's cheek as he waved Jacqueline toward an empty chair so he could continue his lecture.

Miss Atkins and Major Buckmaster hosted a reception that night in the ballroom. Most of the male recruits were hulking fellows with bulging muscles, and looked as though they could single-handedly take out a squadron of Nazis. This contrasted greatly with Odette's slender female classmates, especially the frail Jacqueline. *There must have been another reason for hiring women like us,* she mused, but she wasn't sure how to tactfully query the rationale of Buckmaster and Miss Atkins at the dinner table.

"Everyone's so pretty here," Odette stated instead. "I didn't expect that."

"Of course they are," Miss Atkins replied. "Pretty women can elicit information from any man, not to mention their looks can be a layer of protection should the Gestapo get ahold of them." She said something else under her breath that Odette couldn't quite hear, but it sounded like, "hopefully."

Odette didn't necessarily see the logic, but maybe in time, all that physical endurance de Wesselow claimed they'd experience would carve them into brawny mercenaries like their male counterparts.

Although the alcohol was flowing freely, the atmosphere in the room was guarded. Odette didn't drink more than a glass of sherry; she was afraid this was one of Buckmaster's tests to see if their tongues became looser after consuming liquor. The other girls, except for Claudine, seemed as reluctant as Odette to talk about themselves.

As Odette sat, pretending to listen intently to the piano music, she saw a few men look toward Jacqueline with an admiring glance. One or two even looked Odette's way—she had taken off her wedding ring since her alter ego Céline wasn't married—but none of them approached any of the women. The males spent their time comparing boxing scars and football injuries in boisterous voices while chugging beer. *Apparently they have no qualms about drinking in front of Buckmaster*, Odette decided.

Odette was awoken the next morning by a loud knocking on her door. An older woman entered and set a cup of tea down on the nightstand. "If you please ma'am, your presence is required on the tennis court."

Odette raised herself sleepily. "The tennis court? What time is it?"

"Seven-thirty. You have half an hour to get ready. May I suggest shorts and gym shoes?

Odette threw the covers back with a sigh.

After a few minutes of batting a ball back and forth with a handsome man in a white sweater, while a bespectacled man with a clipboard looked on, Odette was sweaty and fully aware of muscles she'd previously forgotten about.

The Greek Adonis, who was quickly turning into Odette's personal torturer, finally paused his relentless racket swinging. "It's time for a breather." He wiped his face with a towel as he walked toward her. "Do you mind if I ask you a few questions, Céline?"

Odette gulped water from a bottle.

"Céline?"

She realized he was talking to her. "Yes?"

"Suppose a burly SS man came for you. What would you do?"

She was too distracted by her aching muscles to recall what *SS* meant. "How big did you say?"

"Over two meters."

She considered the problem. "I would probably run away in the opposite direction as fast as I could."

"Judging from your performance just now, I don't think that would be overly fast. What if he caught up to you?"

"I would pinch him."

"Pinch him?" The Adonis's face broke out into a wide grin. "Anything else?"

"Pull his hair?"

The grin, if possible, grew even more extensive. "Well, I do have to say that I've never heard that before, though if they insist on letting women into the F Section, I might hear it more." He set his water bottle down. "I'm going to teach you a better way to disable a would-be aggressor than pinch him and pull his hair. The average time an agent survives in France is three months. My job is to extend that."

Odette, unsure how to reply, held up her water bottle in mock salute.

The recruits were treated to a full English breakfast, including pickled herring—known to the Brits as "kippers"—eggs, toast, and marmalade. Afterward they were each given a vest with a number on the front and back.

"What's this?" Odette inquired, sniffing the foul-smelling vest. It had obviously been used before.

"Probably more P.T.," Claudine answered.

Odette apparently wasn't the only one who didn't know what she meant, as Jacqueline asked, "What is P.T.?"

"Physical training," Claudine said loftily as she headed outside.

They were taken on an arduous run along the grounds of the

mansion. Odette thought she'd keel over as she passed the entrance gate guarded by armed Field Security police.

"Do you want to trade places?" she breathlessly called to one of them who had just come off duty.

He held up his rifle. "You wouldn't be able to handle this."

"Not yet, but maybe next week." Odette suddenly got a second wind, and managed to even pass Jacqueline before the run was finished.

The training got progressively harder as the week went on. Instead of what Odette would have now considered a leisurely morning tennis game, the women, along with the men, were forced to go on ten-mile runs through the surrounding woods fueled by nothing but a cup of tea.

Adele was the strongest, her short but powerful legs carrying her faster than the other women. Odette was the second fastest and made it her goal to pass the slowest man before her training finished. When she changed into her pajamas, she noticed how shapely her calves had become. While somewhat pleased and proud of herself, she found it ironic that, when they went to France, they were supposed to blend in as ordinary civilians. Yet here they were, getting their muscles ready as if they were going to swim across the Channel to get there.

After lunch, the exhausted women trainees were taken into the sitting room, where the afternoon's instruction consisted of coding messages, identifying the different German uniforms, and ways of escaping if they were caught by the enemy.

"When are we going to learn how to shoot?" Claudine asked their instructor one day.

"Shoot?" He looked taken aback, as if he'd never heard the likes of women agents aiming a gun. He rubbed at his chin. "I'm not sure that's strictly necessary."

"You can't possibly want us to supply guns to rebels when we don't even know how to use them, can you?" Claudine demanded.

He waved his hand. "I'll look into it."

The most relevant lesson thus far, in Odette's opinion, had been on how France had changed under Nazi rule. They had to learn about rationing and which bread and meat tickets were available to use on certain days. They were also taught the distinctions between the German secret police, *the Schutzstaffel,* or SS, and the Vichy *Gendarmerie.* Jacqueline had nodded her head throughout that particular lecture, having obviously been in France far more recently than any of the other women.

If learning about life in the Occupied Zone was the most meaningful lesson, Odette's least favorite was Morse Code. The dots and dashes just wouldn't stay in her head.

"What's the Morse sign for L?" her instructor asked.

Odette thought for a moment. "Dot-dash dash-dot."

"Wrong!" he shouted, spit flying out of his mouth.

She narrowed her eyes. "No, that's it, I'm sure of it."

"Morse code is a matter of fact, not opinion, and I know the facts better than you. You are wrong, and lives depend on you knowing the right code."

"But I'm not going to be a coder or an operator; I'll never need to use Morse."

He threw up his hands, muttering under his breath about how it had been a dangerous decision to send women into the field. He turned to Jacqueline. "Do you know the answer?"

She shook her head numbly.

His arrogant manner had irked Odette and she racked her brain. "L is dot-dash-dot dot!" she shouted.

"Finally." He walked over to the chalkboard and erased it, dust flying everywhere. "Now, let's discuss the best method of disposing a parachute other than chopping it up into panties for your girlfriends." He glanced over at Odette. "Er, that is to say pajamas for your boyfriends."

Miss Atkins popped in from London that night to check on how the training was going. She'd obviously heard about the Morse faux pas that afternoon, as, after greeting her girls, she said casually to Jacqueline, "I'm told your sister Didi has quite the mind for Morse."

Jacqueline dropped her fork. "Is that so?"

Odette glanced from Jacqueline's stricken face to Miss Atkins' impassive one.

"You have to promise me you won't send Didi to France," Jacqueline begged.

"Your sister would make a fine agent."

"No, she wouldn't," Jacqueline insisted. "I know my sister better than anyone. She's too young and impetuous." She touched the sleeve of Miss Atkin's uniform. "Please. I told her she has to be 25 to go to France. I hoped by then this infernal war would be over. If you don't reinforce that idea, she will beg you every day to go into the field."

Miss Atkins nodded. "Just concentrate on your training. I'll make sure your sister never gets to France."

CHAPTER 9

MATHILDE

*I*nterallié expanded more quickly than even Armand had imagined. Just as he had predicted, each new recruit was the source of many more, and the network grew by leaps and bounds. Every time they added a contact, Armand would connect him or her to the other branches until the map of France in the living room looked like a spiderweb stretching across the Occupied Zone. Next to his map, Armand had posted a sheet he'd painted with a quote from Charles De Gaulle's rousing speech after the Nazis had invaded Paris: 'Whatever happens, the flame of French resistance must not, and shall not die!'

Naturally, with so many different agents in various parts of the country—both Occupied and Free France—communication became one of Interallié's largest problems. By the time the intelligence was obtained from the letterboxes, passed to other agents to be carried over the demarcation line to Spain, and finally on to London, it was often too late for the Allies to act upon it.

The final nail in the coffin was when Uncle Marco, through his contacts in the railway, found out the exact route for Hermann Göring's Paris-bound train. Armand sent the report as soon as Mathilde typed it out. Their courier, known as Rapidé, followed his usual itinerary by boarding a train to Marseille. Once onboard, he would unscrew the lavatory mirror in a previously agreed-upon car, and then plant the message before restoring the mirror to its proper place. After finishing his task, he would disembark and another contact would board the same train in time to retrieve the information.

Three days later, Mathilde and Armand stayed glued to the radio, hoping to hear a break in the program announcing Göring's untimely death.

At 2 pm the doorbell rang—a long ring followed by two short ones —signaling it was someone in the network.

Mathilde looked up as Armand opened the door to see their courier, Kiki, standing there, his eyes red. "What happened for God's sake?" Kiki asked in a shrill voice as he stepped into the apartment.

Armand shut the door behind him. "What do you mean?"

"What do I mean? I just watched Göring's train return, an untouched shiny silver, perfectly intact train, Reichsmarshal Göring laughing as he disembarked, also perfectly intact."

Armand threw up his hands. "Unbelievable!"

Mathilde walked over and stroked his arm. "Uncle Marco will be so disappointed."

Armand shook his head. "Something went wrong." He turned to Kiki. "Please inform Monsieur Marchal that we sent the message through the right channels but something went wrong." His tone softened. "Tell him that even though Göring arrived unscathed, he wouldn't have been laughing if he had known that our network observes most of his Luftwaffe activities in France."

The young man's face brightened. "So even though he survived today, his future is not looking promising, is it?"

"No." Armand agreed, reaching out to shake Kiki's hand. "We have our disappointments, but we don't exactly make the Boches happy, do we?"

"And that's why we carry on," Mathilde said, leading Kiki to the door. "Give my love to Uncle Marco, I'll be seeing him soon."

Kiki tipped his hat to both of them before he left.

When Armand received London's reply over a week later, he read it aloud to Mathilde. "Regarding the Göring train: sorry we got the news too late to use it for the RAF." He crumpled up the message and tossed it into the fire. "Do you know what a coup killing Hitler's right-hand man would have been?"

"What's the solution?" Mathilde asked. "Our people are working hard enough already."

"It's the communications." Armand went to his wall map and stared intently at it. "There's got to be a better way." He tapped his finger first on Paris and then on London. "I'm going to Marseille in a few days to meet up with some London agents. Maybe they can help."

Armand returned from Marseille with a large suitcase in addition to his small bag.

"What's that?" Mathilde inquired as he hoisted the case onto the desk, not without effort.

"It's a transmitting set," Armand replied proudly. "Take a look." He snapped open the suitcase, revealing a black box full of dials and gadgets. "I met an English agent named George Noble," he went on while he fidgeted with one of the dials. "It seems that Baker Street, home of the SOE, has come up with a coding system to use for their agents. And get this…" he grinned. "The BBC is going to regularly transmit messages during their evening broadcast."

Mathilde's mouth dropped open. "How? The Boches monitor it constantly." The Vichy government and the Germans had tried to ban listening to the BBC in favor of a Nazi-propaganda program called 'Radio Paris;' an effort stunted in no small part by the BBC slogan: 'Radio Paris lies, Radio Paris is German.' Most of Interallié's contacts, like Mathilde and Armand, covertly tuned in to the BBC every night. The announcer ended every broadcast with *les messages personnels* from natives stranded in England to relatives back home in France. It was like a light shining on an otherwise darkened Paris, reconnecting it briefly to the rest of the world.

"The directive will be encrypted, of course," Armand explained. "It will sound like a personal message, or even nonsensical to Nazi ears, but will make complete sense to the right person."

Just then, the doorbell rang the signal and Mathilde opened it to find two burly men standing in the hallway.

"Ahh, wonderful timing," Armand stated. "Marcel and Kent, I'd like you to meet 'Madame la Chatte,' my business partner." He turned to Mathilde. "Kent is going to help us get the wireless working and Marcel will be our operator."

Marcel nodded at Mathilde as he set up at Armand's desk. He took out a pen and several pieces of perfectly square paper. "What shall our first message to London be?"

Armand paced up and down the small room. "How about, 'From Interallié STOP very happy to establish the direct link STOP.'"

Marcel nodded as he started writing a series of numbers on one of the cards. Kent fiddled with the transmitter as Armand stood over him. Mathilde decided to leave them to their work while she went out to queue for bread.

When she returned, Armand told her Kent had left to go scrounge up more parts, but they were ready to send the message. Mathilde and Armand watched anxiously as Marcel tapped away on the Morse key.

"Is it working?" Armand asked when he had stopped tapping, but Marcel held up a finger with one hand while keeping the other clamped to his headset, appearing to listen to something. He motioned for his pen and Mathilde placed it, along with one of the square pieces of paper, in his hand. He furiously copied something down before signing off.

Mathilde peered at the sheet as Marcel handed it to Armand. It appeared to be a string of letters in groups of five.

Armand grabbed *B. Kieski's Dictionary* before sitting on the couch. He started by subtracting numbers then rapidly turned pages in the dictionary. Mathilde fetched him a cup of tea while he worked. Finally he pushed the paper toward Mathilde. "We did it, Lily!"

She picked up their first decoded message and read it aloud: *"To Interallié STOP Congratulations, we're receiving you."*

Armand stood up and enveloped Mathilde in his arms. "We did it!" he repeated before planting a kiss on her cheek.

"The reception was perfect," Marcel stated.

Armand released Mathilde to get back to business. "How many transmissions do you think you can make a day?"

Marcel thought for a moment. "We can fix up to four times a day. I suggest no more than five to ten minutes at a time, but I could convey about a hundred groups of figures that way."

"That's still four hundred words a day." Armand's voice was shrill as he shook his head in amazement. "Direct contact with London with four hundred words to send them." He took a sip of tea. "What about safety?"

Marcel went to the wireless case. "I have quartz crystals for four different wavelengths. I will change the wavelength every two or three minutes, so even with such a strong transmitter, provided we work rapidly with short intervals, I think we can avoid detection."

Mathilde made dinner as Armand and Marcel discussed ideal places from which to transmit. She had mostly tuned their voices out, but still overheard them agreeing that Mathilde and Armand's apartment was unsuitable for operating the radio set.

In due time, Mathilde found a more accommodating apartment on the Colonel Moll with an extra room that Marcel could use for transmissions. Their new landlady had claimed to have a hatred for Germans—as she told it, they thrust a bayonet into her buttocks when they had first entered Paris—but that didn't stop her from renting the apartment across from Mathilde and Armand's to some Boches. Members of the Gestapo, if Mathilde was interpreting their uniforms right.

Armand seemed merely amused by their close proximity to the enemy; nevertheless, it made Mathilde nervous, especially given the presence of the wireless. She settled for keeping the radio playing dance music day in and day out and tasked one of their contacts with the duty of listening to the BBC and reporting any important messages.

Though her work and the presence of Armand kept her warm in their little apartment, the weather that fall became frigid and there was not enough coal in the city to go around. One particularly chilly evening, when Mathilde was queuing for food outside a butcher's shop in the avenue d'Orleans, she had a sudden memory of when she had first moved to North Africa with her husband. She never thought that she—a graduate of the Sorbonne—would end up a teacher, married to the destitute headmaster of a European school in Ain-Sefra, Algeria. The first night they arrived in Africa, Mathilde had watched the sun set beyond the sand dunes, which had turned a bright scarlet, in contrast to the deep blue hue filling the rest of the sky as night fell. She'd thought then that everything would be all right, but when she returned to their cramped new apartment, she felt immediately stifled, a sentiment that never changed during the five years she'd been married.

She now gave an involuntary shiver, not from the cold, as the line moved forward. She might be hungry and freezing, but even in Occupied France, she had more freedom than when she'd been living with her husband. Though it was one of the frostiest Octobers anyone could remember, she'd found her place in the sun through Interallié, not to mention Armand. And she wouldn't trade that for anything, not even a lifetime of warm weather and clear skies.

Identity papers were among the most important precautions with which Interallié armed its agents. Boby Roland, the policeman husband of Mathilde's friend Mireille Lejeune, provided Armand with blank identity cards straight from the offices of the Prefect of Police. Another contact contributed the proper stamps, and Armand spent several long nights creating false identity cards for some of their contacts, using his own forged ID as an example.

He told Mathilde the next day that he'd had a scare as he was stepping off a Metro train. A policeman had demanded his papers, and Armand had opened his wallet only to find it empty. Too late, he realized he had mistakenly placed his own card in the apartment safe the last time he'd locked up his extra cards and stamps.

"What did the policeman do?" Mathilde asked after she finished rinsing the dinner dishes.

"He held the whistle up to his mouth, but he didn't blow it. He just stared at me, and after what felt like an eternity, he waved me on my way."

"What would you have done if he had whistled for more policemen?" She wiped her hands on a towel. "Would you have run?"

Armand looked thoughtful. "I don't rightly know. I suppose you never know what you would do in a dangerous situation like that until it actually happens."

"I guess not." She opened the closet door and retrieved her coat.

"Where are you going?"

"I'm going to the store. After a scare like that, I think you could use some good tea and biscuits."

"Wait." He got up from his desk to pull a box down from the closet. "Open it," he told Mathilde. The box contained a shabby black fur coat.

"I know it's not much to look at, but it will keep you warm," Armand said.

She tried it on, admiring the way the coat matched her dark hair in the hallway mirror. "Where did you get it?"

"Remember that widow I told you about? The one who saved my life?"

Mathilde nodded.

"It was hers—I found it when I was unpacking. It's too small for me, obviously, but it did its job. And now it will do it again, for you."

"Thank you, Toto."

CHAPTER 10

ODETTE

*O*nce their initial training was completed, Odette, Jackie, Adele, and Claudine were sent to "finishing school" at Lord Montagu's mansion among the vast trees of New Forest. Odette was beginning to think that the SOE really stood for "Stately Old Estates," with all the old manors being requisitioned to train secret agents.

She did have to admit that the large grounds provided good cover for the would-be saboteurs while they were mastering outdoorsy skills such as canoeing, navigating through the woods using constellations as their guide, and cooking rabbits and chickens pilfered from neighboring coops.

The endless lectures continued as well. One day Odette and the other women sat in the library as their instructor pointed to the picture of a Boche on a colored chart. "Claudine, who's this chap and what do his badges of rank mean?"

Claudine blinked rapidly as she thought. "He's a feldwebel in the Luftwaffe."

"Jacqueline, what's the medal on his chest?"

"Iron Cross, Second Class," Jackie promptly replied.

"And Adele, what about this one?" He gestured to another picture.

"He's an oberleutnant in the Panzergrenadiers."

"Céline, what about his medal ribbons?"

Odette shrugged, breaking the rhythm. "I don't think that medal ribbons are of any importance."

He tapped his hand with his pointer impatiently. "Your opinion does not happen to be shared by the staff. Céline, I must insist you pay attention to what we, the experts, know to be of importance."

"Yes, sir," Odette replied.

He fixed his unblinking gaze on her. "Can you tell the class about the topographical requirements for a Lysander pick-up?"

That was an easy one. "I would look for a flat field with a hard surface for it to land and no trees or poles or ditches around. The field would have to be at least six hundred yards long and four hundred yards wide. I would arrange for the pick-up to take place under a full moon."

"It is London who organizes the pick-ups and drop-offs," he answered dryly.

Odette frowned as the lecturer asked Jackie about the requirements to land a Hudson bomber. It was beginning to seem as though she could do nothing right.

They were always being watched, especially at mealtimes, by men with clipboards, who carefully noted which spoon they used for eating soup or how they cut their meat. It was essential to do everything the "French way," for as soon as someone suspected they were British agents, they would find themselves under arrest.

It seemed the only place the men with the clipboards were blissfully absent from was their psychiatric evaluations. Odette's doctor, a balding, bespectacled man in his late 40s, used a pad of paper to document everything she said and did. Sometimes he would show her ink-splattered pictures and record what she claimed to see, but other times he would just fire questions at her, like today. "Tell me your biggest fear."

"Something happening to my children."

He waved his hand. "That's every mother's biggest fear. I'm talking about recurring nightmares, the ones you've had all your life. Some people fear snakes, some twisters, some falling from heights. What keeps you up at night?"

She hesitated this time, weighing her words. "The dark."

He picked up his pen. "Just being in the dark?"

Odette shook her head, thinking about those three years she spent completely blind, her vision robbed from her by polio. Her mother had dragged her from doctor to doctor, finally hiring an herbalist—some might have called him a "witch doctor"—who had provided a curing elixir. Once Odette's sight had returned, the unnerving dreams began. "I'm running through a forest."

The doctor started scribbling. "Go on."

"Something is chasing me, some sort of beast, but I can't see it. I have to make it through the woods, but there are trees everywhere and it's so dark, and the beast is on my trail, I can hear its breath coming closer..." She stopped and pinched the inside of her hand to bring herself back to reality.

He nodded as if satisfied with her response. He flipped his pad to a clean page. "Tell me about your husband. Your instructors say you never mention him."

"We're required to remain undercover here, remember? We're not supposed to disclose anything from our real lives."

"Yes, but no one sees you pull out his picture and kiss it before you go to bed at night, or peek twice at a man who reminds you of him. It's as if you were never married."

"I don't talk about my children, either. We're not supposed to," she repeated.

He pointed the tip of his pen at her. "Your face softened when you mentioned them just now. The same cannot be said regarding your husband. How old were you when you got married?"

"Young," Odette replied, grateful for the distracting conversation. "I was barely eighteen, and twenty when Françoise was born." She smiled to herself. "The night we married, I panicked about going away from home for my honeymoon, and made my mother and new mother-in-law go to the cinema with me instead."

"You didn't have a father growing up." He folded his hands in front of him. "Your early marriage was an attempt to fill the male void in your life, but you don't like to have any man dictate what to do. You were relieved when he went off to war so you could have your autonomy back. If he died, you would grieve for a bit, but gradually realize your life is more fulfilled without him."

Odette stood. "Are we quite done?"

"For now." He picked up his pen again.

"What's the point of these evaluations, anyway?"

"We're trying to make sure you have the right kind of grit, that you won't go to pieces under the intense pressure of living undercover in France."

"And what does any of that have to do with how I feel about my husband? And, by the way, you are completely wrong about him."

His pen moved even more rapidly. "It has a lot to do with it. And I don't believe I'm wrong at all."

Odette left his office, shutting the door behind her with a little more force than necessary.

Early the next morning, Odette was jostled awake by someone shoving her. She opened her eyes to an intense light shining in her face.

"Get up!" a man in a black mask shouted.

Odette, suspecting that it was just another test, wanted to retort that she was tired and needed her sleep to get through the rest of her training, but then she saw other men in black hauling Jackie out of the room. She was shouting curses at them in French.

The men took Odette into one of the downstairs rooms and pushed her into a chair.

"What is your name?" one of the men demanded in a gruff voice.

The light was back in her eyes. "Céline," she replied automatically.

She heard a trigger cock. The spotlight prevented her from seeing the gun, but she could sense that it was aimed at her head. If this was a training exercise, it was certainly an authentic one. Odette's heart was beating at a terrifying pace and she could feel pinpricks of sweat forming on her forehead under the heat of the lamp. "What do you want with me?"

"What is your real name and what is your occupation?"

"I told you, my name is Céline, and I'm just a widow from Somerset."

The light left her face for just a second as the man holding it gestured to another, who came up behind Odette, cracking his knuckles.

The cajoling, blinding light, and threats continued for over an hour, but Odette never wavered. Finally, as the sun ascended above the horizon, they switched off the spotlight. Odette blinked several times as the men removed their masks to reveal themselves as Major de Wesselow, her Morse instructor, and the Greek Adonis from the Wanborough Manor tennis courts.

"You did well, Céline," de Wesselow told her.

She rose to her feet, planting her hands on the desk. "What gives you the right—"

"It's just part of the training," de Wesselow interrupted, waving his hand as if the experience they'd put her through had been no big deal.

The alcohol that evening, as with most evenings in finishing school, flowed freely in the parlor. Odette, not usually one to partake, asked the bartender for a glass of wine.

When she noticed the normally reticent Jackie doing the same, Odette took her arm and led her to a remote corner. "Did you…" she trailed off with a glance around the room.

"Yes. You?" Jackie replied.

"With the major and the Morse and tennis guys."

"I had Roger and the psychiatrist."

"Only two? Lucky." Odette took a sip of wine. "Who's Roger again?"

As if on cue, the dark-haired man who'd informed Odette that London—not her—arranged for bomber pick-ups appeared. "You'll have to forgive us, of course," he told the two of them. "We want to make sure that you don't break under pressure."

"Does that happen?" Odette inquired.

"Yes. Two men today, in fact. Started weeping like babies. Don't bother," he said as Jackie and Odette searched the room, looking for tell-tale guilty expressions. "They've already been sent on."

"To France?" Jackie covered her mouth with a giggle. "No, I suppose not."

"No," Roger agreed. "They'll find places for them in other, less secret areas of F Section. Secretarial or Morse work, most likely."

"Not back to their ordinary lives?" Jackie asked.

He shook his head and Jacqueline murmured something that sounded like, "Good."

"You'll thank us for all this training, eventually," Roger said. "For setting such a high standard. It means anyone who is in your spy circuit has gone through similar trials, passed with flying colors and is as reliable as you are." He turned to Jackie. "I received an application just the other day from someone with the same last name as you, and I'm told you're their next of kin in England."

"My sister," Jackie said. Then, in a halting voice, she begged Roger not to take her on. "She's too impulsive, too stubborn. She might make it through the training all right, but she wouldn't last more than a minute out in the field."

"Stubborn seems about right: she's already been rejected twice, though she'll probably keep applying. And anyway, stubbornness isn't necessarily a bad thing in this line of work."

"Please," Jackie reached out to touch his sleeve. "Can you tell her that she's too young?"

Roger studied her face for a moment before nodding.

"Hallo, Rog, what do you have here?" The Adonis, looking even more flushed than he'd been on the tennis courts, stumbled his way across the parlor to join them. "Picked out the two loveliest birds in the room to chat up, didn't you?"

Roger smiled apologetically at Odette and Jacqueline. "This is Captain Mackintosh. He once trained here as well, but it was determined that the best cover story in the world could never hide his English accent and mannerisms, so we kept him on as an instructor. We call him Mac."

Mac took a long sip of his drink. "That's right, I failed, and here I am now, training damsels in distress." He raised his finger toward Odette, nearly toppling over from the effort. "This one damn near soiled her knickers this morning."

"That's not true." Odette forced her voice to remain calm, thinking that this might be yet another test. "Major de Wesselow said I did well."

"You did a somewhat adequate job, for a woman." He pointed at her again, only slightly steadier this time. "But you nearly blew your cover. You do that in front of the Boches, you're going to get yourself killed. And everyone else in your circuit too. I suppose you've heard of Hitler's newest decree: that anyone caught in an act of sabotage will be handed over to the SS for torture and then death." He grimaced, his beautiful face contorting grotesquely. "This is the exact reason they shouldn't allow women in this program. They're too emotional—that porcelain veneer of yours cracks easily."

"That's where you're wrong." Jacqueline said simply before she walked off, clearly believing this repugnant man was not worth her time.

Odette had also had enough and was not about to stand down this time. She stuck her finger directly into Mac's chest, forcing him to take a wobbly step backwards. "We women are going to become agents, whether you like it or not. And we will spark the resistance that brings down the Nazis, you'll see."

As Roger led Mac away, Odette's words echoed in her own head. It was abundantly clear to her now that she did have the strength that Buckmaster, Miss Atkins, and Jepson all believed she did. *I will agree to go to France,* she decided. *Now all they have to do is ask me.*

As if reading her mind, the next day, Major de Wesselow informed Odette that Major Buckmaster had driven out to New Forest to have a talk with her.

"Well, Céline, I've received the final summary of your training," Buckmaster said by way of greeting.

"And?" She wiped her hands on her trousers, suddenly nervous that they had deemed her inadequate.

"It's not as good as I would have liked."

She narrowed her eyes, thinking that the appalling Captain Mackintosh probably had something to do with her report. "What did he—they—say about me?"

"They said you have determination, but you are temperamental, sometimes without the clarity of mind that is required to get you out of dangerous situations." His lips turned up into what almost resembled a smile. "They also said your main weakness is 'a complete unwillingness to admit that she could ever be wrong.'"

She could feel the blood drain from her face. She'd come so far, and to be declared a failure now, after all of the trials she'd just been through, seemed almost cruel.

Buckmaster's expression softened. "Would you be terribly disappointed if I recommend you for coding work here in England?"

"Coding?" Her hands tightened into fists. "No. I want to go to France."

"Do you? Have you officially changed your mind?"

She sank into a chair. "You knew I was hesitant?"

"Of course I knew. That's my job. But I can also see that you have a certain determination about you. You aren't going to let anyone else tell you that you can't do something." He tapped an unlit cigarette on the desk. "Don't bear too much of a grudge toward Captain Mackintosh—he was only going off the script I gave him."

Odette felt slightly duped. *Even blockheads like Mac were not who they pretended to be.* "Major Buckmaster, I won't fail you. That I can promise." She leaned forward. "Who would you rather have in the field, someone who is willing to bow down to the Boches or someone with an unshakeable moral compass, a person who refuses to admit she is wrong because she knows she isn't? Someone with that 'certain determination' you so readily perceived?"

He sighed. "I suppose there is no use in doing things by the book."

She sensed that she had hit her mark. "Is there a book?"

The smile appeared with full force this time. "No. Not yet, anyway." He reached out his hand. "Congratulations, Agent Céline. You have become a fully-fledged member of the SOE."

Odette shook his hand.

"We will start the process of getting you a new identity and passport. The time is approaching, so make sure to get your arrangements made."

She knew he was referring to her family. "Yes, sir."

CHAPTER 11

MATHILDE

*I*nterallié obtained intelligence from people in all walks of life — dockmasters reported German submarine and ship arrivals while farmers watched truck convoys driving across the countryside and street-sweepers picked up on which hotels were hosting the Gestapo. All of this information was sent across France to Mathilde's Parisian network of letter boxes. Each afternoon she would travel to different areas of the city and retrieve the dispatches. She would then cull the most pertinent findings and type them up, always beginning with her signature greeting, "The Cat Reports...." to be communicated to the SOE in London.

René Aubertin paid a visit to the Colonel Moll apartment soon after they moved in, to inform Mathilde of Uncle Marco's latest coup. Industrial chemist that he was, Uncle Marco had created an acid solution to remove the bonding from the cement mortars in an underground hangar, resulting in the collapse of the entire airport wing.

René was just finishing his story when Armand walked in. As Armand had never officially met René, Mathilde gave them a proper introduction over cups of tea. As she filled Armand in on the latest news, René cast his eyes around the living room. "Do you think those are wise?" he asked when she'd finished, nodding toward Armand's collection of maps pasted all over the walls.

Armand frowned. "They keep track of the Boches' every move-ment, from sea to land to air."

"Don't get me wrong," René held up a hand in conciliation. "They are amazingly well kept, but I'm not sure they are exactly discreet." He nodded toward the door. "Mathilde told me you have Gestapo neighbors. Suppose they take a wayward glance inside? Something like that could get you thrown in Fresnes Prison with no questions asked. Not before you're arrested, anyway. I hear the Gestapo are quite efficient with their interrogations once you're their prisoner."

Armand seemed agitated by the comment and inched forward in his chair. "You and Mathilde have been friends forever, and—I would imagine—it would be hard to trust a stranger such as myself. If it helps, I will gladly tell you my real name and how I came to work with Mathilde."

René nearly spit out his tea. "For God's sake, don't do that. The less information you have about the people you're working for, the better."

Just then Marcel, their radio operator, let himself into the apart-ment using the key Armand had supplied him. After introducing himself to René, Marcel picked up Mathilde's latest report and then went into the little room he used to transmit.

René set down his cup. "Forgive me for asking another question, but is it prudent to send out your radio transmissions from the same apartment you are living in?"

"Transmitting here is better than having Marcel traipse around the city after curfew," Armand replied tersely.

"It's just that the Boches have gotten wind of the Resistance. They're cognizant of the fact we're sending out secret messages, and their detection vans are more ubiquitous than ever. I would hate for them to pick up Marcel's signal."

Armand loudly drained his tea before replying. "Rest assured, Marcel is an expert in avoiding detection."

After a few moments of uncomfortable silence, with Mathilde racking her brain for a neutral subject to discuss, Marcel headed into the kitchen and began searching through the cabinets. "Have you any champagne?"

"No," Mathilde said rising, grateful for the disruption. "But I think there is a sparkling white wine somewhere around here."

"What's the occasion?" Armand asked.

Marcel handed Armand his latest decoded message while Mathilde scrounged up four wine glasses.

"It's a congratulations from London," Marcel stated, the pride obvious in his voice. "They want us to know our intelligence is being received and the RAF is taking action immediately."

Armand beamed down at the little square paper. "Well, isn't that something?"

Mathilde handed him his wine first, not missing the inquiring glance he shot at René. It was obvious Armand was seeking approbation for his wounded ego.

René bestowed his characteristic smirk on them as he held up his glass. "To Interallié."

"To Interallié," the other three repeated.

The next day Mathilde took a break from traveling between letter boxes to have a cup of coffee in the café across from the Montparnasse station. She was warming her cold hands indulgently on the coffee mug when the chair in front of her was abruptly pulled out. "May I join you?" a German officer asked in halting French.

By the time she removed one hand from her mug to gesture to the chair, the officer had already settled into it. He had no food or drink in front of him. "If you don't mind, Fräulein, I would like to ask you a few questions."

"Of course," Mathilde set her cup down. "Only if I can inquire something of you first."

"By all means."

"You are wearing the uniform of an officer of the *Luftwaffe* but I don't seem to recognize the markings on your shoulder. Are you a flier?"

"No," he replied proudly. "I'm what you call—how do you say it in French—a Colonel of the Materials section. I'm responsible for the *Luftwaffe* supplies for the whole of the Bordeaux area."

"You are a long way from Bordeaux. What brings you here?" Mathilde tried to take a casual sip of coffee. Was it possible his presence had something to do with Interallié? Was he a member of the Gestapo, come to arrest her?

"I'm here on leave, and I was hoping you could instruct me on where to buy a box of tennis balls."

"Oh." She shot him a genuine smile. "Of course."

The German flagged down a waiter and requested a coffee, obviously not planning on leaving any time soon. As he waited for his order, he told Mathilde his life story: that he was the son of an important businessman in Stuttgart and, ever since he was a student in Paris, greatly admired the French culture.

"Yes, but what will happen to that Parisian culture now that your country has annexed our city?"

"Don't you see?" he leaned forward. "Paris is going to become part of the new and glorious Europe the *Führer* is creating. Thus far, his master plan has proceeded flawlessly."

Mathilde, who had no use for Nazi propaganda, noticed her coffee had gone cold. "I apologize, but I have just realized I am late for an appointment." She stood and gathered her fur coat. As she started for the door, she heard a man across from their table whisper, *"Collaborateur."*

The German gave Mathilde a sympathetic smile before shooting a warning look at the Frenchman and touching the gun at his holster for emphasis.

The Frenchman's hate-filled eyes occupied her thoughts as Mathilde left the restaurant. He had obviously thought she was one of those native traitors who abetted the Boches in order to save their own hides. *If only you knew what I've been up to,* she silently chastised him. *You wouldn't be so quick with your judgment.*

Mathilde discovered that Armand was in another one of his moods when she returned to the apartment. He'd been in a highly agitated state for the past few days, which she had originally chalked up to him working too much.

"Where have you been?" he demanded. "I have friends coming over and there is nothing on the stove."

Not for the first time she wondered how someone as brilliant as Armand could so easily take on the demeanor of a spoiled child. "I've been out."

"Just out? I heard you were in deep conversation with a Boche officer at a café."

How quickly information travelled these days, especially through a spy network. "Only to gain intelligence." She told him about the Luftwaffe supply officer as she opened the refrigerator and took stock of its contents. "Why are you having friends over? I thought we were going to have a quiet evening together."

"My mother is dead."

"What?" Mathilde shut the refrigerator. She knew how close Armand had been to his parents, how he regretted leaving them behind in Poland. "I'm sorry."

She moved to wrap her arms around him, but he shrugged her off. "Lucien and Bernard will be here any moment."

Both Poles. Mathilde refused to be put out, musing that Armand invited them because he wanted some hint of his homeland tonight. Besides, she liked Lucien de Roquigny, a slim, gray-haired Polish aristocrat, not least because he was always attentive to her.

She couldn't say the name of Bernard Krutki, however. The former lieutenant who'd been Armand's aide in the Polish Air Force—and who was now heading one of Interallié's sectors—usually acted stand-offish, almost to the point of suspicion, around Mathilde.

"Did you hear about the arrest of Raoul Kiffer?" Bernard demanded to know, before Mathilde had even taken his coat.

"Kiki?" Mathilde's mouth dropped open as she glanced at Armand. "He's one of our couriers."

Armand shrugged. "You have to break a few eggs to make an omelet."

Mathilde was not so sure she was willing to sacrifice anyone's life for the network, but she thought it wise not to say that aloud.

"It's nice to see you again, Mathilde," Lucien said, taking her hands between his thin ones. His normally amiable expression had taken on a pinched look, as if he were more worried about Kiki's arrest than he let on.

Between the tragic news of Armand's mother and Kiki, the dinner was as miserable as to be expected. Mathilde sat next to Armand, occasionally touching his arm to reassure him of her presence, but he acted as though she wasn't even there. All through the main course he was silent, as if in another world, perhaps back in Poland with his parents, while Bernard and Lucien talked business.

Mathilde was too distracted over worrying about Armand to notice how much wine he had consumed. The other two men matched him glass for glass until all three of them were drunk. As Mathilde made tea, Armand thought it would be a great game to hurl their empty wine glasses at the fireplace. None of them made it in, and they crashed into varying lengths of shards on the wood floor.

After that display, Mathilde declared it was time for Bernard and Lucien to leave. She retrieved their coats and escorted them out, Lucien whispering that she could call on him at any time. She shut the door behind them and then cornered Armand on his way to the kitchen for more wine. "I realize you are upset about what happened back in Poland, but don't forget, Interallié—and I—am your family now."

"Family?" he scoffed. "How can I be sure they—or you," his voice had taken on a mocking tone, "won't betray me at a moment's notice?"

She thought back to what he had said the day he was almost arrested. "Well, I guess you don't. You never know how a person might act when threatened by the Gestapo. But," she reached out to rub his arm, "you can have faith in me, at least. I would never betray you."

Once again he shrugged her off. "I'm not sure I believe that."

"What?" Mathilde had the mind to shake him. "How can you say such a thing?"

"Well, you were seen this morning talking to a Boche. And Bernard says—"

It was her turn to imitate his tone; she slurred her words and exaggerated the vowels as she retorted, "I don't care what Ber-nard says." She picked up the dinner plates, stepping carefully over the broken glass. "And I told you why I was talking to that *Luftwaffe* officer."

As she brushed by Armand's desk on her way to the kitchen, a stack of papers fell over. She dumped the dishes in the sink before gesturing to the pile on the floor. "And who should not fully trust whom? During my training in Vichy, Captain Sardanapalus said to destroy all records, not keep them around like some kind of flashing sign pointing to every member of our network."

Armand narrowed his bloodshot eyes as he frowned at the mess. Then without a word he spun on his heel and lurched to their bedroom, slamming the door and then locking it for emphasis.

Mathilde gave an audible sigh before she turned on the sink and began washing the dishes.

She was so involved in her work that she didn't hear the front door open and shut again. She looked up with a start to see Marcel standing in the living room, staring dejectedly at the scattered papers. "Is the night's dispatch in there?" he asked upon catching sight of Mathilde.

"No. I didn't have time tonight to type one up."

"Is there nothing to send to London then?"

She gave him a regretful shrug. "You can tell them Armand's mother has died. That's why there is no report tonight."

He muttered something about not letting personal matters get in the way of winning a war before he went into the little room.

CHAPTER 12

DIDI

*D*idi started her six-hour shift that night in the usual manner, tuning in to the established frequency and adjusting the wireless to lessen the background noise. Sometimes the interference was so harsh she couldn't imagine hearing a voice over the din, but tonight it was barely noticeable. She hunched over her desk, her headphones blocking out the click-clack of the other FANY's Morse keys, a cacophony Didi's trained ears couldn't translate to anything discernible, even when she could hear clearly.

She waited for her operator to make contact. He was usually punctual, and when the time for his sked came and went, Didi grew anxious. She shifted in her chair and restacked the square cards she used to take down Marcel's code. After that, she polished the Bakelite box and knobbed lever of the Morse key that she used to tap out her dispatches.

Finally she heard a transmission coming through. Didi grabbed the pencil and took down his Morse signals. They employed the Q-system commonly utilized by ships, which consisted of a series of 3-letter combinations, most beginning with Q. Marcel had tapped, 'QRK IMI' which meant, *How are you receiving me?*

Didi replied with, 'QSA 4,' on her Morse key. The 4 indicated the strength of the signal; anything less than 3 and Marcel would attempt to resend his message. But since the signal was strong tonight, Marcel continued with 'QTC,' *I have a message for you.*

Didi faithfully translated the clicks of his key into letters on the square card until she got to 'QRU,' *I have nothing more.*

If there were messages to send from the SOE, Didi would then type out her own 'QTC' and then the coded reply. Tonight, however, there was nothing to relay and she ended the transmission with 'VA,' *Close down.*

She took off her headphones, relishing the cool air of the hut on her warm ears before she picked up her pencil again and began to decode Marcel's message.

She was so involved in her work that Captain Smith's voice startled her. "Was that the latest report from The Cat?"

"Yes." Didi set down her pencil and pushed the card toward him.

"What's this? Nothing to report?"

She shook her head. "Something about a family emergency."

He tossed the card back onto the desk. "There's going to be a lot more family emergencies if that devil Hitler's allowed to keep moving about France. Don't they know there's a war going on? We've no time for 'family emergencies.'"

"Yes, sir." Didi replied for lack of anything else to say.

"That Cat's reports are usually quite informative. Sometimes even as little as a few hours after you end the transmission, our bombers are on their way to France to blow up something they've told us about—an ammunition dump or a German train carrying more troops across the border."

"I know, sir," Didi said, not without a bit of pride this time. It was luck of the draw that she had been assigned as Marcel's home operator. She wasn't quite sure who The Cat was or how he/she was related to Marcel—or whether it was Marcel himself—but she knew that anything that came in beginning, "The Cat Reports," was given priority by the higher-ups of the SOE.

Captain Smith shook his head. "It's not right. I hope their so-called emergency had nothing to do with the gonios that have started circling Paris."

Didi recalled what Archie had told her about the Nazi signal-detecting vans. "I hope so too."

"How did Marcel sound to you tonight? You sure it was him?"

Didi nodded. If there was such a thing as, 'Intimacy in Morse,' which is what the other girls called it, then Didi had experienced it. She had become so well-versed in Marcel's fist—his personal touch on the key—that she could compensate for any 'Morse Mutilation' from interference. "It was him, sir—of that I am sure."

"Well, maybe we should get the head of that circuit out here to London—make sure he's trained in all ways of the SOE."

"Pardon me for asking," Didi was hesitant, figuring Captain Smith would refuse to divulge any information, but she decided to pursue it anyway. "Who is The Cat?"

"She's not technically one of ours, nor is the real head—the one they call Armand. They got their start well before we did, but, as their circuit is up and running and ours are just getting off the ground, they're still the best we've got. I'm going to see if Buck can arrange a Lysander pick-up for this Armand as soon as possible." With that, Smith did a rapid about-face and walked away.

CHAPTER 13

ODETTE

*W*hen Odette returned to London, she met Miss Atkins at the Trocadero, a baroque-style restaurant near Baker Street. It fell under Miss Atkins' jurisdiction to finalize logistics, and she asked Odette to make a list of all of her personal possessions and whom she wanted them to go to in the event Odette did not make it back from France.

Odette agreed to do so, fighting down a pang of panic at the possibility Miss Atkins so politely alluded to. Luckily she was distracted by the food's arrival. Miss Atkins watched with her eagle-eyes as Odette picked up her knife and fork, holding the knife loosely in her right hand in the proper French form.

Miss Atkins nodded approvingly. "There are informants everywhere in France, whether they are spies, Vichy-supporters, or just fools wanting to get in with the Nazis. We must make sure that nothing can unwittingly expose you to suspicion. Above all, remember to look left to right when crossing the street. Traffic is on the right side of the road in France, and looking the wrong way is a dead giveaway that you are foreign." She went on this vein for quite some time, advising Odette how to interact with the local Resistance population, explaining which rationing coupons could be used on which days, and updating her on curfew times. Odette tried to absorb it all, thinking if only she could obey every one of Miss Atkins' commands, her mission would be triumphant.

After lunch, Miss Atkins accompanied Odette shopping, where she picked out a French-made dark grey jacket and skirt. "This gray will hide the dirt in prison," Odette said, fingering the heavy material.

"Do you think you're going to prison?" Miss Atkins asked.

"I don't know." She'd been in a melancholy mood ever since Miss Atkins suggested she might not come back. "But it's better to be prepared, don't you think Miss Atkins?"

She frowned. "I suppose so."

Miss Atkins purchased the suit, along with a new French valise and heeled shoes, courtesy of the SOE. She also added a Parisian perfume, gloves, and an umbrella to the booty before dropping Odette off at a hairdresser's with explicit instructions on how to cut Odette's hair in the latest Parisian style: shoulder-length, with layers to help it curl.

The next morning, Odette approached the gates of St. Helen's Boarding School for Girls. Her training had been relentlessly thorough but nothing had prepared her for the agony of saying goodbye to her daughters. She smiled through her tears as she watched them approach in their plaid jumpers, one of the head nuns trailing after them.

"Mummy!" Marianne began to run. She reached her thin arms through the garden gates and Odette did her best to embrace her.

"I've come to say good-bye, girls." Odette wiped her eyes as the nun finally opened the gate. Marianne and Lily flung themselves at her while Françoise stood back and looked on.

"Where are you going?" Françoise asked.

"Scotland." She pulled her oldest daughter close. "You'll look after your sisters, won't you Françoise?"

She nodded solemnly. "When will you be back?"

"I don't know." A tear coursed down Odette's cheek. She licked her thumb and rubbed at an imaginary spot on Marianne's face. "You will all be good girls while I'm gone, right?"

"Of course, Mummy," Lily replied.

"I don't want you to go," Marianne wailed, grabbing one of Odette's legs. "You can't leave us."

"I have to." Odette's voice was barely above a whisper. "Someday you'll understand why."

"Are you going to fight the Nazis?" Marianne asked through her tears.

"Yes, but I'll try to come back as soon as I can." Odette nodded at the nun, who clapped her hands. "Come on, girls, we must be getting back to class."

Each girl hugged her once more before grudgingly following the nun back inside.

Hitler could do his worst to me, and it wouldn't be nearly as hard as what I just went through, Odette mused as she slowly walked away from St. Helen's. Saying good-bye to her girls, not knowing when or if she would be back, had been the worst experience she'd ever had to endure.

After a tearful night alone in her London hotel, Odette met with Buckmaster the next morning.

"Good morning, Lise," he said as she entered his office.

Odette looked around the room. "Who is Lise?"

"You are."

She sat down. "What happened to Céline?"

He shrugged. "She's done, her ashes scattered over Manchester. Rest in peace. Oddly enough, another woman with her same coloring and features has emerged, although she's a bit…" he gave her a meaningful look, "more amenable than Céline. She will have many other aliases," he pushed an identity card across the table, "but to the SOE she will be known as Lise. We decided to keep your first name for your on-the-ground pseudonym. That way if someone calls you on the street, you'll know they're talking to you."

She took the card, trying to hide her shaking hands. 'Odette Metayer' was printed in bold lettering. Her own expressionless eyes stared back at her from the photograph. From here on out, like Céline, Mrs. Sansom had officially been buried, to be replaced by the various aliases callously provided by the SOE. It gave Odette a cold feeling, like ice water running through her veins, and she did her best to shrug it off.

"Tell me about yourself, Mrs. Metayer," Buckmaster demanded.

Odette cleared her throat. "I grew up in Dunkirk. My father's name was Gustav Bédigis, a bank official. My mother's name was Lil Lienard."

Buckmaster nodded at her to continue.

"My father was killed at Verdun. I married Jean Metayer, a shipping clerk. He was quite a few years older than I, a kind man while he lived. He died in 1936 of bronchitis." She touched a handkerchief to each eye for good measure.

"And, Mrs. Metayer, have you any children?"

She hung her head with real emotion. "No children, sir."

"I think that's good for now." He clasped his hands. "Now Lise, the circuit you'll be working with is Clothier. You'll be their courier in Auxerre." Odette recalled from her training that the SOE's networks, or 'circuits' were organized around three main people—the "head," or organizer, courier, and the wireless operator. It was the courier's job to carry dispatches to and from the different circuits and the local recruits. She also knew that women were preferred as couriers because they could move about the countryside easier than men, not to mention the Germans being less likely to conduct thorough searches on women for messages hidden in their hair or undergarments should they come under suspicion.

Buckmaster opened a drawer and pulled out a small purse. "Here is 50,000 francs. You will receive instructions at a later date on how to obtain more money." He handed her a piece of paper filled with contacts and addresses. "Memorize this, and then burn it by tomorrow morning before you depart for the airport. You should be in France in a few days."

He took out another pouch and emptied it onto his desk to reveal an assortment of differently-sized pills. He separated the white ones into a little pile. "These are responsible for violent stomach issues. You can give them to the enemy or use them yourself to feign illness. It won't be pleasant, but it will get the point across should a doctor need to examine you." He then pushed the green ones forward. "These are stimulants and should only be taken when you are too tired to do your duty, but have to keep going."

She picked up the purse and scooped the pills into it.

"And this," Buckmaster held up a small brown one. "This is the 'L' tablet. L for lethal. It's a cyanide tablet, and once chewed, it can kill you in a matter of 15 seconds. Obviously it would be used as a last

resort: if you get captured by the enemy and feel there is no escape…
well, this little pill can be your permanent way out."

Odette tried not to visibly balk at Buckmaster's suggestion. She
wasn't sure she could ever willingly commit suicide, not even if being
tortured by the Nazis was the alternative. She did her best to steady her
fingers once again as she accepted the pill and placed it into her bag
with the others. The question of the L-pill could wait for another day.

"One last thing," he reached into the breast pocket of his jacket
and pulled out a small gold ring. "This is your good luck gift."

"Good luck gift?"

He dropped it into her hand. "We give them to all of our departing
agents, just to let them know we're thinking of them. If worse comes to
worst and you run out of money, you can always pawn it."

The ring was too big for any of her fingers, so she slipped it on her
thumb for now, vowing to take it off later. "I think I'm ready."

"Do you have any other questions?"

"No questions." Odette reached into her handbag and pulled out a
packet of letters. "But I do have a favor." She pushed the letters across
the desk. "These are to my daughters. They are all undated, so if you
would be so kind as to post them to St. Helen's once a week, I'd be
grateful. I don't think I'll be in a position to write to them on a regular
basis."

Buckmaster tucked the packet into his drawer. "Will do. And good
luck, Mrs. Metayer."

She stood. "Thank you."

CHAPTER 14

DIDI

*A*s Captain Smith had predicted, the SOE requested the presence of Interallié's chief in London as soon as possible, and Didi dutifully communicated the invitation through the wireless. Over the next few days, a great number of her dispatches to and from Marcel were about finding a place for a Lysander to land.

Didi had just sent out a message, translated as, *Pick-up for Armand fixed for full moon on first October eleven thirty PM STOP, On this day confirm safety and give weather conditions STOP*, when Captain Smith approached her station.

He took out a handkerchief and rubbed a fingerprint off her Morse key. "I'm going to arrange for you to give Armand instructions on how to code and send messages, SOE style."

"Me, sir?"

"Yes." He tucked the handkerchief back into his front pocket. "You are aware that, as the biggest Resistance network in France, they are still a little raw in the way we do things around here."

She nodded.

"He won't have a lot of time on this side of the channel, and his 'dance card,' as you might say, is already full. I'm assuming he's going to want to send Marcel a personal message through you, and you might as well take the opportunity to show him the proper way to code."

"Yes, sir."

. . .

The first week of October, Captain Smith walked into the wireless hut accompanied by an unfamiliar man. "This is the director of Interallié," Smith said. "The first official pick-up we've ever made from German-occupied territory."

Armand was tall and lean, with dark hair and matching eyes that studied Didi's every move. She held out her hand, casting her gaze downward rather than meet his penetrating one. As he reached forward to shake hands, a newspaper fell from his briefcase.

"Look at this," Captain Smith bent down to pick it up. "It's the *Paris-Soir*."

"The main underground newspaper for the Resistance," Armand stated, sensing that Didi did not understand the significance.

Captain Smith tucked it under his arm. "I will see that this is on the King's breakfast-table in the morning. I can't imagine how surprised he will be to personally read about Resistance activities firsthand!" He clasped Armand on the back. "I'm glad we are finally able to unite France and England's endeavors to stop Hitler."

"Me too." Armand tapped Captain Smith's shoulder in solidarity, but his eyes were once again on Didi.

"Would you like to send a message to Marcel?" she asked after Smith had left.

"Yes." His smile widened. "So you are the one we've been communicating with. I always thought it would be a man."

"Most of the men in England have gone off to war." Didi set a pencil and stack of white cards in front of him. "We FANYs are responsible for all but the extremely sensitive communications."

"Very well, very well." Armand started writing something. After a minute, he put his pencil down and pushed the card toward Didi. He'd written, *Safely arrived STOP The wireless operator you've been in touch with is simply wonderful STOP if you don't mind I might try my own with her STOP.*

Didi refrained from heaving a deep sigh as she took it.

"What's wrong?" Armand asked.

"Nothing." Didi began to code as he stood over her shoulder, his breath smelling of brandy. "It's just that…" she searched for a possible explanation for her rudeness. "I thought we would be sending this to The Cat."

Armand waved his hand. "Lily would only get this message second-hand and Marcel knows enough not to pass it on. She's incredibly jealous, you know."

Didi pretended to be intensely focused on her task. She was done in a matter of minutes and Armand remarked, the admiration clear in his voice, on how little time it took her.

"I've been doing this day in and day out for months now," she replied.

"That's your only job, to code and transmit?"

"Yes."

He rubbed his chin, his dark eyes thoughtful. "It takes Marcel much longer. Perhaps if I found someone more adept at translating codes, it would take less time and Marcel could focus more on the transmissions."

"Perhaps," she agreed.

"And now, if you don't mind, I'm starving. As I'm a foreigner, would it be too much to ask for you to accompany me to one of England's finer restaurants? Your choice, of course."

"Well," Didi glanced at the clock. "It's too dark to go far, and there's not much around here. I suppose there might be something at the Spread-Eagle pub." She couldn't keep the twinge of regret out of her voice, as the last time she had frequented that particular pub was when she'd met Archie.

Armand was incredibly talkative at dinner and filled her in on the dramatic story of being picked-up by the Lysander and on the functions of Interallié in France. He had several beers, telling her that he was sick of French wine, and, with each beer, grew more animated until he began to remind Didi of a very excited child. "In France, the Gestapo is everywhere. There's even some occupying the apartment across from Lily and I."

"Do you live with this Lily, then?" Didi asked, swirling her sherry without drinking it. Based on this conversation and his earlier mention of Lily's jealousy, she'd surmised that Lily was The Cat's alter ego.

"My mother, God rest her soul," he crossed himself, "would have never approved of me living with a woman before marriage. But Lily is my secretary, and *C'est la vie. C'est la guerre,*" he continued in poorly accented French.

It is life. It is war. Didi motioned for the waiter to bring the check before Armand could order another beer.

"I will be in England for a month or so," he told her, draining the last sip of his pint. "I would like to see more of you."

"I'm sure your agenda must be filled at this point," she replied, hoping that was true.

"I would make time for you," he said, his chestnut eyes so full of mirth that she couldn't tell if he was serious.

Didi drove him back to the mansion grounds. It was well past dusk now, and she could see his grip on the door handle eventually relax as she zipped through the darkened streets with ease.

"You're a very good driver," he said before turning to gaze out the window. "It's so quiet. I expected to see bombed out buildings everywhere. And there's no German sign posts. It's like the war has never come here."

She slowed down as they approached the checkpoint to enter Fawley Court. "When you go to London to meet Major Buckmaster, you'll probably see a lot more damage there."

"You're so smart, and I've never seen a woman more at ease driving during the black-out. Have you ever considered becoming an underground agent?"

"Yes." Didi pulled into a parking spot and shut off the car. "But for some reason the SOE won't take me."

"They will," Armand replied confidently. "You keep doing what you do and someday they'll realize they have no choice but to recruit you."

"I hope so." Didi exited the car. "It was nice meeting you," she continued truthfully, her earlier irritation having dissipated with his last comment.

"Same here. You know, I have my own room here. If you want, you can…"

She stretched into a fake yawn. "Not tonight, Armand. But thanks for the companionship."

"Good night, Didi."

"Good night." She could feel his gaze on her back as she walked into the mansion and headed off to her attic bed.

· · ·

A few days later, Didi received a strange message from Marcel.

Important STOP Marcel to Armand STOP Have serious trouble with La Chatte. She refuses to cooperate and is threatening secession STOP What should I do STOP.

"Captain Smith?" she called as soon as she'd finished decoding it. "Is Armand still on the premises?"

Smith frowned. "I think he's in London, but I can send for him."

"I think that would be wise." She handed him the decoded message. He scanned it before tossing it on the table. "Right then." He turned and headed out of the hut.

Armand reported to Didi's station a few hours later. Without a word, she gave him the message and then watched his lips move as he read it.

He crumpled it in his hand. "I should have known. Lily is so emotional. I knew I couldn't leave her to direct such a vast organization. She doesn't have the physical endurance nor the proper military training."

For some reason, Didi felt indignant about him insulting The Cat. "She helped you form the network."

"Of course, of course." Armand was back in his highly-strung adolescent mode. "As far as the work is concerned, we are perfect partners. She finds the right people and keeps in contact with them while I know how to use them most effectively, what to ask them, and how to best utilize the news they report."

Upon spotting Armand, Smith hurried over. "Well, what is to be done about this new development?" He nodded toward the crumpled message in Armand's hand.

"I wasn't aware that Lily and Marcel had bad blood, but I guess it makes sense. Marcel is the head of radio service, and he can be a little hot-headed sometimes. He probably made some remark to Lily and she overreacted to it…"

"And?" Smith demanded. "Is it serious enough that you will need to return to France?"

Armand considered for a moment before answering, "Lily can be quite temperamental. If we leave it too long, it could develop into serious trouble."

Smith nodded. "I will start making the arrangements, though this time won't be by a Lysander landing. As a former naval man, I'd suggest going by boat to the coast of Brittany, or the other alternative is to parachute in."

Armand held up his hand. "As an Air Force man, I choose parachuting."

As if suddenly remembering Didi's presence, Smith told her to let Marcel know Armand would be back in a few days.

"And make sure you put a stop to this petty fighting within your network," Smith cautioned Armand. "We've got a war to win."

"Yes, sir!" Armand saluted Smith before the captain walked off.

"Such a shame," Armand stated, winking at Didi. "I'm under orders to return to London tonight to finish the meeting they pulled me from to discuss this mess in Paris. I guess we won't be having that drink after all."

"I guess not." She decided to ask the question that had been burning in her mind ever since she'd decoded the fateful message. "Does Interallié have other wireless operators?"

"A few, none as good as Marcel, and none of them know how to code."

"Oh," she said, disappointed. She wasn't sure with whom she'd rather part ways, the operator whose Morse fist she'd gotten to know so well over the last few months, or the woman head of Interallié whose reports had provided so much valuable information.

"Take care, Didi," Armand said. "And good luck to you."

"Same to you," she called as she watched him stride away.

CHAPTER 15

MATHILDE

*D*espite the somewhat wounded alliance between its co-leaders and its wireless operator, Interallié was flourishing. Mathilde was occupied day in and day out, almost too busy to think about Armand. Almost.

As soon as he came back to their apartment, looking admittedly travel-weary, she threw her arms around him. "You are back, Toto! It's so good to see you in the flesh! Yesterday you must have still been in England and now here you are."

Armand released her embrace to look at his watch. "Yes, at this time yesterday I was having dinner with the RAF."

"The RAF?" Mathilde echoed, trying to hide her stung feelings at Armand's indifference.

"The Royal Air Force," he strode past her to look through the messages on the table. "I suppose there's been no communication since Marcel…"

"Quit," Mathilde filled in.

Armand went into the kitchen and fixed himself a drink before plopping into an armchair with a heavy sigh. "Well," he said, taking a sip of his bourbon. "Tell me what happened."

Mathilde began pacing the length of the room. "Marcel quarreled with me on several occasions over the slightest details. I think he resented a woman being in charge of him."

"I told you before I left, Lily, you weren't technically in charge of Marcel. He works on his own accord."

"The network needs to be a fully functioning machine. Marcel was a nail in the tire, so I let him go." Too late she remembered that only a few minutes previously she'd said Marcel quit.

If Armand noticed she'd changed her story, he didn't say anything. "Again, you did not have the authority. If I had it in my power, I would hire him back, but he's moved on. He'll be working with the first SOE men coming in from England. It's probably better they have one of ours anyway—I got the feeling they don't quite know what they're doing yet." It was clear that Armand's already inflated ego had grown even larger while he was in England.

She sat down across from him. "Tell me what London was like. Is it much damaged? What is the morale over there? What about the blackouts and bomb shelters... and when are they going to liberate us?"

"I would have perhaps acquired more information had I not been forced to return so quickly."

"I'm sorry. I had no idea Marcel was going to tell you about... our little situation."

"Listen..." Armand drank the rest of his bourbon and then set it down with a clink. "I didn't realize this before I went to London, but we are currently the largest Resistance organization in France. While it's a great honor, it should also inspire in all of us a sense of responsibility for the role we are playing."

"Great honor?" His attitude was beginning to irritate her even more than the news that René had shared with her that morning. All the same, she was thankful that she now had the opportunity to change the subject. "I doubt you would say such a thing if you saw the German vans outside our apartment like René did."

Armand frowned. "Radio detectors?"

"Yes."

"I suppose that means it's time to move." He ran a hand through his hair. "We'll have to find another safe house, and soon."

"I've already found one."

His eyes twinkled. "That's why we make the perfect pair, you and me. Where is it?"

"A little house in Montmartre, owned by a widow of a colonel in the First World War. A Frenchwoman," Mathilde emphasized. "I told her that my 'cousin' would need to be out late at night since he—you

—is involved with trading on the Black Market. You know, to get by."

He hugged her, the distance that had grown between them in the last month disappearing as their bodies touched.

The next day Mathilde led Armand to the little brick house on the Rue Villa Léandre, a little cul-de-sac of three-storied rowhouses. The rent was cheap, but Mathilde had mainly been drawn to the narrow, vine-yard-ringed streets on Montmartre because, despite the intimidating presence of the Occupation, it had not lost its quintessential Parisian character.

Armand was both impressed and dismayed by the amount of intelligence that had piled up in his absence. He picked up a piece of paper off the top of the stack of papers they'd brought with them and scanned through it. "I don't think there's any way I could code this all by myself."

"What do you mean?" Mathilde asked.

"With Marcel gone, I'm not sure what we're going to do. All of our contacts are already overwrought and I wouldn't want to trust just anyone with our code. I met this coder in England, a woman, who..." he trailed off.

Mathilde did her best to suppress a fiery feeling of jealousy at his simple mention of another woman. "What are you going to do?"

Armand replaced the paper onto the stack. "I'll think of something."

The next morning, Uncle Marco requested that Mathilde accompany him to Brest for a reconnaissance mission. When she returned to the red-roofed house a few days later, she found an unfamiliar woman in the living room.

"Where is Armand?" Mathilde demanded before eyeing the woman up and down. She was pale, her pathetically thin figure clad in a dowdy dress, of a style typical in provincial France.

"Who are you?" The woman's voice held more than a hint of challenge.

"It is none of your business." Though she longed to put this horrid woman in her place by informing her that she was Armand's partner, Mathilde had no idea if the woman was trustworthy.

The other woman met her eyes, and the two sized each other up with equal amounts of hatred. "That's my coat you're wearing," the other woman spat out.

Mathilde ran a hand up and down the sleeve, as if she were petting the fur. "It's mine now. Armand gave it to me."

Armand chose that moment to enter the room. "Ah, Lily, I see you've met Viola Borni."

Mathilde whipped her head toward her lover. "What is she doing here?"

Armand slipped past her to stand by the woman, this Viola.

"I'm the one who helped Armand after he escaped from a POW camp and provided him with his French papers." Viola looked up at Armand with wide eyes as she added, "They once belonged to my dead husband."

"Is that so?" Mathilde pulled the worn fur tighter around her body before turning to Armand. "That still doesn't explain why she is in Paris."

"I thought she could help me code your reports now that Marcel is gone. She's an accountant and very good with figures."

"So she's just your secretary."

If it was possible for Viola to display any more animosity toward Mathilde, it happened. Her eyes narrowed into slits, she replied, "He brought me all the way here to assist him. He even offered me a room in this house."

Mathilde held up a hand in defeat. "If that's how you want it, Toto, then so be it." She wasn't going to make a scene and demand that Armand rid the house of this new woman. She had never begged a man for anything in her life, and she wasn't about to start now. If it was so easy for her to abandon her husband, then giving up Armand should be a simple task.

Mathilde moved out of the Rue Villa Léandre house as soon as she could find an apartment, one still in Montmartre, on the Rue Cortot. She poured herself into her work, vowing to forget all about Armand and his little secretary. She still made her daily rounds to the letter-boxes, particularly the one at the Café La Palette, and typed her reports of all the compiled information. She made René Aubertin bring each edition of The Cat's reports to Armand so that Viola could code them before they were transmitted to London by their new wireless operator. Coffee in the morning and wine in the afternoon and at night helped the gnawing feeling that Armand had deserted her.

Her efforts worked for a week, until Armand decided to call together his Interallié associates to celebrate the one-year anniversary of the network.

"I'm busy that night," Mathilde snapped when Armand stopped by her apartment to invite her.

"But you have to come, Mathilde."

She noted the absence of his pet name *Lily*. "No. It's too dangerous for all of us to be together, with the Gestapo on the prowl."

He put a tentative hand on her shoulder. "You and I were the founders of this thing. We started with two people and have grown it into hundreds—Gestapo threat or not, you have to come," he repeated. "Plus, I have a surprise for you."

"Will Viola be there?"

He raised his eyebrows, seeming surprised at Mathilde's onerous tone. "Of course."

Mathilde pursed her lips, a million questions forming as she waited for Armand to say something, perhaps deny that he had romantic feelings toward Viola or declare that he missed his black-haired mistress, his *petite chatte*. She'd settle for anything that resembled an apology. But he said nothing, so Mathilde let her questions die. "I will be there for Interallié," she finally relented.

Armand nodded before he left. Mathilde went to the window and watched as he walked down the street, whistling to himself.

René took Mathilde out to dinner the night of Armand's celebration. It was a Category B restaurant, which meant that it had a fixed menu price of less than forty francs for a meal, more than Mathilde could afford, but René had managed to scrounge some black-market money from somewhere. René carefully studied the menu before ordering the pasta. Mathilde did the same.

"What I wouldn't give for a steak," René commented.

"Or coffee with cream," Mathilde said. Most restaurants were forbidden to serve coffee after three in the afternoon.

"We could have gone to one of the *collaborateur cafés*," he replied. "I hear they pay no attention to rationing, serve meat on non-meat days, and charge way beyond the set prices."

"But then we'd have to eat amongst the Nazis. It's bad enough they're all around our new neighborhood." Mathilde managed to finish her thought before the waiter arrived with their food: watered down, butterless noodles with dried turnips on the side.

"Did you hear of the Hugentoblers?" René whispered once the waiter was out of earshot.

"No." The Hugentoblers were a couple who let Interallié use their house for gatherings.

Despite its unappetizing appearance, René dug into his meal with gusto. "It seems the Gestapo paid a little visit to their home, searching through their things."

"Did they find anything?"

"I don't think so. The couple were obviously shaken up, but they weren't arrested. Why the Gestapo would set their sights on them, I have no idea, but it's a disturbing coincidence. That and the arrest of Kiki last week would put anyone on edge."

"Indeed." Mathilde paused, her fork halfway to her mouth. "You don't think Kiki would divulge any information about Interallié, do you?"

René sighed. "Not under usual circumstances, but the Germans have ways of making people talk."

While she did not think Kiki would bow under pressure, it was, as René said, disturbing. Mathilde set her fork down. What little appetite she managed to conjure up had now disappeared.

The evening did not improve. Everyone at the party knew of both the Gestapo's visit to the Hugentoblers and the arrest of Kiki and the room was filled with awkward pauses in conversation. Mathilde sat helplessly as Viola took over the hostess duties, getting people drinks and refilling the snack table.

"Why is she here?" René hissed.

"I don't know," Mathilde replied honestly. "Armand and I have been working together every night and day for the last ten months. And then he suddenly casts me aside for that simpleton."

Though he'd been moderate with the wine at dinner, René now

had a full glass of champagne in his hand. He took a great gulp of it before saying, "Could it be…"

"What?" Mathilde knew René's brutal honesty might bruise her ego, but she was tired of wondering what had happened to Armand's affection. And if anyone knew her better than Armand, it was her oldest friend.

René sized the new woman up, his adroit eyes missing nothing. "She has no societal ties, no interest in being a debutante, clearly her education did not even reach secondary level." He now gazed at his friend in the black beret, her fur coat shed to reveal a fitted dress. "You are her complete opposite: so dynamic, so blazingly direct." He drained his glass. "Could it be that Armand wanted someone simpler, someone more… uncomplicated?"

While flattered by René's summation, it did not soothe the ache in Mathilde's heart. "If that's what he wants, then he sure got someone… as you said, 'uncomplicated'."

"But at the same time, he seems to have made this whole thing that much more complicated." He put his hand over hers and gave her his customary half-smile. "Don't let this situation change your work ethic. You are more dedicated to the cause than anyone."

Mathilde nodded, trying to keep her gaze from wandering to Armand, who had his arm around Viola's waist.

"I almost forgot!" Armand exclaimed before disappearing into the next room. He came back with a large box and Mathilde watched with narrowed eyes as Viola opened it. She squealed as if she were a calf playing in the field, pulling out a brand-new fur coat.

Mathilde raised her chin, hoping René wouldn't notice the tears that were forming. "I would never let anything interfere with my work."

"Shh!" Armand shouted, rushing toward the radio and spilling most of his drink in the process. He turned up the volume as the BBC announcer began with his usual salutation: *"Ici Londres."* Mathilde leaned forward in her chair.

"And now," the voice continued in French, "here are some personal messages." This was the moment that the BBC sent messages from the SOE in code, rightfully assuming most of the German higher-ups did not speak French. "We wish a happy anniversary to the little family reunion happening in Paris. Happy anniversary!" he repeated.

For a moment all strife was forgotten as the Interallié agents rose from their seats, congratulating each other.

"And a special thanks to my partner, *La Chatte!*" Armand declared, clinking his glass with Mathilde's. "This network wouldn't be what it is without her!"

Mathilde took a sip of dry champagne before casting a triumphant look at the hostess, who crossed her arms over her chest.

"Viola!" Armand shouted, causing the little woman to look up at him, the hopeful look all-too obvious on her face. "Code a little message to send back to London. What should we say?" he asked the room.

Mathilde pasted on a fake smile and held up her glass. "*Vive la liberté!*"

"*Vive la liberté!*" the rest of them echoed.

CHAPTER 16

DIDI

*W*ith Marcel gone, Didi's wireless transmitted nothing but static. Rather than assign her to another "Joe," or on-the-ground agent, Captain Smith told Didi she'd been selected for a different task altogether.

A few days later, she and several other FANY's, including Yvonne, were bussed back to London. Didi was under the impression that civilians in the area thought the women bunking at Fawley Court were there to train as ambulance operators, but, as the women disembarked, the driver glanced back at the empty bus and asked if there were, "any more spies onboard."

Yvonne giggled, but Didi worried that perhaps they hadn't been secretive enough.

They were taken to a basement room with no windows, which was predictably chilly and poorly lit. There were not enough chairs for all the FANYs. Didi stood, keeping her fingers warm by flexing them over an imaginary Morse key while the other girls chatted animatedly.

After almost an hour, the door was flung open and a short man with wild black hair entered. He didn't look that much older than Didi, but he carried himself with maturity. He flicked the switch next to the wall and the room was suddenly flooded with bright light.

He nodded at a uniformed officer, who held up a small speaker. After another nod from the young man, the officer pressed a button.

Although by this time the FANYs had all ceased their gossip, the tinny sounds of their voices could still be heard.

"He recorded us," Yvonne's voice was hushed. Even in the dim light, Didi could see Yvonne's face redden as she heard her taped voice say, "What's with the lack of chairs? Do they think us FANYs have no fannies?"

Another girl's voice postulated that reason for their instructor's tardiness was because "he must be having it off with Phyllis Bingham herself."

By this time the girls were too embarrassed to look either at their instructor or each other. Thankfully the officer switched off the recorder.

The young man cleared his voice before he addressed the room. "You've been kept waiting in a freezing room so you will become tired and irritable. Tired and irritable people grow careless, and when you're careless, you're inclined to be talkative. This is something we are going to need to fix. Next time you feel like talking, remember that the Nazis have recorders too, stored in places where most of you ladies wouldn't think of putting them."

Didi glanced at the originator of the Phyllis Bingham remark, who stared at the floor.

The young man continued, "The Gestapo is hoping you're green enough to want to brag about your position. I know what it is like to be young, to be suddenly hired into an organization such as the SOE, thinking that you've made it. You're going to be told about things most people don't know and should never be allowed to know. We are trusting you to keep these things secret, maybe forever. If you ever talk about any of them, men will die. It's as simple as that."

He began to pace the perimeter of the room. "You might think you're tired, you who've had yourselves a decent night's rest last night. Imagine the field agent who has not found time to sleep for more than a few hours, three nights in a row. The Germans are all around his so-called safe house, but he has to keep his sked in order to send an important message to London. Now, I'm going to ask you a question: Doesn't that agent have an excuse for making mistakes in his coding?"

The girls who'd gotten past their initial embarrassment nodded vigorously.

"There's an indecipherable upstairs with your names on it. It's from a Belgian agent whose cover is completely blown. He's sent us a message telling us his coordinates. A Lysander is ready to pick him up and bring him home, but the message is unreadable. In his panic, he's made too many mistakes. At ten o'clock this evening he's due to come on air and repeat his message, but if he does, the German signal-detectors will close in and we will lose him, just as we lost another agent last week. The SS shot him while he was retransmitting an indecipherable message."

A few girls murmured, and he waited for the room to get silent again. "If any one of you finds the key to break this message, you all will have broken it. You're part of a team now, an indispensable part."

Didi's chest swelled with a sense of importance—she might not be in the field, but she was still doing a crucial task for the war. Despite his pretentious attitude, there was something endearing about the young man's dedication to his work.

"Before I leave you to it, I want to apologize about the recording. If you girls can think of a better way of reminding you to never talk about your work, please mention it to me. I'm going to end now by wishing you good luck—good coding, and remember, you are the only hope an agent has got!" He gave them an unofficial salute and then darted from the room.

"What a strange man," Yvonne declared loudly.

"Hush!" another girl stated. "They could still be recording us."

Didi used her voice for the first time since she entered the room. "How 'indecipherable' can it be?"

"I don't know," Yvonne replied. "But something tells me we are about to find out."

Didi and the rest of the girls filed into a small room, where the young man was waiting. The young man, who finally introduced himself as Leo Marks, had been given permission to train groups of FANYs to decode indecipherables.

Because the agents were using famous quotes in their heads, and were coding under duress, they often made mistakes. A small slip, such as a spelling error in one of the poem words, could result in the whole message becoming unreadable, or, as Marks called it, an indecipherable.

"As much as 20% of SOE traffic ends up as gibberish. The powers-that-be think it best that the agents recode it the next night," Marks told them.

"Well, if it's the agent's mistake, I suppose he is the best person to correct it," one of the other girls said.

"No," he replied, pointing a bony finger at her. "That's the last thing they need to do. A wireless operator is the most dangerous position there is. Why should they have to resend a message and risk being found by the German detecting vans probing the area?"

The girl who asked, her face bright red, was too busy taking notes to answer.

"It's our job to solve their puzzle, to figure out what they are trying to say. To break the indecipherable. Or else they might end up in the hands of the Nazis." He kept his eyes on Didi as he spit out his next statement. "If we do our job well, it means we save lives."

Didi nodded. "No more indecipherables."

"Right," Marks sounded pleased. "No more indecipherables."

CHAPTER 17

MATHILDE

*T*he morning after the anniversary party, Mathilde went to meet Michel, one of their agents, at a café near the Lamarck metro station. She ordered a cup of coffee and read the morning paper, but, after almost an hour with no sign of Michel, decided to go home.

"Madame la Chatte?" Mathilde was startled to hear her code name on the street.

It was Mireille Lejeune, one of the couriers Mathilde had recruited, who had also become a friend. She was sitting on the stairs outside of her apartment building.

"Yes?" Mathilde asked.

"The German police have been along the Avenue Junot all morning." Junot was the street into which the little cul-de-sac of Rue Villa Léandre fed. The street Armand lived on. "You'd better not go to that area today," Mireille continued. "It might be dangerous."

Mathilde's face grew hot as she recalled the thick file René had given her after the party. It now sat on the counter in her Rue Cortot apartment. She sighed. "I've got to get back home and hide all of the maps and intelligence stored there." Mathilde looked at Mireille. "If you don't hear from me later today, make sure to burn all the papers you find."

Mireille reached for her hand. "Don't go, Madame la Chatte. It's too dangerous."

Mathilde shrugged her off. "Don't you worry about me," she said, starting toward the Rue Cortot. "And see if you can find out what happened to our mutual friend!"

Mathilde climbed the many steps of the Rue des Saules, her heart heavy, her eyes darting around the brick walls surrounding the stairs. The steep avenue would normally be deserted at this hour on such a cold November morning, but, as she reached the Rue Cortet, she saw with dismay that there were many men on the street. They stood on the corner, seemingly uncomfortable in their civilian suits and ties, and their air of forced idleness indicated they were clearly waiting for someone. Mathilde passed by her street, continuing to the Place du Tertre like a tourist on a shopping mission. The stores were closed, and, as she glanced over her shoulder, she noted that the men in the suits were following her.

She stopped in front of a print shop, as if to gaze in the window, but really she was sizing up the reflection of the man behind her.

"You're up quite early this morning," the man said, his accent heavily German.

"I'm just looking around." She pointed at something in the display window. "That etching would make a perfect present for my lunch companion."

"Why don't you have lunch with me instead?"

She turned to look at him. He looked no less sinister than his reflection, his yellow-toothed grin even larger in real life.

Despite her fur coat, Mathilde felt her veins run cold. She shook her head before turning back the way she came. She could hear him trailing her but did not know where else to go besides her flat. She cursed herself for not heading in the other direction, toward the Sacrè Coeur. She was no longer *La Chatte*; she had become *La Souris*, the mouse, the prey.

As soon as she arrived at the gate outside her apartment building, her arms were seized from behind by someone with a forceful grip. "We've been waiting for you all morning," another man said.

As Mathilde was hustled into a van, her landlady appeared, stepping over the outside door, which had been torn off its hinges and cast aside. Betrayal was written all over the elderly woman's wrinkled face.

"Don't hurt her!" the landlady called, looking as defeated as the door. "She's done nothing wrong!"

"I'm not sure that's strictly true," the driver replied.

"Where are you taking me?" Mathilde demanded, her voice strangely confident despite her panic.

Though there were at least two other uniformed men in the van besides the driver and her handler, no one answered her. She stared out the window as the car turned down Rue d'Amsterdam, noting that the leaves had fallen off the vines. The glorious Parisian foliage had all but disappeared in anticipation of a long winter.

The van pulled to a stop in front of the Hotel Édouard VII. The driver turned off the car before nodding to the man in the passenger seat, who got out and opened the door. He extended his arm toward Mathilde to help her out, but she swept past him, only to feel his hand on her back as she walked toward the hotel.

Mathilde's eyes narrowed as she caught sight of Viola smoking outside. "That's her!" Viola cried, pointing. "That's The Cat!"

Mathilde refrained from spitting on her as the man poked her in the back, urging her along. She complied, thinking that whatever the Germans had in store, it had to be better than the way Armand had treated her.

She was wrong. After a few hours of interrogation at the hotel where they asked her the same simple questions over and over: what was her name, where was she from, was she of 100% Aryan descent, etc., she was taken to La Santé prison. On the way out of the hotel, Mathilde caught sight of Michel, the agent she'd been supposed to meet that morning, sitting in a corner of the lobby, his hands cuffed behind his back.

It wasn't until Mathilde was shoved into her cell that her hopeful outlook came crashing down. It was pitch-black, the stale air frigidly cold.

Though still armed with her fur, she spent a restless, freezing night in prison. It finally occurred to her that all she had worked for—and everything she and Armand had achieved—had been destroyed. If the Germans had captured Viola, they must also have Armand. Her face crumpled and she could feel the tears coming, but then she remembered how Armand had treated her. *Maybe it was time he and Viola got what they deserved.* But how could she make that happen when she was stuck here in this hellhole?

The tears subsided, she closed her eyes, only to have them fly open with a start as the prison clock chimed the hour. It was followed by the hospital's clock, the asylum's, and then those of the various buildings in the Santé district. The process repeated itself every half hour. Mathilde focused her mind on the incompetence of the clock-makers—*couldn't the usually efficient Boches have synchronized them all?*—instead of her possible fate. For one terrifying minute she allowed herself to imagine the unimaginable: what it would be like to stand in front of a firing squad, before another clock began its relentless clanging.

By morning, death was almost a welcomed notion. Anything to be out of that prison, away from the cold, the darkness, and, most of all, the clocks…

CHAPTER 18

DIDI

*A*fter solving one of Leo Marks' indecipherables—she'd figured out that the agent had misspelled just one word—*bugle*, in Rudyard Kipling's poem 'Gunga Din'—Didi was transferred to Norgeby House, one of the SOE's London coding locations. She'd told Captain Smith she would have rather been relocated to France, but he just shrugged.

Didi was put up in a hotel off Baker Street. When she went to check in, the desk clerk told her she would be sharing a room.

"I'm not sure—" Didi began, but the desk clerk interrupted her. "I'm told that you are quite familiar with this person." He handed her a key. "I was also told there would be no problem."

Clearly the desk clerk wasn't in the mood to handle any unforeseen issues. Didi's heart started beating rapidly as she walked up the stairs and accelerated even more as she put the key into the lock. *Who was it going to be?* Armand? What if it was Archie having returned from the field?

The voice that greeted her was indeed familiar. "Hey Deeds."

Didi let out a heavy breath as she caught sight of her sister standing in the middle of the room. "What are you doing?" Didi asked.

"Packing. I'm leaving for France in the morning."

"I just got here."

"I know." Jackie put a jacket on top of the heap of clothing on the bed and walked over to her sister, embracing her. When she let go, Didi could see that she had tears in her eyes. "I hear you are one of the best coders they've got."

"It doesn't matter." Didi flopped onto the bed, careful not to destroy Jackie's pile. "They won't send me out."

"No?" Jackie pulled out her handkerchief and wiped at her eyes. "It's probably because you have to be twenty-five to be an agent."

Didi had never heard that rule before. "Jack, you didn't say anything about me to anyone in the F Section, did you? I just can't figure out why they keep rejecting me."

Jackie tossed the handkerchief on the dresser. "Of course not, Deeds. I would never do such a thing."

Didi searched her sister's face for a hint of insincerity, but couldn't find anything. Either she was telling the truth, or her spy training had been that good. Didi forced a smile. "Show me what you're taking with you."

Jackie sorted the clothing into organized stacks: two skirts with matching jackets, two blouses, and two pairs each of pajamas and shoes. "All French labels," Jackie stated. "Courtesy of Miss Atkins and the SOE."

Didi fingered the pajama top. "These will shrink to nothing the first time you wash them."

Jackie folded the shirt before putting it into her suitcase. "I know, but that's the only fabric available in France right now. I can't wear English ones—if they captured me while I was sleeping, it would be the nail in my coffin." Her voice softened. "I'm glad they afforded us some time to say goodbye. I suppose I have Miss Atkins to thank for that as well." She walked over and put her arm around Didi. "You'll be all right while I'm gone?"

"Of course," Didi replied, hugging her once more. She and Jackie had been both best friends and fierce rivals as far back as Didi could remember. Well maybe rivals only in Didi's mind: for her part, Jackie never seemed threatened by her determined little sister. They'd had no one else to rely on except each other during the long journey from France, and now Jackie was leaving her again. "I can take care of myself," Didi declared. "Since my twenty-fifth birthday is not too far off, we'll probably meet again in France."

"Or else England, God willing."

CHAPTER 19

MATHILDE

*A*fter a breakfast of stale coffee and even staler bread, Mathilde was returned to the Hotel Édouard VII. Coming from a night in a silent prison cell, the lights of the hotel seemed overly bright but the hustle and bustle of day-to-day operations made the marble-floored lobby seem blissfully clamorous.

She was taken upstairs to a room with a spacious living area and dining room. On the table was an enormous breakfast spread, including eggs, rolls, butter, and black, steaming coffee. Her mouth watered in remembrance of both the horrid meal she'd been given earlier that morning and the privations of Paris's rationing.

"Help yourself," a man stated, nodding at the table. In her haste to pick up her plate, Mathilde barely registered him as the yellow-toothed detective who'd confronted her on the Place du Tertre the other day.

A tall, heavy-set man in tortoise-shell glasses entered the room. Mathilde could feel his eyes on her as she helped herself to a mountain of scrambled eggs, but refused to acknowledge him. She finished heaping food onto her plate and balanced it with one hand so she could carry a mug of coffee with the other.

The man was already seated at the table; he kicked out the chair across from him so she could sit down, though he remained silent as she dug into her breakfast. She abandoned her manners as she ate audibly, chewing the buttered bread with relish and swallowing the eggs and sausage by the mouthful. After her plate was finally empty, the man offered her a cigarette.

She turned the cigarette over. "These are my favorite brand."

"I imagine they would be, seeing as we found several cartons of them in your apartment. These are confiscated from your own supply, and at your disposal whenever you desire one."

"How kind."

As Mathilde angled toward his match, he stated plainly, "We've arrested your friend Roman Czerniewski—or Armand, as you knew him."

She took a puff of her cigarette, not wanting to show him any sign of her inner turmoil.

"We've also detained the woman that was in his bed when we found him. A little one, good-looking, though not nearly as pretty as you."

Mathilde blew out a ring of smoke. "Oh?"

"We have in our possession all of the documents we need to put you in prison for life, or possibly in front of a firing squad."

He paused to gauge her reaction, but once again Mathilde declined to give him one. "Is that so?"

"However," the man leaned forward, "my colleagues and I have decided that you are much too intelligent and interesting a person to languish in prison."

She ashed her cigarette in lieu of a reply.

He lit a cigar. "You know everything. You could be a valuable asset in helping us destroy the Interallié network."

"Why should I help you destroy what we have worked so hard to build?"

"Yes," he nodded enthusiastically as Mathilde reprimanded herself for admitting her guilt. "You and this Armand formed Interallié. You do know that his girlfriend had nothing nice to say about you when we questioned her, don't you? She thinks you betrayed the network to us and that you were a more revolting beast than a cat. She said, and I quote, 'It was up to me to convince Armand that that deceitful trollop would double-cross him one day. I managed to get her to move out, but that didn't stop her, did it?' She even told us you'd be wearing a bright red beret, 'a tasteless blood-colored thing, along with a tattered, moth-eaten fur.'"

Mathilde's painstakingly cultivated veneer finally cracked. "That bitch!"

From his spreading grin, she knew she'd committed a great blunder.

He glanced around the overstuffed room. "This is not really the place to continue this conversation."

She bit her lip, afraid he'd demand for her return to prison. But instead he reached over, placing a thick hand over hers. "I think you're due for an even more substantial meal, and a big glass of wine at that. That will put us both in the right mood for a real tête-à-tête."

She searched his face, but he kept his expression as neutral as hers. "Are you mocking me?" she asked finally.

"Of course not." Though his countenance gave nothing away, his voice sounded sincere.

She slid her hand out from under his. "How could I, an accused spy, go anywhere in public with you? If you insist on making jokes, you might as well..." she couldn't bear to suggest he send her back to La Santé.

"I didn't get to where I am by making jokes." He moved his hand as though to shake hers. "It just occurred to me I never introduced myself. I am Sergeant Hugo Bleicher of the Abwehr and I would be delighted to take you to lunch. I suggest La Tour d'Argent."

She'd heard of the Abwehr before—it had something to do with military intelligence. *At least he hadn't said he was with the Gestapo.* Her stomach, despite its fullness, grumbled at the thought of her favorite pre-war restaurant.

"I only have one stipulation," Bleicher continued. "You must give me your word that you will not try to escape. It would pain me very much if I had to shoot such a beautiful woman."

Mathilde shut her eyes for a second, at the same time shutting her mind to her plight, focusing only on how Armand's new girlfriend had betrayed her. That, and the choice that this man had put before her: a few hours of eating, drinking and conversation in a pleasant setting versus returning to her prison cell.

She reached out to shake his hand. "I give you my word, monsieur." She drew back to touch her hair, desperately tangled from a night spent tossing and turning on a filthy bed. "But I couldn't possibly accompany you to La Tour d'Argent looking as I do."

His eyes brightened as he nodded to a uniformed guard, who opened the bedroom door. Another guard entered, pulling a rack of clothes behind him.

"My things!" Mathilde exclaimed. She quickly recovered her calm stance. "You've been busy," she commented as dryly as she could before taking a sip of coffee.

"Indeed." Bleicher snapped his fingers and a guard, with typical German efficiency, pulled a hanger from the rack and walked to the table, displaying the outfit with a flourish.

Mathilde ran her eyes over her favorite black pantsuit, forcing her lips to curl upward. "Perfect. Now, if you gentlemen will allow me the pleasure of a shower."

A few hours later, Mathilde found herself sitting across from Bleicher at La Tour d'Argent's best table, overlooking Notre Dame. The sun had begun to set and the hulking towers of the cathedral appeared black against the orange sky.

La Tour d'Argent was a *catégorie exceptionnelle* restaurant, which meant that it was even higher than Category A and subject to neither rationing nor price setting. Bleicher ordered mutton chops for himself and duck for Mathilde.

Mathilde suppressed a shiver as she took in the jovial diners, the immaculately white tablecloths, the gleaming silver candelabras. She'd only spent one night in prison, but it was enough to know she never wanted to go back. Her mouth wouldn't stop watering at the thought of the impending meal.

The waiter presented Bleicher with the wine cork. Despite herself, Mathilde was impressed with the worldly way her dining companion tasted the wine, letting it linger on his tongue before nodding his approval at the waiter.

"The world has certainly turned on its end," Mathilde commented as the waiter retreated. "Who would have thought that a German Abwehr officer would have a suspected French spy for his dinner companion?"

"Indeed, who would have thought that women, instead of raising children and running a household, would go off to gamble their lives in the French Resistance?"

"I never had children," Mathilde said, as though he were directly referring to her.

"I know. I know all about your husband and his... problems."

"Ex-husband. I filed for divorce." As soon as she said it, Mathilde realized the words weren't strictly true—she had been so busy with Interallié that she'd forgotten to file. But she had intended to, and supposed that intent versus action made little difference to the Abwehr.

"The men in your life—French like your husband or Polish like the one you call Armand—have done nothing but hurt you. Why remain true to the Allies?"

"The brave Allied soldiers are no reflection of the men in my life," Mathilde commented as the waiter arrived with their food. Nearly melting at the taste of the duck, she started in on her meal as Bleicher told her what seemed like his life story.

"My father owns a bicycle shop in Tettnang, Germany, which is located only a few miles away from the Swiss border. He wanted me to take over the business, but I refused. I tried enlisting in the Navy, but," he gestured toward his glasses, "was rejected due to my impaired vision. Nonetheless, I was drafted into the army when the Great War began. In 1916, I stole a uniform off a Tommy and crossed enemy lines. The British arrested me, accusing me, of all things, of being a spy and kept me as a P.O.W. for two years." He paused to take a bite of his meal. "Between the wars, I was a businessman, working for an export company and traveling, which helped me learn both Spanish and French. That's probably why, when war came again, they made me part of the Secret Police."

"The Nazi Police."

He shrugged. "I'm not sure how much you know about the Abwehr, but, unlike the Gestapo, most of us do not belong to the Nazi party. Those goons are more interested in upholding Hitler's racist decrees than they are in uncovering Resistance intelligence."

This clarification made Mathilde feel only slightly better.

After another large bite of food he continued, "I don't have political ties myself, but if anyone has a reason to loathe England, it is I. The British refused to show me any humanity when I was their prisoner—Christmas of 1917 found me in both handcuffs and manacles around my ankles."

A thought suddenly occurred to Mathilde and she voiced it aloud. "Are you married?"

He pushed his empty plate aside. "Yes. Unlike you, I have a son. But my wife knows not to expect me to remain faithful while I'm away."

Mathilde turned her nose up at what he might be implying. "You and I are on opposite sides of this war. Whether you agree with Nazi politics or not, you are still a member of the German Police, and I was arrested for being a member of the French Resistance."

He waved his hand. "The French, and all of the Allies for that matter, are going to lose this war. And you will have nothing to show for all your efforts with said Resistance, except poverty, forced slavery... and a broken heart."

Mathilde took a sip of wine to cover up her consternation.

"The war is a forgone conclusion: Hitler is bound to win and those who were foolish enough to oppose him are doomed."

Doomed. She closed her eyes, picturing the prison walls closing in on her. Although she longed to think of herself as self-sufficient, a female warrior, she'd never in her life been without a protector for long. Armand had abandoned her, even before he was arrested, and now she felt desperately alone. *How could he?* Mathilde could once again feel tears forming behind her eyes as she thought of his unfaithfulness with Viola.

Bleicher must have sensed he'd hit his mark, for he reached for her hand and caressed it with his thumb. The rest of her dissent evaporated with this slice of kindness. He lifted his other arm to glance at his watch. "A few hours until nine o'clock, when The Cat usually reports to London."

At these words, Mathilde was filled with a sense of defeat. There would be no more transmissions to London, and soon no more communication with the rest of the world. Only long days in a cold, dank prison cell.

"You were never truly on their side," Bleicher said as the waiter delivered dessert: chocolate cake and real coffee with cream.

Mathilde blinked at this non sequitur.

He helped himself to a heaping teaspoonful of sugar. "You became a spy out of a misplaced sense of duty, and a misguided attraction to Czerniawski. He never even disclosed his real name, nor did he tell you about Viola Borni. How could you have loved a person who was dishonest with you from the start? He used you, and when you ceased to be of service to him, he cast you aside for the widow Borni. All of your network knew of this deception and probably had a few laughs at your expense."

"I never said I loved him." Even Mathilde could detect the contempt in her voice.

"No," Bleicher said soothingly. "I don't have a high opinion of him either. Do you know he was in his pajamas when we arrested him?"

The combination of coffee, wine, and sugar was getting to her: she was beginning to fall under this man's—this Hun's—spell. She glanced around the restaurant with blurry eyes. Her fellow patrons, most of them also Huns, laughed uproariously, indifferent to rationing, to the war, to the life and death struggle carrying on outside the restaurant doors. Impervious to the turmoil going on inside her head. Would it be a noose waiting for her, or would she have the honor of a firing squad?

Bleicher's deep voice interrupted her thoughts. "The hour grows late and we must be getting home."

"Home?" Mathilde was brought back to reality. "To what home are you taking me? Back to prison?"

He leaned forward, his eyes suddenly stony, his voice grave. "That, *mein Fräulein,* is for you to decide."

CHAPTER 20

ODETTE

Odette's passage to France had been nothing but delay after delay: a few times because of bad weather, once because Buckmaster had received word that her French reception committee had been captured by the Gestapo, and once because her appointed plane had been damaged during landing.

When a new plane had finally been scheduled, she was directed to spend the night at a hotel in Cornwall, near the airfield. The War Office told her to be ready for a 2 am flight and to grab any rest she could.

She thought that might be an impossible request, but, despite her nerves, she fell asleep right away.

At one o'clock in the morning, she was awakened by someone opening her door. "I was told to rouse you," a woman in a FANY uniform said.

Odette sat up in bed, glancing at the still undrawn shades. "It's raining. The plane can't leave in this weather." She wasn't wholly sure that was true so she added, "Can it?"

The woman shrugged before setting a cup of tea on the bedside table.

Odette gave a deep sigh before she reached for the tea.

. . .

When she arrived at the airfield, it was still pouring. She could just see the bulky outline of the plane, a Whitley, through the driving rain.

The Scottish pilot told her that the Whitley's engine had a small issue. "Dinnae fret, hen," he said, which she took to mean that she shouldn't worry. He pointed to a pair of bedraggled mechanics examining something underneath the fuselage. "Mah lads'll hae it right soon. I'll take care o' that fer ye while we wait," he added, picking up the bag at her feet.

When the plane was finally ready, Odette found that the seats had been removed to make room for the cargo, and her lone bag was perched atop a mountain of crates. She settled on the floor, leaning against yet another pile of wooden boxes.

"Sorry, miss. It's no' going to be a comfy ride," the pilot told her as he started running his checks.

At least France isn't far, she consoled herself. Maybe this time she'd actually leave English soil.

She closed her eyes as the engine started, hoping she could catch a few minutes of sleep. She felt the Whitley jerk as it left the ground. Her eyes flew open as a box tumbled off the pile behind her. Something was wrong.

The pilot fiddled desperately with his instruments. Odette's stomach lurched as the Whitley surged upward only to fall again. It reminded her of being on the see-saw as a child.

She tried to close her eyes yet again, but then she felt the entire fuselage start to convulse. "What's happening?" she shouted.

The pilot glanced back at her, the panic obvious on his face. "I cannae control her!"

Odette planted her feet as the cargo boxes plummeted toward the Whitley's nose.

"We're going down!" the pilot cried.

Odette felt herself rise from her perch before her stomach dropped once again as she fell to the floor. *So this is how it ends*, she thought. *I never even got the chance to see a Nazi, let alone thwart any of their plans.*

Boxes descended upon her as she covered her head and braced for impact, nearly too late. She felt the plane hit the ground, swerving unsteadily before finally coming to a stop.

A heavy crate landed on top of her arms, which were still covering her head. She felt a rush of cool air as the pilot pulled the weight off her. "Get out now!" he yelled. "She might catch fire!"

Odette flew to the door. She pulled the latch down and then shoved at it with her shoulder but it refused to open. The pilot, taking a running start, rushed forward. The door finally opened and the pilot, recovering his composure, waved Odette out first.

Once outside in the still-driving rain, she gulped in a few breaths of air, then, remembering the pilot's dire warning about fire, took off in a sprint, stopping just short of a cliff that led 30 meters down to the Irish Sea.

"I don't know if it's Fate, or if you're doing something to cause all these disasters to keep happening," Buckmaster commented when Odette returned to London. "Are you sure you want to go to France?"

"What powers do you think I have, that of a witch?" Buckmaster raised his eyebrows at her, and Odette laughed at his foolishness before adding, "Of course I still want to go. Perhaps at this point it might be better if you arrange for me to cross the Channel by sea."

"Yes, I will get you a boat," he agreed. "We can't afford any more planes for you."

CHAPTER 21

MATHILDE

*M*athilde huddled against the cold November afternoon in her customary fur, this time accompanied by a matching hat, a gift from Hugo Bleicher. He directed her into a BMW with French plates and told the chauffeured driver to take them to the Pam Pam.

He turned to Mathilde to lament, "The Pam Pam is home to two of my most despised American exports: hamburgers and jazz."

"It was Duvernoy's idea." Mathilde's voice contained no emotion. Duvernoy was a contact from Vichy's Deuxiéme Bureau that Bleicher had demanded she arrange to meet. She half-suspected the Abwehr officer was using her as a lure so he could arrest Duvernoy.

When they arrived, Bleicher followed as a waitress led Mathilde across the restaurant. "A corner table, the mark of Allied spies in the Occupied Zones," Bleicher quipped as he pulled out Mathilde's chair.

Her stomach turned over, but she said nothing.

Duvernoy entered the restaurant, smiling openly as he caught sight of Mathilde, but his expression turned into a glower as he approached. "Who is this?" he asked, jutting his chin toward Bleicher.

"Don't worry about him," Mathilde replied, spreading a red-and-white checkered napkin over her lap. "He can be trusted."

"Is he a friend of Armand's? René told me about the arrests."

"He's—" Mathilde cast a helpless look at Bleicher, who answered,

"Yes, I am one of Armand's associates. We were all saddened by his capture, but, as they say, the show must go on." He looked up as the waitress arrived. "Three hamburgers."

"Have you heard from Binet?" Duvernoy asked as the waitress walked away.

"No," Mathilde's response was terse.

"Well, what information do you have on the Germans? Anything new with the Resistance that I can take back to Sardanapalus?"

She refrained from another bewildered glance at Bleicher.

"It's been quiet lately, what with the arrests and all," Bleicher supplied.

"Indeed." Duvernoy got down to business: two cargo vessels carrying much-needed supplies had left from South America and were headed toward Casablanca and Bordeaux. He then spoke about a German coal ship that was loading at Diego Suarez and was expected to set sail within the next few days.

He finally fell silent as the waitress arrived with the food. Mathilde wondered when Bleicher would make his move. Perhaps he had decided against arresting Duvernoy, or maybe he was just trying to avoid making a scene in the restaurant.

Finally Bleicher set his steak knife down and tossed his napkin onto the table. "I must get going." He turned to Duvernoy. "Can I give you a lift in my car?"

Duvernoy glanced at Mathilde, who nodded. "Thank you," he replied.

As the car sped down the Champs Elysées, Duvernoy seemed to sense that something was amiss and became uncharacteristically subdued. When they'd passed the Place de la Concorde, Bleicher announced, "Monsieur Duvernoy, you find yourself in the company of the German Police, and you are now under arrest."

The normally pasty Duvernoy turned a sickly green. "You deceitful slut!" he shouted at Mathilde.

"She had nothing to do with this," Bleicher stated, slapping a handcuff around one of Duvernoy's wrists. "But you could save yourself quite a bit of trouble if you denounce your comrades."

Duvernoy gave a resigned sigh. "What do you want to know?"

"Well, to start with, who is this Binet you spoke of?"

Duvernoy cast a hateful glance at Mathilde before answering. "He is a commerce inspector."

"And I presume I will find him at the Ministry of Finance?"

Duvernoy nodded.

Bleicher brought the handcuffed Duvernoy into the Hotel Édouard VII. When he returned to Mathilde, who was waiting at the curb next to the BMW, he asked, "Who is René?"

Mathilde cursed to herself. Nothing seemed to get by the astute officer. "He's an old friend."

"And, I take it, also involved in Interallié?" His piercing eyes searched her face.

The words wouldn't form, so she nodded instead.

He marched over to a phone booth. "You will call this René and arrange for him to meet you at the Café Graff at six tonight."

"But—"

"Six o'clock at Café Graff or you will find yourself back in La Santé at the same hour."

With a shaking hand, she picked up the receiver. As she gave the operator René's number, she crossed her fingers at her side, hoping he wouldn't pick up.

But he was as reliable as ever. "Hello?"

"René."

"Mathilde!" The relief in his voice was all much too much to bear. "What happened?"

We should have arranged a code word in the event one of us was forced to betray the other. Mathilde blinked back a tear, wishing she, or René, could have had such forethought. She glanced at Bleicher, wondering if he could detect the change in her tone as she repeated his instructions: Café Graff at six o'clock.

Bleicher didn't seem to notice the higher pitch any more than René did. After she'd hung up, Bleicher rubbed his hands together. "And now to arrest Mireille Lejeune."

The mention of yet another friend was too much for Mathilde. "No."

He put a vise hold on Mathilde's arm before opening the door to his car. "La Santé prison," he told the driver loudly, his grip tightening as he pushed her inside.

She moved over to the other window, feeling numb. Bleicher sat as close to her as he could.

"La Santé prison," the driver repeated as he started the car.

"You won't change your mind?" Bleicher asked Mathilde.

"No. Prison would be better than helping you do this to my friends."

"They will be arrested no matter what—Armand kept an index file of all of Interallié's agents, not to mention he had a box full of copies of messages sent to the SOE."

Oh Toto, what did you do? I told you to get rid of those records.

Bleicher continued, "Viola gave us the cipher and we've read all of the messages. And chances are, most of your agents will talk and we will make more arrests. But if you aid us, you will save yourself from such a fate."

"I won't do it."

"Duvernoy, Binet, René, Mireille Lejeune, her husband Roby Roland," Bleicher tapped his fat fingers with his other hand as he counted, "Uncle Marco, Armand, Viola…"

"Stop." A migraine was rapidly forming and Mathilde held a hand up to her temple. "Please stop saying their names."

"If you have a headache now, think about how much worse it will get as you sit in your cold, stinking cell." He touched her leg. "Help us," he beseeched.

Mathilde's hand dropped back into her lap. "You know about all of them?"

"We do. As I said, their fates have already been set." He could tell she was weakening. "Where does Mireille live?"

Mathilde leaned forward and gave the driver the address.

They entered Mireille's apartment with Mathilde in the lead and Bleicher just behind. Mathilde introduced her companion as a "trusted friend" before inquiring about her papers.

"I burned them just as you told me to," Mireille stated.

Thank you, Mathilde thought as Bleicher's face fell. "And these?" Mathilde asked, pointing to a vase that had come from her flat. She walked over to touch a wilted tulip. "Why did you take them?"

"I was going to water them until you got back." Mireille's tone was full of confusion.

Bleicher's voice reverberated through the small room. "They were going to die no matter what. You didn't have to try to save them."

"Did you take anything else?" Mathilde found it hard to focus her racing mind.

"Just the money. I figured the organization could use it, or maybe it could be a bribe to get you out of jail."

"You shouldn't have touched anything."

Mireille's mouth dropped. "Why, Mathilde, if it's the tulips you are worried about, I will see to it that you will have more flowers than ever."

"What about the money?" Bleicher asked.

Mireille went over to an empty vase near the purloined flowers. She reached inside and pulled out a wad of bills. "It's all there. You can count it if you don't believe me."

"That is quite unnecessary," Bleicher seized the money. "But it does prove your guilt."

"What do you mean?" she demanded.

Bleicher pocketed the bills before pulling out his handcuffs. "You are under arrest."

Mireille's eyes became little slits as she looked at Mathilde. "You did this."

"Of course not," Bleicher's voice cut in, convincing no one. Mireille didn't say a word as Bleicher placed the handcuffs over her wrists, kindly keeping her arms in front instead of behind her. "Now, tell me where your husband is."

"I don't know. He is a police officer and is often assigned to different parts of the city."

"Then I guess we will be taking a tour of our fair Paris."

Even though the women were separated by Bleicher's presence between them, Mathilde could feel her friend fuming as he directed the driver to the first police station. Tears pricked her eyes, but she wouldn't give Bleicher the satisfaction of letting them fall.

They found Boby Roland outside the precinct off the Champs-Élysées. Mathilde stayed in the car, watching as Bleicher forced Roland to his knees beside his stunned wife. Bleicher waited beside the couple, now both with their hands cuffed behind their backs, until a white van came to collect them and deliver them to the Édouard VII.

. . .

When Bleicher returned, he once again directed his chauffeur, his voice dripping with satisfaction. This time it was to the Café Graff. Upon their arrival, Mathilde saw that yet another white van waited next to the curb.

"You go ahead in," Bleicher said as he helped her out of the car. "I'll be there in a minute." He gestured to a man wearing plain-clothes standing outside. "Stay at the doorway. Patrons are free to enter, but do not let anyone leave."

Mathilde took a wobbly step toward the restaurant before turning around to address Bleicher. "I don't think I can do this."

"Your life and liberty depend on it." His face softened as he realized the extent of Mathilde's turmoil. "Just act as you would normally."

René was waiting at a table. He stood up as Mathilde approached. "*Ma petite princesse*, thank goodness you're safe. I thought the Germans had arrested you too." He kissed each of her cheeks before embracing her.

He didn't seem to notice his old friend's shiver. As they broke apart, Mathilde squeezed his hand. *Run*, she wanted to say, but her tongue once again refused to work as she caught sight of Bleicher at the bar.

René ordered a double whiskey before commenting, "Boby Roland told me something really bad was happening within the network."

"When did you see him?" Mathilde asked, her voice unnaturally high.

"Two days ago, when I was supposed to make my weekly report to Armand. Roland told me of Armand and Viola's arrest, and also said that you'd been apprehended that morning in the Rue Cortot."

"Roland doesn't know the full extent of what happened."

"No?"

The waitress returned and distributed their drinks.

"Someday I will explain it all to you." She nodded at his glass. "For now, enjoy your whiskey." She wanted to add that it might be his last for a long time, but two burly men approached the table from behind René.

One of them held a pistol to René's back as he announced that they were members of the German police. "If you move," the German said, pushing the gun harder into René, "we will shoot you."

"You can arrest me, but leave the woman alone," René commanded.

Mathilde closed her eyes to the swimming room. She opened them as René said, "If you don't mind, I'd like to have a drink before we go."

The man relaxed his pistol, and René downed his whiskey. Mathilde pushed her glass across the table and he quickly finished that as well before he rose, dumping enough money on the table to pay for both drinks.

As one of the men handcuffed René, Bleicher approached. "Put your cuffs on my wrists," Mathilde hissed under her breath.

"What? Why?" Bleicher's voice was equally low.

"Just do it."

René caught her eye before they led him off and gave her that familiar half-smile. Her ruse had worked—her oldest friend suspected nothing of her betrayal.

She watched sadly as the Germans escorted him out of the restaurant, suppressing the urge to demand they take her as well. *After all,* she consoled herself, *they already know everyone who worked for Interallié.* There was nothing she could do to save René… or any of her other associates, for that matter.

Afterward, Bleicher took her to another fancy restaurant, where Mathilde drank too much champagne in an effort to forget the long day which had seen the arrest of her friends. Whenever the guilt tried to penetrate her alcohol-infused thoughts, she would remind herself that the plush-covered restaurant booth was infinitely better than the freezing, rat-infested cell of La Santé.

When Mathilde found herself once again in Bleicher's car, she was conscious enough to realize that, instead of returning to her room in the Rue Cortot as she had expected, the car was speeding away from the city. "Where are we going now?" she asked Bleicher.

"We are going to bed."

"What?"

Bleicher's voice was rushed. "You are free, Mathilde, but, given the circumstances of the day, I don't think you should be left alone tonight. You shall come and live with me at Abwehr headquarters, at least until suspicion about you should die down."

Exhaustion took over Mathilde's outrage and she said nothing more as they drove out to Maisons-Laffitte, a baroque château in the north-western suburbs.

And she was too weary to fend off Bleicher when he appeared that night in her room, clad in his striped pajamas. He climbed into her bed, and pulled up her nightgown. When he entered her, she made a cry of surprise, but not of protest. She was too tired to fight anymore.

CHAPTER 22

ODETTE

O dette was able to board a troopship, which brought her as far as the British colony of Gibraltar, on the southern tip of the Iberian Peninsula. After she was escorted to the safe house, she found a young man in a naval uniform waiting for her. With his lithe body and blonde hair, he could have been a poster boy for Hitler's Aryan race.

He introduced himself as Jan Buchowski before offering her a cup of tea.

"Do you have anything stronger?" Odette asked. "I've been tossed about on rough seas for nearly a week."

He gave her a wry smile before pulling a flask from his pocket. "Whiskey?"

Odette nodded.

After opening several cabinets, Jan finally produced two glasses. He poured a healthy amount of the amber liquid in each before handing Odette one.

"You are Polish?" she asked before taking a drink. It was somewhat watered down but still potent. She took another sip.

"Yes. I am commander of the boat *Dewucca* and I'm in charge of the Gibraltar-to-French Riviera run, which is a difficult route for even the most experienced of soldiers. I'm not sure how they expect a woman to manage it."

"If you are Polish, I don't suppose you've heard of the women of the SOE's F Section, then?"

"No," his gaze was still haughty, though now it had developed the tiniest hint of curiosity.

"We've been thoroughly trained in all matters of warfare. You needn't worry about me."

"Trained?" he laughed. "Trained in what? How to fight the Nazis? How to avoid being taken as a prisoner of war and how to die like a man?"

Odette found a bottle in one of the cabinets and poured him more whiskey. "All of the above."

"Ah." He finished his drink in one gulp. "If you don't mind me being so bold, I don't suppose you would dance with me when I return to Gibraltar on my next run?"

"But I won't be here when you return. Your job is to conduct me to France, remember? By orders of the War Office."

He waved his hand drunkenly. "The English War Office is nearly a continent away."

She suppressed the urge to throw her glass at him, remembering something her grandmère used to say: *you can catch more flies with honey than vinegar.* Odette stuck out her lower lip. "But I've had so many setbacks in getting to France. At this point I'd almost swim."

"You would look quite fetching in a bathing costume," Jan agreed.

She set her glass down with a clunk. "We will depart for France. Tomorrow."

"No," Jan returned. "I refuse to escort a woman such as you in my meager, unkempt boat across, as you called them, rough seas. You should stay here, in Gibraltar, enjoying a life away from the front. I will take you dancing when I come back."

"No." Odette's voice was equally adamant. "I have my orders." She reached for Jan's glass to refill it. "Someday you young men will realize that women have just as much to gain in this infernal war." She poured up to the rim. "Not to mention lose."

After he'd finished nearly the entire bottle of whiskey, Jan turned his glassy eyes on Odette to ask, "I suppose they gave you a gun, this F Section."

"No, they did not." An idea suddenly occurred to Odette. "Do you have one?"

Jan reached into the pocket of his trousers and displayed a pistol. "If I ever meet a German battleship, I plan to sink it with my Vis 35."

Odette didn't bother with the logistics of that statement. "If I hit a target of your choice, you have to take me to France."

He frowned but handed her the pistol anyway. "Be careful of the recoil—this gun makes a very big bang. Maybe too big a bang for a small girl like you." They walked outside together, Jan holding the empty whiskey bottle. "I'm going to throw this off the cliff over there. If you shoot it before it hits the waves, I will guarantee you a dance."

"Not in Gibraltar. In France," Odette clarified. "But first you will bring me to the coast in your boat."

"Sure. If you can hit the whiskey bottle, I will abide by whatever you say."

She could tell by his wry smile that he didn't believe she'd be able to accomplish the feat. She cocked the gun and nodded at him. He flung the bottle, which soon exploded with the gratifying sight of breaking glass. Odette turned to him expectantly.

"We will leave for France tomorrow," he said, his voice resigned.

CHAPTER 23

MATHILDE

*B*leicher set out to destroy the Interallié network agent by agent, and Mathilde was his unwilling accomplice. She saw herself as helpless to intercede—since Bleicher had all the documents from Armand's apartment, the arrests would have taken place no matter what.

After René Aubertin and the Lejeunes, it was time for Armand's Polish friends from that fateful dinner party: Bernard Krutki and Lucien de Roquigny. Krutki put up a fight, of course, stating that he had nothing to do with Interallié, but, after a few prying questions from Bleicher, he finally gave in.

The arrest of Lucien was harder for Mathilde: she'd always liked the diminutive Pole and suspected he had amorous feelings for her. Indeed he seemed pleased to see her when he'd answered the door to his flat. "*Ma chère Chatte*, it is good to see you. Come in, come in."

She had just entered his lavishly furnished living room when Bleicher and his men rushed in, shouting their usual line, the one that Mathilde heard in her sleep. "German police!" The immense Teutons towered over the terrified Lucien. Mathilde decided to wait in the courtyard rather than listen to them grill yet another of Armand's closest friends.

They must have gotten what they needed as, after a few minutes, Bleicher led a handcuffed Lucien to the van. As they passed Mathilde,

Lucien shot her a faint smile and asked, "The weather is quite lovely today, don't you think?"

She nodded, wondering if she should apologize to him for what had just happened. As she wrestled with her thoughts, the oblivious Germans loaded Lucien into the van. She took a forlorn drag on her cigarette as she watched it drive away.

Bleicher had also managed to penetrate the letterbox drop at Café La Palette, which meant that he would soon know about the rest of Inter-allié's couriers. Mathilde was only too pleased to lead Bleicher to her old enemy Marcel, and though he refused to give the Abwehr any information about his new network, they learned the identity of Kent, Armand's radio technician, through papers they'd confiscated.

"And now for Rapidé," Bleicher said, watching Kent being taken away in one of the ubiquitous white vans.

Rapidé was the dispatcher who moved between Occupied and Unoccupied France. Mathilde thought carefully before replying, "I don't think Rapidé will give anyone else up. He's not worth our time."

"Rapidé or La Santé," Bleicher snarled. "Besides, Viola already told us everything we needed to know, except his address."

Mathilde had just made up her mind to have them return her to prison, but the mention of Viola hit its mark. Her heart felt as freshly broken as when she first found the woman in the house she'd shared with Armand.

Mathilde relented, as she so often had to these last few days, and sputtered Rapidé's address, secretly convincing herself that she was biding her time in order to win Bleicher's confidence and ensure her ability to escape someday.

"Good," Bleicher declared. "Viola said Rapidé was one of the founders of Interallié. He'll be able to give us more information about Tudor, the Polish network in Marseille."

"I've only met Rapidé a few times, but I can tell you Viola is wrong —he will say nothing of the sort."

"We'll see," Bleicher replied as the car came to a stop.

Rapidé lived in a small apartment off the Rue des Deux Ponts. As had become the pattern, Bleicher decided to use Mathilde as the bait and she walked up the crumbling, narrow staircase to his third-floor dwelling alone. "It's Madame la Chatte," she called through the door.

A plump, sweaty woman holding a baby greeted her with a smile.

"Is Stanislas here?" Mathilde asked, using Rapidé's real name.

"I'm here," he said, coming over to the doorframe.

Rapidé's wife invited her in, but Mathilde waved her off. "Listen, Rapidé," she said. "Things are not going well with Armand."

"Yes, I heard he was arrested."

Mathilde cast her eyes to the wife, who was playing with the baby, pretending not to hear them, though she flinched at the word, 'arrested.'

"I need the address of Tudor's headquarters," Mathilde stated.

"But I thought you'd been there yourself," Rapidé's reply was casual. "Surely you know where to find it."

"No. Give it to me quickly."

Rapidé, detecting the urgency in her voice, frowned. "I would think that someone so high up in Interallié as you are would know how to locate the Tudor operatives."

"Well I don't." Mathilde could hardly hide her agitation. She hoped that, if Rapidé would just give her the address, she could save him and his family.

But to no avail. She could hear heavy boots pounding up the stairs behind her and moved aside. She took a shallow breath as she felt a gun press into the small of her back.

"German Police!" Bleicher shouted. "Get inside and put your hands up."

A shocked Mathilde did as commanded. Rapidé and his wife followed her to the center of the living room as several Germans filed in and started tearing the apartment apart.

Mathilde felt Bleicher withdraw the gun from her back. She refrained from bawling him out, knowing he was trying to protect her from Rapidé's suspicion.

One of the Germans returned with a bottle he'd found in the bathroom. "Strychnine." Another man pulled a revolver from a pile of couch pillows.

"Okay, that's enough." Bleicher nodded at his captives. "You'll be coming with us now. But don't fret, it's just an inquiry into the possession of black-market goods."

Rapidé's wife began to wail as she set her baby down in a crib. A girl in her early teens appeared from the back bedroom. "Don't worry, *Maman*. I'll take care of Louise until you get back." The girl patted her mother's back, but it only made the woman cry harder.

"It will be less than twenty-four hours," Bleicher spoke with an unexpected show of empathy.

The heartbroken mother continued to sob as she and her husband were pushed into a car. Mathilde sat frozen in the middle.

Rapidé was not fooled. "This is fine work you've done, Madame la Chatte," he said as the car started.

His wife stopped crying and glanced at Mathilde. Her nose was red and her eyes, though still wet, filled with an unequivocal hatred. "You did this? Why?"

Mathilde had no answer, though her already evident betrayal became unmistakable the moment they arrived at the Édouard VII, when the couple were shoved inside and Mathilde was allowed to stay on the sidewalk to smoke a cigarette.

"I can't do this anymore," she told Bleicher when he came back out.

"They'll be fine," he told her, the sympathetic timbre back in his voice. "Especially his wife, as she clearly knew nothing of her husband's betrayal."

"I just…" Mathilde felt faint all of a sudden and placed her hand against the brick wall to steady herself.

Bleicher put his arm around her other shoulder. "Come on. It's been a long day of manhunting. Let's get you something to eat."

Bleicher took her out to another *catégorie exceptionnelle* restaurant to fill up on black market food and wine before they returned to the Abwehr headquarters at the Maisons-Laffitte villa. Bleicher then went off to drink brandy with his colleagues while Mathilde went to bed. Later, he stumbled into Mathilde's bedroom, where he again pulled down the pants of her pajamas and had his way.

Afterwards, Bleicher threw some clothes on and then stood in front of the bed. "Get dressed and come downstairs," he commanded before leaving.

Mathilde took stock of her image in the mirror. She smoothed down her hair, but kept her black silk pajamas on, figuring they were more than presentable for a bunch of tipsy Germans.

Bleicher had been tinkering on the piano but stood when Mathilde entered the parlor. He poured her some champagne before introducing her to Captain Erich Borchers, an exceedingly fat, balding man and Lieutenant Kayser, a short man with dark eyebrows and a thick mustache.

"What are we celebrating?" Mathilde asked.

Bleicher lifted his glass. "To the success we've had this past week, thanks in part to you. The prisons are filling with your colleagues. Your friend Lucien de Roquigny had papers in his château that gave away another member, alias Observer, who then led us to another agent called Coco."

"Now we need to find the Russian Communist Jew known as Uncle Marco," Borchers remarked.

Mathilde felt her stomach drop. Uncle Marco might have had some Russian and Jewish blood, but she also knew that he had been a Frenchman in heart and spirit even before the Great War. She took a hesitant sip of champagne as Bleicher sat on the couch across from Kayser and Borchers. He patted the seat beside him.

Mathilde forced a casual tone to her voice as she sat down. "So tell me, how did you find out about Interallié?"

Kayser laughed, causing some of his drink to form droplets on his mustache. "We were informed by a Mademoiselle Boufet that we'd be able to round up an entire network of agents if we arrested a man named Kiki on his arrival at Cherbourg."

"I am not familiar with Mademoiselle Boufet," Mathilde commented.

"Ah," Borchers folded his hands over his protruding stomach. "She was just a lover whom your man Kiki scorned. The vengeance of women!"

All three men laughed this time as Mathilde took another drink.

"Some vengeance," Bleicher added. "Kiki gave us all the names of your Cherbourg circuit, and we arrested Mademoiselle Boufet as well. She's in La Santé now, along with the rest of the women, including Viola."

Kayser nodded. "Once we raided Armand's apartment, we seized all the messages you had sent and received, and, thanks to Marcel, we also have the transmitting set from the house on Rue Villa Léandre and from the painter's studio." He sat forward. "But tell me, Fräulein, what happened to the third?"

Mathilde set her glass down. "I don't know. I never had anything to do with the radio. I didn't even know we had three wireless sets."

"You're lying." Borchers' voice was a growl. "We know that only you and Armand had the right to compose messages."

"Yes, but I never handled the wireless and I knew nothing about the technical side. That was all Viola and Marcel," Mathilde spat out.

The bitterness in her tone must have been obvious even to the drunk Bleicher, for he raised a knowing eyebrow. He was clearly an intelligent man and Mathilde couldn't help comparing him to the invariably idealistic Armand, the complete opposite of Bleicher in almost every way. Armand—and even herself to some extent—had operated Interallié as though espionage were a sport. Compared to the methodical tactics of the Abwehr, Interallié's procedures appeared haphazard and amateurish. Bleicher had proved that he was no rookie, and they had lost the game. *No,* Mathilde reminded herself. *Armand and Viola have lost. I still have a chance.*

Bleicher sat up as though an idea had suddenly occurred to him. "What if we continue the Interallié messages to Britain?"

"What do you mean?" Mathilde brought herself back to reality. "You just said all of our agents have been arrested. London must know of the collapse of the network."

"No. We've covered our tracks well, and it hasn't been that long since your last transmission," Bleicher insisted.

"Marseille and Vichy know nothing of your plight, and no one still at large knows you are in our hands," Borchers agreed.

"But," Mathilde spluttered. "Why continue? You've thoroughly pulverized Interallié. The Resistance has been annihilated."

"No." Bleicher pointed his fat finger at her. "Interallié was only one piece of the Resistance, albeit a large one. Some of your satellite members will be left without an organization and will try to find another one. That is my ultimate motive—capturing spies."

There is one thing Bleicher and Armand have in common, Mathilde thought. An appetite for complete domination.

Bleicher nodded to himself before catching Mathilde's hands in his. "You are going to send messages to London, and sign them as The Cat. We will carry on a secret radio war, using your contacts to feed them false information."

Mathilde dropped his hand and turned away, wondering how she could possibly justify collaborating with Bleicher's newest scheme to herself, let alone playing an important part in it. Maybe now it was time to reconsider returning to La Santé.

As if reading her mind, Bleicher stated casually, "I've given permission for Viola and Armand to exchange messages with each other from their respective prison cells."

"Aren't you afraid they will discuss escape plans?" Kayser asked.

"No. We are inspecting them first and will censor them if necessary." Bleicher chuckled to himself. "So far it's been nothing but trite: 'I miss you, I love you, the worst torture is not seeing you,' etcetera."

He glanced at Mathilde to gauge her reaction, but she kept her face blank as she held up her empty flute. "May I have some more champagne?"

CHAPTER 24

ODETTE

*W*hen Odette finally stepped ashore, she was greeted by the heady scent of palm trees, violets, and sea spray that was as unique to the French Riviera as the smell of Chanel No. 5 and warm croissants were to Paris. She felt so appreciative to be able to aid — in whatever small way—the country of her birth that she could feel tears spring to her eyes.

A tall, gruff man approached Odette. He introduced himself as André Marsac and told her he had been instructed to bring her to the head of the Spindle network's apartment.

Cannes proved to be nothing like what Odette would have expected. The city seemed untouched by the war: the sidewalks and buildings were all perfectly intact, and the beaches were full of revelers taking advantage of the bright sunshine and turquoise waters.

The apartment Marsac brought her to was also too tastefully decorated for Odette's liking, as if the owner knew nothing of wartime austerity. "This is Peter Churchill, our boss," Marsac told her, nodding to a man almost as tall as he was.

"Are you a relation to Winston?" Odette held out her hand, suddenly conscious of her wind-and-sea-tossed hair.

"No," Peter replied simply, his eyes raised over his tortoise-shell glasses. Those eyes held a hint of amusement in them as he said, "I suppose you would like to freshen up after your journey."

"I'm fine," Odette snapped, though in truth she'd been dreaming of a hot bath for the past several days.

"Yes, I can see that." Peter took off his hat and scratched his head, his arm muscles moving admirably under his civilian t-shirt. Odette noticed that, though his hairline was slightly receding, his hair was thick and wavy. "At any rate," he continued, "there's cake and coffee in the kitchen."

"Cake and coffee? Is that how Free France works now? Because in England, we've been rationing our food."

Peter spread out his hands. "Our circuit went through a lot of trouble to gather this feast, using forged bread coupons. Don't expect to be fed like this for every meal." He gestured toward the kitchen. "But in the meantime…"

After she'd had her fare—just enough to fill her empty stomach, nothing indulgent—Odette asked Peter about the next steps.

He cleared his throat. "Usually we don't task our operatives until at least their second day on the Continent."

"But the War Office said I should report to Auxerre as soon as possible."

Peter took off his glasses and rubbed at his eyes. "Auxerre is over the demarcation line. You will need a guide who is adept at helping others evade detection by German patrols. I'll have to ask Carte if he knows of one."

"I've finally arrived in France, after all this time, and you're telling me I need to wait still?"

"Yes." Peter replaced his glasses, but not before Odette noticed what a sorrowful brown his eyes were.

"Surely there must be something for me to do."

"Why don't you take a nap?"

"A nap?" Odette waggled her finger. "I was instructed to go to Auxerre, not wait around in Cannes, eating forbidden food and watching the pampered wives of collaborators walk their immaculately manicured poodles along unscathed sidewalks. Where I've come from, the damage from the *Luftwaffe* is everywhere."

Peter sighed. "I suggest you get some much-needed rest. I have a busy afternoon ahead of me, but I will see what I can do to make arrangements for your travels."

"I'm not tired," Odette grumbled.

He gave her a weak smile. "No, I don't suppose you are. But perhaps you could lie down while I conduct my business?"

She could see she was getting nowhere. "Do you have a book for me to read?"

He went over to the desk and pulled out a *Figaro* newspaper. "Read the local news. You'll see the war through German eyes. I'll wake you up about six for dinner."

She snatched the paper from him. "You won't be needing to wake me up."

As she lay in a strange bed, Odette stared out the window at the endless, sparkling ocean rimmed by palm trees. She focused her breathing, reminding herself that she was once again inhaling French air. She'd made it, at least to Cannes, and soon she would be starting her mission. She took another breath, thinking as she did so that there were other newcomers—enemies of France—also breathing French air at that very second. As far away as they seemed from this idyllic view, she was here to fight those invaders, to get rid of the Nazis so they would no longer breathe the air of France, or stomp their jackboots over its soil. With that, she fell sound asleep. If Peter came in to wake her up for supper, she didn't hear him. At any rate, her stomach was full enough to allow her to slumber peacefully until morning.

She woke to the smell of black-market coffee boiling away. Odette threw a robe on over her pajamas and headed to the kitchen.

Peter was already up, perusing the morning's *Figaro*, clad in a pair of red-striped pajamas.

"Am I to go to Auxerre today?" she asked him by way of greeting.

He put the paper down. "As I informed you yesterday, these arrangements take time. Buck suggested you stay here for a few days to rest and acclimatize."

Odette helped herself to a cup of coffee. "How long do you think I would need to 'acclimatize?'"

"Three or four days maximum."

She sat down across from him. "Is it possible for you to arrange some work for me to do? I would think it would be most beneficial for my acclimatization that way."

Peter set his coffee mug down with a clank and studied her determined face. Finally he stated, "I do have a job. But it's rather dangerous, especially for a woman unfamiliar with the area."

"I'll do it."

"Four new men have just arrived and need to be escorted to Marseille."

Odette nodded.

"Marseille is overrun with Vichy troops," he continued.

"I can handle—"

"And the Gestapo," Peter finished airily.

She met his curious gaze, knowing he was testing her by offering her such a trying mission when she'd only just arrived herself. "I'll be fine."

"You will leave the men at the station and then go into town." He told her which streets to use, naturally avoiding the Gestapo headquarters, to get to the Hôtel Moderne. Odette filed away everything he said, knowing he was purposely overloading her with information.

"A frumpy old dame runs the place," Peter stated. "You will ask to see Monsieur Vidal. If he is in, you will state to him, in French, that you have news of Monsieur Ternier of Lyon. He will respond that he knows of no Monsieur Ternier."

"But why—"

"It's our password. This will assure Vidal that you are one of our agents."

"Of course." She cursed herself inwardly at her naïve question.

"Good luck, Lise."

Once she'd arrived in Marseille and parted ways with the four men, Odette followed Peter's detailed instructions to the Hôtel Moderne. As she was leaving the train station, she saw a man standing on the street in a grayish-green uniform. Her eyes widened as she recognized his collar adornments. A German Hauptmann.

She tucked a strand of hair behind her ear. This was the type of man she'd been warned about—the kind who had directly or indirectly caused the death or imprisonment of thousands of her countrymen.

She narrowed her eyes at his back. He looked nothing like the depictions of Nazis at Wanborough Manor—there was no way this fat, balding man could ever have been considered to belong to a "superior race."

As if sensing her stare, he turned. "Bonjour, mademoiselle," he stated in tortured French. As he raised his arm in mock salute, Odette caught sight of a Luger tucked into the leather holster of his belt.

And therein lies his power, she decided.

She gave him the most cursory of smiles as she passed by him. She headed straight to the Hôtel Moderne, keeping her eyes on the pavement rather than make eye contact with any more fat Boches on the street.

The woman behind the desk was just as Peter had described. "Monsieur Vidal is currently out," she told her, "but we expect him back around six this evening."

Odette frowned. The last train for Cannes left just an hour later, and if she missed it, she'd have to find somewhere to stay. But going back to Peter without accomplishing her mission would have been a worse fate. "I'll be back then," she told the woman.

Odette toured the town of Marseille, finding that once again Peter had been right about the quantities of Vichy and Gestapo men. She bought a movie ticket and spent a few blissful hours away from prying eyes, returning to the Hôtel Moderne just before six.

"He's not here yet," the woman told Odette, gesturing toward a seat in the lobby.

Forty-five minutes later, a tall, handsome man in a gray beret entered the hotel.

"Monsieur Vidal?" Odette inquired.

"*Oui*," he answered. "And you are?"

"I have news of Monsieur Ternier of Lyon."

He frowned. "I know of no such man." He gazed up and down Odette's form. "Perhaps you would join me for a drink?"

She refrained from glancing at the clock. "*Oui*."

He led her to the café next door. Once they were seated, Vidal asked in an undertone, "How's Buck?"

For a moment she forgot herself before quickly descending back to reality. *Buckmaster.* "He's fine."

He continued, his voice barely audible. "The man I am meeting here is Bernard, one of our couriers. It would be a good thing for you two to become acquainted so you can recognize one another in the future."

"I'm not sure I'll be returning to Marseille anytime soon," Odette replied. "My orders from Buck are to report to Auxerre."

"I'm sorry to hear that. But you should meet Bernard anyway."

She checked her watch. "I suppose it would be no problem for me to find a hotel at this hour?"

"I know of plenty. But let's get dinner first."

The waiter came and Odette said her order in perfect French, waving the exact number of rationing coupons as she did so.

"You enjoy being back in France." Vidal stated after the waiter had left. It was not a question.

"I do."

"How long has it been since you've arrived?"

Odette tallied the time in her head. "Thirty-seven hours."

His lips stretched into a smile. "Wait until you've been here one hundred, thirty-seven hours and then we will have this conversation again." His eyes traveled to a spot over Odette's shoulder. "Ah, here's Bernard, at last."

Bernard was a smooth man in his late thirties. "The oysters here are outstanding," he remarked as he sat down.

"Oysters?" Odette asked. "I've just used the last of my rations on some onion soup."

Bernard motioned for the waiter. Not only was he adept in what to order, but he was a never-ending source of information and gossip concerning the goings-ons in Cannes, which he demonstrated after the waiter had poured each of them a glass of red wine, leaving the bottle on the table.

"I'm sorry to interrupt," Odette said after a while. "But I was just telling my friend here," she gestured toward Vidal, "that I will need a place to stay for the night."

"I will arrange for one where they don't ask any questions," Bernard replied.

She nodded as the waiter arrived with the oysters.

. . .

The hour grew late and Odette knew the ten o'clock curfew was quickly approaching. "The hotel?" she finally reminded Bernard.

"Ah yes." He told Odette to order another drink before he left the restaurant.

"I'm sorry, madame," Bernard stated when he returned. "The hotel is all booked with those Boches that plague our fair town, and not even I," he pounded his chest for emphasis. "have been able to make suitable pleas for a friend." He took a sip of Vidal's wine. "But I've managed to make other arrangements. It's not exactly the Ritz, but it will do for one night."

Bernard led Odette to the Vieux Port. He marched purposefully, his voice keeping cadence with his steps. "People like us, who undertake the kind of work we do, should expect to find themselves bedding in unusual places from time to time. The goal is to avoid anyone asking questions, and for yourself to sidestep filling out any unnecessary paperwork." He abruptly stopped walking and shook her hand. "This is where I leave you. Keep heading down this street until you get to the sixth house on the right. Tell the woman there you are acquainted with me and that you need a room with a key in the lock."

"Why can't you accompany me?" Odette demanded. "What is this place?"

Bernard sighed. "It is a brothel."

Her mouth dropped open. "Why are you sending me there?"

He drew her closer to him, his voice lowered to a whisper. "It's actually the safest place in Marseille to spend the night—the Nazis don't usually raid the brothels because they would only find their own soldiers."

"Can't I just sleep in the train station?"

"You could, but it's not wise. The Vichy would want to know why a lone woman was spending the night in such a place." He waved his hand in the direction of the brothel. "I've got to get back before curfew." He squeezed her hand. "You'll be safe. Trust me."

Odette set off down the dark streets. The only sound besides her heels clicking on the cobblestones was the thud of her heart. At the sixth house, she paused before pushing the door open.

The woman behind the counter put down the sock she'd been darning to give her a curious look.

144

"I've just come from Monsieur Bernard. He said you could help me: I need a room with a key for the night."

The woman folded her fat arms across her chest. "You know what sort of business we conduct here, don't you?"

Odette nodded.

"Come on," the woman said, hobbling down the hall. "Any friend of the Monsieur," Odette noted that she was careful not to say his name, "is a friend of mine. You don't need to worry; I'll make sure no one disturbs you." She opened the door and, after handing Odette the key, headed slowly back down the hall.

The room smelled of cheap perfume and cigarettes, but it was reasonably clean, apart from a filled ashtray and dingy dressing gown hanging on a hook. Odette moved the only furniture in the room—a threadbare armchair—in front of the door before taking off her shoes. She fell into the bed still wearing her dress and stockings. She closed her eyes, thinking sleep would never come, but she was out in only a few minutes.

She awoke to the pounding of many boots. "This is a raid!" a man shouted in German.

Odette crept to the door, standing on the chair she'd placed in front of the door to listen.

She could hear the proprietress's tired voice raise in inquiry.

"We are looking for an army deserter, one who betrayed his beloved Führer," the German's voice boomed. "We need to conduct a room-to-room search."

The woman murmured in consent. "But not that one," Odette heard her say. "My niece is in there, recovering from smallpox."

The German said something else, and then there was the sound of jackboots retreating down the hall.

Odette had a much harder time sleeping after the incident with the Gestapo. At dawn, she headed to the train station still exhausted. Luckily she managed to catch a miniscule nap on the train back.

Peter met her at the Cannes station. "Where have you been?" he demanded, his voice heavy with relief.

Odette sighed. "It's a long story." She cast her eyes over his rumpled suit and bedraggled appearance. "Have you been here all night, waiting for me?"

"No." He took her bag from her and slid his other arm through hers. "You must be very tired."

"I am," she admitted, "though I'm so hungry I could eat a small horse."

"I'm not sure about the horse, but I think I can arrange a small cow for you." He gave her forearm a little squeeze. "What held you up, anyway?"

She gave him a weary smile, her arm tingling from his touch. "It's a long story."

"Why don't you tell me about it over lunch?"

After she'd finished recounting her tale over stale bread and cold soup at the Chez Robert, Peter told her she'd done a good job.

"Thank you." Odette broke off a piece of bread and dipped it into the soup. "I would like to do more such jobs, if you would let me."

"You are supposed to go to Auxerre."

"Yes, I meant until then, though I do have to say I'm looking forward to being closer to the front. The Riviera is a little too," she thought for a moment, "impassively plush for me, if you don't mind me saying so."

Peter nodded as he took in a spoonful of soup. "It is, but we do important work here as well." He set his spoon down. "What would you think if I asked you to stay here and work for the Spindle network instead of moving on to Auxerre?"

"Here? In Cannes?" She thought for a moment. "Even if I wanted to, London would never permit it. I have my orders."

Peter smiled. "Is that so? I think I could probably persuade old Buck to change your orders."

She raised her eyebrows. "I don't think anyone is really capable of persuading Buckmaster to do anything he doesn't want to. Except maybe Vera Atkins."

"Are you willing to bet on it?"

"How much?"

"Fifty thousand francs."

Odette met his smile, knowing neither of them had that much money. "How about one hundred thousand?"

He reached across the table and shook her hand.

When Odette walked into Peter's office the next day, he told her she had won the bet and handed her a telegram.

She read it aloud, "*Send Lise to Auxerre as originally planned STOP. Surely Carte can provide means of crossing the demarcation line,*" before setting it on the table. "I told you." She still thought Cannes a little too decadent. So why was she feeling a twinge of disappointment at Buckmaster's response?

Peter crumpled the telegram. "Will you give me another day before we officially declare you the winner?"

She shrugged. "Of course."

Peter approached her at lunch the next afternoon. "About that hundred thousand..." He showed her another telegram. This one was short: the only words on it were *Oh very well.*

"Looks like you are going to be part of Spindle now." Peter tucked the telegram into his front pocket.

Odette bestowed a genuine smile on him. "Looks like it."

CHAPTER 25

MATHILDE

*B*leicher and Mathilde relocated to a smaller villa in Saint-Germain-en-Laye in order to carry out his new plan, termed, *Das Funkspiele*, or, 'The Radio Game.' The villa had a large garden, which might once have been beautiful, and played host to grand, pre-Occupation parties. Now the grass had turned brown and the trees withered from lack of care. Even before they moved in, Bleicher, who seemed to want a pseudonym for everything, decided to call the house, 'The Cattery.'

Mathilde had one request before complying. "I want you to free René Aubertin," she told Bleicher as he set her bag in a second-floor bedroom.

"I can't." He unzipped the bag and tossed her black pajamas on the bed. "He's already been sent on to Germany."

"To prison?" she demanded, making no move to unpack.

"Sort of… more like an internment camp."

She thought back to how brave René had been when he was arrested. "What do they do to people there?"

"Well," Bleicher pulled at the collar of his uniform. "I'm not exactly sure—Hitler set up these types of camps because the prisons were becoming overburdened."

"Overburdened because he was arresting innocent people." She folded her arms over her chest. "I thought you told me that you weren't a Nazi."

"I'm not. I prefer to outwit my enemies rather than resort to torture to get information out of them." He dumped the rest of her things on the bed. "The René situation was out of my hands—Hitler's latest Führerbefehle states that 'all enemies encountered by German troops on so-called Resistance expeditions with or without weapons are to be annihilated to the last man, and all mercy shall be refused to them.'" He lowered his chin, the glare from the electric lightbulb lighting upon his glasses and obscuring his eyes. "You're lucky you're here with me now—he might have said 'to the last man,' but that doesn't mean women will be spared from his vengeance."

Mathilde ran a hand through her hair, considering what Bleicher had said as he left to unload more of their belongings. *I could leave if I wanted to.* She went to the window and looked out at the garden. There was a layer of snow on the ground and roof, but not enough to provide much of a deterrent. She could sneak out of the window, climb down to the ground, and then exit through the back gate. *And then what?* She tightened her fur coat around her body. She had no idea where to go after that: everyone connected with Interallié had been captured, and, like René, probably sent to Germany to suffer Hitler's worst.

She was still staring out the window when Bleicher returned. "This house is perfect," he confirmed. "We'll set up the radio station on the third floor and Borchers and Kayser can share the bedroom next to ours." He shot her a grin. "Which means we might have to cool our passion a tad."

"Why are they forced to room together? There's an extra bedroom on the first floor."

"It's not extra," he corrected. "Another person will be moving in there shortly."

"Who? One of your Abwehr lackeys?"

"No. Viola Borni."

Mathilde's mouth fell open. "You cannot be serious."

Bleicher peered at her over the rim of his glasses. "Have I ever not been?"

"Why her?" Mathilde's voice was shriller than she wanted. "Why?"

"As you said, you had nothing to do with the coding. In lieu of all of the arrests that have gone down, we wanted to make sure London detects some semblance of the old network: hence Viola's presence."

She stamped her foot. "I refuse to be in the same room with her."

Bleicher shot her a sly smile. "I can arrange for that."

Borchers and Kayser joined them that night for dinner, though Viola was mercifully absent.

"Mathilde, say you had indeed been sent before a firing squad," The mouth of the already-drunk Borchers was full of food. "What would your last request have been?"

Her reply was immediate. "To have a superb dinner, to make love, and to hear Mozart's Requiem."

"That's three demands," Bleicher commented.

She turned to him. "I believe, after all that I've done for the Abwehr, I deserve all of them."

He picked up a morsel of meat with his fork. "I fully agree."

Kayser decided it was time to change the subject. "When will Mono arrive?"

"Who is Mono?" Mathilde asked.

Bleicher gave her a funny look. "He became Interallié's main wireless operator after Marcel left. We need him to send the transmissions. As with Viola, we want to maintain the facade of normal operations as much as possible to keep London from becoming suspicious."

"And I take it Viola will be here tomorrow as well?"

"Yes," Bleicher nodded at his colleague. "Kayser is going to retrieve her from La Santé prison." His lips turned upward into an oily grin. "Tomorrow will be our first attempt at tricking the SOE."

And so it was arranged: the next night, three former Interallié colleagues and their Abwehr counterparts met in the frigid attic room. To prevent any of the erstwhile Resistance operatives from somehow warning London of their circumstances, Kayser painstakingly rearranged Mathilde's message before giving it to Viola. As Bleicher had stated previously, The Cat would inform London that Armand and a few others had indeed been arrested, but she had managed to escape and would carry on the network along with Viola and Mono.

Mathilde broke her own rule and stayed in the attic to watch Viola encrypt the message. Borchers hovered over Viola's shoulder to ensure that she didn't try anything suspicious.

Mono then tapped his call sign out on his Morse key while Mathilde bit at a hangnail, waiting to see if Bleicher's plan would work.

In mere moments, Mono held up one finger as he listened. "Message received," he stated dryly. He handed the Morse to Viola, who quickly decoded it and then passed it to Bleicher.

"*Have news for you,*" Bleicher read aloud, the excitement obvious in his voice. "*Stay at your receiver.*" He released the paper from his hands and Mathilde watched it float to the floor.

"They're falling for it!" Kayser said, pulling Viola out of her chair and hugging her.

Mathilde narrowed her eyes. Kayser was a simple man, clearly lower on the Abwehr chain of command than Bleicher, and up until now she'd not paid him much attention. "Indeed they are," she said, putting a slim hand on Kayser's shoulder. He immediately dropped Viola to enfold his arms around Mathilde.

"What do you think they could want?" Bleicher asked, his voice stony as he watched Kayser twirl Mathilde around.

This question was enough to bring Kayser back to reality. "Whatever they ask, we will make sure to spin it so Germany will benefit."

"Shhh," Mono commanded as the wireless once again came to life. He wrote down what seemed like gibberish to Mathilde. Once the wireless went quiet, Viola decoded the message. This time she didn't bother handing it off and read it aloud: "*Report whereabouts Armand.*"

"Tell them he is in Fresnes Prison, but it is impossible to contact him," Bleicher instructed. "Tell them The Cat is out of funds and is requesting more money."

"You can't possibly think—" Mathilde started to say, but Bleicher held up his hand. "Do it, Viola."

A few minutes later, Viola decoded a message stating that Mathilde could retrieve more funds from the concierge at 10 Boulevard Malesherbes, near the Madeleine.

CHAPTER 26

DIDI

*D*idi laid her latest solved indecipherable on Leo Marks' desk.

He looked up. "Nice work. Was it his mistake?"

"No. Morse mutilation."

He nodded. "I figured. Archambault doesn't usually make errors in his coding."

Didi felt her knees grow weak and sat down in the chair opposite his desk. *That was Archie's message.* The fact that Archie had sent that dispatch made what she had to tell Marks even worse. "He didn't do any security checks, sir."

Marks raised an eyebrow. "No?"

"None, sir."

Marks frowned before he picked up the phone. "Get me Fawley Court," he barked into the receiver.

Since Marks seemed to have forgotten she was there, Didi remained sitting, curious as to what he was going to do. "Captain Smith?" Marks asked after a minute. "I need you to find Archambault's wireless operator."

Didi remembered how Archie had promised he'd send her a personal message and felt a ridiculous twinge of jealousy that he was communicating with another FANY operator.

"I need to know if he's been performing his security checks. Well then, yes, put her on." It took a minute for the girl to get on the line and then Marks demanded, "When was the last time——" He paused to listen. "But——" It was clear Archie's operator was quite talkative. "He doesn't make those kinds of mistakes. Ever." Another pause. "I need Captain Smith again." As he waited, he looked over at Didi. "She should have known—his last three messages didn't have checks, but she didn't pay it much thought." Marks turned his attention back to the phone. "I think it's safe to say that Archambault has been compromised."

Didi felt tears well up, but she blinked them back as Marks hung up the phone, only to pick it back up. "Get me Buckmaster," he commanded.

CHAPTER 27

ODETTE

*O*dette was up early once again a few days later and found Peter in his customary place in the kitchen. He waited until she had settled herself at the table before asking, "Can you ride a bicycle?"

Having spent several years blind or in bed with a serious illness, Odette had never learned, but how hard could it be? "I've just endured a night in a Marseille brothel. I think I can manage a bicycle."

He reached into the bag at his side. "Though I fail to see the connection between a bordello and riding a bike, I would like you to cycle up to the Villa Diana and deliver this," he put an envelope on the table, "to the Baron de Carteret. It's about seven kilometers away so it shouldn't take too long."

"De Carteret," Odette repeated as she took the envelope.

Half an hour later, Odette lay in a ditch with ripped stockings, the bicycle on top of her, its wheels still spinning. She sat up, pushing the bike to the side before removing both stockings. She climbed back on to continue her precariously wobbly journey to the Baron's villa, thinking that Peter had indeed been correct: the connection between spending the night in a brothel and learning to ride a bike was very slim.

· · ·

When she returned, she found Peter out on the balcony standing next to a brawny man smoking a cigar. "Ah, Lise," he said, obviously pretending not to notice her disheveled appearance. "I'd like you to meet Alec Rabinovitch, Spindle's radio operator."

Alec reached out a meaty hand.

"I would have never thought you a radio operator," Odette stated. He had clearly seen his share of fights; his nose was misshapen and he bore several scars on his face.

Peter laughed. "Alec is one of the best in all of France, not to mention he can swear in four languages."

Alec's firm mouth turned up into a smile. "And there's nobody else I'd work for."

"Lise is our newest addition to the network," Peter told him.

Alec's eyes traveled down from Odette's face to her stocking-less feet before he raised an eyebrow at Peter.

"Well," Peter cleared his throat. "Alec, why don't you go back and look for those messages?"

"Yes." He gave Peter a wink. "I'll leave you two alone while I see if I can find the bastards."

Odette walked over to the balcony railing, pretending not to hear Peter admonish him for speaking that way in front of a lady.

After Alec had left, Peter joined her. "Did you know your knee was bleeding?"

She looked down at the trickle of blood dripping down her scraped leg.

"Why didn't you tell me you didn't know how to ride?"

Odette turned to him. "You seem to take for granted that everyone is as competent as you are. I couldn't let you be wrong."

He laughed. "You certainly are an extraordinary woman, Lise. I'm not sure I've ever met anyone quite like you."

She glowed under his praise. "Oh, I assure you, I am most ordinary. I am a better cook than a British agent and far more accomplished at wiping little girls' noses than sleeping in Marseille brothels… or riding a bike, for that matter."

He gave her a brief smile before his face grew serious. "How do you like working here in Cannes?"

She thought about what she'd seen on the road that morning: people lounging on the beach, batting balls about and sun-tanning. "It's not quite the France I knew as a girl, or the resentful, rebellious France I expected to find. It doesn't seem the war goes on here."

"No," he agreed. "But appearances can be deceiving."

"I do like working for you, though," she said, surprised by the earnestness in her own tone. "I think you work very hard—you don't like to dally around. You are dedicated to your operations. I appreciate that."

"And I am glad that you've decided to stay on."

She met his gaze, noticing once again how kindly his eyes were beneath his glasses.

"Don't take this the wrong way, Lise, but I'm going to try to send you back to England."

She took a step back. Hadn't he just said he was glad to have her there? "Why?"

"It's Carte."

"The leader of the Southern Cell?" Odette knew that Carte was a Frenchman who'd founded his own Resistance group consisting mostly of students, artists, and Riviera sycophants. Peter had been sent to Cannes to make sure the Carte network was worthy of SOE money and protection.

"Yes." Peter took off his glasses and cleaned them with his shirt. She couldn't help admiring how sculpted his cheekbones were, as if they'd been chiseled from marble.

He replaced his glasses. "Despite the vast network he claims to have grown, Carte's an arrogant fool. One of his couriers was carrying a suitcase full of sensitive information—names of networks, contacts, anything you can imagine we wouldn't want the Nazis to know—and it disappeared after he fell asleep on a train. Now even Carte's right-hand man, Paul Frager, wants nothing to do with him." He turned to Odette. "I'm sending Carte back to London, along with five of his generals, for a consultation and I was hoping you would accompany them and give Buck a full report of what I've just told you. Does that sound like something you would be up for?"

Odette had no desire to return to London, but she wasn't about to refuse Peter. "Yes."

"Carte's a stubborn nincompoop, but this should be no more diffi-cult for you than…"

She held up her hand. "Riding a bike. Now if you'll excuse me, I should go clean up."

His gaze dropped to her bare legs before he nodded.

CHAPTER 28

DIDI

*I*n the first week of November, Didi was given eight indecipherables and managed to solve all but one of them. That one she took straight to Leo Marks.

"It's from Peter Churchill," Didi told him as she put it on his desk.

"Ah, Peter. Yes, I remember him, and his operator, Alec Rabinovitch, the beast." Marks smiled. "That was the first time I'd met Buckmaster. Alec was showing me one of his boxing moves when Buck walked into my office." He frowned. "Miss Nearne, do you recall when we talked about Archambault and his lack of security checks?"

"Of course." She took that as an invitation to sit down.

His frown deepened and Didi wondered if she had done something wrong, but instead of looking at her, he fixed his gaze on something beyond her right shoulder. "I warned Buck about it, and do you know what he did?"

"No."

"He had the FANY operator admonish Archie that he'd forgotten his security checks and must never do it again."

"But, if he really was compromised, then the Nazis—"

"Know about our security checks." His voice was grave. "I don't know why Buck would do that."

Didi had no explanation either, and she didn't want to think of the fearless Archie being a prisoner of the Nazis. "About Peter's indecipherable…"

"Ah, yes, Peter." Marks seemed grateful for the distraction. "I wrote his poem code myself."

"Really, sir?" Didi had the poem in her purse and took it out to read it again.

I danced two waltzes
One fox-trot
And the polka
With no partner
That they could see
And hope I did not tire you.

I glided round
The other ballroom
The one called life
Just us alone
And have to thank you
For giving me
The sprinkling of moments
Which are my place at the table
In a winner's world.

Keep a space for me
On your card
If you are dancing still.

"It's beautiful," Didi told him, "though a touch sad."

"Yes. Completely different from Peter Churchill, who could probably charm the pants off Miss Atkins herself."

Didi cleared her throat.

"Oh, sorry," Marks said. He took out a pencil and a pad of paper. "During his training, Peter occasionally flip-flopped the order of the letters, which changed the numbers underneath." He looked up at Didi. "This results in what I call 'hatted' columns, and sometimes takes a little coding surgery." He worked for a few minutes before shouting, "Got you!" After a round of furious writing, he pushed the pad toward Didi.

It was a message mostly complaining about someone called Carte's lack of competence and that he was sending an agent named Lise back to London.

"So, if you run across another of Peter's indecipherables, watch out for hatted columns: that seems to be his Achilles heel."

"Yes, sir." Didi scooped up the poem code and put it back in her purse.

"Sometimes it's the people who are the real puzzles, not the code itself," Marks declared as she let herself out.

CHAPTER 29

ODETTE

*C*arte had taken it upon himself to make all the arrangements for his and Odette's trip to London. Odette had been present when he proposed his plans for the Hudson's arrival to Peter and couldn't help finding the situation ironic since her SOE trainer had insisted that it was London who made all the preparations for bomber pick-ups. At any rate, Peter was not exactly impressed with the landing spot Carte had picked out.

"Peter, my dear boy, I don't believe there is any reason for you to examine the field personally. My distinguished subordinates," Carte spoke the words with uncontained pride, "are all aviators and have told me that the field is in every way suitable for the reception of a bomber. If you were to inspect it yourself, it would prove an insult to the integrity of my men."

Peter glanced at Odette, who shrugged before she said, "If you did want to take a look at it, it'd be a hike—it's a couple hundred miles away."

Peter rubbed his forehead in thought. "How long did you say the field was?"

"Over sixteen hundred meters," Carte replied.

"And the surface?"

"Flatter than my sister's chest."

Odette narrowed her eyes. "How broad? And by broad, I don't mean in reference to a woman."

Carte's lips turned up in an oily grin as he stared at Odette's own bosom. "Eight or nine hundred meters across, with no trees or any other obstructions." He reluctantly directed his gaze back to Peter. "You should summon your bomber for the next full moon, and trust me to arrange the rest."

As much as Peter and Odette had their doubts, everything seemed to fall into place. The BBC faithfully broadcasted the fictitious sweethearts' message, "*Joseph embrasse Nicole*," which was their signal to be ready and the five generals scheduled to go to London with her and Carte all arrived miraculously on time. Odette's first major operation seemed to be going off without a hitch.

The night of the pick-up was freezing, but Odette had thought to pack a perfectly suitable French brandy to keep the reception party warm while they waited. As the generals toasted to the steak-and-kidney pudding they would soon be indulging in next to Big Ben, Carte congratulated himself on the careful preparations he'd made in order to carry off this coup.

Peter peered at his watch. "All right, men. The plane should be on its way. When it gets close, point your torches at it until it touches the ground. This is our agreed upon signal that it's safe to land."

One of the generals piped up. "What torches?"

"Your flashlights." Peter's voice contained more than a hint of exasperation. "You were given flashlights, weren't you?"

"No," another general stated.

Carte's gaze narrowed. "You didn't expect me to bother with such trivial details, did you?"

Odette held up her bag, cutting off Peter's sure-to-be-brusque reply. "I have some here," she said.

Even through the enveloping darkness, she could see Peter send her a grateful smile. Carte pretended to take stock of the rising moon as they distributed the lights to the rest of the men.

Peter, torch in hand, started to walk the length of the field. Odette, for lack of anything else to do, followed him. He stopped short after about a hundred yards, and she hurried to his side. Both of them gazed silently into a deep gully.

"Only a lunatic would want to land a twin-engine Hudson here," he stated dryly.

"What should we do?" Odette cried, raising her voice to be heard over the dull hum of an approaching plane.

Peter's reply was drowned out by Carte, who shouted, "Torches at the ready, men!" at the top of his lungs.

The generals looked toward Peter, who crossed his arms in an X-shape and shook his head vehemently. "It'd be suicide to bring that plane down."

She passed him the bottle of brandy. He took a swig before giving it back to Odette, who took a small sip. No man besides Carte made a move as the plane dipped low. Carte ran toward Peter, beseeching him to flash the torch signal to guide the bomber in. Peter repeated his negative gestures, clearly refusing Carte's commands.

The Hudson circled one more time, the pilot noticeably confused at the lack of welcome on the ground, before rising back up and flying off.

Odette, while disappointed that the mission was not a success, was pleased that she had at least a few more days in France. She handed the bottle of brandy back to Peter. "I'll confer with the generals while you deal with Carte."

CHAPTER 30

MATHILDE

Though Bleicher no longer made Mathilde accompany him on arrests, he delighted in telling her about the demise of Inter-allié's remaining fragments. Uncle Marco had been imprisoned, along with Noeud and Lipsky and his daughter Cipinka. Each time the German Police made an arrest, they would confiscate everything in the apartment; the important papers would be added to the growing stacks on the dining room table, and the clothing would be distributed amongst the Huns and their mistresses. Mathilde was aware that some of the ties in Bleicher's wardrobe had once belonged to Armand and René, though the fat German couldn't put a leg into one of Armand's trousers.

One afternoon, Bleicher interrupted Mathilde's nap to hand her a small flat box. "I thought of you when I saw this."

She opened it to find a sparkling necklace.

"Before you get too excited, you should know it's costume jewelry," Bleicher told her. "But it's still nice all the same."

"Where did it come from?"

"Do you remember when we arrested Stanislaus Lach and his wife?"

Rapidé. "Yes," Mathilde answered hesitantly. "Was this hers?"

"It was, but she won't be needing it anymore."

Mathilde shut the box. "Because she's in jail?"

"No. Because she hanged herself the first night she was in La Santé. It was reported that she was hysterical about having to leave her baby. Guess now she won't be seeing either of her daughters again."

Mathilde threw the box on the bed and put both hands over her mouth. "I never…"

"Of course you didn't," Bleicher tried to envelop her in his arms, but she backed away.

She took her hands away from her face. "If you don't mind, I'd like to be alone for a little while."

He nodded and then left, shutting the door behind him.

She laid on the bed and stared up at the ceiling. "I'm sorry, Rapidé," she whispered aloud. "And I'm sorry René." Tears formed and this time she let them fall. "I'm sorry too, Uncle Marco, and Mireille and Boby Roland…" One by one she named all the former Interallié members who were now behind bars, shedding tears for all of the friends she had lost.

When she'd finished, she went to her makeup mirror and dried her eyes before reapplying powder. She couldn't stand to be in that house anymore and needed to talk to someone who had known her before. Of course most of them were not available, so she settled on the bacteriologist Claude, with whom she had become acquainted through Uncle Marco and had always regarded highly. Claude would understand.

She met him in his laboratory after hours. He wore a long white lab coat, his face remaining impassive as she told him everything.

"Well?" Mathilde asked when she'd finished. "Are you surprised?"

"No. The men at Vichy became suspicious when Uncle Marco failed to turn up after an appointment with you, not to mention regarding the arrest of Duvernoy. I'd heard rumors the finger was pointed at you."

Mathilde hung her head. "I'm sorry, Claude." She felt like she'd never be able to stop apologizing.

He reached out to lay a hand over hers. "Don't be, my dear Lily. You've done your duty for the Resistance better than anyone for months now, and you've had the good fortune to come out of it alive, a fate most of our colleagues probably won't share. If the Germans are being as tolerant toward you as you say, then just keep quiet and don't do anything silly. That's what I plan to do."

Mathilde dropped her hand in shock at his easy willingness to forfeit everything they'd worked for.

Claude continued, "Think of your health, your life. What would happen to you if you suddenly refused to cooperate?"

"The same thing that has happened to many of our friends. Arrest, torture, and then off to an internment camp."

Claude shuddered. "I've heard rumors about what happens at those camps. You must take my advice and keep quiet."

Mathilde realized he was right—there was nothing she could do at this point except go along with whatever Bleicher demanded. "Thank you, Claude. I knew you'd understand."

The necklace box was still on the bed when Mathilde returned to The Cattery. She opened it and ran her fingers across the fake diamonds, wondering if she'd ever have the audacity to put it on.

"That's pretty," a meek voice said from the doorway.

She swung her head toward the sound. As she'd thought, Viola was standing there. "Hugo gave it to me," Mathilde said as she placed the box on the dresser.

"May I come in?" Viola asked tentatively.

"What for?"

"I was hoping we could talk."

"What about?"

"Just," she seemed to be searching for the words, "things." She stepped closer to Mathilde. "They let me visit Armand in prison, and he wanted me to tell you something."

Maybe he was finally ready to apologize. "All right," Mathilde snapped. "But not here. I'll tell Hugo to get us some rationing coupons and we'll go to a restaurant."

Viola nodded before Mathilde shut the door in her face.

Viola must have had a few sherrys before she arrived at La Tour d'Argent because she was already stumbling as the waiter led her to Mathilde's table.

"Thank you for meeting me," Viola told Mathilde as she sat. Her words were slightly slurred. "I wasn't sure you were going to."

"I wasn't sure either." Mathilde looked up as the waiter handed them tonight's fixed menu and barked, "We're only having drinks."

"Oh." Viola's face fell. "I thought you had coupons."

"No," she replied, though Bleicher had given her some. The waiter left the menu anyway and Mathilde pushed it to the middle of the table. "What did Armand want to say to me?"

Viola raised her chin. "Did you know we were engaged?"

"I did not."

"He proposed to me right before the night of the anniversary party."

"The night you were arrested," Mathilde corrected. "I heard you were in bed together."

"I'd been so lonely after the death of my husband. I didn't know you and he, that is, had um… a fling… until Bleicher mentioned it."

Mathilde suppressed a visible flinch at the word, 'fling,' wondering if Viola was truly that clueless about their relationship. If so, then Armand's duplicity went even deeper than she had imagined. *But then again,* she eyed her companion's plain dress and make-up, *that girl lies with the same ease as she breathes.* "What did Armand want to say to me?"

"He said I shouldn't provide the Germans with any information about the network, no matter what they promised me. He wanted me to instruct that you shouldn't either."

"It's a little late for that, don't you think?" She meant it was too late for Armand to tell her to do anything, but Viola took it the wrong way.

"Oh, he isn't aware of anything that has happened these past weeks." She refused to meet Mathilde's glare. "He'd heard rumors, of course, that many members of Interallié had been arrested, but not that you or I had anything to do with it."

"So you lied to him."

"I didn't lie," Viola insisted. "And I suggested that he consider working with the Germans—giving them some information they already knew in exchange for his release. I didn't think it would be that big of a deal if he gave them names of some of our collaborators, especially those that had probably been previously implicated."

"And what was Armand's response?" Mathilde demanded.

Viola blinked back tears. "He said… he said he wasn't prepared to betray any of his comrades."

Mathilde stood and tossed the drink coupons on the table. "I could kill you for being so false to Armand."

"I'm sorry, Mathilde. I never meant to..." she obviously couldn't bear to finish the sentence. "And I'm sure you didn't either."

Mathilde repeated something Armand had told her a long time ago. "I suppose you never know what you would do in a situation like this until it actually happens."

When she returned to The Cattery, she found Bleicher in an even fouler mood than her own. "One of our detectives just informed me you are still married."

Mathilde touched her hand to her forehead. "After all that has happened, I've forgotten to follow up with my divorce lawyer."

"And your lawyer is...?"

Still reeling from her talk with Viola, Mathilde spoke the first name that popped into her head. "Maître Brault."

Bleicher picked up the telephone and held it out to her. "Call him now."

"It's late."

"You know lawyers work long hours. Call him."

She went to take the phone from him, but he twisted it in his hand so she could speak into the receiver while he listened in to everything that was said.

"Madame la Chatte," Maître Brault said breathlessly after they'd exchanged hellos. "I'd heard you were arrested."

She gave him the same old story. "Armand was picked up, but Viola and I are safe." She decided to bring up the divorce before he asked any more questions about Interallié.

They discussed it quite thoroughly and Bleicher was clearly growing bored with the conversation. He visibly perked up, however, when Brault stated, "I'm glad you called me, for I've met a very important young man. He has just returned from Great Britain and is tasked with uniting all of the resistance organizations in Paris."

"Is that so?" Mathilde asked, carefully avoiding looking at Bleicher's meddling expression. "What is his name?"

"Lucas," Brault replied quickly. "I shall introduce you to him. Let's meet at my office tomorrow morning."

After a few more details, Mathilde hung up the phone.

"What do you know of this Lucas?" Bleicher demanded.

"Nothing more than what you heard Maître Brault tell me," she insisted.

Bleicher marched into the parlor, which doubled as an office, and began rifling through files. "Do you know anything about a Resistance insurgent named Lucas?" he asked Kayser when the lieutenant entered.

"Lucas?" He smoothed down his mustache. "Yes, I think so." He selected a thin file out from under a nearby pile. "A political agitator, though mostly harmless thus far." He handed Bleicher a piece of paper.

Bleicher glanced at it before letting it fall to the table. "Mathilde, when you meet Lucas, ask as many questions as you can and make sure you remember everything he says so you can repeat it back to me. Also be sure to play up your role in Interallié and offer him anything he might need: fake papers, contacts, especially relaying messages to London. He might just be our enemies' replacement for your dear Armand."

Mathilde stifled a sigh. She had no idea who this Lucas was, but she was sorry she was about to bring him into her trap.

CHAPTER 31

ODETTE

*W*hen Peter sent a message to the SOE complaining about the escalating problems with Carte, Buckmaster decided to summon both him and Carte's lieutenant, Paul Frager, back for a conference. Buck suggested a convening at a small aerodrome that had fallen into disuse outside Périgueux but he wasn't sure about the feasibility of landing a Lysander—which the RAF had declared to be a better choice in lieu of the debacle with Carte and the Hudson.

In order to investigate the aerodrome, Odette and Peter immediately set off for Périgueux, a distance of nearly 500 kilometers. They met a contact at Marseille, who passed Odette a radio hidden in a battered suitcase before she boarded the next train. As she struggled to place it on the luggage rack, a German officer lifted it for her.

"How kind of you," Odette stated, her heart hammering away in her chest. There was no way they could hide what was inside if he demanded to inspect the case.

"It's my pleasure, madam." He made a huffing noise as he heaved it onto the shelf. "Your suitcase is heavy enough to be a radio set." Odette acknowledged his casual remark with a wan smile.

They met up with Paul Frager and André Marsac, one of Spindle's couriers, in the dining car. Frager and Marsac, though weary from their own trip, provided good company. Dinner, made even more merry by a few glasses of wine, turned out to be a pleasant affair.

When the waiter presented Peter with the check, he also delivered two little brown tickets. Peter put down enough money to cover the bill and then two coins on each ticket.

"What are those?" Marsac asked, nodding toward the tickets.

"They're for the 'Winter Relief Fund.'" Odette replied. "The French nationals are required to donate money for children orphaned by the war." She thought of her own girls and the fair possibility that they too might end up fatherless, or even motherless. The notion filled her with fury and she picked up the tickets, glancing at a nearby German officer. "I know just who should pay for this, and it's not the French."

"Now, Lise," Peter put a restraining hand on hers. "Don't you go doing anything foolish."

She shrugged him off before marching over to the German officer and thrusting the tickets under his nose. "I think you, who have been so instrumental in the necessity of this fund, should contribute something to it."

She could feel multiple pairs of eyes on her but the only sound to be heard was the clanging of the train wheels. The officer tightened the monocle over his eye as he perused a ticket. Odette was aware what the challenge could cost her—a beating, or even prison—but she refused to show fear.

The officer signaled for the waiter, who immediately came over, wringing his hands frantically, probably wondering if he had mistakenly set the tickets in front of the Huns. The officer placed a two-cent piece on top of each ticket and waved at the waiter to take them away. He then took off his monocle to peer at Odette with both eyes.

She gave him a satisfied smirk and then headed back toward her companions, who wore looks of admiration on their faces.

All except for Peter, that is, who told her in a harsh whisper as they navigated back toward their sleeping car, "A commendable performance, Lise, but for God's sake, lay off the theatrics—it's dangerous enough as it is."

"I'm sorry, Peter," she said, feeling distinctly unregretful.

They arrived in Périgueux the next day in time for an early lunch. None of them had been to that part of France before, but the worst thing they could have done was to reveal themselves as strangers, so

171

they had to navigate the unfamiliar town swarming with occupying troops without asking questions.

Peter decided his and Odette's cover was to pretend to be married. Frager and Marsac went off to find a different place to stay as Peter and Odette headed to the Grand Hotel. It was nearly full, but they were able to get an attic room which would be perfect to listen to the BBC.

"I hope you don't mind the accommodations," Peter said. He set his bag down and rubbed the back of his neck as they both eyed the lone bed.

"You should take it," Odette said. "I'll sleep on the floor."

"Nonsense," Peter insisted. "I'll make myself a nest out of the extra blankets. Besides, in a few nights' time I'll be back in a London hotel."

"Will you take this to Miss Atkins?" Odette held out a small valise.

"Yes, as long as you let me know what's in it."

"Presents for my girls. Miss Atkins will know how to deliver them."

He took it from her. "Girls? I had no idea you were a mother."

"Well, I am," she shot back.

Peter must have sensed he offended her. "What are their names?"

"Françoise, Lily, and Marianne."

His face softened. "It must have been hard leaving them."

"Yes." Odette was desperate to change the subject. How could she communicate how difficult it had been to abandon them, how disheartening it was every day to wake up without them? "It's a long story, but they are safe and well taken care of."

He nodded. "Is there anything in here for your husband?"

"No," Odette replied softly. After a moment she added, "I don't know where he's posted at this point. And I don't think even Miss Atkins does either."

"And now you're in the company of a complete stranger."

She gave him a shy smile. "I don't think any two people in this line of work are necessarily strangers."

Peter nodded as he tucked the small bag into his larger one. "Would you care for some lunch? Périgueux is known for its foie gras. I might even pick up an extra jar for old Buck."

"Buckmaster?"

"Yes," Peter answered with a grin. "You wouldn't know it, but he has quite the sophisticated palate."

. . .

172

The dining room was crowded with men in German uniforms. Odette and Peter decided to keep up the ruse of being a couple in love and shot each other shy smiles over their lunch of brandy and the requisite foie gras.

Afterward they set off for a stroll about town. As they passed a German officer, Peter gave her a playful nudge and Odette giggled loudly.

The airfield was quiet. Though the hangar was vacant and most of the buildings unoccupied, the control tower seemed operable.

Peter reached for her hand and Odette accepted it.

"What do you think?" he asked.

For a moment she thought he was asking about them holding hands, but Odette quickly realized he was inquiring if she thought the aerodrome would accommodate their objective. "There doesn't seem to be anyone here. But won't the Germans hear the plane landing? It's very close to town."

"True," Peter agreed. "But it would be in the middle of the night, so hopefully most of them will be off duty. And," he dropped her hand to point, "Those woods will provide good cover and that bridge over the creek a feasible escape route should anything happen."

She nodded, her hand empty of Peter's feeling cold.

When they returned to the hotel, Odette sent a transmission for Alec, instructing him to inform London that Périgueux was a go.

That night Odette had trouble sleeping. She lay in bed, staring up at the ceiling and listening to Peter snoring away on the floor. *Had Roy sounded like that?* It seemed like something she should have remembered, but for the life of her, she couldn't recall. It had been a long time in general since she'd thought about her husband, yet she could remember every little detail about her daughters. None of them snored, though Marianne made little cooing noises sometimes, and, when she was really tired, Françoise talked in her sleep.

Suddenly Odette heard loud German voices coming from some-where below.

"Peter," she whispered.

"Wha—" he sat up, taking notice of the commotion. There was a pounding noise, and then the sound of something large like a body being dragged down the hall.

"I think they've arrested someone," Peter said finally.

Odette's gaze traveled over to the suitcase with the contraband radio inside. "Do you think—"

"It will be all right." He came over and sat gingerly on the bed. Odette gave him a stricken look as the bed squeaked.

"Don't worry." He reached over and patted her hand. "They'll just think we're doing what married couples do."

She scooted over to make more room for him.

With Peter beside her, Odette no longer had trouble falling asleep.

The next morning, they were confronted with yet another setback: the plug for their radio had broken off.

"I'm not sure what to do," Peter said, examining the busted plug. "It's illegal to buy or sell any radio parts."

"Surely they must have black markets here just like anywhere else in France."

"Perhaps you could find one in a general store, but..." Peter started.

Odette grabbed her bag and disappeared behind a partition. She emerged after a few minutes wearing her best dress and matching hat. She went to the mirror to apply a dark red lipstick. "I'm going out shopping," she told Peter.

"You look amazing," he replied in an awed voice.

She gave him a little bow before she left.

She returned half an hour later, the purloined plug in her handbag.

Peter told Frager and Marsac to have dinner in the dining room while he and Odette tuned in to the BBC in their room. If the *message personnel* came as expected—for some reason, Peter had chosen '*Les femmes sont parfois volage*,' or 'women can be fickle'—they would go to the aerodrome that night to await the arrival of the Lysander.

"These walls are awfully thin, don't you think?" Odette remarked as Peter fiddled with the plug. She wondered if he was thinking about the same thing she was: namely, the arrest of the man the night before.

"I'll try to keep it quiet," he replied, "though I've never worked with a set like this one." He spun the dial and the room was filled with loud static. He immediately switched it off before wiping his sweaty forehead with a handkerchief.

"Let me see," Odette walked over to the radio. The transmission was scheduled to go on in less than three minutes.

She moved the dial to another station and in moments they heard a booming voice state, "*Les femmes sont parfois volages.*"

"Very fickle," Peter agreed, his face lighting up. Odette followed as he strolled downstairs, carrying their bags. He told the concierge that they had met some friends who had asked them to stay with them and made arrangements for Odette's bag to be dropped off at Frager and Marsac's hotel.

By quarter past eight, the four of them were marching down the road to the aerodrome, their gaze on the orange-red moon rising behind the blackened tree branches.

A mist lay over the fields. The night was cold, but thankfully still. Once they arrived at the field beside the aerodrome, Peter showed them their places. They were to form an L-shaped flare path, standing sentry with their electric torches. As soon as the Lysander appeared, Peter and Frager would run to the top of the L and board the plane as quickly as possible. If they were lucky, the Lysander wouldn't have to be on the ground for more than two minutes, not nearly enough time to rouse the guards from their warm beds.

"We have some time before then," Peter told Marsac and Frager. "Why don't you get familiar with the layout of the terrain?"

They complied and moved out to wander the foggy field.

"You'll be in charge of Spindle while I'm gone, Lise," Peter told her.

"Me? I'm not sure I'm capable—"

"Of course you are," he interrupted. "You are one of the most capable people I've ever met. Man or woman," he added.

"But you'll return soon, won't you?" Odette tried to convince herself she was only concerned about running the circuit without him. Not that she would miss his presence terribly.

"I will. And please take care of yourself. I want to find you intact when I get back, so don't go doing anything too risky while I'm gone."

"I promise you I will, Pierre."

If he noticed her French translation of his name, he didn't remark

175

on it. Both of his hands grabbed for hers. He leaned in, as if to kiss her, and Odette buried her face in his neck.

Just then the low humming of a plane became audible. Peter straightened to flash his torch: one long, then two short.

She could see the Lysander come into view, like a black dragonfly descending into the mist. It flew over her head and then disappeared once again, its roaring slowly fading.

"What happened?" Odette cried, her voice loud against the sudden silence.

"I don't know," Peter replied helplessly. "I'm sure he saw the signal." His eyes traveled to the tops of the trees. "Maybe he'll come back." He nodded toward the white handkerchiefs they'd placed to mark their spots. "Why don't you go wait, lying low, and if he doesn't come back within a half an hour, I'll meet you by the bank of the creek."

Odette squeezed his hand, one long and two short, before she did as she was bid.

She lay down on the freezing ground as she heard two voices. She almost called out, thinking it was Frager and Marsac, but started when she recognized German accents. The men passed so close to her she could hear their jackboots hammering the frost, but luckily they didn't see her. She watched as they approached the spot where she'd left Peter, wondering if they were going to step on his prone figure, but they finally receded from her eyeline.

The tenor of the returning Lysander vibrated the ground. Odette watched to see if Peter would flash again, but another light illuminated the field. The Germans were flashing a countersign to the control tower.

An unfamiliar voice barked, "Put out those lights, you imbecile. Wait until the plane lands and we can grab the whole lot!"

It's a trap! Odette longed to communicate a warning sign to the approaching plane, but she refrained, knowing that she would give herself away. She looked up to see Peter's frame breaking toward the treeline. He was followed by Frager.

The Lysander rose once again as Odette walked purposefully toward the bank of trees near the creek. *Godspeed*, she wished the pilot. *Fly away from here and return to the safety of England.*

Another voice was just behind her. "You make for the right and we'll rendezvous on the road to Périgueux." It was Marsac. She raised one hand, just enough to let him know she'd heard him, and kept up her march.

The quiet after the Lysander's engine was disconcerting. She could feel the hairs on the back of her neck rise as she heard another sound, the frantic breaths of a German Shepherd. A part of her knew that it was her worst nightmare coming true: an unknown beast chasing her through the darkness, but there was not time to dwell on it now. She began to run, listening hard as the dog's breathing quickened. It was chasing her.

She kept up a breakneck pace, her eyes focused just ahead on the copse of trees where Peter told her he'd meet her. But suddenly the ground rushed up to connect with her, and with an audible 'oomph' she realized she'd fallen. She could hear the snap of branches as the dog approached. Odette picked herself up, her knees and bruised hands aching, but she kept moving forward.

She ran to the edge of the embankment, and, knowing she had no other choice, slid down the hill. She gave an uncarthly moan as her body splashed into the creek. The bone-chilling water was waist-deep but she was able to wade through it. She could hear the whining of the German Shepherd, and then a human voice calling, "Frizi, Frizi."

Odette finally reached the other side and climbed out. Her teeth chattering and her soaked wool skirt clinging to her legs, she set off for Périgueux.

She met Marsac about halfway to town, and they continued their weary, frigid walk together. He'd washed his face in the creek and before they arrived at his hotel, he taught her how to clean off her shoes with grass. "It's no good having muddy soles in front of the Vichy police."

Luckily, her bag was waiting at the hotel and he waited in the lobby while she changed into a fresh dress.

"My god," Marsac stated, when she emerged, taking in her outfit down to immaculate hat and stockings. "It's as though you were at a Vogue shoot and not…" he held out both arms, not daring to state last night's adventures aloud.

She shot him a grin before accepting his arm. They sat near the window at the Grand Hotel's café and were able to spot Peter and Frager as they came into town.

"Good morning," Peter called out cheerfully as he pulled up a chair. He looked exhausted but presentable enough.

"Four coffees," he told the waitress before whispering to Odette that he and Frager had spent the night under the stars, managing to catch a little bit of sleep in between a thicket of trees. "Frager's flask of Armagnac was very helpful in that respect," he admitted.

Odette was starving, but she tried to restrain herself as she dug into breakfast. She was immensely pleased to have everyone in their party back safe.

Her hand, holding a forkful of eggs, shook just a little as a group of Gestapo members sat down at the next table. "Did you hear about what happened at the aerodrome last night?" one of them asked in a bellowing voice.

Peter, whose back was to the men, winked at Odette.

"Yes," another one replied, "and I'm sure the swine are still hiding somewhere—unless, God willing, they've already frozen to death. If not, then we'll capture them soon enough: I've got men out there now, combing the woods."

The smallest of them piped up. "I heard a rumor that one of them was a woman."

"Nonsense," the first man replied as the waitress set his order in front of him. "Frenchwomen are not the kind to consent to staying out all night in a freezing field."

Peter gave Odette an appreciative smile as he finished the last of his coffee.

CHAPTER 32

MATHILDE

*W*hen Mathilde arrived at Maître Brault's office, another man was waiting in one of the chairs across from his desk.

"Ah, Madame la Chatte, I'd like to introduce you to Lucas." Maître Brault waved her toward a seat. "As I mentioned, he's recently arrived from London."

She turned her focus to Lucas, who was a slight Frenchman in his mid-thirties with bright blue eyes. "I was trained by the SOE," he said with more than a hint of pride. "I was the first of their men to parachute into France."

Mathilde suppressed an amused smile at his arrogance. "And what is your mission here?"

"To spark the French Resistance."

She sat up. "It's already been, as you would say, 'sparked.' I helped found Interallié: surely the SOE has knowledge of us."

"Yes, of course. But now the SOE is training dozens of recruits at a time with their, shall we say, more refined methods."

Mathilde opened her mouth to retort, but he interrupted her. "Refined as in, with their guidance and expertise, they are hoping to prevent entire networks from being caught."

She shut her mouth. He had her there.

Maître Brault must have decided it was time to change the subject.

"He is planning on leaving again for England tomorrow by plane. Do you have any messages you wish him to relay to London?"

"Leave?" Mathilde asked, then addressed Lucas. "I was told you just returned."

"Yes. I pick up leads on possible local Resistance recruits and then make my way back to Great Britain to pass on their names to Major Buckmaster."

She'd heard that name before but couldn't place it at the moment. "Have you a regular way of getting there? Do you have papers?"

"No. I usually wait all night at a secret airfield near Chartres."

Mathilde refrained from rolling her eyes. It was clear this man didn't have the slightest clue on how to run a resistance network. "Well, if you don't manage to make the plane, I have ways of communicating with London."

He grinned. "Thank you for the offer, I will keep it in mind."

Despite the rocky start to the conversation, there was something about Lucas's cool courage that she took a liking to. *He may not know much about spying, but he could easily be taught,* she decided.

Mathilde's smile was genuine this time. "No problem."

As she walked out into the December sunshine, Mathilde realized she could confide in this young man. Lucas would be her revenge for all the crimes she had been forced to commit.

Bleicher was waiting for her on a bench across the street.

"Well?" he asked as she approached him. He indicated a nearby path leading through a park.

Mathilde understood that he didn't want anyone to overhear them and started down the path, thinking quickly of her best plan of action. "It's as you thought. The SOE sent him in to replace Armand."

Bleicher nodded. "And your role?"

"The same as before." She put a hand on his arm. "You know you can have complete confidence in me. I will run this Lucas affair, and it will be our triumph. You have nothing to fear for I know the price I will pay if it fails."

"Shall I purchase a Mozart's Requiem record just in case?" Bleicher's smile didn't reach his eyes.

"That will not be necessary. As I said, it will be our triumph. But," she continued as an idea occurred to her. "I will need a new apartment, which I will occupy alone."

"No," he replied sternly, and Mathilde's heart sank. "It's too dangerous."

"Although," he paused his walking. "Maybe you do need to move out of The Cattery." She was about to say that was exactly what she'd just suggested when he added, "And I will go with you."

The Abwehr had a list of flats they'd confiscated from British nationals, Jews, or just plain enemies of the Reich. Bleicher and Mathilde inspected quite a few before she finally settled on a suitable one, at 26 rue de la Faisanderie. It had once belonged to an Italian Jew and was beautifully furnished. Bleicher hired a maid to be at Mathilde's beck and call, and she made sure to keep a constant supply of flowers in the apartment, even though it was winter. In addition, they weren't subjected to fuel rationing, and fires blazed day and night in the apartment's many fireplaces.

At Bleicher's insistence, Mathilde paid a visit to Maître Brault in order to determine whether Lucas had made it back to London. As she'd predicted, he had not. She gave Maître Brault her new address and departed, not remembering until she was already several blocks away that she'd forgotten to inquire about the divorce proceedings.

Not a day later, Mathilde received a telegram from Lucas, informing her he'd be walking past her apartment that night around eight o'clock. If agreeable, she could meet him outside.

"And me," Bleicher declared after he'd read the telegram.

"I don't think—" Mathilde started to say.

"But *kleines kätzchen*..." Bleicher appeared hurt. "There is no reason why I shouldn't attend every meeting you have with Lucas. After all, we're in this together."

Mathilde disagreed with all of his statements, but didn't reply.

"You'll introduce me as Jean Castel, your husband. You'll say that I am Belgian to account for my accent. And, I don't know if I need to say this directly, but Jean Castel is a Resistance sympathizer."

She had no choice but to comply.

. . .

Bleicher had hired a new wireless operator and decoder—perhaps he, like Mathilde, expected Viola to betray them both. At any rate, he asked them to meet at their new apartment shortly before Lucas said he'd arrive.

In preparation, Bleicher poured them all heavy doses of schnapps. "Now, *kleines kätzchen* …" he began.

Mathilde was growing to hate that nickname. Translated to "my little cat," it seemed to belittle all that she had done for the Abwehr. "Be sure not to try any gimmicks with us."

"What do you mean?" she demanded.

He threw up his hands. "How do I know you don't have any little tricks up your sleeve?" He got in her face, his breath smelling of alcohol. "Don't you go and double-cross us now."

She shot him a sickly-sweet smile. "I would never."

"I don't suppose you would," Bleicher returned, "knowing the price you would pay if you ever even thought about betraying us."

"You have nothing to worry about," Mathilde lied smoothly. "You can have complete confidence in my abilities."

"Can I transmit a message through your contacts?" Lucas asked after they'd greeted him. His eyes darted from Mathilde to Bleicher, aka Jean Castel, who stood in the corner.

"Of course," Mathilde replied.

Lucas's first transmission to London was simple: he wanted to know if they would acknowledge receipt and if Lucas could use that channel to contact them from now on. Mathilde breathed an inward sigh of relief when the reply came back affirmative.

CHAPTER 33

DIDI

*D*idi was working late one night when Leo Marks' secretary informed her that she was needed in the transmission room ASAP.

"We need your expertise," the captain in charge explained when she'd arrived. "It's about The Cat. We're told you have already been briefed—"

Didi nodded. "Is she live?"

"Yes." He led her to a table where a FANY operator gladly surrendered her headphones.

Didi listened for a moment to the incoming message, faithfully recording it on a white card.

"Is it Marcel?" a man with a thin face and high forehead barked as he approached her table.

Having heard him even through her headphones, Didi took them off and shook her head. "No. It's someone new."

"Well then," the man gestured to the captain. "Let's run them through some of Lucas's security checks."

The captain placed a sheet of paper in front of Didi. "Major Buckmaster, I'd like you to meet..." he paused and looked disconcerted.

"Didi," she replied. Buckmaster shook her hand absentmindedly, clearly distracted.

She typed out the first check, *What is your brother's name?* on her

Morse key. After a moment she looked up. "He's said their names are Jean and Phillipe."

Buckmaster nodded approvingly. "Another one."

Despite her misgivings, knowing that Marks would in no way approve of exchanging such personal information about agents over radio waves, Didi dutifully tapped out the next question. *When is your birthday?*

She repeated the answer aloud. "January 1, 1906."

"That's our man," Buckmaster affirmed. "Apparently he has indeed made contact with The Cat."

"They must have gotten yet another new operator," the captain stated. "I thought for sure it was Marcel."

"Hasn't Marcel been gone from Interallié for quite some time?" Didi asked.

Buckmaster rubbed his forehead. "Yes." He waved his arm toward the white cards scattered around the wireless. "But this is definitely Lucas. Ask him what he wants from us."

Lucas's reply was that he was in need of a radio operator.

"Tell him there are no men properly trained and ready to leave. He needs to have patience," Buckmaster added.

"Sir." Didi took her finger off the key. "I could be of use."

"Is that so?" Buckmaster looked doubtful. "What did you say your name was?"

"Didi—Eileen Nearne."

The captain's eyes grew wide. "Nearne, as in Jacqueline Nearne?"

"That's my sister."

Buckmaster lifted his arm, as if to make some sort of signal to the captain, but Didi missed it as the next message came through. "Lucas also requires funds," she told them.

The captain's focus remained on Jackie. "Jacqueline Nearne is one of our top—"

Buckmaster cut him off with a wave of his hand and fixed his steely blue eyes on Didi. "Nearne, you say. Well, you obviously aren't ready to go off and join Lucas and The Cat just yet, but..." He seemed deep in thought. "After proper training... maybe someday."

CHAPTER 34

MATHILDE

*A*fter the SOE rejected Lucas's request for a wireless operator, he asked Bleicher's new transmitter to beg them for more money. Surprisingly, London returned by directing him to a Vichy diplomat.

Lucas turned to Mathilde with barely concealed delight. "I didn't expect them to be so inclined to replenish my funds. If all is as they say it is with this Vichy chap, well then I owe you an apology."

"Me?" Mathilde asked, willing herself not to glance at Bleicher/Castel, still in his place in the corner of the room. "Why?"

"I wasn't sure how you managed to avoid arrest by the Abwehr. Word has gotten around that their man Bleicher is ruthless."

Even though she was avoiding his eyes, she could see Bleicher start at the sound of his name.

"Well, I was no longer living at the house on rue Villa Leandre with Armand when he was captured." She paused to catch her breath. "How do you know the name Bleicher?"

"We are very well informed of everything happening with the Resistance."

I only wish that were true. Mathilde felt her cheeks grow hot as she felt Bleicher's gaze on her. She kept her face a mask, but sensed Bleicher could see right through her, teasing out her deepest secret: she was attracted to this man Lucas.

"But you've only just arrived," Bleicher/Castel insisted. "You wouldn't know this, but we have on good authority that Hugo Bleicher has released a dozen of our contacts without shooting them."

"That's right," Mathilde added. "He has even treated some of our most important agents as prisoners of war instead of hanging them as Resistance vigilantes."

"Prisoners of war? Do you know he sent René Aubertin to the Mauthausen concentration camp?" Lucas demanded. "Do you know what they do to these so-called vigilantes there?"

She pursed her lips and shook her head, hoping he would understand that she also did not want to think about it.

Bleicher saved her by stating, "Whatever Aubertin's fate, rest assured the Abwehr's sympathy will be tested as soon as the Resistance commits more sabotage."

Mathilde could detect the warning in Bleicher's voice, but Lucas refused to be intimidated. "We will not give in to the Abwehr… or Hitler's demands. We must stand tall no matter what." He stood up from his chair to emphasize his point.

"This Bleicher fellow," Bleicher spat out his own last name with as much vehemence as he could muster. "What orders have you been given with regard to him?"

Lucas's reply was prompt. "Why, to liquidate him of course."

"*C'est la vie.*" Bleicher rubbed at his eyes. "The hour is late. Come, wife, it is time for bed."

Mathilde looked at Lucas. She wanted to tell him he'd just put himself in grave danger and to stay alert, but doing so would be even more perilous for herself. And so she said nothing as Bleicher led her out of the room.

CHAPTER 35

ODETTE

*P*eter decided it was time to relocate the Spindle network. He and Odette had met a contact on the train back from Périgueux who told them that Peter's old Cannes flat had been visited by the Gestapo.

They disembarked at Toulouse, and Peter sent one of his couriers to bring Alec to him.

"Cannes is boiling," Alec told them when he arrived. "The whole circuit looks as if it's been blown. If you return there, Peter, you'd be nothing but a bloody fool."

Peter gestured to Odette. "Once again, Alec, I remind you that you are in the presence of a cultivated woman. Please don't swear."

"Well," Alec leaned forward, casting his eyes around, but the three of them were alone in their contact's study. "The Gestapo paid a visit to Baron de Carteret, asking for information about the whereabouts of Monsieur Raoul Olivier."

Odette knew they were referring to Peter. "And De Carteret gave them his address?"

Alec helped himself to a pickled onion from the dish on the coffee table. "De Carteret believed, as did we all, that you were already in England by then. He sent them on a wild-goose chase to one of your unoccupied apartments."

"Is de Carteret under suspicion?" Peter asked.

187

"Not as far as I know," Alec replied through a mouthful of food.

"What about Lise?"

Alec's eyes darted to her before turning back to Peter and shaking his head. "She's safe, but you should have caught that Lysander to England and cleared out for good. If I'd been there, I'd have shot the bastards stalking you."

Peter sighed. "If you shot everyone you threatened to, we'd have run out of ammunition a long time ago."

"Where shall we go?" Odette asked, mentally agreeing with Alec that Peter should not return to Cannes.

Peter sat back. "I've been thinking. We go to Haute Savoie and find a small town where they don't ask questions."

Odette nodded. "I could forge a doctor's note stating that I need to live at a certain altitude."

"Altitude?" Alec helped himself to more onions. "Are we talking mountains here?"

"In the Alps," Peter confirmed.

"I don't like mountains," Alec remarked stubbornly. "They interfere with my transmissions."

Since Alec was certain Odette had not come under suspicion, she returned to Cannes to discreetly warn the rest of the network to move on. Although Peter wanted to accompany her, she insisted he wait for her in Toulouse, hiding in a sympathetic farmer's shed.

She discovered that Monsieur Raoul Olivier was indeed a wanted man and must now disappear into thin air. She used one of their remaining contacts—a documents expert—to get Peter a forged card with a new identity: Pierre Chauvet, a freelance journalist.

When she presented the card to him, Peter laughed and told her, "You always think of everything."

Peter and Odette left the next day for the little town of St. Jorioz, a little less than 10 kilometers outside of Annecy in the French Alps. They discovered with trepidation that there were Gestapo at the station checking everyone's identity cards before they were allowed to board the train.

"Here goes nothing." Peter retrieved his wallet.

Odette got in line a few people behind him so that, in the event he was stopped, she could avoid detection as well.

She watched Peter hold his head up straight as the queue moved forward. She knew it wasn't the men in uniform that he was worried about. It was the man in a civilian gray suit and hat, standing directly behind the policemen.

She breathed an inward sigh of relief as Peter was told to move on. Now it was her turn.

The policeman gave her card a cursory glance before waving her on.

A railway assistant offered to take her bag and asked if he could assist her in finding a seat.

"No thank you," Odette replied. "I'm meeting my husband aboard."

She found Peter in the second-to-last compartment.

"Now we start all over again," he said quietly as she sat down beside him. "New contacts to recruit, new safehouses to locate. A new life. What do you think about it?"

She shrugged. "I told you a long time ago that I never liked Cannes."

He yawned. "Do you think you'll like Annecy?"

"We'll see." She put a gloved hand on his arm. "Why don't you try and get some sleep?"

"Aren't you tired?"

"I'll be alright."

As Peter fell asleep, Odette gazed out the window as the sun set behind the Alps. She said a grateful good-bye to the warmth of Southern France, looking forward to her next adventure with the man now known as Pierre Chauvet by her side.

CHAPTER 36

MATHILDE

*N*ow that Mathilde—and her imposter husband, Jean Castel —had won Lucas's trust, Bleicher decided they would form a fake network in order to penetrate other Resistance organizations. He told her about it with glee over a dinner she'd made in their new apartment.

"And you want me to do for Lucas and his network what I did for Armand," she surmised aloud.

He gave her a leering smile. "Not everything, of course."

She sat on her hands to refrain from slapping his fat face.

"We'll need to plant more moles." He took off his glasses and rubbed them on his shirt.

"Release René Aubertin and he can be one of them."

"No." He replaced his glasses. "He'd never agree to being a double-agent. I was thinking more along the lines of your man Kiki. Do you think he's the type to betray his own country?"

Am I? Bleicher's words hit home and Mathilde pushed her plate of food away. "Yes, I believe Kiki would."

The next afternoon, Mathilde met Lucas in front of 10 Boulevard Malesherbes. She couldn't help but notice how well his custom-fit

French suit showed off his athletic frame. It had been a while since she was in the company of a handsome man.

Lucas's gaze seemed to be equal in its admiration. "I like your necklace."

She fingered it. "Bl—I mean, Jean Castel gave it to me."

His eyebrows furrowed. "Your husband."

"Yes." Wanting to get away from his curious look, she walked into the building and headed to the front desk.

After informing them the Vichy diplomat was out, the concierge leaned over the desk. "May I ask what your business is?"

Lucas's voice dropped an octave. "I was sent by a man who resides at 6 Orchard Court."

"That is what I suspected. *Pardonnez-moi*." He left the desk and headed through a back door.

His behavior struck Mathilde as odd, and she felt a wave of panic that he was a German informer. She took a calming breath, reminding herself that her relationship with Bleicher meant this type of man was no longer a threat.

But the concierge returned with a large valise. He swung his head around the empty lobby before stating, "Tell Buck I said '*Allo*.'" His French accent had been replaced by a posh English one.

"Will do," Lucas said, giving him a wave as he and Mathilde walked out into the sunshine.

He turned down the first alleyway and checked to make sure no one else was around before bending down to examine the bag's contents. "Just as they said, there appears to be 50,000 francs in here, courtesy of the SOE."

He handed Mathilde a chunk of the money.

"What's this for?" she asked.

"I want you to take it. Even if I only have half of what they gave me on my person, it's still a big enough sum to draw suspicion. Besides," he shot her a lopsided grin, "Now I know for sure I can trust you."

She opened her purse and slipped the money inside.

Lucas stood up. "I think this calls for a celebration. I'm supposed to be meeting one of my contacts for lunch. Why don't you come along?"

"It's a date," Mathilde declared, slipping a gloved hand into the crook of his arm.

"I'm not sure I'd call it that," he looked down at her. "Let's not make your husband jealous."

The Auberge d'Armaillé was a Russian restaurant near the Champs-Élysées. Mathilde noticed one of Bleicher's goons sitting at the bar, but she brushed it off as they were led through a sea of plush red velvet booths. Lucas's contact, an equally handsome young man, was waiting at a table placed directly underneath a stuffed boar's head.

"This is Benny Cottin," Lucas declared as they got settled. "He's a former perfume executive."

"Oh?" Mathilde asked, holding out her hand. "Do you get discounts?"

"Not anymore," he replied.

"Benny's also been trained by the SOE," Lucas said, his voice much lower this time. "We arrived in France together."

Mathilde smiled prettily. "And you said you were the first man to parachute in."

"Well," Lucas spread his napkin onto his lap. "I did land first." He chuckled playfully, and Mathilde couldn't help but return his grin.

"You both seem to be in a jovial mood. Are we celebrating, then?" Benny asked.

"Indeed," Lucas nodded at Mathilde. "The Cat has come through." He looked up as the waiter arrived. "A double vodka for all of us."

"Now it really is a celebration," Benny stated. He turned to Mathilde. "I heard tales of The Cat and Interallié when I was in England. You must have had quite the adventure, especially because it seems most of your colleagues are behind bars."

"That's certainly true." Mathilde relayed her cultivated tale of how she had managed to escape the clutches of the Abwehr and taken over Interallié after Armand's arrest. The waiter returned with their drinks and a platter filled with various cuts of grilled meat on skewers.

"Here's to The Cat!" Lucas held up his nearly empty glass.

"Cheers!" Benny and Mathilde met his drink.

"I have even more news," Lucas lurched forward, his eyes glassy. "There was a message in with the money—the RAF is going to send us arms and ammunition by parachute."

"Where? When?" She took a sip of vodka in an effort to cover her overeager tone. The last thing she needed was for either Lucas or Benny to develop suspicions about her.

"Near Le Mans," Lucas turned to Benny. "I want you to leave tomorrow and scope out the field. It's in a little village called Vaas. The Cat and I will join you the night of the drop."

Mathilde smiled to herself. There was something exciting about journeying out to unknown territory with Lucas.

Benny lifted his drink, and said in a jubilant whisper, "To the Royal Air Force!"

Once again the trio clinked their glasses together. Mathilde tried to catch Lucas's eye, but he was staring off into space, his head probably filled with plans for the Resistance.

Mathilde went straight into the bedroom when she returned to the apartment. She didn't want Bleicher to smell the vodka on her.

He came in a few minutes after she'd finished changing into her pajamas. "What news do you have for me today?"

She didn't want to tell Bleicher about the arms drop but the alcohol had muddled her mind and she couldn't think of another excuse for needing to go to Vaas.

He nodded enthusiastically after Mathilde filled him in. "You can tell Lucas that your husband will arrange for a driver."

Mathilde straightened the hem of her shirt. "You don't need to come."

"Oh yes I do. I'd love to see firsthand how Churchill's Secret Army communicates."

She put up her hands, knowing there was no use arguing with him. "If you so desire, I'll let Lucas know."

He sat on the corner of the bed. "Do you trust this Lucas?"

She shrugged. "Does it matter? The most important thing is that he trusts me."

"I take it the money came through."

She refrained from glancing at her purse. "Yes, Lucas gave some of it to that Cottin fellow for his travels to Vaas."

"Good." He stood up and began to unzip his trousers.

She couldn't stand the sight of his fat belly protruding from his undershorts and shut her eyes. "I have a headache."

"Now?" She heard his pants drop to the floor as he said, "It seems like you always have a headache lately."

Her eyes flew open. "I have a cold and it is creating pressure in my head."

He gave her a searching gaze as he redressed. "I hope that's true, though I don't imagine vodka helped the situation."

CHAPTER 37

ODETTE

*P*eter and Odette disembarked at Annecy, an ancient Alpine town at the northwestern end of a large, sparkling lake. It was less than 40 kilometers from the Swiss border, and with its wooden chalets lining cobbled streets, definitely looked the part. Odette took a deep breath of refreshing mountain air. In her purse was a doctor's order claiming that it was necessary for her health to stay five hundred meters above sea-level. Though the note was fake, she could see why a place like this would be good for both the body and soul.

André Marsac had suggested reestablishing the network in the nearby community of Saint-Jorioz, just south of Annecy. Once again, Peter and Odette took up the guise of being a married couple.

They were both quiet during the 10-kilometer bus ride to Saint-Jorioz. Ever since that night at the airfield, when Peter had, possibly, tried to kiss her and she'd hugged him instead, their relationship had taken on a slightly detached air. Odette longed to tell him how much she'd grown to depend on him, but she didn't want to overstep her bounds as a woman married to someone else, no matter how insignificant that someone else was in her new life. And so she said nothing.

Marsac's wife met them at the bus stop, which was at the crossroads of the town's two main streets. Odette took a look around as she got off. There was a hotel on either side of the street; a telegraph office and an adjacent post office completed the four corners.

"We've taken rooms at the Hôtel des Terraces," Madame Marsac told them. "And so has Paul Frager, but we booked you two a room at the Hôtel de la Poste."

"Good." Peter shielded his eyes against the bright sun as he took stock of his new surroundings. "We don't want to have too many people bombard them at once. I have a feeling Saint-Jorioz doesn't normally see much action."

Odette noted that their hotel had a terrace encircling the entire first floor: an easy escape route should they need it.

Marsac was in the café and rose when they entered. "Peter and Lise, I'd like to introduce you to Jean Cottet, the proprietor of the Hôtel de la Poste."

"Nice to meet you," Peter said as they shook hands.

"These are the friends I've told you about," Marsac stated.

Odette felt indignation at his careless comment. They'd been in town for less than half an hour. Had their cover already been blown?

Cottet looked to only be in his early thirties at most, quite young to be the owner of a hotel. "I will do my best to see they are comfortable," he stated.

Odette wondered what he would think if he knew they were really in town to rebuild their Resistance network. Was he aware of the punishment he might suffer if the Gestapo caught wind that he'd knowingly harbored an enemy of the Germans?

Maybe it's best he's left in the dark, she decided.

Peter found Alec a small house outside Saint Jorioz, strategically located in a gap between two mountains and faced in the direction of England. As Peter continuously stressed to Odette, it was imperative that Alec was content. Without a radio operator, their network, no matter how extensive, would be completely cut off from the rest of the world.

After Peter and Odette had settled into their new room, they paid a visit to Alec's new hideout. The big Russian said the set-up was perfectly adequate. "London, however, is another issue."

"Is something wrong at the SOE?" Odette asked.

"Yes," Alec grumbled. "The other night they had a new operator, obviously straight out of training. She couldn't get out more than..." his voice slowed. "Twelve... words... a... minute. Can you imagine? Next time, I may still be sitting there, waiting for her to finish while the Gestapo closes in on my signal."

Peter indicated the snowy Alps outside Alec's window. "Not here. I think we're safe."

"For a while, perhaps," Alec agreed. "But not forever, and I'll be damned if I am strung up by my ankles because Buckmaster is training some rookie..." he muttered something—probably a foul word—in his native language, "who can't keep up."

"What are you going to do?" Odette inquired.

"Here." He thrust a piece of paper at her. Peter peered over her shoulder as she read it aloud. "*If you put that dolt on again, I quit.*"

Alec folded his arms over his chest. "With your permission, I'm going to send it on to the SOE tonight."

Peter's amused gaze met Odette's. "Go ahead," he said as she handed the message back to Alec.

When they returned to the hotel that night, the owner, Jean Cottet, asked Peter and Odette to join him for an aperitif in his study.

Peter agreed, and, after a few minutes of exchanging gossip about the goings-on in Saint Jorioz, Cottet got down to business. "I remain deliberately detached as to your politics."

Odette, thinking that an odd statement to make, studied his boyish face for a hint of his real intentions, but his expression remained inscrutable. She could feel her muscles tighten in trepidation that he was about to blackmail them.

"I thank you for not inquiring too deeply," Peter replied.

"But," Cottet went on to say, "it might interest you to know that there are a number of men in this town who have vowed to resist being drafted into German forced labor camps, no matter what the cost."

Peter nodded.

"These men have decided to band together in an organization called a *Maquis*," Cottet continued.

Again Peter nodded. "I've heard of such organizations before."

Cottet pulled out a map. "I know you are tourists, here for her health," he gestured toward Odette. "But perhaps on your walks in the fresh air, you might run across the spot where these underground men have congregated." He drew a small circle on the map. "Suppose a person wished to assist these intransient Maquisards, I could indicate to that person what their needs are."

Odette understood that he was offering the location of these rebels to her and Peter, who might want to recruit them for their own purposes. Cottet's roundabout way of speaking of the Resistance reminded her a bit of her interview with Captain Jepson so long ago.

"I think," Peter's voice came out quietly. He cleared his throat and restarted in a more confident tone, "I think I know a man who could assist these Maquisards in the way you are proposing."

Cottet sat back. "I thought you might." He handed Peter the map.

CHAPTER 38

MATHILDE

The hour-long car ride to Vaas for the air drop was nearly silent. Mathilde spent most of the time staring out the window at the cold, bleak landscape. She guessed that Bleicher didn't want to carry on conversation for fear his German accent might give him away. At first, Lucas had taken the announcement that Bleicher/Castel was joining them in stride, but now he seemed nervous—his restless leg never quit moving.

Mathilde longed to put a calming hand on Lucas's leg to let him know they were safe. They were out past curfew and German patrols were sure to be out in droves, but Bleicher had a plan if they were stopped: he would get out of the car and speak to the patrols himself. For Lucas's benefit, it would look like Bleicher was attempting to persuade the patrols they were only out for a leisurely drive, though Mathilde knew Bleicher would reveal his real identity to his comrades if need be.

They arrived at the field around midnight and found Benny. He'd brought a Resistance contact, a schoolteacher who had volunteered to hide the dropped containers in his attic.

The temperature had plunged severely that January and it was now bitterly cold. There was nothing to do but wait so she pulled her new fur—purchased with some of the SOE cash that Lucas had given her —closer and stamped her feet to keep warm.

The schoolteacher bragged to Bleicher about how he scattered pro-Allied propaganda throughout his village. It was too dark to judge Bleicher's reaction to this revelation, but Mathilde was sure he could not have been pleased.

Lucas stood apart from the others, the whites of his eyes visible as he kept his gaze on the sky above. Mathilde would have given anything to move closer to him, but that was impossible with Bleicher there.

But what if he wasn't here? Counting Bleicher and the driver waiting in the car, there were only two Abwehr men. If Mathilde secretly revealed the Germans' identities to the others, the three Resistance men could easily overtake them and steal their car. *But where would we go?* If they were stopped on the way back to Paris, they would need Bleicher for cover.

The time is not ripe yet, Mathilde convinced herself. But someday it will be.

She passed around sandwiches and a thermos of coffee, which quickly ran dry. There was no sign of any aircraft.

At dawn, the half-frozen, defeated team trudged to the school-teacher's farmhouse to get warm. When curfew ended at 5 am, they piled back into Castel's car and made their way back to Paris.

Now Mathilde was genuinely worried. What if London had become suspicious?

The next morning she went to Maître Brault's office to sign her divorce papers. "It's finally over," she declared as she set her pen down.

"Indeed." He picked up the pile of papers and stuffed them into an envelope. "I suppose now you can move on."

"Yes," she replied quickly, wondering how much Brault had known about her and Armand's relationship. "I am determined to do the best I can with my little life. After all, you only get one."

He cocked an eyebrow. "That sounds odd, coming from someone like you, who risks their life daily for the Resistance."

She retrieved her purse. Brault's attitude had grown cold, as if she'd made some sort of social blunder. What it was she had no idea, but she couldn't help feeling a trace of guilt as she left his office.

· · ·

THE SPARK OF RESISTANCE

Kiki was at the apartment when she returned. He was sporting a new overcoat and felt hat.

"Black market?" Mathilde asked by way of greeting, nodding at his smart-looking garb.

"Yes." He seemed a bit embarrassed. "Thanks to Hugo, I've been doing some trading on the side. It's just little things: clothing, alcohol, cigarettes, that sort of thing." He sat down on the couch. "In fact, I am here to speak to Hugo. Do you know where he is?"

"I'm not Bleicher's keeper," she snapped back.

"Mathilde." He gave her a helpless look, as if unsure how to finish his sentence. "I've been tasked to go to Cannes, in the Unoccupied Zone. Apparently there are more Resistance cells down there. Some idiot boarded a train with all kinds of identifying papers—names of networks and their members—in his briefcase, and the Abwehr were able to grab it when he fell asleep. Now Hugo wants me to offer them my services."

"Don't you ever get tired of betraying the Resistance?"

"Don't you?" he returned angrily. After a moment he started again, his voice softer. "Listen, you and I are both doing what we can to survive. I've told Hugo I would never give up any airmen—those men are sacred to me. But everyone else…" he looked down at his hands. "It's war, and people must decide what they think is right, how far they will go to protect their own skin. You shouldn't judge them for that."

Mathilde sunk into the armchair across from him. "You're right, Kiki. In a rather precarious situation myself, I have no right to judge anyone."

They both looked up as Bleicher entered the apartment. "Ah Keiffer, just the man I was looking for. Mathilde, do you mind fixing us a drink? We've got business to discuss."

After Kiki had gone, Bleicher called Mathilde back into the living room. "Is your divorce finalized now?"

"It will be when they deliver Maurice the papers. They'll have to locate him first—last I heard he was in North Africa."

Bleicher nodded. "Then I'm going to arrest Maître Brault tomorrow."

"Why?" Mathilde couldn't keep the shock out of her voice. "We need him if we are going to carry on the infiltration of Lucas's network."

"No." Bleicher waved an unsteady hand. "As you said, he never really joined Interallié, so I don't think it will make much of a difference with Lucas."

She decided to try a different tactic. "If he wasn't technically a part of Interallié, why bother going through the trouble of arresting him?"

"Brault's monetary contributions to the Resistance are well-known. He may never have gotten his hands dirty, but he provided plenty of cash for the saboteurs to carry out their soiled deeds. He's as guilty as you were. We'll go first thing in the morning."

"No." She stood up. "I'm tired and want my sleep. If you're so keen on arresting him, send your goons instead." Bleicher had often complained that his Abwehr associates were lousy at their jobs, and, thanks to their blundering, potential arrestees had a fifty percent chance of escaping. It might be the only chance Brault had. She held out her arm to Bleicher.

"You don't have a headache?" he asked hopefully.

"Not tonight."

CHAPTER 39

ODETTE

*P*eter communicated with the Maquisards hiding in the woods beyond Saint Jorioz through Annecy's ambulance, figuring it was a vehicle that would not invite suspicion.

For several nights in a row, the RAF dropped much-needed supplies for their newfound collaborators: guns, ammunition, knives, medicine, boots, hand grenades, and of course, necessities such as coffee, cigarettes, and chocolate. Once they were fully equipped, the Maquisards were able to mount an enormous attack on the railways and start waging guerilla warfare on the German troops.

"Congratulations," Alec told Odette and Peter the next time they visited him. "Forty new drop sights is quite an accomplishment."

"Thank you," Odette replied, pleased they were finally inflicting the kind of damage on the Nazis she had once only dreamed about.

"And here's this." Alec handed Peter his latest message. "Buck wants you back in England as soon as possible."

Odette felt her heart sink.

"What for?" Peter asked, perusing the notice.

"Maybe they're finally planning the Allied invasion of France," Alec replied.

Peter set the paper down on a nearby table. "Wouldn't that be nice?" His gaze swerved to Odette as if to gauge her reaction.

She gave him the widest smile she could conjure. "Indeed."

"Or maybe it has something to do with the arrest of Carte's wife and daughters," Alec continued.

"The briefcase?" Peter asked.

He nodded.

"What briefcase?" Odette demanded.

Peter sighed heavily. "One of Carte's couriers fell asleep on a train, back in November, and had his briefcase stolen."

"Who was it?" Odette demanded.

"Marsac."

Her mind whirled, wondering how Marsac could have been so careless.

"At any rate, they're sending someone in your place," Alec stated.

Both Odette and Peter focused on Alec. "Say that again," Peter commanded.

"His codename is Roger. If you think some greenie is going to parachute in and bark orders and expect me to obey…" Alec began.

Peter held up his hand. "We all know how you feel about the SOE's newest recruits."

"I'm sure Lise will concur." Alec looked at her imploringly, his heavy eyebrows raised.

For her part, she couldn't imagine anyone, not even Buckmaster himself, daring to take Peter's place. "I agree with Alec."

"I'm sure London knows as well as I do that they can't send some novice to serve as a stand-in for Spindle's director. Not with you two as second-in-command."

Odette weighed his words. Though the Maquisards had proved excellent recruits for the Resistance, it was true that the only remainders of the Spindle Network in Saint Jorioz were Peter, Alec, and herself. It occurred to Odette that the three of them—an English gentleman, a Frenchwoman and a Russian Jew—made for a strange trio.

Once again, Peter met her eyes. "Lise, I'm putting you in charge."

"I—" she began, but he cut her off. "Alec, watch out for her. No matter what."

Alec looked as if he was about to argue, but something else came over him. "Sure, boss. No problem."

Peter extended his hand. "*Au revoir*."

Alec met Peter's outstretched palm with his own meaty one. "Adieu, boss. Be well."

. . .

As they rode home in the gasping motorcar that Peter had managed to finagle off someone, Odette asked why he'd chosen her to be in charge of Spindle.

His reply was simple. "I trust you."

"But Alec is a lieutenant and I'm a woman."

Peter kept his eyes on the road as he repeated, "I trust you."

Odette stared out the window for a few moments, trying not to imagine why Buckmaster wanted Peter back in London. *What if Buck wants to reassign him?*

Peter's gruff voice cut through the silence as they pulled up to the hotel. "Do you have any messages for me to pass on? Either to your daughters or… to your husband?"

"Have Miss Atkins tell my girls…" her voice broke and she paused until she could get the words out. "Tell them I am well and obeying orders from my superiors, just as any good soldier would do."

He turned to her, his eyes full of unspoken emotion. "Will do."

CHAPTER 40

DIDI

*D*idi was working on yet another complicated indecipherable when Leo Marks approached her. He was accompanied by a good-looking middle-aged man with wireframe glasses.

"Miss Nearne, I'd like to introduce you to the one and only Peter Churchill."

"Churchill," Didi said, holding out her hand. "Ah yes, of hatting column fame."

He gave her a wry smile. "Sorry about that. Did it take long for you to figure it out?"

There was something infectious about his grin. "A few minutes. But it's my job."

"Well, I've got Alec Rabinovitch back as my operator so it should never happen again."

"The Beast?" Marks looked surprised. "How is he?"

Churchill shrugged. "Probably chomping at the bit in my absence, but Lise can handle it." His voice seemed to catch at the woman's name.

Marks steered Churchill toward the door. "Well, while I admire Rabinovitch's audacity, if he ever does send in an indecipherable, I'll have to do it myself. There's no way I'd have a FANY try to unscramble it, what with the colorful language he uses. It's bad enough his home operator having to decode all his curses."

Churchill shot Didi one last smile. "I apologize in absentia for my associate's lack of decorum." He turned back to Marks. "If you want to attempt to control him, you can see if you could do a better job than I. But I warn you, he doesn't respond easily to that sort of handling."

"Not many of us do," Marks agreed as he shut the door.

CHAPTER 41

MATHILDE

*J*ust as Mathilde had hoped, Bleicher's comrades cocked up the attempt to arrest Maître Brault. They did not know that most of the larger houses in Paris had a separate servants' staircase. While the Abwehr men plodded up the main stairs, Brault was able to sneak out the back.

After Lucas told Mathilde this story, he mentioned that Brault was on his way to Vichy and needed an official pass to help him get through the demarcation line. Mathilde promised to secure some and deliver them that evening to Lucas's flat.

When Lucas opened the door, Mathilde handed him the pass and some forged papers she'd managed to secure for Maître Brault before heading to the kitchen. As she returned to the main room with two glasses of brandy, Lucas was examining the papers. "These are more than adequate." He seemed preoccupied as he ran his finger over the *Wehrmacht* stamp. "Almost perfect."

She handed him a drink. "I told you my contacts would come through." They were, of course, courtesy of the Abwehr, but she couldn't tell Lucas that.

He sighed heavily. "Mathilde, there's something I've been meaning to ask you." The distraction was gone and his astute eyes now focused on her so intently it made her uncomfortable.

"Is Jean Castel really your husband?"

Lucas looked so handsome. She half-hoped that there was a hint of romantic notions behind the inquiry, but something in his gaze told her that wasn't the case.

She took a sip of her drink. "Of course. What a silly question."

"I don't think it's silly at all, but let me ask a different one. Who told the Germans about Maître Brault?"

She gave him a coy smile, mostly to hide her trembling lips. "What do you mean?"

"Only a few people knew about his involvement with the Resistance, and most of them are in prison."

He had her there. Mathilde realized it was futile to keep lying to him. "Oh, Lucas, there's something you should know." She set her drink down before sinking into the couch beside him. "I too was arrested, the day after Armand. They threw me in La Santé prison and it was so horrible..."

He folded his arms across his chest. "And the Germans convinced you to work for them."

It wasn't a question but she answered anyway. "They forced me to."

"What about your husband—the supposed Jean Castel?"

She hung her head. "His real name is Sergeant Hugo Bleicher. He works for the Abwehr." She reached out to grab Lucas's arm. "You have to believe me. I would never have agreed to such things if my life weren't at stake."

He shrugged her off. "We've all been risking our lives. But the brave men and women I know would rather die than put their networks in peril."

"I, too, would never willingly place mine in peril either."

"Then all of those arrests—nearly a hundred Interallié agents? You had nothing to do with them?"

"No," Mathilde spoke quickly. "I mostly provided Bleicher with false information." She saw no need to confess the full extent of her culpability. It was too late to help any of those agents and would only make Lucas doubt her intentions.

"And all this time they never grew suspicious with your so-called false information?"

"No." She shook her head vehemently for good measure. "But even so, all I want now is a chance to redeem myself, to get back at the Germans for this horrible situation they've put me in."

He folded his hands under his chin as he thought. "We are both in grave danger," he said finally. "The Abwehr has known about my operations all along, and if Bleicher learns you've revealed all of this to me…"

"He'll throw me to the dogs," she finished for him.

"And Benny, and the schoolteacher, Brault, and everyone else I've been associated with since I arrived in France." He took a shaky breath. "I can't have that on my conscience. And, oh, the wireless," he smacked himself on the forehead. "They've been listening to our messages, of course. They know everything. I need to get back to London and warn them that our wireless has been compromised."

"Take me with you," Mathilde begged.

"I'm not sure that's appropriate, though…" he fell silent for a moment. "What if…" At first his voice was tentative, but then it grew more confident. "What if we could infiltrate the Abwehr the way they've tried to do to us?"

"How?"

"Go back to Bleicher and tell him…" Again his mental wheels were spinning, "Tell him I've held a meeting with other heads of Resistance networks and now need to report back to London on our collaboration."

"Did such a meeting take place?"

"Yes," Lucas said, "though that's beside the point."

Mathilde couldn't help herself. "How come I wasn't invited?"

"What?" he looked taken aback. "You've just told me you've been working with Bleicher this whole time."

"But you had no reason to suspect me of that until the night they tried to arrest Brault."

The mark hit home and Lucas had the good sense to look sheepish. "Well, that's not strictly true. I'd had an inkling after you clearly forgot your husband's pseudonym. You said 'Bl—' before you caught yourself. Besides, most people don't continuously call their husbands by their first and last name."

The thought of Lucas distrusting her ruffled her feathers and she felt the need to prove how possessive Bleicher was of her. "Though he's not my husband, he will never give his permission for me to go to London. He hardly lets me out of his sight."

"Explain to him what a grand opportunity it would be to send his own mole to London. That I will introduce you to all the higher-ups in the SOE. Meanwhile you will tell Buckmaster everything you've learned about the inner-workings of the Abwehr."

She sat back, beginning to see that there was a light at the end of the tunnel. A way out of her collusion with Bleicher, and a way out of Paris at the same time, with Lucas by her side, no less. She would become the foremost expert on the German Secret Service, and every man in London would fall at her feet.

Both Kayser and Bleicher were sitting in the living room when Mathilde returned to the apartment. She repeated what Lucas had instructed her to say.

Though Bleicher found the idea ingenious, Kayser had reservations. "We will have to inform the Gestapo of this, and I don't think they'll like it. Their solution would be to just shoot Lucas and the whole lot." Kayser lifted his thumb and pointed his forefinger in Mathilde's direction as though he were cocking a gun. "Including her."

Although she was aware there was a fierce rivalry between the two branches of the German Secret Police, it didn't make sense that they couldn't work together on such a coup. "But I will be privy to your," she quickly corrected herself, "our enemy's top-secret information. Does it matter who gets the credit as long as you outsmart the British?"

Kayser considered her statement.

"I will pay the penalty if she dares betray us," Bleicher was clearly in favor of the plan and tried to drive his point home. "I know her better than anyone else and I can guarantee her intention is not to double-cross us."

"You mean triple-cross us," Kayser stated bitterly.

"She could have had me liquidated at Vaas, but she didn't."

Mathilde gave Bleicher a fake smile, inwardly regretting that she'd not taken the opportunity that night.

"I'll vouch for her," he declared. "And if she does do something, then you can blame me."

Mathilde couldn't help but kiss his forehead.

. . .

Later in bed, Bleicher told Mathilde that her trip to London would be her greatest triumph. "After the war is over, we'll get your story published in the most important Berlin newspapers. You'll be hailed as the number one heroine of the war. And," he rubbed his finger along the bridge of her nose, "we'll be able to pay you even more than before."

"Wonderful," Mathilde said before rolling over. She closed her eyes, dreaming of the day she'd finally be free from Bleicher's clutches.

CHAPTER 42

ODETTE

*A*s Odette herself had predicted, Francis Cammaerts, the man who arrived when Peter left, was not as strong of a leader. He'd brought a few new men into the circuit, including one called Bardet, whom Odette despised upon meeting. As she later confessed to Alec, "He has shifty eyes."

"Shall I drop him in the lake?" Alec asked.

"I don't suppose that would look good on our part. But mark my words, Alec, this man is no good."

Alec shrugged as he pretended to read a message. Odette took the bait. "What is it?" He was about to crumple it up before she snatched it from him. It read: *For Alec STOP Congratulations on your Captaincy STOP The SOE.*

She set it down. "Buckmaster promoted you."

"Thanks to our mutual friend, Peter, I'm sure."

She ran her fingers across the typewritten letters. "Peter has a way with people." She looked up. "But you deserve this, Alec. There is no better wireless operator than you."

He seemed uncomfortable with the praise. "And about this new man, Bardet."

Odette waved him off. "He's going to be running between here and the Occupied Zone. He's staying with somebody named Keiffer so we don't have to worry about him at present."

"Good." Alec took out a lighter and together they watched the paper informing him of his promotion go up in flames.

A few days later, Jean Cottet told Odette that Alec was waiting for her at the Limes. "He asked for you to come right away."

Odette frowned. The Limes was an abandoned villa that Peter had chosen to meet with his contacts since he'd decided it wouldn't be wise to have them come to the hotel.

The Limes was less than a quarter mile away and Odette got on a bicycle and pedaled as fast as she could.

"What is it, Alec?" she asked breathlessly as the door banged shut behind her. She saw with trepidation that he was not alone. The new man, Bardet, was with him and his eyes were as shifty as ever.

Alec was sitting at a battered kitchen table. Even though it was not quite eleven o'clock, he had a glass of whiskey in front of him. He looked at Bardet and nodded.

"Marsac's been arrested," Bardet stated.

"What?" Odette sat down across from Alec. "When?"

"Two nights ago—he wasn't in Paris for 24 hours before we learned he was in Fresnes Prison."

"Why did he go to Paris in the first place?"

Bardet began pacing up and down the room. "We heard they were beginning to crack down on agents in Paris—Marsac had ten contacts there, but most of them had been captured, so we planned on recruiting more. I left as soon as I found out about Marsac and came back here."

"Were you followed?" Alec took a gulp of his drink.

Bardet paused. "I don't think so." He met Odette's glare. "No, of course not."

"I take it he also had supplies and money on him. How much?" Odette demanded.

"Two million francs." Bardet reached up, his hand spanning a rafter. "And four crystals for transmitting. All gone." He lowered his arms and turned to the duo at the kitchen table. "We might be able to negotiate for his release."

"No," Odette replied firmly. "We're not going to do anything until we hear back from Peter." She touched Alec's hand. "Do you think you can send him a message right away?"

He glanced at his watch. "It's not my regular sked, but I might find someone at the SOE on the wireless."

"It's worth a try. And you," she pointed at Bardet. "Don't do anything rash."

"I won't," he promised. He widened his eyes as they once again met Odette's gaze and this time they didn't look shifty at all.

CHAPTER 43

MATHILDE

*M*athilde and Lucas's departure was scheduled for Friday, February 13th. Their eventual destination was the Moulin de la Rive, a spot on the Breton coast where they were to rendezvous with the British navy.

Bleicher wasn't accompanying them. He claimed he needed to go to the Alps for some reason.

He sat on the bed as Mathilde packed her suitcase. "You'll make sure to get a list of all the agents employed by the SOE."

"Of course." She folded her black silk pajamas and put them in her bag.

Bleicher fingered the hem of a flowered skirt. "It's good you are taking your best outfits. London needs to know that Paris hasn't changed: it's still the fashion capital of the world. But even so," he dug out his wallet and handed her some money. "Make sure to pick me up a pair of leather shoes from Oxford Street."

The bills were in British currency. She tucked them in her purse before asking, "Are there a lot of Abwehr men in London?"

Bleicher waved his hand. "Far fewer than we would like."

"Perhaps you should provide me with their contact information."

He stood up and placed his hands in his pockets. "Kayser and I discussed it, and we decided it was too much of a risk. MI6 might have men tailing you."

She studied his face, wondering if he suspected her plan to betray him, but, as always, the detective's face remained inscrutable. She turned to finish packing and he left the room, returning a moment later with her fur coat. "You'll need this. London is quite chilly." As she buttoned it up, he arranged the red beret over her black hair. "Perfect," he said before giving her a quick peck on her lips. "I'll greet you when you return, and we'll celebrate together."

"You'll be back in Paris by then?"

"Yes. My assignment in the Alps won't take too long."

"Okay." She gave him a wide smile, hoping to never have to lay eyes on him again. "Take care."

"And you." He gave her one final hug, wrapping his arms around the bulky fur.

On Thursday evening, the party boarded the Paris-Brest express. Mathilde and Lucas took one train compartment, Benny another, and their two Abwehr escorts occupied a third.

As soon as they were alone, Mathilde informed Lucas of Bleicher's plan for the Abwehr to arrest Benny the moment their boat was out of sight.

Lucas blew out his breath. "I should have expected as much." He rubbed his forehead. "Well, I guess that means Benny is going to have to come with us."

"Will there be room for a third?"

He shrugged. "Hopefully, seeing as London thinks they're just picking up me."

"What about me?"

Lucas stared out the window. "They don't know you're coming."

"What?" She grabbed his arm. "You didn't tell them?"

"I can't just tell Buckmaster I'm bringing along a known Nazi collaborator. I'd have to ask permission, and if he said no, that would put us both in a rather awkward position."

"Not Nazi, just German," Mathilde corrected. "And I would have added the word 'unwilling' in front 'collaborator.'" She moved her hand to grasp his. "Lucas, think of what we can do when we get to England. We could help the RAF blow up the Abwehr's headquarters at Maisons Laffitte, or get them to raid Fresnes and free all of the Gestapo's prisoners. We could even have them poison Bleicher."

He chuckled. "I don't know if I'd go that far, but yes, the information we provide to the SOE can help turn the tide of this war." He leaned back in his seat and closed his eyes. "It's going to be a long next couple of days. I'm going to snatch whatever rest I can, and I suggest you do the same."

But Mathilde couldn't sleep and her mind whirred, imagining Armand's expression when the RAF told him he was free because of The Cat. *Yes*, she decided. *The Fresnes coup would be priority one.* After that would be the demise of Bleicher.

Benny met them on the station platform. Mathilde knew the Abwehr men had gotten off earlier and were going to finish the journey by car while the three spies set off to Moulin de la Rive on foot. The three of them trekking with so many bags would have normally attracted attention, but clearly the German patrolmen had been tipped off, for they weren't stopped at any time during their 10-kilometer hike.

Despite Mathilde's heavy bag weighing down her shoulder, the walk was not altogether unpleasant. It was a lovely, sunny day and she spotted quite a few crocuses popping up alongside the road.

Benny didn't hesitate to find the humor in the scenario. "It's like the beginning of a bad joke: a British spy, a French spy, and a German spy are walking through the countryside…"

Mathilde shot him a conniving look. "Lucas is clearly the British spy, so who is the German one?"

"I meant, that is, the Germans think you are on their side. Not that I suspect you aren't on ours," Benny finished quickly.

"I was also joking," she told him. "I know both of you have faith in me. At least now," she added, remembering how Lucas had confessed his previous doubts in his apartment.

They stopped at a charming bistro on the way and had onion soup, washed down by a house red wine that Mathilde deemed very tasty. Though it wasn't quite as merry as the first time they'd lunched together, it was amiable enough. Lucas hadn't had the chance to tell Benny he was a marked man and would not be returning to Paris anytime soon.

When they emerged from the bistro, they found to their dismay that the sky had turned dark with gathering storm clouds and a penetrating wind had picked up. A few minutes later, it was raining, the kind of rain that stung like little pinpricks. By the time they'd reached the coast, the sea was rough with waves.

A German patrol was marching along the beach, but they paid no attention to the rain-soaked trio. Lucas located a small cave to use for shelter. A freezing Mathilde set her gaze to where the coastline should have been, but at this point she could see nothing but a gray curtain of rain. Even so, Lucas and Benny flashed their previously-agreed-upon signals every ten minutes.

She was just about to declare their departure hopeless when Lucas shouted, "Look over there!" Indeed, two vague forms were approaching.

Mathilde followed the other men as they ran out to meet them. The rain had let up somewhat, and they were able to hear one of the figures say the password: *Le temps d'aller.* Time to go.

"I'm Lieutenant Abbott," the shorter of the two men declared. "Buckmaster's sent me to be the wireless operator for your circuit." He nodded toward the man next to him. "This is Lieutenant Redding, also SOE."

Redding held up his briefcase. "I've brought a new transmitter."

"No, no." Lucas pointed down the beach where the men had come from. Mathilde could just make out two dinghies drifting in the waves. "You're coming with us," Lucas told the new men.

Abbott scratched his head. "This is going against Buckmaster's orders."

Lucas led them to where the dinghies had docked and found the ranking officer. "We're all going back."

"What's this now?" the officer asked.

"I don't have time to tell you the details," Lucas replied. "Let's just say our circuit's been compromised and the Germans know everything. We're all in imminent danger, including these new men," Lucas indicated Redding and Abbott. "There are Abwehr detectives crawling all over these rocks, ready to pounce as soon as you leave."

"Very well then," the naval officer sighed before nodding at the SOE men. "We'll take them back to our freighter waiting just off-shore."

"My companions are also coming with us," Lucas commanded, gesturing to Mathilde and Benny.

Benny opened his mouth as if to protest, but thought better of it. He picked up Mathilde's bag. "Let's get you aboard."

. . .

Mathilde clutched the sides of the dinghy as it started heading for the awaiting ship. The seasoned naval officer proved to be no match for the powerful current: both dinghies were only a few yards from shore when a giant wave washed over, flinging everyone on board into the freezing sea.

Mathilde felt herself going under, weighed down by her fur coat, which now felt three times as heavy. Her mouth and nose filled with water, burning her nostrils. She glanced up to see the moon's reflection in the water growing fainter as she was dragged further under.

She felt pressure on her chest and thought it was the water entering her lungs, but then she was yanked back to the surface. She gasped for air, barely hearing Lucas screaming at her. He wrapped his arms around her and he pulled her to shore.

Finally she felt the wonderful sensation of sand under her toes. She tried to stand up, but the cumbersome fur was like a vengeful animal.

Lucas hauled himself up onto the beach beside her. "I think it's time you lose your fur to the sea gods," he panted.

"No. I love my fur."

He got to his feet unsteadily. "It did almost kill you. And we've got a long walk back to the village."

She hugged herself in it one last time, but it felt, and smelled, like a wet dog. Reluctantly she took it off and laid it across the water as if it were a funeral pyre. It began to sink almost immediately. She shivered as she turned to Lucas. "What now?"

The soaking-wet naval officer approached them. "I've signaled our ship to go back. Even if they did manage to send us new dinghies, there's no way we can reach it with these swells."

They met up with Benny, Redding, and Abbott, who had landed further down the beach. After some discussion, it was agreed that they were much too big a party to go unnoticed. Lucas decided that he, Mathilde, and Benny would go back the way they came, as he remembered seeing an inn along the way.

"And we'll find shelter and hide out till morning," Redding stated. "We've got papers and some cash, so we should be alright until we can make our way to Paris."

With that statement, Mathilde realized the bag containing most of her favorite possessions had been washed out to sea.

"You ought to throw your guns into the ocean," Lucas replied. "Anyone found with a weapon in Occupied France will be shot on sight."

Redding and Abbott immediately did as Lucas suggested, but the naval officer was more hesitant. After he finally chucked his pistol into the waves, he pulled at his soggy collar. "There's not much I can do to hide, being in uniform. I'm just going to have to give myself in."

"Good luck to you, and thank you for your service." Lucas held out his hand.

The officer shook it. "At least I'll be taken with all the privileges of a prisoner of war. If any of you are captured in civilian clothes, you'll be hanged as spies."

Lucas nodded.

"Presumably those Germans you said were patrolling the beach watched everything. So let's see, eh?" The officer held up both his hands in surrender and walked toward the dunes circling the edge of the beach. Nothing happened.

"Right then," Lucas said to Benny and Mathilde. "Let's go."

CHAPTER 44

DIDI

*L*eo Marks called Didi into his office one afternoon in early February. "I'm sorry to say I have to let you go," he said before Didi had even sat down.

"What? Why?"

"Buckmaster wants you to report to him right away—he's at 6 Orchard Court. Looks as if you're going to be recruited for spy work after all."

"Yes, sir." She reached out to shake Marks' hand. "Thank you, sir."

He shuffled a pile of messages on his desk. "I'll be sorry to lose you, but at least the SOE finally got their heads out of their arses and promoted someone worthy."

"Yes, sir. Thanks again," Didi called as she left his office and walked outside.

It was less than half a kilometer to the address Marks had given her. A sign outside read, "Inter-Services Research Building." In contrast to the bustling Baker Street office, the lobby seemed eerily quiet.

"You must be Eileen Nearne." A lanky man stepped out from behind a large ficus tree. "Major Buckmaster has been expecting you." He led her through a maze of rooms until they finally stopped in an office where the well-groomed Buckmaster waited.

"Didi, it's good to see you again." Without waiting for a reply, he removed a pile of papers from an upholstered armchair. "Sit."

"Mr. Marks said you wanted to see me."

"Yes." He sat behind the desk. "We are expecting the arrival of a woman from the depths of Occupied France. I believe you know her."

"Is it Jackie?"

"No," he waved his hand distractedly. "Jacqueline's doing fine work out there. It's The Cat."

Didi couldn't keep her mouth from dropping open. "She's coming to London?"

He appeared disconcerted as he fiddled with a pen. "Yes, and her SOE companions suspect she might be acting for the benefit of Germany."

Didi sat back. "I can't believe it, not after everything Interallié accomplished."

Buckmaster held up his hand. "I completely agree, but we can't be too careful. We're going to need someone to accompany her at all times. Considering your history as their wireless contact, I thought you might be in the best position to help us decide whether or not she can be trusted."

She wasn't being sent to France, but this newest mission was the closest Didi had come to being an agent. "Yes, sir."

CHAPTER 45

MATHILDE

*I*t took another two weeks and two more failed, though not as eventful, beach pick-ups before Mathilde finally found herself on a seaworthy dinghy headed for a Royal Navy ship waiting offshore.

A tall man in a white overcoat stood at the bow of the ship. "What is this?" His grip tightened on the revolver he was holding as he watched a sailor help them aboard. "Oh Christ," he said upon making eye contact with Mathilde. "A bloody woman."

"Sorry, sir," Lucas replied, straightening. "But she'll be of good use to us."

The man introduced himself as Major Boddington as the ship got underway. "Don't like the look of that light," he said, pointing toward a faint glow coming from the beach dunes.

You'd like it even less if you knew the Germans were witnessing your Navy's exact procedures for smuggling Allied agents out of France. Mathilde glanced with disdain at his conspicuous white jacket, deciding that Major Boddington was a first-class blockhead.

Lucas stood next to Mathilde as the ship's motor started. Together they watched the white-capped waves hit the boat with great force. Her stomach began to churn in unison with the choppy sea below. "I think I might need to lie down," she said.

Lucas put his hand on her arm. "But you'll miss the first view of Blighty."

His touch warmed her in a way her lost fur never could. As much as she wanted to stay, her nausea needed to be quelled. "Wake me when we get there."

But Lucas wasn't on deck when she returned. As she stared out at the cliffs of Dover, which formed a jagged, purple border between the gray sea and the pinkening sky, Mathilde's thoughts turned unexpectedly to Armand. She recalled how he used to play with her hair and tell her that she could accomplish anything to which she aspired. She tightened her grip on the hand railing, picturing the people of London standing on the street, heralding her as she made her entrance. *If only Armand could see me now.*

Upon arrival in England, Mathilde, Lucas, and Boddington were escorted to a car. The sun faded into the legendary fog while they approached London and Mathilde—still exhausted from her long journey—fell in and out of sleep.

The traffic in the city seemed endless, especially compared to Paris, where the only people who could afford cars, or their gas, were the Germans. As they pulled up to yet another stoplight, Boddington informed them they'd be staying in his flat that night, and would be shown their private accommodations the next morning. "Madame Carré, we've arranged for one of our secretaries to be your companion, since you don't speak the language that well."

She narrowed her still sleepy eyes. "You mean to guard me?"

"No." He shot an embarrassed smile at Lucas before he asked, "Do you wish to go to dinner? Major Buckmaster is anxious to meet the woman he knows as The Cat."

For some reason that statement enraged Mathilde. "No. Please have dinner delivered. I am far too tired to go out."

"Whatever you prefer," Boddington replied.

Major Buckmaster was a skinny man and Mathilde immediately decided that both his wide-set eyes and his elephant-sized ears were too big for his face.

"You must be The Cat," he exclaimed as soon as he entered Boddington's apartment.

She slipped her hand from his enthusiastic shake. "Madame Carré."

He looked a bit put out. "You'll have to excuse me. After all the times I've read your report, I feel as though I know you personally."

Boddington gestured for the major to sit down. "Madame Carré has expressed that she is quite tired, so I promise to keep this short." He turned to her. "Lucas has already told us that you have been in contact with the Abwehr."

Mathilde shot a curious glance at Lucas, who raised his eyebrows and nodded at her. She sighed before stating, "It was not by any choice of mine, of course, only to preserve what few agents remained in Interallié."

"And what agents were those?" Boddington raised his underdeveloped chin. "From what we've gathered, almost all of them have been sent to internment camps."

"That's not true," she insisted. She thought hard. "There's Maître Brault, Claude, Kiki."

"Kiki?" Boddington demanded.

Lucas cleared his throat. "His real name is Jean Keiffer, and it appears he is willingly supplying the Abwehr with information on members of the Resistance."

"Let me get this straight," Boddington leaned forward. "Of the three men you just named, one only narrowly escaped capture, one was never an agent of Interallié, and one is a straight-up traitor."

Buckmaster raised his hand to halt Boddington's tirade. "As you yourself have said, Madame Carré is clearly worn out and frazzled— now is not the time to interrogate her."

But I'm sure it will come later. Mathilde, who hours ago had felt so free, was now beginning to feel like a bird in the gilded cage of England. "What do you want of me?"

Buckmaster crossed one leg over the other. "Lucas also told us your transmissions have been compromised."

She nodded. "Bleicher called it 'the Radio Game.'"

Buckmaster's already wide eyes expanded even more. "Yet the Krauts still believe you are working for them."

Once again she nodded.

"So we'll play our own version of Bleicher's game and feed him false messages."

Mathilde held a hand to her forehead. "Just so you are aware, Bleicher is an incredibly intelligent man. Your ruse won't work for long."

"No doubt not," Buckmaster quickly agreed. "But maybe long enough for us to change the course of the war."

Mathilde glared at Lucas, wondering why he was suddenly so quiet.

"We want to go back to France as soon as possible," Lucas stated. He rose and stood next to Mathilde. "I will escort her to bed and we can talk more of our plans when I return."

"Goodnight, Madame Carré," Boddington and Buckmaster dutifully responded.

"Goodnight, gentlemen," she told them before Lucas showed her to the guest bedroom.

CHAPTER 46

ODETTE

*E*ver since Peter left for England, Odette hadn't been sleeping well. Though he had insisted on staying on the sofa next to the bed when he was there, she desperately missed his snoring.

One morning she woke up at dawn and laid in bed until the sunlight streamed through the windows of the hotel.

It turned out to be a beautiful day, and she decided to run errands. She went into Annecy to meet with Tom Morel, a member of the Vichy police, who supplied her with blank identity cards and a warning. "I need to tell you, Madame Chauvet, that last night I was told by a coworker that the comings-and-goings of the people in Saint-Jorioz are beginning to become of interest to the police."

"Is that so?" Odette asked, feeling goosebumps form on her arms. She made a mental note to warn Peter as soon as he returned.

After that she went to the hairdresser. Before boarding the bus back to Saint Jorioz, she stopped to pick a posy of forget-me-nots and stuck it in the lapel of her coat.

The bus was nearly empty and she located a seat right away. As she sat down, she glanced back and caught the eye of the only other passenger, a stocky man in a dark gray suit. He looked to be in his early forties, with an oval face beneath dark-framed glasses. He sensed her staring and met her eyes for a few seconds before moving his gaze back to the window.

For no reason at all, Odette felt a sudden twinge of fear, as though she were an animal being stalked by a poacher. Like her, the man disembarked at Saint-Jorioz, tipping his hat as he got off the bus. He walked off in the opposite direction, whistling to himself.

Odette met Jean Cottet's wife for lunch. She would have preferred to dine alone, but didn't want to cancel her appointment. As she sat down, one of Spindle's couriers stepped into the café. "Lise, there is a man in town who has been asking about you."

She put her menu down and looked at him coolly. "You know Peter has said that you should never come to the hotel."

"I know, but this is an extremely urgent matter."

She nodded at Madame Cottet, who was pretending not to hear their conversation. "You see that I have a guest."

The courier glanced back and forth between the two women before shrugging helplessly.

Somehow Odette managed to keep up the guise of civility through lunch. She didn't even startle when the gray-suited man entered the café and approached their table. "Madame Chauvet?"

Odette nodded.

"May I have a word?" He glanced at Madame Cottet, who finished her tea. "I was just leaving," she stated before casting Odette a worried glance.

Odette gave her a casual wave and Madame Cottet, with one last look, left.

"Would you mind if I joined you for coffee?" the man asked.

"You will forgive me, monsieur. I do not know your name."

He sat down. "I am Hugo Bleicher, an officer in the German Army."

Odette kept her expression neutral, though her heart was hammering away. "I'm not sure why an officer in the German Army would want to join me."

"I have a letter for you from Monsieur Marsac, courtesy of Fresnes Prison."

"Please sit down."

He got comfortable in the chair before pulling out an engraved cigarette case. He offered Odette one and she took it, wanting something to calm her shaking hands.

He lit hers before his own. He took a brief puff before stating, "I came from Annecy on the bus this morning."

"Did you?" she feigned disinterest, knowing he had noticed her. "As a matter of fact, so did I."

Bleicher must have sensed they'd arrived at a stalemate and reached into his coat pocket. "Here is the letter."

Odette scanned it. Marsac stated that he'd been arrested, but had not been ill-treated, though he was hungry. He also mentioned that Sergeant Bleicher had requested to discuss a matter with Madame Lise personally. Marsac ended by stating he believed Bleicher to be trustworthy.

Bleicher took another puff of his cigarette. "I would like to inform you of the circumstances of Monsieur Marsac's arrest."

She folded the note and put it into her purse. "Yes?"

"I have already told you I am an officer with the Germany Army, but in fact I am a member of the military Abwehr, a counter-espionage department, whose allegiance is to the General Staff. We are not directly associated with the Nazi Party. I myself arrested Monsieur Marsac in order to keep him from the Gestapo."

She tried to search his eyes to see if he were telling the truth, but they were hidden by a glare of sunlight on his spectacles.

"We of the Abwehr love our country and believe we can save it from the destruction that will be brought on by Adolf Hitler's relentless despotism."

Odette ashed her cigarette to hide her surprise. She was under the impression that all Germans worshipped their so-proclaimed Führer with unrelenting dedication. "Nothing can save Germany from destruction."

"There you are wrong. If Germany is destroyed, so is the rest of Europe. But with Hitler out of the way, Germany could settle in peace. You, madame, can serve as the medium for people who believe as I do. You, and of course, the SOE."

She stabbed out her cigarette. "I am not sure what you are asking me to do, monsieur."

He leaned forward, breathing out smoke, before he said in a lowered voice, "I want you to provide me a transmitting set and the code to get in touch with the British War Office."

She gave him a blank look while her mind raced. She was in over her head and desperately wished Peter were here to tell her what to say.

"I cannot give you what you ask for, monsieur. I don't have a transmitting set, and without it, a code would be useless."

He flicked ash off his still smoldering cigarette. "But you have ways of communicating with London."

She scrutinized his face, but the glare remained on his glasses. "I do," she finally admitted. "But I am not willing to pass on your message unless you clarify your intentions."

He laughed. "You, a British agent, are seeking to impose conditions on me, a German officer with the power to arrest you?"

Odette's pulse quickened at the word 'arrest,' but she wouldn't show this officer how much he intimidated her. "May I speak freely?"

"Of course."

"Monsieur Bleicher, you will forgive me if I say that your occupation does not recommend you to me."

"But Monsieur Marsac has recommended me."

"I do not know if he was forced to write that letter under duress. In light of his message, I'd like more information. Will you allow me to dispatch one of our contacts to accompany you in speaking to Marsac and then report back to me?"

Bleicher hesitated briefly before agreeing.

"I'd also like to send a parcel of food to Monsieur Marsac," Odette continued.

"I will consent to that as well." He lowered his head, finally making eye contact. "You wouldn't run away in the meantime, would you Madame Chauvet?"

"I would never deliver a man into your hands and then run away. I assure you I will stay here in Saint-Jorioz until he returns with his report."

"I believe you." He took a sip of his coffee. "Are you sure you are wholly French?"

"Of course. Why do you ask?"

He gave a hesitant smile. "I might have sensed a bit of German blood in you."

"Not a drop." She stood. "If you will be here at five this evening, I will return with my man and the food parcel. I know your country has no respect for hostages, but I assure you this man will not be worthy of being arrested in light of the importance of your proposal." She crossed her fingers by her side as she repeated her grandmère's favorite expression. "One does not catch flies with vinegar, Monsieur Bleicher. This could be a gesture of your good will."

He lit another cigarette. "I don't suppose I could induce you to come to Paris with me yourself, could I? They are giving a performance of Mozart's 'Magic Flute' next week."

"No, monsieur." She coughed delicately. "My health is quite fragile and I must remain at five hundred meters above sea-level. Doctor's orders," she added.

"I understand." He put out his cigarette before reaching for his hat. "I will see you this evening," he stated before walking out of the café.

Odette wrote a brief report and then mounted her bicycle to deliver it to Alec and fill him in on all that had just transpired.

"If I'd have known you spent the afternoon in the clutches of the Abwehr, I'd have shot the bastard," Alec declared.

"It's always the fifth of November with you, Alec," she said with a laugh. "But," she lowered her voice, "do you remember that English officer, Roger, who arrived on the same Lysander that Peter left on?"

Alec nodded.

"I think we need to send him away. Things are getting too heated around here for someone new. And maybe you too." She glanced around at all of the radio equipment. "How soon could you be packed up?"

"In a moment. But you would be a bloody fool if you think I'd leave without you. Or Peter," he finished with a growl.

"Still… you should think about packing your essentials. Something tells me that zero hour is near."

"Peter should be back next week. Let's not make any hasty decisions without consulting him first."

She nodded, knowing Alec was right. Not to mention she would never willingly leave Peter unless she was absolutely forced to. "Let's send a message to our mutual friend, care of the SOE."

Odette had no other man to send to Paris besides Bardet. He returned in a few days' time to report that Marsac was well enough and thanked her for the food.

"And Bleicher?" Odette inquired.

Bardet lit a cigarette. "I believe him to be entirely trustworthy."

The same cannot be said of you, Odette decided, narrowing her eyes. Those were the exact same words Marsac had written, as if Bleicher was telling them what to say. "Oh?"

"Yes. Monsieur Bleicher has requested that you arrange for a bomber pick-up for you, him, and Marsac, whom he has graciously volunteered to get out of prison. You can introduce Monsieur Bleicher to Major Buckmaster, and together they can come to terms and bring peace to Europe."

"Don't you think that sounds a little far-fetched?" she demanded.

Bardet waved his hand. "Of course, we would need to dispose of Hitler, but these things can be arranged."

Now Odette was more certain than ever that Bardet was going to betray her and the rest of the network. "You've done well. Tell Monsieur Bleicher I will do my best to arrange a pick-up. The next full moon will be in the middle of April. I will let you know the location I've arranged at a later date."

He nodded. His voice was bursting with exaggerated nonchalance as he asked, "What news of Peter? Do you know when he plans on returning?"

"No," she stated firmly and then, in a bold-faced lie, told him that he would be the first to know if she heard anything.

As soon as Bardet took his leave, Odette once again rode out to see Alec. Though she informed him of Bleicher's latest scheme, she decided not to include the part about Bardet's certain betrayal, knowing that Alec would jump at the chance to pull the trigger of his .38 Colt.

CHAPTER 47

DIDI

*W*ith her shrewd green eyes and pinched nose, The Cat definitely earned her nickname. Though she wasn't exactly pretty, Didi could see why so many men had become enamored of her—she had an indescribable magnetism, what her fellow Frenchmen might call a certain *"je ne sais quoi."* That is, before they learned how badly she had betrayed their country.

The Cat was installed in a Porchester Terrace flat overlooking Hyde Park. Unbeknownst to Mathilde (though Didi, of course, was well aware), the apartment was filled with microphones.

Mathilde laid claim to the large master bedroom and Didi took the smaller, "maid's room."

Didi's instructions were to accompany her quarry all over London. Mathilde insisted on wearing her red beret everywhere they went. Didi couldn't understand why, but she couldn't shake the suspicion that it was because The Cat was intending to meet with someone and the beret was their signal.

Soon after she arrived, Mathilde demanded that Didi escort her to Selfridges to buy what she termed "essentials": a nightdress, under-wear, a pair of black silk pajamas, perfume, and a box of face powder. When it came time to pay, Mathilde stepped back, insisting it was the SOE's job to compensate her since she had lost most of her things when their boat capsized. Didi had indeed been given an "allowance" from Buckmaster, but the Selfridge total pretty much wiped that out.

As they left the store, Mathilde pulled out a black velvet choker with a bright red flower on it and put it around her neck. "Here," she said, pulling something out of her bag. "I bought one for you, too." She looked expectantly at Didi, who held the hideous necklace between two fingers.

"Thank you," Didi replied, putting it into her purse. "I'm not sure it quite goes with this outfit, though."

A few days later, they were invited to an SOE-hosted cocktail party at Claridge's. Mathilde insisted on doing Didi's make-up for her in the main bathroom. Despite rarely using much face paint, Didi consented, figuring it would be a good opportunity to pry further into her companion's story.

Didi was used to translating Morse messages and codes, but the real-life Cat was like an indecipherable that gave off visual cues to her true meaning. Her nervous habits, such as endlessly tucking her hair behind her ear, or refusing to meet her interrogator's eyes, led Didi to believe she was more responsible than she was prepared to admit for the eradication of the Interallié network. Still, Didi's objective was to get Mathilde to confess as much as possible in range of the microphones hidden all over the apartment. She could only hope that the SOE had thought to put at least one in the master bath.

"I was always loyal to the Resistance you see," Mathilde said as she began tackling Didi's eyebrows with a pair of tweezers. "Everything that happened was a curse of fate. That and, of course," she plucked a particularly stubborn hair, "coercion by the Abwehr."

"Who are the Abwehr?" Didi asked, trying not to wince from the pain. "Are they in line with Hitler?"

"No," Mathilde replied vehemently. She tossed the tweezers onto the counter. "The Abwehr are not Nazis. Far from it—Bleicher abhorred them, and he especially objected to the Gestapo's methods of torturing their captives."

"I met Armand once," Didi stated casually.

"Oh?" Mathilde did not attempt to hide the surprise in her voice. She uncapped a bright red lipstick. "Then you must have seen how reckless he was."

Didi pursed her lips as much as in thought as to help Mathilde apply the lipstick. "I wouldn't say that… he was more what you might call, passionate." She immediately regretted her words. "What I meant was, he was exuberant, yet dedicated to his cause."

Mathilde took a step back and set her strange gaze on Didi. "He had many lovers, Viola Borni the least of them. And he told them everything. He was completely indiscreet." She snapped the cap back on the lipstick. "Had not Kiki's forsaken lover, Madame Boufet, given Bleicher everything, Armand's carelessness would have eventually ruined us all, somehow."

And what part would you have had in that? Didi noted that Mathilde was doing everything to deny her own role in Interallié's undoing. "Where is the widow Borni now?"

The mention of Viola felt like waving a red handkerchief at the already enraged bull that was Mathilde. "It doesn't matter where she is. It was all her fault, you know."

"The downfall of Interallié?"

"Yes." Mathilde pulled a face puff out of a tin of powder and blew on it. "She gave Bleicher the code so he could read Armand's messages." She lightly dusted Didi's face with the puff. "Armand should have been more cautious, but without the cipher, they could never have interpreted them."

Didi shook her head. Of course they would have worked out the code, eventually.

"There," Mathilde said, plopping the puff back into the tin. "What do you think?"

Didi peered into the mirror. Her face looked as if she'd seen a ghost, and the lipstick was way too red. "It's perfect."

"And now for your outfit. What do you plan on wearing?"

Didi shrugged. "I'm not sure—I don't really own a ball gown."

"It's lucky I bought two." Mathilde led the way to her room and took a black silk dress out of the closet. She handed it to Didi. "It might be a tad long, so you'll have to wear heels."

Didi accepted it, a bit reluctantly, though she noticed the high collar meant she wouldn't be forced to don her new choker. "What about you?"

"I suppose this is my only option." She tossed a spaghetti-strapped, blue beaded dress onto the bed.

"Good choice," Didi replied, for lack of anything better to say.

. . .

Upon entering the elaborately decorated lobby of Claridge's, Didi was immensely grateful to Mathilde. Had it not been for her outfit, and of course, her make-up job, Didi would have felt even more out of place. Though it was probably designed to hug every curve of a more endowed woman, the dress hung loosely on Didi's thin frame, something she wasn't altogether disappointed by.

Her heels sounded like thunder on the black-and-white marbled floor as Mathilde led the way to the ballroom, which was done up in art-deco elegance, including gold-gilded mirrors, crystal chandeliers, and silver columns lining the walls. Didi couldn't imagine what the party, and its attendees would have looked like without war-time rationing—with it, they still looked like they stepped from the pages of Vogue.

Major Buckmaster, wearing a tailored tuxedo, approached them. "Ah, if it isn't The Cat, and her escort, Didi Nearne."

Mathilde accepted the proffered flute of champagne. "It's not that I don't adore Didi, I do, of course. But..." she stuck her red lips out into a pout. "Why do I need an escort at all?"

"Oh, it's just policy," Buckmaster replied. He pointed to another tuxedo-clad man across the room. "You can ask my boss, Lord Selbourne, about it."

"Lord?" Mathilde eyes widened. "You'll have to introduce me to him."

"All in due time. First I'd like you both to meet Miss Atkins."

A tall woman wearing a gown with an even higher collar than Didi's approached.

"You must be The Cat," Miss Atkins said, holding out a slim hand. "I've heard so much about you." After they shook hands, Miss Atkins set her dark eyes on Didi. "And you too, of course. Your sister Jackie has become quite the asset to the SOE."

Didi swiped a glass of champagne from a passing waiter. "Well, we Nearne girls have a special talent in that way." No matter how well Didi was doing, it always seemed that Jackie soared higher. Here she was, finally meeting the mysterious Miss Atkins, and the acclaimed woman could only sing her sister's praises.

"Tell me, Madame Carré," Miss Atkins took Mathilde's arm. "What are the latest fashions in Paris? And how is the rationing?

Forgive me if I pick your brain over all things Parisian." She led her away.

Buckmaster cleared his throat. "How are things going? Have you managed to get anything good from our little Cat thus far?"

Didi shrugged. "She seems to want to blame the demise of Inter-allié on Viola Borni, but I don't fully believe her."

"You shouldn't," Buck agreed. "Some of the agents that were arrested were unfamiliar to Viola—and likewise, some of the ones Viola knew of but Mathilde didn't—managed to escape. If that's not evidence of The Cat's guilt, I'm not sure what is."

Didi took a hesitant sip of her drink. "Viola was only a coder, and coders are not privy to anything besides what they are working with," she said knowingly. "Mathilde was Armand's deputy—and knew the inner workings of the network."

"Yes, and that's why you need to keep a most careful watch on her... Hallo, what's this?"

Didi turned to see The Cat engaged in conversation with the head of the SOE, a balding, short man, his height further diminished by his stooped frame. "Does he know who she is?"

"Well," Buckmaster finished the rest of his champagne. "I should think so. He's read all the same reports I have."

Didi noted that the couple was standing quite close to a table of appetizers. "I'm feeling a bit hungry all of a sudden."

Buckmaster nodded his approval and she took that as a cue to creep toward them.

"I promise you, I will see to it that you have every luxury afforded to you." Lord Selbourne's voice was predictably posh.

"And you will tell Churchill everything I've done for the Resistance?" Mathilde asked.

"Of course I will. Heroines like you deserve to have their praises sung. But in the meantime, I'd love to take you to dinner."

Didi sucked in her upper lip as she watched Lord Selbourne seemingly lose himself in Mathilde's green-eyed gaze. *Even if she wasn't pretty,* Didi thought as she returned to Buckmaster, *somehow The Cat could entrance members of the Resistance and the Gestapo, sorry, the Abwehr alike.* She also realized she might have had a tad too much champagne.

"It's not good," she told Buckmaster.

He glared over in their direction. "What I hear you saying is that my boss is about to make a fool of himself with one of the most dangerous double-agents of the war—one who could betray all of the SOE to the Germans."

"Maybe he's playing up to her to get more information."

Buckmaster shook his head. "Unfortunately, Selbourne isn't that clever."

Didi recalled all the frustrations Leo Marks had unloaded on her regarding the security checks and poem codes. "How unfortunate."

"I'm afraid that sometimes in England, it's who you know, not *what* you know, that leads to positions of power."

Well, that should bode well for me now that I know both you and Miss Atkins. "What should we do about The Cat?"

"Convince her it'd be foolish to pursue Selbourne—not the least because he's a married man. Something tells me that once The Cat gets her claws into a man, she doesn't take kindly to his rejection. I think she's the type to enact the worst kind of vengeance."

"Like with Armand. He hurt her, so she took down his entire network."

"Exactly."

Buckmaster pointed at Didi. "Is that lipstick on your teeth?"

Her face heating up, Didi resorted to a line she'd heard Jackie use a thousand times. "If you'll excuse me, I have to go and powder my nose."

CHAPTER 48

ODETTE

*L*ondon's orders were exactly what Odette had expected: she should have no more contact with Bleicher. She could almost imagine Buckmaster's clipped voice dictating the message, which read:

Bleicher highly dangerous STOP You are to hide across the lake and cut contacts with all save Alec STOP Fix dropping ground for Peter who will land anywhere soonest.

She looked up at Alec after she'd read that last part. "If Bleicher's back in town, he will be on the alert for Peter's return."

"I know of a spot high in the mountains overlooking the lake. It's a hell of a place to drop, but there's enough flat ground for an experienced parachutist like Peter. And we can light a fire so it can't be seen from Annecy."

Odette consented—what other choice did she have? Alec sent off the instructions for Peter to jump by the next full moon.

Bardet was waiting in the lobby when she returned to the hotel. He asked her if she had news of the bomber pick-up for Bleicher.

She lied smoothly "I'm still trying to arrange it for April 18th."

"Do you have any news of Peter?"

She shook her head. "I doubt he'll be back at all."

"Oh." Bardet put on a look of concern. "Lise, do you remember that British officer, what was his name? Roger?"

"Yes? What about him?"

"He's no longer staying at the Hotel de la Plage. It's as if he suddenly vanished."

"He didn't vanish," Odette replied patiently. "I sent him away."

"Where to?"

She waved her hand as if the matter was of no importance. "To stay with some friends of mine. Why the sudden interest?"

He turned up his shoulders, also playing that it was no big deal. "I only wondered, that's all."

"I assure you, he's quite safe."

Odette studied his face as he frowned, probably upset that he couldn't report back to Bleicher on the whereabouts of Roger. But she no longer hated Bardet: she only felt pity and contempt for him. They were all trying to navigate through a world turned upside down, and some people, like Bardet, were content to take the easy way out. "Goodbye, Monsieur Bardet."

"Bye, Madame Lise."

The day of Peter's arrival was extremely hectic. Odette spent the morning in Annecy, warning her contacts to either lie low or get out of town. The BBC message wouldn't air until 7:30 that evening, and then she and Alec would only have a few hours to get to the top of the mountain to act as Peter's welcoming party.

She tried to take an afternoon nap, but found herself too anxious to sleep. She wasn't sure if Peter should be literally jumping into this mess with Bleicher, but at the same time, she had missed him terribly and looked forward to his return.

Alec arrived after dinner with a satisfying announcement: he had managed to secure a motor car that would save them some time and effort in their travels that evening.

At the appointed time, Odette, Alec, and Jean Cottet gathered around the radio. It seemed to Odette that the announcer was particularly slow in getting to the *messages personnels*, but at last he stated in a pithy voice: *Le scarabée d'or fait sa toilette printemps.* The golden scarab is washing in the spring. Peter was on his way.

Alec and Odette left immediately. The old car traveled slowly as Alec turned off the main road and started up the mountain. But the motor couldn't handle the steep incline and it quit before they got more than a quarter up.

Alec got out and gave the useless old thing a hard kick, swearing up a storm, as Odette emptied it of their flashlights and other supplies.

The mountain path was covered with snow and ice and Odette stumbled several times as she tried climbing over the freezing rocks with her hands full. She could occasionally hear Alec's burly body lumbering behind her, cursing loudly at her to slow up, but she had only one thought in her mind: to make it in time to greet Peter.

At last she made it to the plateau Alec had described. The wind had abated and the bright moon had risen. Alec came up beside her, breathing heavily. "Suppose he doesn't come tonight." His words came out in heavy puffs of air. "That whole climb will have been for nothing."

"He'll be here," Odette replied confidently.

Alec lit a pile of dead branches, which quickly started ablaze, the flames reaching high into the night air.

In a few minutes, the roar of a Halifax bomber interrupted the otherwise still night. The Halifax flew over the lake and then passed over their heads. Odette searched the sky desperately for the white balloon of Peter's parachute, but the brightness of the snow reflecting off the moon partially blinded her. The Halifax had disappeared. *What if it had decided not to drop its passenger?*

She squinted, trying not to panic, when she heard a faraway voice singing the Marseillaise. She laughed wildly as Peter finally came into view. In a moment he had landed and was in her arms.

On the way back down the mountain, taking a much more leisurely pace this time, Alec and Odette filled Peter in on everything that had happened in his absence.

"We only have until the 18th until Bleicher gets suspicious," Odette told him. "That's when I told Bardet I was arranging his flight to England."

"We should clear out tomorrow," Peter stated dryly. He squeezed her hand. "You should have left sooner, Lise."

She squeezed back, wishing she could say how glad she was to have him back. "There was just too much to do. We've been quite busy since you went away. I couldn't just leave everything in chaos."

"You should have still gone. You're an obstinate woman, Lise," he said, not without affection.

"I can arrange a boat to take us across the lake at first light tomorrow," Alec said.

"Good. It'll be good-bye to Saint-Jorioz at the crack of dawn," Peter commanded.

When they got back to their room, Peter grabbed some pillows and blankets from the closet to make his usual nest on the couch. "You must be exhausted from your trek up and down the mountain."

"I am," Odette agreed, settling onto one side of the bed. She patted the other. "But not too tired for you to tell me about your travels. How are Buck and Miss Atkins?"

Peter dumped the bed clothes on the couch and then folded his arms across his chest, looking doubtfully at the empty space on the bed. "I didn't see Vera—she was too busy training new women—but Buck was Buck." He sat gently at the foot, curling up against the bedpost as if he were trying not to take up too much room. "But the War Office told me my older brother had died. He was RAF and they shot him down the very day I arrived in Cannes. Seven months ago. They didn't see it fit to tell me while I was undercover."

She reached out to put her hand on top of his. "I'm so sorry."

He met her gaze with red eyes. "My mother... I had to try to console her the best I could. She hadn't heard anything from my youngest brother in over a year, another son was dead, and there I was, about to ship out again."

Odette scooted closer to him so she could caress his arm. "Maybe you should have stayed in England."

"Buck tried to convince me to do the same. He said after Alec sent us the information about Bleicher, they could recall you and Alec, or help you relocate to another circuit. But I wanted to come back and join the Maquisards. It's become my dream to welcome the Allies into France and end the war with a gun in my hands. I'm tired of playing this espionage game. It's an endless duel of wits where, if you make one misstep, you ruin your chances of getting out alive."

Odette had no reply to that.

"Besides," Peter continued, rotating his arm to grasp her hand. "There was another reason I wanted to come back."

At last she'd heard the words she'd been waiting for. They both leaned forward, their lips meeting. They kissed softly at first, hesitantly, and then Peter wrapped his arms around her and this time, there was nothing hesitant in his kiss.

After another minute of passion, Peter broke from their embrace. "And what of your husband?"

"Don't you worry about him. I've already made up my mind to divorce him the soonest I am able. And," she traced the lines of his palm with her finger, "If I never make it back to England, to my daughters, I'd like to make love one more time with someone I care about."

She watched his frown turn to a wistful smile and then a positively glowing grin as her words sunk in. "I'm sure that will happen soon. But not tonight." He reached out to turn off the lamp, and his voice was once again somber. "We need our rest if we're going to leave Saint-Jorioz in the morning." He got comfortable beside her, fluffing the pillow and pulling the blanket over both of them. "Lise... in case our days are indeed numbered, you should probably know that I care about you too, more deeply than I can express."

She cleared the lump in her throat before she replied, "Good night, Peter."

"Good night, Lise."

It could have been the best sleep she'd had in weeks, but sometime before daylight, Odette was awakened by a faint knocking at their door. She tried to ignore it and go back to sleep, but the knocking turned into an urgent pounding.

"Who is it?" she called.

"It's Jean Cottet," a gruff voice answered.

"What do you need, Jean?" Knowing they had a trying morning ahead—and warmed by Peter's proximity—she was reluctant to get out of bed.

"There's a man downstairs who wants to see you. Now. He says it's a most pressing matter." His voice dropped an octave. "There's something about all of this that worries me."

"It's okay, Jean. Tell him I'll be down in a minute."

She quickly threw on the clothes she'd laid out the night before. She was still half asleep, irritated at being woken up, but not terribly worried, despite what Jean had said. She stomped down the stairs, determined to give whoever it was that demanded her presence a piece of her mind.

She stopped short when she caught sight of the man, however. He cocked the Luger in his hand and pointed it at her. She glanced to her left, where another man was in a similar stance. Two more thuggish-looking men were behind him. None of them were familiar to her.

She blinked fast, feeling as though this wasn't really happening, that she was an actress in a movie. But the man who stepped out of the shadows was no stranger.

Bleicher approached her, a gun in his hand. "Congratulations, Lise. You have played your part with great skill. But your game is up. Don't make things any more difficult by trying to escape—we have the building surrounded."

He turned to one of the thugs in the background and growled just one word. "Pierre."

"No," Odette protested. "I am his wife and it is my fault we are back in France. I am a Frenchwoman, and he is English. Let him go and take me."

A pistol was shoved into her back. "Upstairs," the man behind her commanded.

Bleicher led the way back to their room as Odette wrestled with what to do. She could shout for Peter to make for the roof, but then the Gestapo men waiting outside would shoot him dead. Besides, she knew if he heard her scream, he'd try to rescue her, putting both of them in even more danger. *No, we must face the music as the experienced SOE operatives we are.*

Bleicher kicked the door open and turned on the light. Peter, exhausted from his journey, was still sleeping. Odette looked upon his prone form with a sudden stab of affection, willing him not to wake up. She cast her eyes around the room. Her purse sat on the table. She pictured the cyanide pill tucked safely inside the lining. It felt like the last safeguard she had against impending torment and suffering, but she knew she could never take it.

Peter's jacket hung over the back of one of the chairs, the square shape of his wallet just visible in the front pocket. She knew there was damning evidence inside it: new radio codes and thousands of francs for their agents.

The other man pointed his Luger at the bed as Bleicher shook Peter's shoulder. "You are under arrest, Pierre Chauvet."

As he sat up wearily, Odette slipped over to the table.

Peter started to deny his identity, but the gun thrust in his face made him stop. Odette grabbed Peter's wallet and slid it into the cup of her bra as Bleicher ordered him to get up. "You, Chauvet, are a British agent and saboteur."

Peter, under the direction of the two armed men, threw on a shirt and pants.

"Cuff him," Bleicher told one of the thugs.

"I'm not finished dressing yet," Peter insisted.

"All in good time," Bleicher stated. "You are aware that this district is occupied by the Italian Army?"

"Yes," Peter replied tersely.

"Well, which would you prefer: to be the prisoner of the Italians or Germans?"

Peter gave a hoarse chuckle. "The Italians, of course."

This answer obviously did not please the Germans. After Peter had put on his coat, Bleicher repeated his instructions to have him handcuffed. The steel bands snapped over his wrists and Odette and Peter were taken out to the hall while Bleicher dumped out the contents of their drawers and dug through their packed bags. But the only incriminating item was already tucked away in Odette's bosom.

The thugs left the room, one of them taking Odette's elbow, and led her and Peter back downstairs.

Jean Cottet was still in the lobby, a look of panic on his normally inscrutable face. It was obvious he had known nothing of Bleicher's plan.

"Jean, I'm sorry about this," Peter told him. "I didn't mean to cause you any bother. You couldn't have possibly realized I was a British officer."

Cottet feigned a look of surprise as the men pushed Peter out the door. He met Odette's eyes, his sympathetic as he mouthed, "Good luck," and then Odette too was shoved into the cool night air.

There were two cars waiting. Bleicher climbed into one of them and patted the seat beside him. Odette reluctantly followed as Peter was taken to the car behind them. When Bleicher leaned forward to give instructions to the driver, Odette reached under her blouse to grab Peter's wallet. She was mercifully still unhandcuffed, and, pretending to straighten her stockings, she stuffed the wallet under the cushions of the car, sighing with relief that at last Peter's secrets were hidden as best as she could manage. As they drove away, Odette kept her eyes on the mountain they'd been on only hours before, when Peter had been in her arms.

CHAPTER 49

MATHILDE

*L*ucas came to visit Mathilde a few days after the Claridge's party. She invited him into the parlor and asked Didi to make them some tea.

"I am going back to France," Lucas told Mathilde flatly.

"Oh?" She noted that he had said "I" and not "we."

They both fell silent as Didi deposited a tea tray on the ottoman. Some of the liquid spilled and Lucas mopped it up before lifting his tea cup, which seemed way too delicate for his strong hands. "Circumstances in France have changed since we've arrived, and now Buckmaster and Boddington think it's too dangerous for you to come with me."

"If it's too dangerous for me, what does that mean for you? Are they not sending you right back into the lion's den?"

"Yes." He took a sip. "But seeing as how I'm a…" he seemed to have trouble swallowing, "a well-trained, experienced SOE operative, they see no reason not to drop me back in."

Lucas might have been trained by the SOE, but he was also a man. And Buckmaster and Boddington were more than aware that Mathilde was not. "What about our plans? What about blowing up Fresnes and killing Bleicher?"

"I know." He put his cup down and reached for her hand. "I told them I would only go back if the SOE consents to two things. One, that they make sure you are well treated here, and two, that in a few months I'll come back to retrieve you, and together we'll set up a new network."

"A smaller one," she agreed. "Interallié became too big to manage. We'll only have four or five agents, ones whom we trust implicitly."

"Yes." Lucas sat back. "In the meantime, you'll stay here and keep feeding Bleicher false information."

"I don't want to work with those men without you. Buckmaster always looks like a deer trapped in the headlights of a car." She laughed to herself. "And if Buck is indeed a buck, then Vera Atkins, with her long face and beaked nose, is his doe. Either that or a Jewess. And don't get me started on that simpering idiot Boddington."

Lucas held up both hands. "Okay, okay. It's obvious you're not a fan of the SOE. But I've known Boddington for a while now, and he's always done right by me." He dropped his arms to his side. "The British may suffer from a lack of imagination, but I'd rather work for them than anyone else."

She shook her head. "If only you'd experienced Interallié in its heyday." She fell silent remembering all of Armand's missteps and how they'd very nearly caused the downfall of everyone concerned.

Lucas rose. "I won't be gone long, and when I come back, we can set our former plans into motion."

"Thank you." She stood on her tiptoes and kissed his cheek. "*Buena suerte*, Lucas."

CHAPTER 50

ODETTE

*P*eter and Odette were brought to the barracks of the Italian Army's mountain infantry—the Alpini—in Annecy. "Take good care of them," Bleicher told an Italian officer in typical Alpini uniform: a green tunic and calf-length bloomers, which might have looked ridiculous if the officer's facial expression hadn't been so menacing. "I've got to return to Paris now, but we can't afford to lose these two," Bleicher continued.

Odette stood by Peter, whose wrists were cuffed in front of his body. She reached for him, and he looked at her with so much affection it nearly made her blush. She squeezed his hand hard, willing herself to give him strength. She knew that, as the commanding officer of the Spindle Network, he was destined for much worse things than she, a mere woman. More than anything, she wished she could take on his pain and endure it herself.

She was taken to a small room in the barracks, not altogether unpleasant, though the bed was hard.

That first night was spent in a maze of *what if's*: what if Peter had missed the drop-off? What if she had packed up early and left Saint-Jorioz a few days prior? What if Bleicher had waited until the 18th to arrive like she'd asked him to?

But it was no use: as Bleicher himself had stated, their game was up. She and Peter had had a productive run, longer than most, shorter than some. They had accomplished good things, but now it was time to pay the price.

The next morning, she awoke to a guard calling for assistance in a panicked voice, followed by the sound of many jackboots sprinting down the hall, and then a startled cry that sounded suspiciously like Peter.

Next she heard more cursing in Italian, accompanied by kicking and grunting. *They were hurting Peter!* Odette strained her ears, tears running down her face, but there was no more noise after that.

An Italian officer entered her cell a few hours later. He introduced himself as the chief of secret police before stating in an expressionless tone, "Your partner is a criminal, signora."

"He's not my partner, he's my husband," Odette replied, trying to keep the panic out of her voice. "What have you done to him?"

"He tried to make a getaway last night by knocking down one of our guards. It's going to be pretty bad for him now."

Odette could feel herself tearing up again, wishing desperately that the Italian had come in to inform her of Peter's successful escape.

"What sort of work did you and your husband do?" he asked stiffly, refusing to leave his post next to the door.

She looked at him with pursed lips and shook her head.

"You are not in a position to make decisions," he reminded her.

Odette opened her mouth wide, stating her words slowly, as if the Italian were stupid. "I have nothing to say to you."

He narrowed his eyes at her. "We shall see about that."

But the next few days passed uneventfully. For some reason, the Italian soldiers had warmed to Odette. She got a clue as to why when one of them grudgingly told her, "You husband is very brave, though hard to manage. He attacked one of his guards."

"Is he hurt?"

The guard shrugged. "His ego was probably more bruised than

anything else—he almost managed to escape, but we caught him. We had to take his glasses so he wouldn't try anything else."

The thought of Peter being free made her lips turn up wistfully. "Will you permit me to send a message to him?"

He shrugged. "I guess there's nothing wrong with it. It will be something to fill my boring days." He raised his finger and pointed at her. "But nothing military or secret about it."

"No."

In a few minutes, the guard returned with an inkwell and a small pad of paper. As instructed, Odette kept her note impersonal and brief. She scribbled, *Are you quite all right?* before handing it to the guard unfolded.

He read what she wrote and tucked it into his front pocket. "I'll be back in a few minutes."

Odette sat on the bed, her hands clenched into fists. Her agitation stemmed not from whether Peter was hurt, but something else entirely. She'd once compared marriage to living in a gilded cage, and now that she was in a real prison, she realized that being in Saint-Jorioz with Peter was the most free she had ever felt.

Her hands tightened even more as it dawned on her that, somehow, she had accidentally fallen in love with her network leader, a man she wasn't sure she'd ever see again.

Peter's response read, *A little banged up and bruised, but will survive. How are you? Are you worried about your girls?*

"Yes," Odette replied, her pen moving rapidly. She was tempted to say what was really on her mind, but, not knowing if the feeling was mutual, she couldn't bring herself to write that she loved him. Instead, she added, *And I'm concerned for you too.* Without thinking, she signed her real name.

The guard had a reply in a few hours. *Odette. Now I know your true name.* Peter's handwriting appeared shaky this time.

I might still think upon you affectionately as Lise, the fearless courier. But it suits you to have a different name now. I feel as if our sort of predicament is the kind that either brings out the best or the worst in people. Clearly you are showing the former, and my admiration for you has never been as deep as it is now. Stay strong, my lovely Odette/Lise.

Tears blurred her vision as she re-read his words, mentally inserting the word 'love' for 'admiration.'

After a week, the secret police officer regretfully told Odette she was being transferred. She nodded and collected her meager things: two blouses, a skirt, and the gray suit she'd once told Miss Atkins would be perfectly suitable for imprisonment, still on a hanger.

A lorry was parked in the middle of the garden outside the prison. She'd not had a shower or been able to look after any sort of hygiene in quite some time, and she could smell the stink of her own body.

"Oh!" she cried as another prisoner came into view. *Peter!*

He looked similarly disheveled, with a crusty gray/brown beard forming on his normally chiseled jaw. Odette watched as his guards shook his cuffed hands, some of them patting him on the back. It was clear his captors had developed a profound respect for Peter, though it could never rival her own.

Close up, Odette could see that Peter's hair was greasy and his skin was covered in bruises, but to her he looked wonderful. "Are you hurt?" she asked.

"Not too much." He managed a smile. He nodded toward a young guard. "That's the one I knocked over trying to escape."

The man waved and Odette marveled how Peter could make friends out of the worst enemies.

The Italians allowed Peter and Odette to sit together, and she once again reached for his hands. They sat in silence as the lorry started, but soon she was emptying her purse of cigarettes, tucking them into every available pocket space on Peter's jumpsuit.

"Where did you get all these?" he asked.

"The guards gave them to me. I'm sorry they smell—they lit them for me and then I stubbed them out immediately."

"No odor from a cigarette could possibly mask my own foulness."

"You smell, and look, perfectly fine to me," Odette replied honestly.

He gazed into her eyes, and it seemed to her that time had stopped. She was momentarily blind to the fact that Peter was in handcuffs, and armed guards were surrounding them. All that mattered was that she was beside him again.

They fell silent, each of them staring out at the scenery they'd been deprived of for the last week.

"Peter," Odette finally whispered under her breath. "Who do you think betrayed us? Was it Bardet?"

"It doesn't matter, Odette." Her proper name sounded strange coming from his lips. "They could hang me for any of a dozen reasons."

"But they won't," she replied resolutely. *Not if I can help it.* "You can survive this." The incident with the orphanage coupons on the train to Périgueux came to mind, and she quoted him, "So long as you lay off the theatrics—it's dangerous enough as it is."

The memory was not lost on him and he shot her a lopsided grin.

She glanced at the guards behind them, who were preoccupied with a game of cards, their guns at rest. She dropped her voice to a whisper. "From now on, you should tell everyone your real name."

"No. You know they will treat me even worse with the last name of Churchill."

"I've been telling everyone that we are married, and that I too am a Churchill."

"There goes my cover story," he stated dryly.

"Nonsense," she replied loudly. The guards in front looked back at her, and she sat up, rubbing her filthy back on the seat. When they'd lost interest, she continued, again in a whisper, "The Germans are obsessed with names and heritage. They will praise Bleicher to the moon and back for capturing one of old-man Winston's relatives. Who knows, maybe they'll arrange for a prisoner exchange."

"I always thought it was a dangerous name to travel under."

She shrugged. "Maybe sometimes, but it's a gamble worth taking." She gave his hand another squeeze. "And if anyone asks, we've been married since the war broke out."

He gave a heavy sigh. "Sink or swim, our fates will be determined together."

The man in the front seat turned around. "You are not talking of anything political, no?"

"Of course not." Peter's smile reappeared, though Odette could tell the effort pained him. "You think a man and his wife would waste their last moments discussing politics? I'm just whispering *dolce far niente* in her ear."

The Italian gave them a lecherous grin before turning back around.

Odette giggled to herself. "I should add that the guise of our marriage is merely a war-time stunt, designed to save my own hide as well as yours."

Peter's face turned serious. "If I ever get the chance, I shall ask you if you care to make it a permanent thing."

Odette met his gaze, but they both knew she could never promise to love another man while she was still married. Her eyes on the men in front, she bent down to retrieve something from her bag. She handed Peter the gold ring Buckmaster had given her before she'd left England. "*Pour toi, mon Pierre,*" she said, placing it in his hand before closing his fingers around it.

CHAPTER 51

DIDI

*B*uckmaster called Didi into his office one windless spring day to tell her: "Lucas has been arrested by the Abwehr."

"What?" Didi sank into a chair. The hardness of it sprung her back to reality. "It wasn't The Cat, was it?"

"No." He straightened a pile of papers. "The Cat, or rather the SOE, reported to Bleicher that Lucas had been sent to Scotland for training."

Didi couldn't help wondering if it was wise to inform the Abwehr where London trained their agents.

"We're working on getting Lucas back," Buckmaster continued. "But in the meantime, we have to decide what to do about The Cat. To quote Lucas himself when he first met her, she's either brilliant in her ability to outfox the Krauts, or foolish enough to still be working for them. I think he finally decided on the latter." He locked eyes with Didi. "What are your thoughts?"

She spread out her hands. "I've been with her practically every hour of every day and I can't find any evidence of collusion."

"At any rate, I'm not sure we can continue feeding them false information via the wireless. If she's not a triple-agent, then the Abwehr will surely grow suspicious, if they haven't figured it out already."

She shrugged. "With all due respect, sir, I can't imagine the Germans priding themselves on trusting a former member of the

Resistance simply because she was…" Didi could feel her face grow hot but she continued anyway, "sleeping with one of their officers."

"Yet, despite their probable mistrust, they sent her to London. And they let Lucas go too."

"Indeed."

Buck sat back in his chair. "You think they allowed her to come to England because she consented to giving up so many of her colleagues?"

"Allowed yes, but I'm not sure she's acting as an agent for Germany now." Didi shut her eyes, trying not to think of Jackie, Archie, or anyone else in France whom The Cat could have put in danger. "She was a compliant tool in the extermination of Interallié, but I would argue—and I'm afraid the Germans might too—that the ability to betray your friends does not necessarily indicate a willingness to heed their enemies."

He rubbed his chin with his thumb. "Yet she's here. Why?" He closed his eyes, clearly deep in thought. After a few moments, he leaned forward abruptly, startling Didi. "Do you think she's dangerous?"

"What?" Didi asked, stalling for time.

Buck spoke slower. "Do you think she presents a threat to the Allies?"

"Even if I said no, she is now in possession of valuable information about the inner workings of the SOE and I don't think she should be allowed out of England."

He nodded. "If she were to go back, she'd probably be shot as soon as she stepped foot on French soil." He gave an ironic chuckle. "Though by whom—the Resistance or the Abwehr—would be anyone's guess."

"Yes, sir." Didi rose, but Buckmaster stopped her before she got to the door. "Miss Nearne, it has occurred to me that perhaps we are missing an opportunity."

"What opportunity would that be, sir?" she asked, not daring to hope.

"Your sister has done very well for herself, and for the SOE, in France. We are hoping you might follow in her footsteps, especially now that the business with The Cat is about to be concluded."

Didi sat back down. "But what about my age? I'm not quite twenty-five still."

"And?" Buckmaster's confusion was obvious. "There's no minimum age to work for us."

"But my sister—" Didi paused. Clearly Jackie had lied to her about the age limit to keep her from pursuing the matter. "When do I leave for training?"

"Since you've already learned Morse and are well versed in our coding system, you would only need to attend a finishing course for field operators."

"Wait." Didi leaned forward. "Am I being sent to France as a wireless operator?"

"Of course." Buckmaster folded his arms. "How else would we send you in?"

As an agent, Didi replied, to herself. But she swallowed her disappointment. She was still going to France, no matter what the role.

CHAPTER 52

ODETTE

*O*dette and Peter were brought to Fresnes Prison, a hulking, red bricked penitentiary located a few miles south of Paris. Upon arrival, they were taken to different sections of the prison for their respective registrations.

Odette gave her name as "Odette Churchill." Just saying Peter's last name was enough to make her weep, but she forced herself to stay strong. If her SOE training had instilled anything in her, it was that things could—and would—get much worse.

She was told to take her clothes off, which she did without reluctance. To her, decency had become a state of mind, and was no longer subject to her lack of clothing.

The women in gray scrutinized her naked body before digging through her hair and ears, searching for lice. When they did not find any, Odette was commanded to get dressed again and handed a threadbare blanket and bed sheet.

She was then led down an underground passage, dark in places where the pool of light from the overhead electric lamps did not reach. The putrid smell of the corridor filled Odette's nostrils, causing her to cough.

The female guard barked at her to keep walking. Odette obeyed, her legs moving as if not of her own will, through the endless underground maze of darkness and light. Gray doors appeared on either side of the hallway, like tombstones in an abandoned graveyard.

The woman led her up a flight of stairs, where a familiar, bespectacled figure was waiting. The guard suddenly became a woman again and simpered, "*Herr Hauptmann, heir ist Frau Churchill.*"

Bleicher visibly startled at the name as Odette thrust her bags at him. "In France, it is customary for men to carry things for women." She raised her chin. "I see no reason why the same courtesies should not continue in prison."

Bleicher reluctantly accepted her filthy bundle. The guard led them down the hallway, stopping at Cell 108 before digging a large key out of her pocket. Without a word, Bleicher handed Odette her things and then continued on.

Odette entered her cell, putting her things on the soiled mattress atop the rusted bed frame, before looking around. In the corner was a dirty toilet and brown sink. Next to that was a chair with a broken back and above it, a crooked shelf containing a tin bowl and spoon. Twelve-and-a-half full steps one way took her the length of the cell, and eight the width. Like her guard, everything on the inside was grim and gray, save for the rust on the bed frame and the bright yellow mold decorating the right side of the ceiling. A cobweb-covered vent broke the monotony on the left.

On the wall next to the door, there were barely discernible scratches in the paint. She walked over and ran her fingers over the scratches. Someone had etched, in French, *When I was little, I kept the cows. Now it is they who keep me.* It was signed, 'Suzanne.'

A few steps further, she found a series of numbers also scrawled into the wall, most of them run through by a diagonal line. After a moment of contemplation, Odette realized she was looking upon a calendar. The last date crossed out was the 11th of November. Did that date represent freedom for the carver, or was Suzanne already in her grave?

Odette took a hairpin from the one hat she had and made a faint mark. She felt a surge of triumph—keeping track of her days in prison would be one way to pass the time.

She continued on with the perusal of her new surroundings. The window consisted of a series of frosted glass planes, impossible to see out of, but she could sense that the sun was setting by the deepening shadows inside her cell.

She spread out her blanket on the mattress and lay down. She could hear absolutely nothing—no activity, no marching of guards, nothing but a daunting stillness throughout the prison.

She closed her eyes and found the filmy darkness under her lids more soothing than the blackness of her cell. Her body might be in prison, but perhaps she could project her mind to freedom. She squeezed her eyes tight, willing her daughters to materialize in the imaginary screen behind her eyelids. After what seemed like an eternity, they came, playing and laughing in fictitious sunlight. Odette's tightened facial muscles relaxed and a smile formed.

But they disappeared as a blood-curdling scream broke the silence. Odette sat up as another shriek came through the walls. She could hear heavy boots clomping in the hallway. The screams became a raucous cackling, nearly covering up the sound of a key rattling in a lock and then a command barked in German. "*Ruhig!*" But the voice did not shut up, and soon there came the unmistakable ringing of blows, this time accompanied by heartrending wails of pain.

Odette reached out and touched the wall, longing for the blows to stop. Eventually they did, and the German voice called out some final insult and then a door slammed shut. The heavy boots came back down the hall at a much slower pace.

Odette dropped her hands and laid back down. She shut her eyes, hoping her girls would reappear. But they didn't and she finally fell into a dreamless sleep.

She awoke to a strange rattling. Sleepily she realized it was a key in her cell door and she covered herself with the blanket as the door was thrown open. "*Gib mir deine Schüssel.*"

Odette shook her head in confusion.

The woman in gray pointed to the tin bowl on the shelf. "*Schnell.*" Odette rose and took the bowl, holding it out as the guard filled it with a putrid-smelling broth.

When the guard left, Odette tasted the brown liquid. It was cold coffee, probably rendered from acorns. She drank it down in one gulp, her face puckering from the bitterness.

The woman in gray reappeared and this time gestured for Odette to follow her.

She was led to a small room where Bleicher was waiting for her.

"You are now a political prisoner of the Abwehr," he said, as the guard shut the door behind her. He lit Odette a cigarette. She took one puff before putting it out carefully against the heel of her shoe.

He watched her. "You aren't perhaps in love with Peter, are you?"

She shrugged, not wanting to give him the satisfaction of knowing anything more about her than he already did.

He leaned forward. "Lise, I'm sorry to see you here. Fresnes Prison is not…" he looked at a spot beyond her shoulder, as if searching for his next words. "Not for women like you."

Odette sat as still as she could.

"I would have preferred to see you again in Saint-Jorioz, your beauty competing with the mountains. But I had to arrest you."

"Why?" she demanded, breaking her silence.

He looked surprised at the vehemence of her tone. "To save you from the Gestapo, of course."

"Like you saved Marsac? The number of people you are claiming to have rescued would fill a landing field for a Hudson. Abwehr or Gestapo, steel prison or execution, the end appears to be very much the same."

"You may be right for now," he took a thoughtful drag of his cigarette, "but it doesn't always have to be so. You don't have to stay here, Lise."

"No?" She smiled involuntarily at the ridiculousness of his statement.

"Does the possibility of freedom amuse you?"

"I was wondering what bargain you were going to suggest. Obviously I can't offer you a radio or a bomber pick-up from here," she raised her hands, gesturing to her surroundings.

"You are in many ways a wise, brave woman, Lise, but you can also be very foolish." He tapped out his cigarette. "I know a great deal about you, far more than you may think. You told the guards you are Mrs. Peter Churchill, but I know that, in fact, you are married to another man, you have three daughters, and you are an agent of the French section of the British War Office, headquartered at Baker Street, London. Your chief is Major Maurice Buckmaster, educated at Eton."

"Are you quite done now?" she demanded, still stinging at those words he'd used, *married to another man.*

"No. Do you think self-sacrifice is still noble? That mentality went out the window when the tank was invented."

She opened her mouth as if to protest, but he ignored her. "Even so, your prospective sacrifice is misdirected." He tapped a finger on the table. "Your duty is to those girls at home, not to a collection of amateur spies and saboteurs from the War Office. Do you think for one moment that your friend Alec—or your so-called husband Peter Churchill—are prepared to forfeit their own lives for yours?"

"Yes," she breathed. "But even if they aren't, I am only responsible for what my own conscience dictates."

He lit another cigarette before searching her face. "What would you say if I informed you I am trying to arrange a prisoner exchange for Peter Churchill? What would you say if I also told you that he is more than eager to go… despite knowing that it means leaving you here to rot?"

She smiled. "I would say you're a liar, Monsieur Bleicher."

If he was disappointed that he'd failed to sow any seed of doubt in her mind, he didn't show it. He kept his eyes on her as he ashed his cigarette, and, skilled interrogator that he was, he swiftly changed topics. "I told you before about the Mozart concert. They are giving a repeat performance in a fortnight, and it would give me great pleasure to take you to see it. At best, Mozart is exquisite, and even at his laziest, he is lively, delicate, and charming."

It was her turn to study him. He was clearly offering her a way out, but one she could never accept. "You are making a mistake if you think I will go anywhere with you."

"If that is the way you wish to keep it." He stood up. "Though it grieves me to see you here, I will pay you another visit… soon."

The gray woman reappeared and escorted her back to Cell 108. Odette sat on the edge of the bed for a while, mulling over all Bleicher had said to her.

CHAPTER 53

DIDI

$\mathcal{U}$nlike sprawling Fawley Court, The Drokes, where Didi was to complete her wireless field training, was a modern brick house located on the Beaulieu Estate in New Forest. Like Buckmaster's London office, The Drokes dripped with art-deco flooring and furniture.

Upon arrival, a woman with graying hair introduced herself in perfect French as Adele. "I've just returned from my final mission in France," she told the group of new recruits sitting primly in the parlor. "Come, let's show you to your rooms," she called as she walked toward the hallway staircase.

This time Didi wasn't sleeping in the attic but a second-floor bedroom, though she still had the requisite several roommates. Adele gave the women some time to unpack before reappearing half an hour later. This time she announced it was time for their first lesson.

Didi was the last to leave the room, and found Adele waiting in the hall. "You're Jackie's sister." It wasn't a question.

"How did you know?" Buckmaster had instructed Didi not to tell anyone her real name; her codename for training was 'Alice.'

Adele started down the stairs. "I saw the name on your chart and put two and two together. I trained with Jackie here at Beaulieu over a year ago, though we were at the main house."

Training to be real agents, Didi bitterly surmised.

"We weren't supposed to talk about anything personal," Adele continued, "but Jackie did mention her determined little sister."

Didi figured that Jackie had used a less-kindly word than 'determined.' Maybe Adele could explain why Jackie had lied to her about the minimum age for the SOE. "Do you know if my sister..." She paused, struggling to find the right words. But they'd reached the bottom of the stairs, and she could hear the women gossiping in the parlor. She shot Adele a sheepish grin. "Never mind."

Didi sat down in an armchair just moments before a uniformed man entered the room. He greeted them and introduced himself as their propaganda instructor, Kim Philby, before warning them that, from there on out, everything would be spoken in French.

"Why do we need a propaganda instructor?" a pretty, exotic looking woman asked.

Philby pointed a surprisingly manicured finger at the speaker. "I'm not sure if you know this, but France has been invaded by the Boches. Some of the natives have become complacent with the German intruders. Part of your job will be to convince them to stop being so complacent and join the Resistance. And likewise, Vichy and the Nazis have their own propaganda, the kind that can threaten your very existence and that of others in your network." He dug a red poster out of his briefcase and put it on the table.

Didi leaned forward to examine it. The headline across the top read, in German, 'Liberation... by crime.' Below that were photos of blown-up tracks, derailed trains, and dead bodies, and at the bottom were several pictures of men in civilian clothes.

Philby picked up the poster and walked over to show the woman behind Didi. "The Gestapo referred to these men as 'Judeo-Communist terrorists.' To our knowledge, they are all dead."

"But I thought we were going to be wireless operators," the same woman from earlier said in a hushed voice.

"That doesn't mean the Gestapo can't capture you." He waved at a well-dressed man standing in the hallway. The scent of his cologne entered the room before he did.

"Speaking of ways to avoid capture, this is Monsieur Bisset," Philby informed them. "He's come all the way from Max Factor in London."

"Max Factor? Are we getting a lesson in make-up?" someone called.

"Not the way you think," Philby replied.

. . .

For the next hour, Monsieur Bisset taught the new recruits how to alter the jawlines by inserting pieces of sponge into their cheeks, how to change their hair color by lightening it with lemon juice or darkening it with charcoal, and how to emphasize minimal wrinkles with eyeshadow.

The exotic woman turned to Didi. "And here I thought all this time we wanted to hide our age lines."

"Not that you have any," Didi replied, thinking that the woman was one of the most beautiful she had ever seen.

The woman extended a slim hand. "I'm Nora."

"Alice," Didi returned.

"And one more thing," Bisset interrupted. "Occasionally it might be your responsibility to alter the appearance of a male colleague." He used his own-clean shaven face to demonstrate how to use a make-up pencil to add whiskers.

Finally it was time for dinner. After getting her tray of admittedly delicious-smelling food, Didi sat next to Adele.

"Is any of this really necessary for us?" she asked. "The make-up, the hair coloring…"

Adele shrugged. "Maybe, maybe not. They've certainly become more thorough since I was recruited, probably because some of the women I trained with are missing in action."

Didi felt her heartbeat speed up. "Not Jackie?"

Adele shook her head. "No. Not…" She left her sentence unfinished, but Didi mentally filled it in for her. *Not yet.*

"Listen," Adele put her hand on Didi's arm. "Being in the field, whether as a courier or wireless operator, is not easy. You don't have anyone to truly confide in. Sure you have the other people in the network, but you can't reveal yourself to them fully. They can never learn your real name or who you were before the war. But—" she relaxed her grip, "you must remember how important the job is: you're going to be part of the Resistance. You will play a critical role in the liberation of France and, hopefully, victory for the Allies."

Didi gave her a grateful smile before digging into her meal.

CHAPTER 54

ODETTE

The next morning was the same for Odette: more bitter brown liquid for breakfast and then the guard took her to the room where Bleicher was waiting.

Once again Odette took a quick puff of the cigarette he offered her before carefully putting it out.

Bleicher watched her intently. "I visited Peter," he said finally. "He's in cell number 220 in the Second Division."

Though her heart leapt at the mention of Peter's name, she refused to show Bleicher any reaction.

"Peter is well and sends his love. I've given him some cigarettes. As you know, I'm trying to arrange an exchange for him."

Again, Odette said nothing.

"But it is you that I want to talk about," he continued. "I have hoped that two days and nights in this place might have softened you."

"Did you now, Hugo?" Odette replied, deliberately dropping the formal 'Monsieur Bleicher.'

He frowned. "If you choose to stay here in Fresnes, the Gestapo will send for you. They are determined to find the whereabouts of your wireless operator Alec and the British officer Roger." He fixed his eyes on hers. "They know, as I do, that you have this information. I frankly fear for you if you are summoned to 84 Avenue Foch. The Gestapo is not as patient as I am."

She sat forward. "Tell me, Hugo. Are you going to offer to save me from the Gestapo again?"

"Yes," he replied eagerly. "I can get you out of here. All you have to do is ask."

She folded her hands in her lap. "You seem to know much about the French Section of the War Office, but there is one important point on which you're lacking knowledge. If one of us is captured, then we've got to take what's coming to us. I tried to play games with you once, and I lost. It's why I'm here. And I won't play anymore—I'm not clever enough to leave here under your protection and keep my silence and, therefore, my self-respect. So I choose to remain."

"I impose no conditions, Lise. I know I would be wasting my time if I asked you either to give your friends away... or work for me."

She sighed. "Do you think I could ever return to England and look my daughters in the face while telling them that I was captured, but they let me out again because an Abwehr man took me under his benevolent wing?"

"Maybe don't tell them. It is war, and people must do what they can to survive. Others have done worse than what you believe I'm proposing and are thriving."

"There is no way I would thrive if I betrayed anyone. I couldn't even live with myself, let alone face my daughters." *Or Peter.* She stood. "You will forgive me if I ask that this interview come to an end."

His reply was unexpected. "Are you hungry, Lise?"

She folded her arms around her chest. She was unsure where his question would lead, but decided to answer honestly. "Very."

"I could order you extra food."

"Do other women get extra food?"

"Some. The ones that do chores, such as push the food trolley around."

"No thank you. I can manage on what they've been giving me."

"Would you like books to read?"

"Do other women get books?" She didn't want it to look as if Bleicher was giving her special treatment.

"Yes."

"Then I should like some books."

"I will arrange that for you. Is there anything else?"

She hesitated. "Yes," she finally said softly. "On my cell door there

268

are some notices in German. I don't know what they say, but I'd like to learn."

The corner of his mouth turned up. "I will translate them for you."

"Thank you, Hugo."

He knocked on the door and, when the woman in gray opened it, he told her, "I will accompany Mrs. Churchill back to her cell."

The guard nodded and led them to Cell 108. Bleicher rubbed his chin as he read the signage outside her door. "That one means that you are a grand secret." He pointed. "This one says "no books, no showers, no favors, no contact with anyone, that sort of thing."

"Wouldn't it have been simpler to only have one notice stating, *Nichts, Nix*, nothing?" Odette asked.

Bleicher considered. "I suppose, but it might upset the system. It's all carefully planned, you see."

She nodded. "Wouldn't it upset the carefully planned system if I walked out of the prison with you?"

He bent his head, the glare of the lamp overhead hiding his eyes. "You are quite incorrigible, Lise. I don't suppose there is any point in you coming to talk with me anymore."

She gave him a polite smile before she sauntered away. He left and the guard slammed the door shut.

Odette sat on her bed, triumphant that she had managed to outwit Bleicher. She was still congratulating herself when she heard a faint call. She stood up, tracing the sound. It seemed to be coming from near her window. "'*Allo, 'allo, la nouvelle,*'" the voice repeated in a lilting tone.

La nouvelle, the newcomer.

"'*Allo, la nouvelle* in Cell 108, if you can hear me, stomp your feet."

Odette pounded both feet on the floor and then stopped to listen again.

"Bonjour, *la nouvelle,*" the disembodied voice said. "I am Michelle. I am in the cell directly under yours. Near the ceiling in your cell is a grating for the furnace, which connects to my cell. If you wish to speak, talk into the grating."

Odette pulled a chair over. By standing on her tip-toes, her mouth could just reach the lip of the grating. "Hullo, Michelle," she said.

"Aha," Michelle returned. "Welcome to Fresnes, *la nouvelle*. What is your name?"

Odette hesitated. She didn't want to use her real name, but couldn't bear being called Lise by anyone else. "I am Céline."

"*Allo*, Céline. How have you come to join the ranks of the *mortes vivantes?*" The living dead.

"I am a political prisoner," Odette said, and then for good measure, added, "I am English."

"*Oh là là*, an English prisoner!"

"And you, Michelle, how did you come to be here?"

Michelle replied that the Gestapo had found an incriminating letter in her home. She'd been in Fresnes for four months without a trial. "One day I will either be allowed to go free, or else be shot by the Gestapo. If it is the latter, I hope I will go with dignity. Dignity is the best weapon we have against the Boches, Céline, for they do not understand it."

"I agree with you, Michelle." Odette paused before asking, "What about the women here who scream and then are beaten?"

"Oh, them." Even through the indifferent medium of the heat vent, Odette could detect the scorn in Michelle's voice. "They have no self-respect. Sunday is the worst day because it is so quiet, and the stillness makes them scream all the more."

"The stillness is awful, but the screaming is worse."

"Have you broken a window pane yet?"

"No," Odette replied with surprise. "Is that possible?"

"Yes. You will be punished by not being given soup for a day, but it is worth it to see the sky, especially because you are new and don't know the pangs of real hunger yet." She paused. "Try it and we will talk again this afternoon. The best times to speak are between twelve and two, when the SS women are at lunch, and then again when they are making dinner between four and five in the afternoon. *Au revoir,* Céline."

"*Au revoir,* Michelle." Odette stepped down from her perch. She considered the window for a moment before lifting the chair over her head and smashing it against the panes. To her delight, one of the panes cracked. She repeated the motion, and a piece of glass fell out. She set the chair upright and climbed on it once again as she heard Michelle call, "Bravo, Céline."

By peering through the small hole, Odette could catch a glimpse of the blue sky. A tiny wisp of cloud rose up from the south. She marveled at the idea of it, forming over the olive groves of the Mediterranean and drifting its way to Paris. For a few minutes, Odette watched the cloud change shape and, as it passed over and then faded from view, she felt as though she'd lost a friend. *But now I have Michelle,* she reminded herself. She got back into bed, her eyes focused victoriously on the broken window.

CHAPTER 55

DIDI

The SOE had recently developed a manual for field wireless operators, and Didi had to suppress herself from continuously pointing out the many contradictions it presented. The manual stated they should not be contacting other members of their network directly, yet, two paragraphs later, they were instructed to "room with friends as the key taps are quite loud and can be detected in other rooms."

"How are we to find 'friends' to stay with if we are not to have contact with anyone in our network?" Didi asked Nora one evening. They were supposed to use this time to study, but Didi's mind was often too filled with questions to concentrate, questions that plagued her long after lights-out and kept her from getting a good night's sleep.

Nora shrugged from the bed across from Didi. "I don't suppose they mean to make friends with random people off the street. The Gestapo has ways of turning even the most patriotic French citizens against their own people."

"And this." Didi ran her finger across the words as she read them aloud: "Wireless operators in the field must constantly move their sets in order to prevent detection." She looked over at her friend. "Do they know how hard it is to locate a suitable safehouse from which to transmit, let alone several safehouses?"

Nora's voice had grown sleepy. "Let's ask Adele in the morning. Since she's already been to France twice, she'll probably know."

"It's because they want you to only transmit at certain times," Adele told them at breakfast the next day. "If you do so enough, then the Germans can lock onto your schedule and trace your wireless. They have direction-finding vehicles camouflaged to look like ordinary laundry vans with antennas that can pick up a signal within half an hour." She put her fork down. "You do know that a wireless operator is the most dangerous job of all, don't you?"

Didi nodded. Marks and Archie had told her something similar.

Both Didi and Adele's eyes turned to Nora, who, for a moment, looked panicked. She blinked hard, and the panicked look faded. "Of course," she replied.

Adele watched intently as the woman next to Didi prepared her coffee. "Don't ever put the milk in first," Adele stated.

The woman looked up in confusion. "What?"

Adele nodded at the little pitcher of milk next to her. "Not that there's a lot of milk to go around in France, but if you do get your hands on some, add it to your coffee, not the other way around. Putting the milk in before the coffee is a dead giveaway that you are English."

"Does it really matter that much?" the woman asked.

"Yes," Adele said simply. "A little gesture like that could get you killed."

The panic was back on Nora's face as she met Didi's gaze.

After lunch it was time for interrogation training. Philby started by saying that, thanks to returning agents like Adele—and agents who'd miraculously escaped after being caught—the SOE had learned a lot about the Gestapo's methods of questioning. "They rely more on terrorizing their subjects into confessing everything rather than accumulating much intelligence," Philby stated. "If you find yourself in the hot seat, remember to talk slowly. Think before you speak and try to stay calm. No matter what, stick to your cover story—you're just an ordinary French citizen trying to make a livelihood, but don't get too indignant. These Gestapo thugs don't take kindly to people who challenge their authority. If all else fails, just count to yourself, especially if they give you an injection. If you can make it through the first fifteen minutes of whatever they do to you without giving up your network, chances are you can make it through the next fifteen days, or even fifteen months, provided they don't gas you first."

Didi filed these useful tips away in her brain, hoping they'd become as second-nature to her as Morse code.

Didi was too mentally exhausted to even flip through her manual that night. She fell asleep much earlier than usual, only to be awoken shortly before dawn when the bedroom door was flung open.

"Get up!" a man whom Didi didn't recognize demanded. He and his companion were dressed all in black.

He nudged Nora with the butt of a gun. "There's been a leak among you trainees," the man spat out. "You are all to report for questioning."

Didi reached for her robe, but the other man stated, "Now."

Once downstairs, Didi, Nora, and the rest of their roommates were taken to separate rooms.

Her interrogator wore a long black coat and wide-brimmed hat and spoke with a German accent as he barked questions at her. "Who are you?"

Didi blinked as a spotlight was directed at her. "Alice Wood."

"Say it again," he commanded.

Didi repeated her code name, feeling her face growing hot under the heat of the lamp.

"What were you doing at 7 pm yesterday evening?"

She kept calm, knowing this was yet another test. "I was reading in bed."

"No you weren't. You were at the train station." There was a swift motion and Didi suddenly found herself on the floor, the chair next to her.

"Get up!" he barked and she rose shakily to her feet, her backside already sore.

"I'm going to ask you again: where were you at 7pm yesterday?"

"I was reading in bed." He did another sudden movement and now her face stung from where he'd slapped her.

She could feel her eyes fill with tears of shock. *If this was a test, why were they getting physical?* He shoved her against the wall, and Didi bit back a surge of rage. Remembering what Philby said that afternoon, she started to count in her head. *Un, deux, trois…*

The interrogation continued this way for what seemed like hours, with the masked man repeating his questions and Didi answering them the same way every time. Occasionally he'd deliver another slap or shove until Didi no longer thought it was a test.

When the light was finally switched off and the man removed his mask, Didi was amazed to see the seemingly mild-mannered Philby.

"Why did you hit me?" she asked dazedly.

"I'm sorry Miss Woods,"

"Wood," she corrected.

"Miss Wood. Since we've gained more knowledge about what the Gestapo are doing to our captured agents, we've had to get much harder with that particular test." He wiped at his forehead with a handkerchief. "Go and snatch some sleep and we'll talk after breakfast."

Nora was already asleep when Didi returned to the room, but her own heart was still racing and she lay awake, staring at the ceiling.

After breakfast, the women were brought into a small room. "We've had time to review your individual sessions, and there are some things we want to point out. Some of you did very well, and some less so," Philby told them.

Didi crossed her fingers at her side, hoping she was in the former group. Suddenly her voice filled the room, "I was reading in bed." She cringed as she heard the sound of Philby slapping her. Another dull noise. Didi rubbed her arm where she'd hit the wall when he shoved her. Then there was nothing but the sound of the tape spool.

Philby stopped the recording. "As you've heard, Alice did a great job. She never wavered on her story, no matter what I did."

Didi kept her outward expression neutral, but inwardly she felt like cheering.

"However," Philby continued, "we must examine another's experience." He again fiddled with the machine and this time they heard Nora's voice. "I was talking to Alice, and we were discussing the notion of our safehouses."

"What about the safehouses?" a disguised voice asked.

"Well… I mean, they say we shouldn't let the other members of our networks know about them, but yet we rely on our contacts to find them. So… what should it be? Should we…" There was the sound of a sharp noise, followed by a moan from Nora.

Philby paused the recording. "I'm sure you'd agree that Nora gave too much away."

Didi glanced at her friend's fallen face. A purplish bruise was forming on one of her cheeks.

"These are stupid mistakes that can compromise a network, or, worse yet, the entire Resistance," Philby continued. "But, with more training, we can get past them."

Nora lifted her chin. "I'm willing to do whatever it takes."

"Me too," the other women chorused.

Philby nodded. "That's the spirit." Almost to himself, he added, "The spirit of Resistance."

CHAPTER 56

ODETTE

*T*rue to his word, Bleicher did not return again. Odette's days fell into a monotonous routine, broken only by intervals of staring at the window and speaking with Michelle.

The day she most feared occurred a week after she'd arrived at Fresnes. The day when the SS guard opened her door and shouted, "Tribunal!" Both Michelle and Bleicher had told Odette about this: it meant she would be taken to 84 Avenue Foch and grilled by the Gestapo. Michelle had also said that some women returned, but the woman who had occupied Cell 108 before Odette had not.

She dressed in her gray suit and ran her fingers through her hair, trying to untangle it as best she could. She was then bundled into a black, windowless van and driven down the tree-lined Avenue Foch. Number 84 was a beige edifice checkered with wrought-iron railing balconies. It had once been a residential building before the Gestapo had confiscated it and inside, with its marbled lobby and high ceilings, it still maintained its old grace.

Odette was taken to an upstairs room and instructed to wait. She must have been there for two or three hours before a tall man dressed in civilian clothes entered. He smelled strongly of cologne.

She had been told of these clean, non-uniformed Gestapo men. They had been handpicked by Himmler, the chief of the German Secret Police himself and their training in Himmler's *Geheime Staat-*

spolizei school had been extensive. Odette knew their job was to make people talk, and she willed herself to not give anything away.

The man sat down and pulled out a pad of paper. "I have two questions for you." He set a pen down and adjusted it so it sat perfectly parallel to the paper. "The first is this: where is your wireless operator, the man you call Alec?"

Odette's response was simple. "I have nothing to say."

"My second question is, where is Francis Cammaerts, the new head of Spindle?"

She repeated her previous statement.

He looked at her over the top of his glasses. "I find your parrot-like replies most irritating. Once again, tell me the location of your men, Roger and Alec." He glanced at his wristwatch. "You have one minute to provide your answers."

The silence that followed was almost worse than the stillness of Fresnes. Odette could hear the tick of his watch and counted to herself. At fifty-nine seconds, the man gave an expectant, "Well?"

"I have nothing to say."

"That is very foolish of you. As you must know, we have ways of making you talk."

"I do know," she replied, feeling a drip of sweat make its way under her collar from the back of her hairline. "Do you think I came to France without knowledge of what you do to people?"

Another man entered the room and walked behind Odette. She could feel his presence but refused to look back. Suddenly he grabbed her arms and twisted them painfully behind her chair.

"Unbutton your blouse," the first man commanded.

Odette did not move even as the second man released her.

"Unbutton your blouse," he repeated, "or I will do it for you."

With shaking fingers, Odette undid the first two buttons. The man behind her pushed her shirt down. She could feel cool air on her shoulders, but then a searing ache blazed down her spine, bringing tears to her eyes. She tried not to picture the hot poker being held to her vertebrae.

The first man's voice seemed to come from somewhere very far away. "Where is Alec?"

She forced her voice to stay calm. "I have nothing to say." She allowed herself a deep breath as the poker was removed, though her spine still burned.

He now approached her, his cologne tingling her nose. "You are still refusing to say anything?"

Odette nodded.

"Do you prefer to take off your nylons and shoes yourself?" He smiled, his white teeth glowing under the fluorescent light. "I can assure you, I am well versed in the art of removing female suspenders."

"I will do it." Slowly she slid her feet out of her shoes and unrolled her stockings before readjusting her gray skirt.

The interrogator gestured to his colleague. "Stefan here is going to rip your toenails out one by one, starting with the little toe of your left foot as I repeat my questions. As soon as you give us a satisfactory answer, he will stop."

The other man came around to kneel down beside Odette's legs. He glanced up and Odette saw that he had large brown eyes. She was not overly surprised to note that he, too, was handsome. He didn't make eye contact with her, seeming to look past her, and Odette found his detached manner alarming. With freezing hands, he took her left foot and placed steel pincers at the tip of her nail.

"Where is Alec?" the other man demanded.

Odette shook her head. More than six weeks had passed since her and Peter's arrest. Surely Alec had heard by now and made the appropriate arrangements to disappear. She could give them his former location in Saint-Jorioz and the Gestapo would most likely find no trace of him there. *One address and this would end.*

But refusing to give these men what they wanted had become a match of wills Odette was determined to win. She glanced down to see the blood emerge from the cuticle as her nail was pulled out. Her little toe felt as though it was on fire before a coolness settled over it.

"Where did Roger go?"

Odette tried to summon her customary answer, but no sound came out. The interrogator nodded at her torturer, who opened his pincers to drop her toenail onto the ground.

The agony spread to her next toe, and then the next. *Trois, quatre, cinq.* The perfumed man's voice was once again far away. Now the burning extended to her other foot. *Six, sept, huit.* Odette bit her lip until it too began to bleed. *Neuf, dix.*

In a few minutes, it was all over and the kneeling man stood and glanced at his superior, who shrugged.

Odette gazed first at the bloodied spectacle of her feet and then at the pile of pale ovals on the floor, counting them to herself. Ten. They had removed every one of her toenails. She was grateful that she had lost the power of speech, so intense was the pain. *Now they will never know the answers to their questions.*

The interrogator put his hands in his pockets. "Though I didn't take you for a fainter, I am surprised at your endurance. Congratulations, Lise, you've made it this far." He looked at the other man, who still held the blood-soaked pincers in his hand. "Stefan, why don't you fetch her a cup of tea?"

A wave of nausea washed over Odette and she squeezed her eyes shut, willing herself not to throw up. The wave passed, and she opened her eyes to see the perfumed man staring at her. "Well," he asked. "How do you feel?"

Though her tongue felt as though it were coated with sawdust, she managed to eke out a reply. "I have nothing to say."

"Conversationally, you have become quite a bore to me. No doubt you feel somewhat heroic for managing to not reveal anything. At the same time, you must think of me as a monster." He sat in the chair beside her. "But you are wrong. I am a servant of my Führer, Adolf Hitler, and I do not regret what I do."

She gazed at him, thinking that he was the one who was mistaken: he was indeed a monster, as hideous as Hitler himself. "It is interesting to me that you consider it necessary to defend what you have just done." The speech was an enormous effort, but she refused to show him how much it cost her.

"We Germans do not need to make excuses to inferiors. Last night your RAF dropped thousands of bombs upon Dortmund. I do not know how many good German men, women, and children were killed or are hurt, but I do know that I care nothing for the sufferings of a single, obstinate Frenchwoman." He stood, towering over her. "Are you going to answer my questions?"

"No."

"Then it is time for your fingers to receive the same treatment as your toes."

Odette looked dully at her fingernails as another man in civilian clothes entered the room. He glanced down at the drying blood on the floor and then at Odette's feet before turning to the perfumed man and speaking rapidly in German.

Her interrogator gave a resigned shrug as the other turned and walked out, the crunching of one of Odette's toenails audible under his jackboot.

The perfumed man's tone was slightly defeated as he informed Odette, "That was my major. He says that you will never talk and I am wasting my time. While I do not agree with him, I have no choice but to take you back upstairs."

Odette's torturer entered the room carrying a steaming cup. The perfumed man barked at him as Odette gathered her shoes and stockings. "You will find it more convenient to walk on your heels for some time," the interrogator said before he left the room.

The other man, Stefan, held the door open for her, his hands stained with Odette's blood. "*Après vous,*" he said in perfect French. It was with even more horror that Odette realized she had just had her toenails ripped out by a fellow countryman.

CHAPTER 57

MATHILDE

Though London in spring was quite pretty, Mathilde began to chafe from boredom. Lucas had yet to return, and everything she did was scrutinized by Mrs. Brown, the woman who replaced Didi. She didn't even have the courtesy to buy Mathilde flowers for her birthday. And for that matter, neither did Lord Selbourne, whose affection had cooled quite considerably in the weeks following the reception at Claridge's.

The day after her, rather uneventful, birthday, Mathilde was relaxing with a glass of wine when there was a knock on her door. "Can you get that please, *chérie?*" she asked Mrs. Brown.

"I think you should," was the terse reply.

With a sigh, Mathilde got up from her perch to find two plain-clothes men standing in the hallway.

"May we come in, Mrs. Carré?" one of them asked.

She swung her arm in a welcoming gesture, the ostrich feathers from the sleeve of her robe fluttering. "Of course."

The men looked uncomfortable once inside. The shorter one pulled at his collar as he said, "We've come to arrest you."

"Pardonnez-moi?"

The taller man stepped forward. "You're being arrested by order of the SOE."

Mathilde tightened the belt of her robe. "Is this from Colonel Buckmaster? He would never dare…"

"Yes, that's exactly right." The shorter man seemed to have regained his confidence as he declared, "*Major* Buckmaster decided you are a danger to our missions in France and that, according to Article 12-5A of the Aliens Order, you must be detained."

"Here in England? Why? I could understand if maybe Hitler wanted my arrest, but not His Majesty."

"I don't know all the details, other than, yes, you will stay here in England for the duration of the war."

"The duration of the war? Who knows how long that will last?" She decided to try to reason with them. "This is all just a misunderstanding. If you would please just contact Lucas, you'll see."

"Lucas has been captured," Mrs. Brown called from the kitchen. "But even if he were here now, I don't think he'd vouch for you."

Mathilde stamped her foot. "Whatever do you mean? Lucas trusted me implicitly."

She could barely hear Mrs. Brown's mumbled reply. "You're not the only one who can use charm to deceive people."

The shorter man glanced over at his companion before stating, "I'm sorry, Mrs. Carré, but if you'll come with us now, there will be no need for handcuffs."

"Of course there's no need for handcuffs." She was fully aware that if she protested, they'd take her against her will, and without ample time to pack her things. As she swept by them on her way to the bedroom, she asked rhetorically, "What do you think I am, some kind of criminal?"

Neither man replied as they started to follow her. She shut the bedroom door in their faces.

She threw a few things into a suitcase, including the robe she was wearing, the dress she'd worn to the Claridge's reception, and the necklace Bleicher had given her. She decided to leave on her customary black silk pajamas in lieu of changing. Finally she opened the bedroom door and announced, "If you insist on arresting me, I am ready."

Mrs. Brown could hardly contain her look of glee as the two men led Mathilde out of the apartment.

CHAPTER 58

DIDI

*D*idi was summoned back to Buckmaster's office a few days
after the interrogation practice. Once again she was told to
sit in a cushioned chair while Buckmaster sat behind his desk. He
started by saying, "I've heard the recording of your inquiry training."

She folded her shaking hands in her lap. "Oh?"

"You were so convincing I couldn't tell when, or even if, you were
lying."

"Does that mean I've passed?" Didi was so nervous she could
barely get the words out.

Buckmaster laughed. "I'd be a fool to fail you. Not only are you one
of our best wireless operators, but you lie seamlessly. On top of which,
your sister's field work has been extremely valuable for the SOE."

Didi didn't see how Jackie's success had any bearing on her own
prospects, but she nodded anyway.

Buckmaster turned serious. "You do know this is no ordinary job:
there will be no time off for holidays, no regular hours, and you will
not be able to contact anyone here on a regular basis."

"I know that. Besides," she shrugged, "I don't really have anyone to
keep in touch with."

"And your mission is what we refer to as 'unacknowledgeable.' We
obviously cannot claim you as an SOE operative, for that would
admit to Hitler that there is such an organization." He lifted his

eyebrows in inquiry. "You've heard of Hitler's *Nacht und Nebel* decree?"

"Yes." Didi's voice was soft. "Night and Fog. If you are captured as a suspected member of the Resistance, his secret forces will make sure you disappear."

"We've lost a few members of the SOE already. Miss Atkins is, of course, trying her best to find them, but the trail is hard to pick up. The Geneva Convention offers no protection for spies."

"I know."

He cleared his throat. "Well, I just wanted to make sure you are fully aware of what you are getting into, especially in light of..." he paused. "Well, as I'm sure you know, our losses have been especially heavy lately."

"Yes, sir. I'm fully aware, and I'm ready to do my duty for the Allies."

"Good." He reached into his desk drawer and took out a heavy envelope with the words TOP SECRET stamped on it. "This is everything you need to know about the person you'll become in France: where you were born, your birth date and star sign, your brothers and sisters, et cetera. Memorize it down to the last detail and then burn the whole darn thing."

"Yes, sir," she repeated.

"To summarize, your new identity will be Jacqueline du Tetre, a rather empty-headed shopgirl. You will travel with your new boss, Jean Savy, who is to become the head of the Wizard circuit in a suburb just outside of Paris. There you will help Savy in his mission to raise Resistance support in preparation for an Allied landing in France."

"Yes, sir. Will I be receiving parachute training then?"

"No," Buckmaster replied, a bit cryptically, Didi thought. "Jean has no use for a parachute." He reached into the pocket of his trousers and pulled out a small velvet box. "This is for you."

"What is it?"

"Just a little thank you from Miss Atkins and me. It's not much, but it might come in handy one day."

Inside was a gold cigarette case containing an unfamiliar brand of cigarettes.

"Those are Gauloises," he told her. "I suppose it's worth mentioning that you can't smoke your English brand over there."

"Thank you, sir."

"You're welcome. And good luck, Miss Nearne."

Buckmaster was right about Jean Savy: it turned out her new boss had a handicap: his left arm was much shorter than the other, and his left fingers were fused together.

Savy caught Didi staring at his arm the first time they met. "I know what you are thinking: how can a spy work under the radar with such a glaring deformity?"

"No, not at all," Didi replied, though that was exactly what she was thinking.

"I'm also a fairly well-known lawyer in Paris, so there's no sense in using a codename. I just have to outwit the Gestapo the best I can. Don't you worry about me… I can shoot a gun just fine," he said, lifting his disfigured arm in the air.

"Never mind that," Didi said. "Are you going to tell me I'm too young for this position?"

Savy chuckled. "A child and a cripple. We make quite the pair, don't we? Buckmaster is going to be thoroughly surprised when we establish the best underground network in France."

"I don't think he'll be too surprised, after all, he's the one that gave us the job."

"Not that he had much of a choice, with the networks floundering as quickly as they do nowadays." He laughed again, as if to take away the ominous meaning of his words, but Didi felt her heart start to pound anyway. "What's your guise?" he asked.

"Jacqueline du Tetre, a boutique clerk with a weakness for cheap wine."

"That was prompt."

She shrugged, acting as nonchalant as she could, though last night she'd practiced in front of the mirror for hours. She decided to change the subject. "How long have you worked for the Resistance?"

"Since it began, really. I believe we have a mutual friend."

Didi expected him to mention Jackie, but he named Adele instead. "She introduced me to France Antelme, of the Bricklayer circuit, who then brought me to Buckmaster." He frowned. "One of the first things on my docket when I get back to Paris is to find Antelme. No one has heard from him in weeks. His new courier, Martine, also went missing as soon as she was dropped in."

"Do you think their circuit was compromised?"

He gave a heavy sigh. "I certainly hope not, but the Nazis seem to have a way of penetrating much further into the Resistance than we'd like." He held out his good arm. "What do you say we try our damndest to keep them out of Wizard?"

Didi earnestly shook his hand. "Agreed."

CHAPTER 59

MATHILDE

*M*athilde was taken to Aylesbury Prison in Buckinghamshire, a red-bricked Victorian monstrosity complete with an arched gate. Her accomplices took her through the front door of the prison and into the office of a gray-haired woman, who stood upon seeing her. "You must be Madame Carré."

Mathilde nodded.

"I'm Miss Mellanby, steward of Aylesbury. The SOE has asked me to make special arrangements for your detention, and, consequently, you will be staying in the D-wing with three other women, who've also been detained under the Aliens Order."

"Do I not get a private room?"

Miss Mellanby gave her a tight smile. "Under the circumstances, I'm sure you will find little fault with the accommodations that have been bestowed upon you by our benevolent government." She reached into her desk and took out a long key.

The two detectives trailed behind Mathilde and Miss Mellanby as she led them down the main alleyway of the prison. Some women in baggy striped uniforms gave them despondent looks as they passed by. Mathilde noted that most of them were younger than herself.

"Here we are." Miss Mellanby opened a heavy steel door to reveal a large space containing a long wooden table, a tiled shower and sink, and a forlorn-looking refrigerator. Four beds lined the walls, each with a nightstand and metal chair. There was a small nook in one corner, which, Mathilde guessed, housed the toilet.

"Thank you, gentlemen." Miss Mellanby asked them to wait in her office as she pulled the heavy door shut. She moved to the middle of the room, gesturing for Mathilde to follow her. "Ladies, I'd like to meet your new companion," Miss Mellanby called.

The other women, all dressed in plain-clothes of varying styles and degrees of extravagance, walked over. The woman who introduced herself as "The Duchess de Château Thierry" wore a floral dress and pearls while May Erikson, a dark-haired woman clearly of Jewish descent, sported unkempt trousers and a wrinkled shirt.

"I'm Stella Lonsdale," the youngest of them stated. She was wearing a faded striped dress. "What's your name?" She took a step closer and peered into Mathilde's eyes. "You look like a cat. Are you French?"

Mathilde nodded.

"Then we'll call you 'Mitou.' It means 'Queen Cat,'" Stella told the others.

"What is she the queen of?" the Duchess asked, eyeing Mathilde's black pajamas with disapproval.

"We're all here because of expected collusion with the Germans," Stella told Mathilde. "Are you a spy?"

"For the Allies," she replied. "I helped found one of the first Resistance networks."

"If that's true, then why are you in an English prison?" the Duchess demanded.

Mathilde, who had no answer, set her bag down on the empty bed and began to unpack.

Miss Mellanby cleared her throat. "I will be taking my leave of you ladies now. Miss Kate will be here at the usual time with dinner." She turned to Mathilde. "Now, who will be providing your monthly allowance?"

"Allowance? Am I not in prison? I would think it is up to the British government to pay for my meals and lodging."

"Indeed," May stated. "But seeing as you are a political detainee, you should be afforded some additional cash for incidentals. The Swedish consulate takes care of my meager fees."

"And mine are paid by my ex-husbands," the Duchess declared. "As you can see, it allows me to afford new clothes, linens, and extra food, among other things."

"Yes," Stella added. "While the meals here are not horribly distasteful, they don't feed us nearly enough. You can make arrangements with one of the guards on what you want purchased from town." She pointed to the fridge. "But make sure you keep your hands off other people's stuff."

Mathilde didn't miss the glance exchanged between May and the Duchess and imagined that very scenario had recently caused strife among her fellow prisoners. But who would be willing to send cash in her name? Not her ex-husband, not Armand, and certainly not Bleicher.

"I'll see if I can negotiate with your escorts," Miss Mellanby told Mathilde. "We can probably work a payment out via the SOE."

Mathilde's eyes widened. Perhaps prison life wouldn't be so bad after all. "Please do."

CHAPTER 60

ODETTE

Odette floated in and out of consciousness for the next few days, her destroyed feet bound in a shredded bedsheet.

Just as she was once again beginning to feel human, she was summoned again. "Tribunal!" the woman in gray shouted.

Odette limped behind the guard, forcing a single phrase to occupy her thoughts. *I have nothing to say, I have nothing to say.*

This time when they reached 84 Avenue Foch, she was taken to a new room and offered a chair. With a sense of dread, she wondered what they could possibly do to her now, though she did not have to wait long for the perfumed man to enter the room. "What do you know of Peter Churchill?"

Her customary answer on her lips, Odette realized this was her chance to convince him that Peter was completely innocent of any wrongdoing. "He's my husband," she replied instead. "I was a Frenchwoman, and angry about the Occupation. I was the one who told him to take up with the Resistance, but he didn't do much for them before he was arrested."

"No, I don't suppose he could have, seeing he's the most asinine imbecile I've ever had the chance to query."

Odette wanted to shout back that the interrogator was lucky to even have been in the same room with someone as irreproachable as Peter, but she bit her lip, knowing this was just another game. "Yes, I realize my husband is no prodigy. I had to tell him what to do, both in life and in espionage."

"Did you plot against Germany for money?"

"No," she replied honestly.

"A shame." He scribbled something on the pad of paper in front of him. "You will probably be killed without question, but your husband might live."

She couldn't help smiling. "Why do you say that?"

He shrugged. "He's an English officer, and a Churchill at that. He'll most likely be exchanged."

She breathed a sigh of relief. Peter would survive the war, and, despite what the interrogator said, maybe she would too. *But what then?*

The interrogator left Odette alone with her thoughts for at least an hour before the door banged open again. Four uniformed officers filed into the room followed by an older man in civilian clothes, whom she decided must be a senior member of the Gestapo. He addressed Odette in rapid German as the other men nodded in unison, as if they were puppets being controlled by the same master.

The civilian finished his tirade, looking at Odette expectantly.

She shook her head. "I do not understand German."

He looked put out for a moment. One of the officers stepped forward and seemed to ask permission of the Gestapo man, who handed him a piece of paper. The officer turned to her, speaking French in a thick accent. "Madame Churchill, you have been sentenced to death on two accounts—for being both a French spy and a British operative."

"Well which is it?" Odette demanded. "As you know, I can only die once."

The man cleared his throat and reread the sentence to himself, his eyebrows furrowing in confusion. "Both," he replied finally. "You are condemned once for France, and once for England."

I guess I shall never know for which country I will give my life. Odette tried to cheer up by telling herself that for every tragedy, there is an element of comedy.

When she was brought back to Cell 108, she noticed a new symbol on her door—a little red cross. Upon spying it, the SS guard asked curiously, "*Avez-vous été condamné à mort?*"

She nodded. *"Condamné à mort."*

She repeated the phrase in her head as she lay back in bed. *I've been condemned to death.* But the words had no effect on her. She, Odette Sansom, who had delivered a few messages to other members of the Resistance, had made herself as useful as she could to men like Peter Churchill and Alec Rabinovitch. Her lips turned up into a smile as she thought of the brawny Russian Alec who still roamed free, wreaking havoc on the Nazis. Perhaps he had helped with the RAF raid on the perfumed man's precious Dortmund. It was as it should be, and she would gladly take on a thousand death sentences if it meant Alec could still do his job.

Or that Peter would be safe. She buried her face in her arm—just the thought of Peter made her want to weep for days. *But then again...* She sat up, thinking about the conversation with the perfumed man that morning. Maybe, just maybe, she did manage to save him by taking on the double death sentence.

For the first time since she'd been arrested, she slept soundly that night, dreaming of a thousand little red crosses decorating her cell door.

CHAPTER 61

DIDI

*M*iss Atkins came to the airfield to see Didi off.

"If my sister returns, will you let her know where I am?" Didi couldn't help but feel a little pride when she pictured the astonishment on Jackie's face once she learned Didi had finally been sent to France.

Miss Atkins' lips pursed. "I don't imagine Jacqueline would be pleased to hear of your mission, though she knows as much as anyone how desperate we are for wireless operators in the field." She straightened the collar of Didi's jacket. "Good luck, Miss Nearne."

The Lysander could only fit two people comfortably, and, with Didi, Jean Savy, their luggage, and items meant for the Resistance —guns, ammunition, and medical supplies—it was a tight squeeze. She gripped the handle of the bag at her feet so hard during lift-off that her knuckles turned white.

Her unease finally diminished when she saw the reception committee's red lights flashing the right code in Morse. The touch-down was only moderately bumpy, but Didi still felt her stomach lurch as the plane came to a stop.

When she disembarked, she was greeted by two shadowy figures. For a moment she was terrified they were Germans, but then one of them told her to hurry in a heavy French accent. With that, she felt the rest of her panic disappear.

Savy appeared beside her and grabbed her hand with his good arm. "We'd better get going."

"Jean Savy," another French accent declared.

Savy turned. "Henry." He let go of Didi to shake the other man's hand. "On your way back to England?"

"Indeed." Henry nodded at his companion, who tipped his hat at Savy before entering the Lysander.

"This is Jacqueline du Tetre," Savy said. "She's going to be Wizard's wireless operator."

Henry peered at her. "Aren't you a little young for this? You know that Nazis have no discrimination for age: they kill young and old alike." He gestured to the Lysander. "We can still bring you back to London and tell Buckmaster, if he insists on recruiting females, at least they should be women and not girls."

Didi raised her chin. "Buckmaster's orders are to follow Savy to Paris. And I always obey orders."

"And this 'girl' is one of the best wireless operators Buckmaster's got." Savy gave Henry a mock salute. "Safe flight."

When the men had boarded, Savy shot Didi a wry grin. "Sorry about their rudeness."

"It's okay—I've gotten used to it by now."

Savy once again took Didi's arm and led her further into the woods, where their reception committee awaited. They showed them to a barn, stating this would be their hideout until morning.

After longing to work for the Resistance for so long, a restless night in a barn was not quite what Didi had pictured. She spent most of the time lying on a dirt floor staring up the spider-filled eaves, scratching at the hay which poked at her entire body, and trying to forget that she was freezing.

In the morning, Savy said his goodbyes before going off to locate the missing France Antelme.

One of the men of the reception committee informed Didi that he would take her to a safe house in Orléans. Didi felt a twinge of regret as they left the sight of the barn, for as horrid as the previous night had been, at least she'd felt a modicum of safety. Now they were going out into the open, to see firsthand how well her training had prepared her to be amongst the enemy.

The sun was just rising as they made their way to the train station and, to Didi's relief, they encountered few people along the way. The station master merely glanced at Didi's papers before waving her aboard the train.

As soon as they reached Orléans, however, Didi felt a mounting sense of terror. German soldiers were everywhere, stalking the streets in their grayish-green uniforms.

"For God's sake, don't stare at them like that," her companion hissed.

Didi felt her face grow red and glanced down at the sidewalk, willing her looming tears to dissipate. *How could I have been so stupid?* She not only had to reinvent herself as Jacqueline du Tetre—she also had to act as though she were used to the presence of the German Army.

Her companion led her into the station and set her bag down. "This is where I leave you."

"Thank you," Didi said, hoisting the bag.

The young man turned to depart, but then hesitated. "Will you be all right? It's not an easy job, you know. Especially—"

"I'll be fine," she snapped. She was tired of people underestimating her. Jackie might be off gallivanting around France as a master spy, but Didi was still being treated as the inferior little sister, a child to watch over or dismiss.

When the train arrived in Paris, Didi immediately set off to find her contact. Buckmaster had told her it would be a woman named Louise.

It was snowing heavily. Luckily Didi was quite familiar with the Left Bank of Paris, for she could barely see anything, not even the towering spires of the Notre Dame Cathedral. She could still see the gargoyles on top of the cathedral in her mind's eye, their faces taking on those of the Boches she had seen on the train.

She'd been told Louise would be waiting for her on the bridge. As Didi arrived, she could see a small woman around her own age standing just to the left of the statute of Henry IV.

"Jackie!" the woman shouted.

Didi's first instinct was to tell the woman she had the wrong sister, but then she remembered her codename. The two women hugged each other as if they were old friends.

"I'm so excited you've come to visit me." Louise tucked her hand into the crook of Didi's elbow. "It's about time you came to visit fair Paris."

"Yes," Didi's voice was hoarse. "I am glad too."

Louise chatted amiably about nonsense all the way back to her apartment in the Place Saint-Michel. Didi, guessing that the act was for the benefit of any Germans in the vicinity, tried to chime in whenever Louise paused for a breath of air. Though the white-out also blinded them to the despised German soldiers she imagined were everywhere, Didi had to refrain from glancing over her shoulder every now and then.

Once they were safely behind closed doors, Louise's expression turned serious, but she did not slow her speech. Now the gossip had turned to instructions. "You will need to find a new accommodation as soon as possible. You can have your messages delivered here, but you cannot yourself stay for long. It's too dangerous to my family. I live with my mother and sisters, and they don't know I've joined the Resistance."

"I'll look for a room in the morning."

"And a place to transmit from?"

Didi, impressed with Louise's knowledge, nodded.

"I can help you," her new friend told her.

Didi suddenly felt exhausted. "Thank you."

"Come on." Louise once again linked her arm through Didi's. "Let's get you a nice warm bed."

"That would be so wonderful." Didi told her about her dreadful sleep the night before as Louise gathered pillows and blankets.

She led Didi down a small hallway. "You can sleep in my brother's room."

"Is he…"

"Dead." Louise started to make the bed. "And now you know why I've joined the Resistance." She handed Didi another blanket. "It's not the most comfortable bed in the world, but it should be loads better than a dirt floor in a barn."

"Oh, I'm sure it will be."

"Good night, and…" Louise paused at the bedroom door. "Thank you for what you are doing for the Allies."

"Thank you," Didi said again, feeling the words were a bit inadequate for the amount of gratitude she felt.

Louise departed, leaving Didi in admiration of someone who, despite being what some might consider "too young," was clearly confident in her own abilities.

Didi fell into a blissful sleep, pleased that, though she couldn't stay there permanently, at least she had a roof over her head and a friend to help her in her new mission.

CHAPTER 62

ODETTE

One rainy afternoon, Odette was drawn to her cell window by a commotion outside. A middle-aged man, British by the look of his trousers, was being marched around the yard. As she watched, the man's bare feet slid in the mud and a guard barked an order. He righted himself and continued. Round and round he paced, and if he slowed even by a hair, the eagle-eyed guard would raise his rifle before once again shouting at him. Odette's stomach turned at the way he was being treated—like a caged beast—and she walked away from the window, only to be drawn back by the diversion.

She watched him for hours. Johnny, as Odette now referred to him, kept his pace as best he could, through what she imagined was stinging, freezing rain. As though monitoring Johnny was an arduous task, his guards were changed every hour, and, a few minutes after the fourth change, Johnny fell to his knees.

Have courage, Odette thought, and then decided to shout it through the window. Someone else took up the cry, and another voice started to sing "God Save the King." Odette faintly heard Michelle join in by humming the melody and figured she must not have known the words.

Johnny picked himself up and waved toward the windows of the women's wing before starting his relentless march again, his back straight and what almost looked like a smile on his face. Though she knew he couldn't see it, Odette waved back, thinking she was proud to be in the same prison as a man like that.

She heard the key in her cell door and jumped down from her perch, fearful that she had been caught. But it was not an SS guard who stood in the doorway. "May I come in?" Bleicher asked.

She pushed the chair toward him, but he walked the length of her cell instead, looking almost embarrassed. At long last he sat down and offered her a cigarette.

She accepted it. "Thank you."

Bleicher lit his and inhaled, the smoke leaving his mouth as he stated, "You've been to the Gestapo."

She nodded.

"I heard what they did to you." He glanced at her bound feet. "And I'm very sorry. You have to believe me that there was nothing I could do."

"I know."

"Is there anything I can do now?"

She sat down on her bed. "Have you seen Peter lately?"

"No, but I was going to see him this afternoon when I leave you."

"Then there is something you can do." She pulled a blanket over her legs. "You can keep silent about this. I'm sure you know that after we were arrested in Annecy, he tried to escape from our Italian prison."

"I heard that he was badly beaten."

"Yes. And I don't want that to happen again. If he caught wind what the Gestapo… what they did to me, he'd probably do something even more foolish. So please don't say anything about my feet… or about my being sentenced to death."

He put his hand over his heart. "I won't say a word." He dropped his arm. "Lise, do you ever think of yourself as much as you do others?"

"I've had far too much time of late to think about me. I'm becoming a very selfish woman."

He blinked hard behind his glasses. "I hate to see you here, Lise, among these people."

"These people are no more contemptible than ones you might meet on the street." She gave a wry smile. "Especially here in Occupied Paris. Being in prison doesn't really change people. All it serves to do is make a strong person stronger and a weak person weaker. If you look out the window, you will see one of the bravest Englishmen I've ever laid eyes on. Besides Peter, of course."

Bleicher went to the window. After a moment he turned away to wipe his foggy spectacles with a handkerchief. "To use your favorite expression, Lise, I have nothing to say."

"Give my love to Peter Churchill, but not a word about anything else."

He nodded and started for the door before turning back to her. "Lise, do you mind if I come see you again sometime?"

She raised her eyebrows. "Isn't it rather awkward for a member of the all-powerful Abwehr to ask a condemned prisoner for permission to pay them a call?"

"I don't think it's awkward at all."

"All right, then. I will see you soon. *Au revoir,* Hugo."

"*Adieu,* Lise."

CHAPTER 63

DIDI

*W*ith Louise's aid, Didi rented a room in northwest Paris near a Metro station. Finding a place to transmit was a different matter, however. It needed to be private enough, but not somewhere it could attract the Germans' suspicion since she would have to visit it on a regular basis.

Louise managed to locate an abandoned house in the suburbs belonging to a couple by the name of Dubois who had fled the city. The neighbor who'd been tasked with looking after it agreed to let Didi make her transmissions from the attic.

Didi's next obstacle was to deliver the transmitting assemblage to the Dubois house. The transmitter, receiver, sixty meters of wire, extra batteries, a Morse Key, frequency crystals carefully packed in a Bakelite container, and various other necessities were all stored in an attaché case. Carrying the ten-kilogram case all the way to the suburbs would be a rather arduous task, and any German on the street could ask to search her. Taking the Metro was another possibility, but she could once again be subjected to an inquiry and escaping the train would not be easy. Didi knew from her training that the invaders had grown much more hostile after four years of occupation, and stories abounded of German soldiers assaulting French citizens for the slightest provocation.

After careful consideration, Didi decided on the Metro. She'd taken the train to Paris without incident, so it seemed like the safest way to transport the wireless set.

Didi set out for the Dubois house in Bourg-la-Reine the next morning. As she made her way to the station, she knew she'd made the right choice—there was no way she could have lugged the heavy case much farther. When the train arrived, she managed to find an empty car and settled into a seat gratefully.

At the next stop, several German soldiers boarded her car. Two of them sat in the seat in front of her and the others across from them. Didi refused to acknowledge them and stared out the window instead.

"Bonjour, mademoiselle."

Didi turned to see one of the soldiers leering at her from across the aisle. She nodded at him before turning back to the window.

"What's in the case?" the soldier in front of her asked in halting French. The confusion must have been obvious in her face as he gestured toward the wireless set.

"It's just a gramophone." She crossed her fingers beneath her skirt. *Please don't ask to see it.*

Thankfully he didn't and Didi moved toward the window again but then the German across the aisle reached over to offer her a cigarette.

"I don't smoke," Didi replied in a glacial tone hoping to discourage him enough that he left her alone.

But when his eyes fell to her nicotine-stained hands, his friendly smile turned into a sneer and she instantly regretted her snub. He said something in German that Didi couldn't catch. All four of them were now staring at her.

Her mind told her to run, but she stayed put as the train made another stop. She returned her gaze to the window, watching the people at the station coming and going—as free as anyone could be in a country occupied by the enemy—while she sat trapped in a train car with the very same enemy soldiers, a case full of contraband that would spell her condemnation should any of them ask to open it by her side.

Through the reflection in the window, Didi could see that the German in front was gazing at her. She felt her face grow hot. When the train slowed again, she picked up the case, suppressing a grunt at its considerable weight. Pretending that this was her stop, she made her way down the aisle as nonchalantly as she could, half-expecting to hear one of the soldiers commanding her to halt.

Her heart hammering, she stepped onto the platform. She turned as the train started again, relieved to see the Germans still seated in the car, gaping at her as it pulled away.

She checked the Metro sign and found she was more than two kilometers away from the Dubois house. Her legs still shaking from the close call, she began slowly heading toward Bourg-la-Reine.

Didi let herself into the abandoned house, dreading that there would be more German soldiers waiting to trap her. "Hello?" she called out tentatively. When no one answered, she decided to explore the house.

The best place to transmit would be from the attic, and consequently, after much effort, she hauled her case up two flights of stairs.

In the attic, more trepidation set in: what if the transmitter was damaged? What if there was too much interference and she couldn't get through to London?

With trembling hands, Didi began to set up the wireless. Once she'd fastened the aerial antenna under the eaves of the roof, she inserted the sugarcube-sized crystal into the transmitter and tuned in to the predetermined frequency. After fiddling with the dial, she was relieved to hear a clear signal. She transmitted an update to the SOE: "Met my contact as directed. Waiting for Savy to return." She then disassembled everything and hid the set underneath a bunch of old blankets.

This time, thankfully unburdened by the case, she picked a rather packed train car, hoping there would be no more surprises.

She got off at the stop near Louise's apartment. Louise's family had a radio even though Hitler had made it illegal. If the Germans caught them listening to the BBC, they would be arrested. But Didi hoped the SOE would send a message through the *messages personnels* to let her know they'd received her transmission. Indeed, right before the end of the broadcast, the announcer stated that he was, "happy to know that the duck had a good trip."

Louise turned to Didi, her eyes wide. "They mean you, don't they? Are you the duck?"

Didi nodded, feeling a wave of satisfaction wash over her. She had officially established contact with the SOE, and now she was ready to work. All she needed was to reunite with Jean Savy and they could begin their task of changing the course of the war.

CHAPTER 64

ODETTE

"Céline!" It was unusually early for Michelle to be calling. Still half-asleep, Odette pulled the chair over to the grate. "Yes, Michelle?"

"Céline, I've been released!"

"Oh, Michelle, I will miss you!"

"And I you, Céline." Her voice softened to a barely audible level. "Is there anything I can do for you before I leave?"

Odette thought quickly. She recalled a Parisian address from Buck's briefing before she left for France, which she repeated to Michelle. "Can you tell them you have spoken to the woman named Lise and that she and Peter are in Fresnes?"

"Yes, of course. Anything for you, Céline—or should I say Lise? At any rate, good luck to you, and to this Peter as well."

"And to you," Odette replied sadly. She had never laid eyes on Michelle, and now she never would, but she had been the best friend she'd had these past few months. She smiled to herself as she stepped down from her chair, picturing the look on Miss Atkins' face when she at last got news of Odette.

. . .

Bleicher seemed ill at ease when he came into her cell that afternoon. "They are clearing out Fresnes to make room for more Allied prisoners. I would hate to see you be sent to Germany."

"What do you mean? Do you think they are planning to move me?"

"I haven't heard, but one is helpless against the wishes of the Gestapo."

"Maybe they'll release me like they did Michelle."

"Who?"

She pointed to the floor. "Another prisoner."

He let out a heavy sigh. "No, I doubt they will release you or any of the other SOE women who are housed here."

Odette's mouth dropped open. "There are more?"

"Yes, many men and women: the Gestapo has been busy busting up Resistance networks." He began pacing up and down her cell. "I'm going to fetch you tomorrow and take you to Paris. You can have a shower, dress in nice clothes, and I will take you to lunch."

She shook her head. "You asked me that before, when I first arrived here. I told you then that I could not compromise."

He stopped walking. "And now?" he asked hopefully.

"My answer is the same. The time I've spent behind these walls has only made me more determined. Thank you for asking, but I prefer to stay here."

"Is that final, Lise?"

"Yes."

He stared at her for a few moments before putting his hand out. She looked down at her feet instead of accepting it. He frowned as he thrust both hands into his pockets. "Then this will be my last visit. I shall not come to see you again."

"As you wish, Hugo."

"Goodbye then, Lise." He opened the door before hesitating. "And may I say, you are one of the bravest women I've ever had the pleasure to meet."

She flexed a nailless toe. "Let's hope I can stay that brave."

"You will." He gave her a sad little wave before he left.

CHAPTER 65

DIDI

A few days after Didi arrived in France, Louise told her that Savy was back in Paris and waiting to touch base with her in a flat belonging to a Resistance sympathizer.

After greeting Didi, Savy told her that France Antelme had been captured.

"What?" Didi sat in an armchair. "How?"

Savy remained standing. "Upon arrival. Antelme, his wireless operator, and their courier, a woman codenamed Martine, are all missing. They were supposed to land near Poitiers, but somehow they were dropped off in Sainville. Their reception committee must have been Germans because no one's heard from them since that night."

They'd been scheduled to arrive only two days before Savy and Didi herself. "What should we do?"

"I don't know," Savy answered. "But my best prediction is that the whole Prosper circuit has been compromised, and for our safety, I should find new contacts."

She nodded.

Savy had been tasked with preparing for the much-anticipated Allied invasion of France. While the actual date was top-secret, most people, including the Germans, assumed it was coming soon. Savy spent his days training new Resistance recruits and securing funding from trust-worthy Parisians.

The would-be Resistance financiers were often nervous that their loans would not be backed by English banks. Savy would then ask them to name a word or phrase which Didi would dutifully send back to the SOE. A day or two later, the BBC would repeat the phrase in their *messages personnels*, convincing the nationals to finance the loan. It was also Didi's job to pass on Savy's communications to London and arrange for more Resistance supplies to be dropped into fields near Paris.

Her daily itinerary was dictated by the cadence of her skeds. The maximum time Didi could transmit was twenty minutes—any longer would run the risk of the Gestapo vans locating her signal.

It was taxing work, but every time Didi put her hands on the dials of her wireless, any weariness was replaced by feelings of power and patriotism. Gone were the pangs of helplessness that had plagued her since the beginning of the Occupation, when her family was forced to move from Paris to the countryside. The Germans might still be over-running France, but for once there was something she could do about it.

When she wasn't with Savy or listening to the BBC broadcasts in Louise's flat, she was completely alone. She'd often pass by warm-looking cafés, and dream of a steaming cup of coffee coupled with casual conversation, but she knew the only patrons in such indulgent places were the Boches. Besides, she'd become used to the solitary life of a spy: a life spent in shadows, always looking over her shoulder. She wondered if Jackie lived a similar life, if her sister indeed were still alive. The Germans were getting increasingly paranoid and every day Savy told her of more Resistance contacts who had been arrested.

One day, while meeting Savy once again in the safehouse, he informed her he'd discovered something that could only be relayed to Buck-master in person.

"What is it?" Didi inquired.

He looked around the empty apartment. "I saw V-2 rockets in an ammunition dump located about 60 kilometers northeast of Paris."

"Are they aimed at England?"

"I'm afraid so."

"I'll arrange for a Lysander pick-up right away." Her sked time wasn't for another couple of hours, but Didi left for Bourg-la-Reine anyway, hoping a capable FANY would be scanning the transmissions.

Didi was too occupied with the possibility of London's demise to worry much about her own safety, though she found herself pretending to gaze into a shop window when a German passed her on the street, to make sure she wasn't being followed.

CHAPTER 66

MATHILDE

*M*athilde's life in the D wing of Aylesbury Prison fell into a routine. As Stella had declared, the food wasn't overly terrible, and a guard delivered fresh fruit a few days a week, courtesy of the allowance provided to Mathilde by the SOE.

Stella was by far Mathilde's favorite of the other prisoners. The younger woman could sometimes be a bit too raunchy for Mathilde's taste—that first night after lights-out, Stella had spoken in depth of the difference in lovemaking between Englishmen and the French—but she made a better companion than the other two, who were much older and inclined to be stand-offish. It was clear the Duchess and May had known each other before, and Mathilde gradually worked out that May had been one of the domestic servants at Château Thierry, as she often stood over the Duchess's shoulder, waiting for instructions.

"May spied for both Russia and Germany," Stella confided to Mathilde one day as they walked in the prison garden.

"Wasn't she aware they are on opposite sides of the war?" Mathilde replied.

Stella shrugged. "She claims it was not out of allegiance for either country, but because her lover asked her too. He was shot by the Germans and then May was arrested."

Mathilde felt a twinge of sympathy toward May's plight. "I know what it is like to go against your morals because of a man."

"Is that why you are here?"

Mathilde nodded. "One man in particular." She was thinking of Bleicher, but then it wasn't really Bleicher's fault that she agreed to go along with his ploy. *No*, she realized. *It was a misplaced sense of anger toward Armand.* Mathilde put her hand over her mouth as it occurred to her that she had almost single-handedly destroyed Interallié—and possibly sacrificed her friends' lives—because she was upset at Armand for choosing Viola over her. "Oh," she said aloud. Her legs felt unsteady and she stumbled over to a garden bench.

Stella joined her. "Are you alright?" When Mathilde didn't reply, she carried on, "They say you are a double-agent for Germany. Is that true?"

Mathilde shook her head. "I think maybe I was only ever looking out for one entity: myself."

"I wish I'd thought of that. When they interrogated me for possibly being a German agent—I returned to England from there in 1941—I suppose I was a bit too lewd for them. Maybe had I reigned it in, they'd have let me go."

Mathilde couldn't help giving her an amused smile. "You, lewd?"

Stella shrugged. "I never played for the other side, but they weren't sure what to do with a woman like me, so here I am."

"Here we both are: imprisoned because of the whims of men."

"You have to admit, Aylesbury is not such a horrible place." Stella shuddered. "You should hear the stories about what they do to 'undesirables' like us in Germany. They put them in concentration camps. Most of them don't last long, and if they do then they're tortured and starved, and made to do slave work."

Mathilde felt her chin quiver as she thought of René Aubertin. *Was that his fate now, thanks to her?* "You're right: Aylesbury is not bad at all."

"Still, you have to watch out for May," Stella continued. "She tells the guards everything that goes on in the D-wing, so if there's something you don't want people to know, keep your mouth shut around her."

Mathilde acknowledged the warning with a nod.

CHAPTER 67

DIDI

*T*he Allies landed on the beaches of Normandy on June 6, 1944. After that it seemed everyone in France wanted to join the Resistance, to prevent Hitler from providing reinforcements for his massive army. Countless men were recruited to bomb roads, armaments, bridges, and railroad tunnels. In retaliation, Germany's determination to destroy the Resistance mounted.

Since Didi's boss, Jean Savy, was still in England, he missed witnessing the results of his hard work, though Didi received word that the rocket depot he'd discovered had become one of the RAF's latest targets.

With Savy gone, Didi didn't have much to do, and she chafed for more assignments. Finally an SOE transmission came through, instructing her to contact a man named Dumont-Guillemet, head of the Spiritualist network. Thankfully this circuit operated in the Seine-et-Marne, just east of Paris, which meant she wouldn't have to relocate her equipment.

Whereas Savy had been reserved and cautious, Dumont-Guillemet was buoyant and brash. The mission he had been given by the SOE was to reunite the Prosper and Farmer circuits, which had been splintered by the arrests of their leaders and many of their agents.

However, Didi quickly discovered that the head of Spiritualist had several unofficial projects in mind. The first was to find the where-abouts of his friend and fellow SOE agent, Sidney Jones. When that trail went cold, Dumont-Guillemet made contact with a group plan-ning an attack on Fresnes Prison, where many of the captured SOE operatives were housed.

Didi, wondering if Jackie were among the prisoners, dutifully relayed Dumont-Guillemet's message to London. Buckmaster was not enthused, but Dumont-Guillemet was ready to go through with the scheme until he found out the lead architect of the Fresnes coup had been jailed in the very prison he'd targeted.

Dumont-Guillemet next set his sights on kidnapping two German rocket scientists, who had probably helped develop the V-2s Savy had seen. This time Buckmaster sent a message back stating, *There's no way in hell I'm agreeing to that STOP.*

Even with all these extra plans, in the month after D-Day, the members of the Spiritualist network were able to inundate the SOE (and Didi, for that matter) with information on troop movements and locations of German trains transporting soldiers to the frontlines, making for still more RAF targets.

Though Didi knew that, following the successful Allied landing, the liberation of Paris might only be weeks away, she became exhausted from working non-stop. Dumont-Guillemet was not immune to Didi's plight and brought in another wireless operator, whom he introduced as 'Maury.'

They met in Savy's old safehouse. Maury was a short man with coke-bottle glasses, but he seemed nice enough. "Maybe now that I'm here, you can have a day off," he told Didi.

"Thank you, but I don't take days off," Didi replied.

Dumont-Guillemet raised his hand. "While I appreciate your dedi-cation, you both should be aware that all of the increased shelling we've done on German communication and transportation lines means the Boches are getting angry. They'll only increase their efforts to pene-trate our Resistance networks."

"Yes, sir," Maury replied.

Dumont-Guillemet turned to Didi. "How long have you been transmitting from the house in Bourg-la-Reine?"

"About four months, sir."

"Four months?" Maury asked. "You've been using the same safehouse for three months and two weeks longer than we were instructed during training."

Didi shrugged. "No one knows I'm there and I get an excellent signal."

"You might want to think about moving sooner rather than later," Dumont-Guillemet told her. "The Gestapo vans are everywhere now, searching for our signals."

As if Dumont-Guillemet and Maury had predicted it, that very evening, Didi thought she detected interference on her transmission, as though someone were listening in. She told herself not to be silly, that it was just nerves, but she cut her transmission short anyway, using her call sign to let London know everything was okay.

Less than a minute after she'd ended, she heard a police siren. She hid in the attic under the blankets, fearing that a host of German soldiers would burst in at any moment and arrest her. She managed to make it home just before curfew, promising herself that she would find a different location to transmit in the morning.

CHAPTER 68

ODETTE

*T*he next time Odette was taken to 84 Avenue Foch she sensed
something was different. Indeed she was shoved into an unfamiliar room, where she discovered several other women were waiting.

A beautiful, dark-haired woman approached Odette. "I'm Denise. I
worked for the Prosper network."

Odette numbly shook her hand. "You're with the FANY?"

Denise winked. "Yes. And this is Simone, courier with Inventor, and
Yolande, the radio operator for Musician." One by one, Denise introduced the F Section women by their code-names and circuits. Though
Denise looked as prison-weary as Odette felt, some of the other girls
were fresh-faced, and obviously new arrivals to Fresnes.

"I'm Lise," Odette said. "With Spindle."

"When did you train?" Denise asked.

When Odette told her, she nodded. "I thought so. You must know
Adele."

Odette recalled the undeniably brave, blue-eyed woman. "I did."

All told, there were seven other F Section women in the room, each
with a different story leading to their arrest. The woman named
Martine had parachuted right into German hands.

"How do they know so much?" Odette asked.

"I think there is at least one mole in the SOE," Denise replied
matter-of-factly.

She seemed about to say more, but the door burst open and the commandant entered. "You will be leaving for Germany in a few hours. Are there any requests? Keep in mind this might be your last."

"Yes," Odette said without thinking. "We could all use some tea. And," her eyes traveled over the other F Section women, "be sure to make it in the English way, with milk and sugar."

The commandant's eyes narrowed and he left the room without further comment. But a few minutes later an aide entered the room carrying a tray with a tea pot and eight china cups.

The women drank their tea, chatting animatedly about their Resistance adventures and the Allied landing in Normandy.

Yolande had a tube of lipstick with her, and all the girls passed it around: to Odette it was bliss to feel like a woman again. She'd been in solitary for so long with only Michelle to talk to, and here were women just like her: Buck's recruits, trained by the SOE while being looked after by Miss Atkins. They'd been dispatched to France as part of the Resistance, and, just like her, were arrested because of it. Odette wasn't sure where they would be going—maybe to another prison or sent off to their deaths—but she hoped that wherever it was, they could remain together.

"Have any of you been condemned to death?" Odette asked.

They all replied in the negative. "Have you?" Yolande asked.

"Yes." Odette's lipsticked lips stretched into a smile. "Twice, in fact."

When the door burst open again, the commandant had more instructions. "You will be handcuffed in pairs. If any of you attempt to escape, you will be shot immediately."

"Where would we go?" Odette asked. The whole scene was becoming outrageous: there were at least ten armed guards for eight defenseless women.

"I don't know," he replied, "but my superiors aren't taking any chances."

Odette was handcuffed to Yolande, a fresh-faced, curly-haired woman in her early 30s, who shot an ironic smile at her.

As they were led downstairs, Martine started singing *Le Chant Des Partisans*, the unofficial Resistance song, until one of the guards told her to shut up.

There were several black vans waiting outside, their engines running. Odette shielded her eyes against the sun to take one last look at 84 Avenue Foch. Her perfumed interrogator had come out onto one of the balconies to watch the spectacle.

Odette raised her unbound wrist to wave at him. "Good-bye!" she called. Even from the ground she could sense the ferocity of his glare. He stepped back inside, but she saw him continue to observe from the shadow of a curtain.

The Germans had reserved two second class train compartments. Yolande and Odette were seated across from Denise and Simone. An SS woman sat behind the latter two and a male guard was placed near the door of their cabin.

Odette scooted closer to the window as they entered the countryside, and stared out at the ubiquitous debris and burn scars.

The male guard walked over to stand in front of her. "That's the work of your RAF. They've also destroyed my mother's house in Dortmund."

Odette sat back in her seat with a satisfied air.

His already narrowed eyes became slits. "I only wish that they dared to bomb the train now. It would give me great pleasure to crush your skull underneath my boot and save the German hangman a job."

"It is your duty," Odette spat out, "to deliver us to Germany. If an accident were to indeed happen, your first care should be to the safety of your prisoners."

"I would never sacrifice my own well-being for swine like you."

Odette shrugged. "You are definitely not the brains of your outfit, but as a German, aren't you supposed to be efficient?" She held up her now unshackled wrist, which she had been working to free since they left the station.

The guard turned on his heel and left the cabin.

Yolande gave her an admiring look. "How clever of you, Lise," she whispered as the guard returned, brandishing a key. He pushed Odette forward and then snapped the handcuff on her so tight that she could feel it cutting into her skin. *It had been worth it.* Any little thing Odette could do to cut down the pompous Boches gave her a feeling of accomplishment.

. . .

As dusk fell, Yolande whispered that Odette could lay her head on her shoulder. Odette tried shutting her eyes, but her wrist hurt and she couldn't get comfortable enough to sleep more than a few minutes at a time.

As dawn was beginning to break, Yolande shifted in her seat and Odette leaned against the window to give her more room. She watched the gray mist fade, thinking that the same sun was rising over Somerset. She pictured her daughters playing in the sunshine. She realized it would be Francoise's birthday in a few days and hoped Miss Atkins would be able to send her daughter one of the cards she'd written.

The train glided over a shining river, and the SS guard announced that they were crossing the mighty German Rhine and would be entering the Fatherland.

"It's not the German Rhine," Yolande declared. "I know Hitler thinks he can possess everything, but even he can't own a river."

Odette tightened her free hand into a fist. They had just left the comfort of France and now were in the monstrous Hitler's domain. "What is our destination?" she asked the SS guard.

"Karlsruhe," he replied. "As you can imagine, I'm pleased they've decided to kill you in Germany and not France. I received a 48-hour leave to accompany you, and I get to see *meine liebste Mutti*."

She gave him an insincere smile. "How glad I am to sacrifice myself so you can see your mother. Even the devil has family, I suppose."

When the train arrived in Karlsruhe, Odette and the other F Section women were unloaded and escorted, once again by armed guards, to a nearby office.

"Can you please unlock these so we can use the restroom?" Odette asked, lifting her bound wrist.

"No." The guard's brusque tone left no room for argument.

Yolande shrugged at Odette. "Nice try."

Two by two, the women were led out into awaiting taxis and then were driven to the Karlsruhe Criminal Prison. They were finally released from their handcuffs to use the dirty bathroom before being strip-searched and inspected for lice. When the endless check-in process had finished, the women were taken to separate cells, situated as far away as possible to cut off all contact.

. . .

Odette was immensely disheartened to be alone once again, though she and the other F Section women were permitted to walk solo in the yard once a day. Odette would watch her comrades from her window, calling and waving. "Hullo, Yolande, how are you? Good morning, Denise, it's a fine day for exercise." The other women did the same when it was Odette's turn.

But after about a week in prison, Odette no longer saw any of the F Section women.

A guard came to fetch her, stating that she was wanted for an interview. She was led to the Commandant's office.

The Commandant, a hulking man with a pencil mustache that was much too small for his face, told her that a reporter wanted to talk to her.

"Where's the rest of the women who came in with me?"

The Commandant looked confused. "Who?"

"The women I arrived with. I was handcuffed to Yolande, and then there was Denise and Simone and…"

He held up his hand. "Some of them were returned to France a few days ago."

"France?" Odette sank into a chair. "Thank God."

"Oh, I don't think that's necessary." He gave a sadistic chuckle. "They've been taken to Natzweiler-Struthof concentration camp."

"But why? Why would you go through the trouble of transporting them here only to be brought back? That seems very unlike you Germans."

The Commandant shrugged. "They are probably slated for execution."

Before Odette could process this news, a short man with a crooked nose entered the room. He introduced himself as a reporter with the *Völkischer Beobachter.*

"The Nazi Daily," Odette commented listlessly.

"Well, Frau Churchill, you will be pleased to know we already have three of your relatives in German prisons. We look forward to the addition of another—Mister Winston Churchill."

"I don't think you will have to wait long for his arrival." Odette leaned in. "But when Winston Churchill comes to Berlin, it won't be as your prisoner. He will be the one driving through the rubble of your city in triumph."

The reporter blinked his shrewd eyes rapidly, his pen posed over his notebook.

"That's enough!" the Commandant snapped. "This interview is over." He motioned for a guard to take Odette back to her cell.

Two weeks later Odette was summoned once again and told to pack her meager things. They gave her the daily ration of one slice of bread before taking her to a station where she once again boarded a train, this time not handcuffed to anyone.

She was told to remain in the narrow passage next to a compartment which was packed with disheveled, emaciated men. The men seemed to be in good spirits, and she occasionally caught snippets of them singing "It's a Long Way to Tipperary."

The train was headed east, and she saw more of the RAF's exploits: fields pockmarked by bombs, destroyed factories, and piles of contorted metal.

As the train's wheels shrieked to a halt, Odette peered outside at the warped tracks, which must have once been another RAF target.

"*Encore un peu de patience, mes camarades,*" one of the men inside the compartment shouted. "Hitler's day will soon be over."

The guard next to Odette put his finger on the trigger of his Luger as he stared morosely at the ruined track.

The train had to backtrack and ended up in what remained of the city of Frankfurt. Even though night had fallen, Odette could see that most of the half-timbered houses still standing bore bomb scars, and the ground was littered with rubble.

The roof of the Frankfurt station had also been destroyed. When the train stopped, Odette was shoved into yet another black van and taken to yet another prison, where she was searched yet again.

This time, however, the cell that she was crammed into was nothing more than a barred cage set in the middle of the police station. Odette's throat was burning with thirst, but there was no sink or even a toilet in the cage.

She lay on the stone floor in between the other two occupants, who were loudly snoring. Odette held her hand over her eyes to block the naked electric bulb overhead, which still blazed at this late hour. She heard the faint buzzing sound of an airplane, and hoped it was a British bomber returning to blow this horrid place into oblivion.

The next morning, a guard put a large bucket of raw potatoes into the cell. The other two women each reached for a potato with their grimy hands and began to peel it.

"You help," one of the women told Odette with a toothless grin.

Odette completed three potatoes and then quit.

"Guard!" the first woman shouted as the other woman stared at Odette with dull eyes. The first woman pointed a trembling finger. "The Frenchwoman stopped."

Odette crossed her arms over her chest. "I have peeled three potatoes because that is enough for me to eat. I am a political prisoner and decline to do anything more than my fair share."

"If you refuse, you will be taken before the Chief of Police," the guard threatened.

Odette wiped her hands on a towel before replying, "Let's go."

When she was brought before the chief, she was informed that she was going to be transferred again, this time to Halle, and then on to the Ravensbrück Concentration Camp.

"Good," Odette told him. "Anything's better than here."

"Oh, I don't think so," he cackled, throwing his head back and revealing yellowed teeth. "I'd tell you to report back to me in a month to see if you still think so, but you won't be alive."

She shrugged and allowed the guard to lead her away.

This time she was taken to an attic and shoved into a stifling, windowless room. She could hear the sound of many bodies breathing raspily, and when her eyes became accustomed to the darkness, she saw that there were some forty women lying in various states of exhaustion on the floor. Odette saw with horror that the women had relieved themselves wherever they found convenient, and the room reeked of body odor, urine, blood, and excrement.

The Germans had strewn sand all over the floor to hinder fires if the Allies dropped bombs upon the attic. It got into Odette's eyes as she marched over to one of the most cognizant-looking women.

Odette tried introducing herself to the woman, but she shook her head and replied something unintelligible in a scratchy voice. It might have been Ukrainian, Odette decided. Nonetheless, she took the woman's skeletal arm and led her under the skylight. She got down on all fours and then gestured for the woman to do the same. Odette stood up and took off her shoe before mounting the woman's bony back. She slammed her shoe into the glass with all her might, noting with satisfaction as it shattered around them. The little breeze whipped more sand into Odette's eyes, but she managed to take in a much-needed breath of fresh air.

Even with the occasional gusts from the broken skylight, the attic was boiling hot and Odette spent yet another sleepless night crushed between atrophied women's bodies.

In the morning a bucket of soup was placed in the sand and the women became snarling, clawing beasts as they thrust their hands into the bucket. Odette turned away, trying not to think about the contaminated, thin soup, no matter how much her stomach growled. Instead, she stood under the skylight and breathed in the morning air.

Once the bucket had been licked clean, the women went back to their spots and lay down. Odette curled up in a corner and tried to sleep. In the afternoon, bread was thrown into the attic and the horrid scene from the morning played out again as women snatched sand-covered stale bread from one another.

As dusk fell, the door opened again and a man's voice called up the stairs. "Frau Churchill? *Ist Frau Churchill hier?*"

Odette got unsteadily to her feet, wondering if the time of her execution was upon her. At this point, she almost welcomed it. She crept over the Ukrainian women and went down the attic stairs holding tightly onto the banister.

"I am Mrs. Churchill," she told the man, a portly shadow against the light of the hallway.

She felt a whoosh of air and then a crushing blow landed squarely on her mouth, causing her to nearly tip over.

"That's for Winston Churchill!" he shouted before he slammed the door so hard it shook the walls.

CHAPTER 69

DIDI

*T*he new wireless operator, Maury, found another place in Le Vésinet, a western suburb of Paris, to transmit from, though he warned Didi that the reception there wasn't the greatest.

One warm afternoon in early July, Dumont-Guillemet gave Didi an urgent message to send to London: he had discovered his friend, Sidney Jones was now in the hands of the Gestapo. "Tell the SOE that one of their men, someone named Bardet, has been working with the German Secret Police for the better part of a year."

Didi sighed. "I guess that explains the rise in missing agents."

"Yes." Dumont-Guillemet's normally ebullient tone was subdued. "But don't go back to the Dubois house," he cautioned. "It's not safe."

She nodded and took the message before letting herself out of the safehouse.

Luckily Maury had already set up the wireless in the new place, so she wouldn't have to move the suitcase across town. Didi perused a Metro map and started to find Le Vésinet with her finger, but then paused as a thought occurred to her. *Maury also said the reception was poor at the new house.* What if she couldn't communicate Bardet's betrayal right away? What if her transmission was garbled by Morse mutilation? In the time it took to solve the indecipherable, Bardet could betray even more agents.

This will be the last time, Didi promised herself as she boarded the train for Bourg-la-Reine.

When Didi reached the Dubois house, she found that the suburb's power was out. It didn't come on for hours, forcing her to miss her evening sked. Still desperate to deliver the Bardet information as soon as possible, she decided to sleep in the attic and wait for her morning sked.

She awoke to the light of the small lamp next to the wireless. She hastily went to the small attic window and threw it open, noting a few more lights coming from the other houses in the predawn hours. *The power was back on.* She pulled the wireless case out from the pile of musty blankets beside her and assembled it. Once it was ready, she placed her finger over the Morse key and typed out her message.

From the open window, she could discern the sound of a car engine, but, as she was engaged in her task, paid little attention. She completed the message and then had begun dissembling the transmitter when she heard a car door slam.

She forced her trembling hands to set the Morse key down before once again peering out the window. Two white vans were parked across the street and another was pulling in. Her heart froze when she saw several men exit the vans, holding tracking devices.

The Gestapo. The moment she'd been dreading had come. She had only a few minutes before the Nazis would come knocking on the door of the abandoned Dubois house. Or, worse yet, bursting in.

She ran to the back window and frantically pulled down the aerial. She threw it into the case, not caring if she damaged it in doing so. She started to bury the case in its customary spot in the blankets, but, after a desperate moment, decided that was too obvious and hid it in a second-floor closet instead.

She continued downstairs to the kitchen, where she hurled Dumont-Guillemet's handwritten message into the fireplace. She grabbed a set of matches from the mantel and struck one, but, because her fingers were shaking so badly, it refused to light.

After a few more tries, she finally got one lit, which she held to the message. To her relief, the paper quickly caught fire. She grabbed a poker and spread the ashes out.

Didi was moving so fast that it seemed as though the Germans were taking forever, but then a heavy hand knocked on the door. She stirred the ashes once more. The fire had mostly been extinguished, luckily after the evidence had been burned, but there was no explaining why she had chosen to light the fire on a sizzling July day.

She took in a deep breath, attempting to calm herself, before opening the door.

A man in plainclothes was on the other side. He lowered his gun before barking an order in German.

Didi shook her head.

She caught the German words for "search" and "house" before the man barged in.

I am Jacqueline du Tetre, a simple shop girl, she reminded herself. "Who are you and what do you think you are doing?" she demanded.

The German took one look at the still smoldering fire before sticking his head out the door and beckoning to his comrades, who were at the house next door.

Didi, knowing that her life depended on her demeanor, clasped her hands together in an attempt to still them.

A new man stepped into the living room. "We know that you have been using an illegal wireless set," he told her in French. "You have been sending messages, which means you are working against Germany."

Didi started to shake her head.

"Show us where the wireless set is."

She finally found her voice. "What do you mean sending messages? Aren't wireless sets used to listen?"

More men entered the house. Most of them were carrying guns, and Didi felt herself start to panic. She took in another deep breath. "I've never seen a wireless set like what you say."

The man in front of her frowned, and for a split second Didi thought he believed her. But then he nodded and his men began opening cupboards, tossing out whatever they found inside. Finding nothing of importance, they headed upstairs. Didi started to follow, but one of them told her to stay where she was.

"*Hier ist es,*" a triumphant voice called. A soldier walked downstairs, holding the wireless case in front of him.

He placed the case at Didi's feet. "What do you think this is?" he asked in halting French.

Didi's eyebrows rose as the soldier's eyes narrowed. She thought about denying that she knew anything of the set, but then quickly surmised that the Germans would demand to know whose equipment it might be. Since she appeared to be alone in an abandoned house, she decided that the best solution was not to say anything at all.

The man who had brought down the wireless dug into his back pocket and pulled out a pair of handcuffs. He slapped them over her wrists and then nodded at another man, who shoved her forward with the butt of a rifle.

She was under arrest.

CHAPTER 70

ODETTE

After four torturous days in the stifling attic, Odette and the Ukrainians were taken by train to Fürstenberg, where they were then unloaded and forced to hike three miles to the Ravensbrück Concentration Camp.

Odette had nearly nothing to eat for the past week and she walked slowly, both because she was feeling weak and because the gravel hurt her mangled feet.

The camp had been built next to a sparkling lake rimmed by a forest of dark-green trees. A few charming chalets were sprinkled along the shore, their windowsills brimming with white gardenias, whose scent filled the summer air. *All in all, I can think of worse places to die,* Odette decided.

A few people were lying on towels next to the lake, catching the last rays of sun. They did not look up as the morbid line of women straggled past them. Odette mused that they were probably guards off duty.

Soon monstrous towers came into view, and after that, gray walls at least five meters high. Feeling very small, Odette followed the Ukrainians through the mammoth iron gates.

The little group paused as a band of skeletons in black and white striped sack dresses marched past. With a start, Odette realized the skeletons were women. She imagined many of them had once been beautiful with womanly curves, but now their heads were shaved, their

329

emaciated bodies marked by purple and yellow bruises. None of them made eye contact with the new recruits. Odette looked back to see the massive gates open once again to let them out. As one of them stumbled, the female SS guard behind them cracked her whip, landing on the back of the offender, who didn't even cry out.

When the newcomers reached a sandy clearing about the size of a soccer field and void of any greenery, the guards stopped them and went into a little building, probably to announce their arrival.

Odette's shoes sank into the sand as she paused to gaze around. The wall blocked them off from the pretty village, and had barbed wire on top, most likely electrified, judging by the stenciled skull and bones every 20 meters or so. A gravel alleyway lined with poplar trees led to the main part of the camp, where around 15 gray sheds formed right angles to the road on either side.

Odette and the Ukrainians were ushered down the trail to a cinderblock building. Inside were long pipes, interspersed with nozzles, running along the ceiling. *The showerhouse.*

Odette turned on a tap and was thankful to be confronted with a trickle of rust-colored water. She opened her parched mouth and sipped in as much water as she could, not even noticing that it tasted of copper. A guard informed them that the camp was over capacity and that they would be staying in the showerhouse until further notice.

Odette undid the little bundle she'd carried from Fresnes. Besides the somewhat tattered shirt and trousers she wore, she had the gray suit, a blouse, a pair of silk stockings and heeled shoes, and an extra set of underpants. She washed them all with a tiny piece of soap before turning to her own battered, shrunken body. After she was suitably clean, she spread her meager wardrobe out on the concrete floor to dry. Still dripping, Odette then lay down next to her belongings and fell asleep.

She awoke before dawn the next morning to a woman's hoarse voice shouting, "*Appell!*" Odette splashed cold water on her face, noting that her companions had already left. Remembering the defeated, starved women from yesterday, she decided to cling to her femininity for as long as possible and put on her gray suit and red blouse.

She walked out into the cool darkness only to be greeted by another line of prisoners drifting slowly past, the whites of their striped dresses glowing in the electric searchlights.

She joined them in their ghastly march to the clearing in front of the gates. Thousands of wretched waifs in sack dresses were already lined up in rows, standing as still as possible, as both male and female SS guards marched up and down, taking roll.

"*Achtung!*" an obviously well-fed, heavyset woman shouted. "Ranks of five, hands by your side." She carried a hefty accordion folder, occasionally thumping the women in the head with it if she felt they were not standing at attention.

She paused at Odette's side, taking in her red blouse and shoes. "You are new?"

Odette nodded.

The woman called for another guard, who came over. "Take her to Sturmbann-Führer Sühren," she commanded.

He looked at Odette expectantly. When she didn't move, he got behind her and whacked her in the back with the butt of his rifle. "*Los!*" he shouted, hitting her again. "Get moving."

Odette did as he told her, albeit slowly, walking on her heels as much as possible, but the gravel kept getting caught in her soles. As they approached the showerhouse, Odette paused. "Do you mind if I change my shoes?" She slipped her foot out of one to show the guard her disfigured toes.

His upper lip curled in disgust. "*Klar,*" he agreed. "*Schnell, schnell.*"

She went inside, where she brushed the dust off her gray skirt and coat with her hands and then ran her fingers through her tangled hair. If she was going to give the impression she was a Churchill, she'd better at least try to look the part. The familiarity of primping calmed her, and when the guard threw open the door, tapping his jackboot impatiently, Odette announced that she was ready.

With his predictably blue eyes and blonde hair, Sühren was as Aryan as they came. His face was round and his eyebrows were so light they were barely visible. He looked too young to be responsible for the fates of the thousands of prisoners that occupied his camp. "*Sprechen Sie Deutsch?*"

Odette, musing over how ineffectual his voice sounded, replied that she spoke no German, and then half-heartedly added a "Monsieur," at the end.

His forehead furrowed above those non-existent eyebrows as he looked down at the paper in front of him. "Frau Churchill." He looked up. "You are related to Mister Winston Churchill?" he asked in halting English.

"My husband is a distant connection of his."

He lifted a manicured hand. "Here in Ravensbrück you will no longer be Frau Churchill and will answer to the name of 'Frau Schurer.'"

She recalled the slap she'd gotten in the attic simply for being a Churchill. "I have had many names in my life, monsieur. One more makes no difference to me at all."

She could tell by his frown that he didn't understand. "You have been condemned to death and will therefore be taken to the Bunker, the prison of the camp."

She wanted to laugh at the term 'prison'—as if the rest of the camp were a delightful getaway for those who had fallen on the wrong side of Hitler's regime. "Very well," she replied instead.

Sühren called for her guard. Odette was able to pick up the gist of his German commands: she was to receive the normal rations of the Bunker, no more no less, no exercise, no books, and no bath.

"*Jawohl, Herr Kommandant*," the guard responded before leading Odette back out into the sunshine. They crossed the dusty grounds to an elongated L-shaped building. "*Das ist the* Bunker." He knocked on the steel door and a short, dark-haired woman with a hawk nose nearly obscuring her receding chin answered. She barked something at the guard and then stepped back, indicating that Odette should walk inside.

Odette took one last look at the blue sky, trying to imprint it in her memory, before she entered.

The woman led her down into the depths of the Bunker, the daylight receding with each step until buzzing electric bulbs provided the only illumination. The woman paused in front of a door and unlocked it before shoving Odette inside and slamming the door.

There was absolutely no light whatsoever in the cell. Odette held out her arms, but could not see anything except impenetrable blackness. As she did when she was blind, she used her hands to feel along the room, locating the lumpy mattress and laid down.

CHAPTER 71

DIDI

*D*idi shut her eyes. *It's nothing more than a drill,* she told herself. *Remember what they taught you: show no fear.* She tried to take a deep breath, but instead she swallowed water. The water was everywhere, in her eyes, in her mouth, up her nose. Everything burned.

And then it was gone, and Didi was gasping at fresh air, which also stung her lungs.

"Who are you?" a German voice demanded. "Are you French?"

"Of course," Didi insisted. "I live in France, don't I?"

The voice growled at her to shut up before the water was back. He'd shoved her head into a bathtub. He held her long enough that her lungs felt as though they were on fire. Didi's mind began to wander. Just as she thought she'd drowned for good, he pulled her back up by her hair. "Who do you work for?"

"A company," Didi gasped. She tried to remember her cover story, but found her brain wouldn't function right. Her eyes wandered around the bare room. *Focus,* she commanded herself as water dripped down her face. There was no way she would reveal the truth, but she couldn't think fast enough to outwit her interrogator.

"Do you speak German?" he demanded.

She coughed. "No."

"Are you French?"

"*Mais, oui.* I work for a businessman. He tells me what messages to send, and I do it. He pays me well," she finished, her words coming out in halting breaths.

"What messages?"

She shook her head. "They are in code. I don't know what they mean. The money he gives me helps me survive."

The man grasped her head, as though to shove her under the water again.

"Please," Didi insisted. "I don't know. I told him I could learn the code when he hired me, but I could never remember, so he did it himself." She made her eyes wide. "I never had a head for numbers."

The German's grip on her scalp relaxed.

"I was terrible in school," Didi babbled. "I lied to my employer, but he needed a wireless operator so badly…"

"We found a gun on the premises." A short man stepped out of the dark corner by the door. "I suppose that belonged to your mysterious boss as well."

"The gardener had a gun. I don't know why… I thought it was to shoot rats." Her voice was higher than normal and sounded false even to Didi's own ears.

The short man's tone was milder than his partner's. "Your boss was obviously a spy and tricked you into sending his messages to England."

Didi forced her eyes to open even wider. "England? Why England?"

The mustached man, the one who'd been holding her head underwater, said in a gruff voice, "You're the spy, you dumb bitch." He reached out and smacked her cheek so hard that she fell.

She touched her hot face. "I'm not a spy." She began to cry real tears. "I'm not what you say I am."

The short man put his hands on his hips. "You really don't know anything about the London circuit? That they are parachuting agents into France, who are stirring up trouble." He got into her face. "They call it the 'Resistance.'"

"Resistance? But who would tell me something like that?" Through her tears, Didi could see the short man exchange a bewildered look with his partner. *The ruse is working.*

They took her into a different room, this one luckily without a bathtub, and asked her more questions. Didi kept up the new storyline for

Jacqueline du Tetre: that of an innocent girl who'd been duped into sending coded messages for a mysterious boss.

She didn't delude herself that the Germans would accept her story for long: she just wanted to give Dumont-Guillemet and Maury enough time to realize she'd been compromised so they could take whatever precautions necessary to preserve the network. She'd been caught, but she was determined no one else in her circuit would suffer her fate. She would protect them to the end.

The lies came easily, the same as when she was in training. Though the Germans tried all sorts of tactics to confuse her, she never hesitated, never faltered.

"Didn't you think it was strange what your boss was doing?" the short man asked

"No," Didi's answer was firm. "He offered me money, and I took it. I was desperate, don't you see?" Her gaze fell to her handbag, which they had tossed into a corner of the room. The L-pill was hidden safely inside, but Didi knew she would never consider swallowing it.

"When is the next time you will meet with your boss?" the mustached man demanded.

Didi thought fast. Perhaps if they went to a restaurant, she could escape through the restroom window. "He asked me to join him at 7 this evening, at the café opposite the Gare Saint-Lazare."

The short man nodded. "We will get him then."

Part of Didi was pleased that she had convinced her captors to chase after a fictitious man, but the other part wondered exactly how she was going to get out of the situation she now found herself in: in a speeding car heading toward the Gare Saint-Lazare. She pretended to hate the man who had supposedly manipulated her to become an unwilling traitor to her country.

"The least you can do is buy me a glass of sherry," she told the short man once they'd been seated. Her hair and shirt were still damp.

He flagged down a waitress and ordered the suggested drink. After a minute, he asked Didi, "You do think he is coming, don't you?"

She nodded, her eyes on the waitress as the woman set the sherry down. The mustached man took a seat at the bar, his gaze never leaving Didi as she took a sip. *How exactly was she going to get out of this mess now?*

As she stood, the short man did as well.

"I need to use the lavatory. The ladies' room," she added for emphasis.

"Hurry back," he told her.

The only window in the restroom was too high and too small for Didi to escape from. She banged her fist on the wall. *So close, yet so far.*

She coddled her throbbing fist as an air-raid siren began to resonate. Now there was really nowhere to go. She glanced once more at the tiny window before exiting the restroom.

The short man was waiting in the hallway.

"I'm sure you've guessed that my boss will not venture out during an air raid," Didi told him.

"Where does he live? If he does not show here at the restaurant, we shall pay him a visit at his home."

Didi gave him an address near the Edward VII hotel.

The short man reached for his pistol. "We'll find this man yet."

Didi was brought back to the Gestapo headquarters on the rue des Saussaies. She was held in a cell while the two men tried to find the address she'd provided.

When the short man returned, he informed her that the address didn't exist.

She put her hand under her chin, pretending to be deep in thought. "I suppose that he was playing me for a fool all this time," she finally stated.

The short man gave a heavy sigh. "I was trying to protect you." He threw both hands up in the air. "But now I give up. You are clearly lying."

Didi's reply was a simple, "No."

His mouth turned up. "How do you feel about being sent to a concentration camp?"

The blood drained from Didi's face. Until now she'd been feeling slightly triumphant about always being a step ahead of the Germans. But they'd resorted to the punishment Hitler always dangled in front of his enemies. Her expression crumpled as she thought of Jackie. *I've failed. It's over.* If only she'd listened to Dumont-Guillemet and moved houses, she wouldn't be in this situation. Her only consolation was that she'd never compromised him or anyone else. Now if she could only keep it that way...

CHAPTER 72

MATHILDE

*I*n July 1944, Mathilde and her companions were moved unexpectedly to Holloway Prison. In contrast to the communal accommodations they'd had at Aylesbury, they were put into separate cells in Holloway's E-wing.

The E-wing was three stories high, opening to arched windows on either end, which gave the central corridor plenty of light. Between each level was a nylon net so that the prisoners on the third floor could not try to commit suicide by flinging themselves over the metal railing. Mathilde and the others were put in cells on the second floor, and not, thankfully, on the first, which was reserved for those women who'd been sentenced to death. The "hanging" room was only a few meters away from where the condemned women slept.

Mathilde's cell held a metal bed frame and mattress, a wooden chair and small table, and the requisite water closet. There was a barred window on the far wall, which could be opened to the outside. The solid wood door also had small windows for the guards to peer in from the hall.

She was served her meals in her cell. Breakfast consisted of tea and toast, with a tiny pat of margarine. For supper there was more bread and margarine, sometimes with a piece of spam, and cocoa. She was allotted three books a week from the library, and spent most of the time reading and ruminating over her plight.

THE SPARK OF RESISTANCE

After many days of deep contemplation, Mathilde decided that the demise of Interallié had indeed been Armand's fault, not hers. He should never have left those incriminating papers all over the apartment. As Bleicher himself once told her, all of the arrests would have happened no matter what; the only difference being that she would have suffered the same fate as the others had she not agreed to work with Bleicher.

Yet because she chose that path to save her own life, the English had imprisoned her. Even though Holloway was worse than Aylesbury, it was surely far better than those German concentration camps where they'd sent René and, most likely, other former Interallié affiliates.

Should the war end, surely the English would allow her to go back to France. But what if some members of Interallié survived? They might have the wrong impression of her, especially those who were arrested in her presence, like Stanislaus Lach, Mireille LeJeune, Boby Roland, and Lucien de Roquigny.

She decided to write a memoir to emphasize her innocence. After she'd completed it, she'd prevail upon her London contacts Lord Selbourne for one—to help get it published. She'd just taken out a pad of paper when someone knocked on the heavy cell door.

"Yes?" Mathilde called.

"Mrs. Carré?" The man who stood in the doorway was not one of her usual guards.

"Yes?" she repeated.

"This letter has come for you, all the way from Paris." He dropped an envelope next to her before retreating.

The envelope contained several stamps. Someone, possibly Bleicher, had crossed out her Paris address and written in *6 Orchard Court, London, care of Major Buckmaster.* Mathilde used her long nails to open it. It was an official letter declaring the death of Maurice, her once husband. He'd been killed at Monte Cassino in January. Even though the divorce was finalized before she'd left France, she was still listed as his next of kin. She refolded the letter and tucked it in a library book before picking up a pen. *"My earliest recollection is one of weariness."*

Mathilde poured herself into her writing, only stopping for meals and her daily walk with Stella. They usually went down the path leading from the mortuary through the lawn and then onto the little garden surrounded by brick walls. A few days after she'd found out Maurice had died, they found a black cat in the garden.

"Mitou, it looks just like you!" Stella exclaimed. She tried to coax it to come closer, but it escaped through a small hole in the wall. Though she longed to touch something soft and furry, Mathilde couldn't help but feel jealous that the cat was so free.

The next day Stella came prepared with a little piece of bread. This time she and Mathilde were able to pet the cat a few times before it again ran off.

The Luftwaffe had returned to London, and the shriek of the air raid sirens became a frequent occurrence. That night Mathilde slept under the little table in her room to protect herself from shattering glass if the bombs were to come too close to the prison. A tear streaked down her cheek at the thought of dying alone in her cell, huddled on the floor. The SOE must have forgotten about her, as she was no longer given an allowance, and the rest of the world, even Maurice had abandoned her, save for Stella and perhaps the garden cat.

She said as much to Stella the next day on their walk.

"I fully agree— you are my closest friend here. Look," Stella dug into her pocket and pulled out a bar of chocolate. "A guard took pity on me when I complained that I was still hungry after the evening meal." She split the chocolate bar and handed half to Mathilde.

"He took pity on you?"

"Well," Stella shot her a grin. "Maybe I did have to resort to my powers of persuasion. I only gave him one kiss, but believe me, I'm willing to do more if it means getting more food."

"At any rate, I'm going to savor it as much as possible and only eat one square at a time," Mathilde declared.

Stella looked skeptical. "Why? What if tomorrow one finds the chocolate melted in the pocket of our burned bodies after the prison was hit by a Luftwaffe bomb? What if the SOE decides we are a mortal threat to their agents and signs our death sentence?" She took a large bite of the chocolate. "I'm going to live for today and pretend that tomorrow doesn't exist."

After a moment of thought, Mathilde, deciding that Stella was right, stuffed the rest of the chocolate into her mouth.

CHAPTER 73

DIDI

*D*idi was transferred to the towering Fresnes Prison in late July 1944. As the car drove through the Parisian streets, she stared out the window, thinking it might be the last time she would look upon her native city. She blinked back tears as they passed Louise's apartment, remembering the warmth and laughter they'd shared listening to the outlawed BBC broadcasts. She vowed she would never say anything that would put Louise or her family in any danger, no matter how much the Nazis might torture her.

They were putting her in Fresnes until they could figure out what to do with her. Didi was well aware that the chances of surviving a concentration camp were slim, at best, but also realized that she could not give in to the blanketing wave of despair that threatened to drown her. *I'll find some way to escape,* she promised herself.

But the looming shadow of the prison was intimidating and, with its peaked roof and barred windows, appeared to be completely impregnable.

Didi's first full day in Fresnes was marked only by a guard coming in the morning and evening to deliver putrid liquid that was supposed to be coffee, and a piece of bread.

In between, Didi explored her cell. The window had a small crack in it, and she was able to look out at the gray sky by standing on a chair. After darkness had fallen, she walked the length of the room, which was illuminated by one bare bulb.

She noticed two separate calendars carved into the wall and ran her fingers on the date of one the scratches. November 11th. The other calendar ended on May 12. There was one word scrawled underneath that date: *Lise*.

Suddenly she heard a faint knocking sound coming from the room next door. She paused to listen. It was a sequence of short and long raps, and then it stopped, only to start over again. With a gasp, Didi realized the tapping was Morse code. It said, *"Welcome, are you with the Resistance?"*

"Yes," she answered back. "Who are you?"

"RAF officer."

The tapping was wearing on her knuckles, so she decided to ask the most pertinent question. "Is there any possibility of breaking out of here?"

"No," came the reply.

Still, Didi refused to give in and spent the next several nights plotting different ways to escape.

Didi was shoved awake early one August morning. "Get up!" her warden told her. "The Allies are on their way to liberate Paris."

Didi's heart leapt. Maybe Dumont-Guillemet had caught wind of what happened to her and was planning another coup.

"You're being transferred," the warden said, tossing Didi's skirt at her.

Still not fully awake, and certain she was about to be set free, this statement confused Didi. "What?"

"The train leaves in half an hour."

"Train to where?" Her voice was desperate.

"Ravensbrück. The women's concentration camp."

It was an unbelievably warm day in a month of warm days. Even at the early hour Didi was taken by bus to the Pantin train station, the sun was blazing.

"There's no passenger train," another prisoner commented.

"No," Didi answered, catching sight of a man in a white uniform with perpendicular crimson slashes. "But the Red Cross is here."

"At least that means they'll keep the Germans in line."

Didi thought the same thing, up until they were told to board the freight train. "Like cattle," she remarked aloud.

The train didn't leave for hours. The day turned even more sweltering, causing the packed cattle car to become unbearably hot. Didi had been lucky to get a spot on the floor near the car door, where at least she could feel the hint of a breeze. She leaned against the wall and closed her eyes, willing herself to fall asleep.

"Can we get some water?" a woman begged one of the men standing outside the car.

"*Nein*." The man slammed the door shut, ending the little breeze.

"Now you've done it," a man's gruff voice chided the woman. "Did you really think the Nazis were going to give you something to drink?"

"We've been here for almost two hours already," the woman said, folding her arms in front of her.

"Well, there are no bathrooms, so be glad you don't have water," the man replied.

"I would have sweat it out anyway," the woman said, fanning herself. "It's so hot."

Didi wanted to save her strength for whatever was in store. *I'll escape*, she decided. Just as soon as the train stops. The thought cheered her, and, as the train started moving, she closed her eyes.

As darkness descended outside, the temperature inside the cattle car fell to a more tolerable level, but soon climbed again the next morning. At that point, they had been on the train for nearly 24 hours without food, water, or a place to relieve themselves. Some of the older prisoners looked near death.

Didi worriedly eyed a sweating, gray-haired woman whose breath was coming out in gasps. The woman swayed as the train slowed.

Didi felt a blast of cool air as someone opened the car door. "*Raus!*" a soldier commanded, gesturing for them to exit the car.

The prisoners got to their feet unsteadily. When Didi walked out

343

into the sunshine, she saw the reason they had to evacuate: the track in front of them had been blown to pieces.

Her legs, after sitting so long in the same position, felt numb. As she shook them out, she noted the large field that lay beyond the train tracks. Without thinking, she started running.

She soon heard rapid footfalls behind her. Someone was chasing her. "*Halt oder ich schiesse!*" a voice commanded.

Didi didn't need a translator to know he was threatening to shoot her. She kept up her pace, convincing herself she could still make it, even if she were in desperate need of both food and water. But then there was the unmistakable crack of a pistol firing. A bullet whizzed past her and blasted a hole in a nearby tree.

She stopped.

A guard grabbed her arm. "You're lucky I didn't kill you," he said in clumsy French. "I will, though, if you dare try that again."

He brought Didi back to the rest of the prisoners, who were ordered to march beyond the demolished part of the tracks.

Didi met the eyes of a farm worker, who paused in his hoeing. He picked up his thermos and, ignoring the guard's orders for him to stay back, approached Didi. "Here," he said, shoving the thermos at her.

"Thank you." Didi took a gulp before relinquishing it to a pale-faced woman across from her.

"Move on now or you will join these prisoners!" a guard shouted.

The farmer tipped his hat before walking away, but other field workers repeated his kind gesture, handing off their own supply of water to the prisoners. "Good luck," one of them said. "God will be with you."

Soon, another train arrived and the prisoners were once again herded aboard. The guard barked something in German and once again used his rifle to underline his point.

A young man next to Didi translated, eyes down. "If anyone else tries to escape, we will shoot them and everyone else in their car." With that, Didi knew her plans were finished—even if she did manage to get away, she'd never be able to live with the guilt of causing someone else's death.

The young man now looked up at Didi. She expected him to scold her for daring to put their lives in danger. But all he said was, "You almost made it."

She attempted to smile.

"I don't know if you know this, but I saw two other women sneak away while they were dealing with you."

Now Didi's smile was genuine. Though she was still a prisoner, thanks to her, two others were not.

The young man stood up and tried to peer out of the small opening at the top of the wagon.

"Do you recognize where we are going?" Didi asked.

"Toward Germany."

She swallowed back her terror. They were taking them to the heart of the Third Reich: the homeland of these monsters. How could she possibly escape now? Even if she did manage to get away from the guards, she would not know where to go, and she couldn't speak the language.

When the train stopped again and the doors were opened, the same young man from before stated, "We're in Weimar."

"Near Buchenwald," someone else replied.

"All men, off now!" a guard commanded.

"What's Buchenwald?" Didi asked.

"A concentration camp," the young man said before walking down the ramp.

The train rolled on for a few more hours before it once again stopped to allow a few Red Cross nurses to come aboard. They handed Didi a small bag. Inside was an apple and some bread. She took a large bite from the apple as the woman next to her eagerly opened her own bag.

"What's that?" Didi expected to see similar items, but the woman held up a nurses' uniform. A pass fell out. The woman started crying as she stripped off her own clothes and put on the uniform. She tucked the pass into her pocket.

"Hold on," Didi told her. She felt immensely overlooked for not being given such a prize bag, but she wouldn't deny the woman's chance at freedom. She spit on her thumb and wiped at a smear of dirt on the woman's face. "There," Didi said. "Now you look the part."

The woman's eyes were still red as she thanked Didi.

"Good luck," Didi called as the counterfeit nurse left the train.

Didi managed to fall asleep again, using the woman's discarded clothes as a pillow. This time when the train stopped, the women were ordered off. They'd arrived at Ravensbrück.

CHAPTER 74

ODETTE

*D*espite the ubiquitous black curtain of her cell, Odette found that she was still able, vaguely, to distinguish time. It helped that every morning, or what she presumed was morning, the door was opened and a blinding light filled her eyes, reminding her of the flashlights of her supposed interrogators during SOE training. A mug of thin, bitter-tasting coffee and a slice of crumbly bread were dropped on the floor before the door slammed shut once again. A few hours later, the routine was repeated, this time with a bowl of watery soup, and another mug of coffee, signaling evening.

Odette surmised that her cell was next to the "beating room," for not long after the last delivery of the day, the night's gruesome entertainment started with the creaking of an iron gate, followed by the marching of several competent jackboots and the dragging of another's feet. Soon the repetitious sound of a German voice counting numbers was heard, accompanied by the maniacal screaming of a tortured female.

Forced to listen, Odette concentrated on the German's detached monotone. "*Eins, zwei, drei...*" she counted along, touching her indiscernible fingers. It was rare that the voice would announce, *fünfundzwanzig*, German for twenty-five, without a lull in screaming. Odette took the pause to mean that the victim had fainted. She would then hear the metallic clang of a bucket and a splashing of water, and the flogging would continue where the count had left off.

On one particularly disturbing evening, the counting went all the way to *vierzig*. Forty. She detected the tinny voice of Sturmbann-Führer Sühren in attendance that time.

Odette felt a tightening of her stomach every night this scenario was repeated, trying to muffle the screaming with her extra shirt, but to no avail. When she finally fell into a fitful sleep, the wailing of innocent women haunted her.

Though she couldn't see her body in the blackness, she felt it getting thinner. When she first arrived at Ravensbrück, she could encircle the forearm directly above her wrist with her other hand. As the days crept slowly by, Odette could fit the space just below her elbow in between her forefinger and thumb, and then above her elbow, and then her upper arm. Soon she could do the same to her calf and she knew she was on the brink of starvation. The glands in her neck felt like rocks and her throat was always parched.

One morning—or was it afternoon?—the door burst open and the light was switched on. Odette shielded her eyes as the unmistakable voice of Sühren asked in English, "Is everything all right?"

Odette's voice hadn't been used in months. "Yes, thank you," she managed to reply.

"Do you wish for anything?"

"No, thank you." Odette refused to ask anything of these monsters. She could feel him make a sudden movement, probably a salute, before he turned off the light and shut the door.

It must have been the end of summer when Odette felt her room become insufferably hot. It wasn't from the heat of the August sun, Odette surmised, but more like they had turned the furnace on full blast. Odette groped for the sheet and pulled it from the mattress before saturating it with cold water. She sat on the bed, wrapping the wet sheet around her. In no time, the intense heat had dried the sheet and she repeated the process.

This went on for six days, though it was hard to mark the time as no food was delivered. She could feel her already fragile will disintegrate. Her skin became bumpy with scabs and her hair fell out by the handful. Though she hadn't eaten, her bowels emptied themselves hour after hour and she knew she'd contracted dysentery.

Just as she thought she'd succumb to her misery, Sühren reappeared. "Have you any complaints?"

Odette swallowed. "Yes, I have. For no reason that I am aware of, the heat was turned on in my cell and I went a week without food."

"There was a reason," Sühren replied. "The so-called Allies have liberated Fresnes Prison, where you once were held as a British spy. By order of the Gestapo, you were punished for that exact crime."

She licked her dry lips and steeled herself for the effort of what she was about to say. "The Gestapo ordered the deprivation of food from a woman in solitary confinement because the Allies released prisoners from a place where she's no longer being held captive?"

"Yes."

She gave a weak chuckle. "Monsieur, I find the actions of the Gestapo rather droll."

She could hear him shuffle his feet. "Do you wish for anything?"

"No."

CHAPTER 75

DIDI

*A*lthough Didi was dehydrated and hungry, the five-kilometer march to the concentration camp did not seem to take long at all. She inhaled each breath as deeply as she could, knowing these might be her last gasps of freedom for a long time. Or possibly her last gasps at all.

They traipsed past a pretty village, which someone said was called Fürstenberg, and then a lake bordered by a heavy forest. Didi filed the deep woods away as a place to hide when she escaped.

But, just as when she arrived at Fresnes Prison, Didi realized she'd probably never be able to break free from Ravensbrück. The camp was surrounded by a brick wall more than twice as tall as herself and seemed to extend from one horizon to the other, a maze of barbed wire covering the top.

They were marched through the camp, which mostly consisted of wooden huts and a huge open space, before entering a long cinderblock building. Here they were told to strip naked. All of their clothing and anything else on their person, including their wedding rings, went into communal paper bags. The woman next to Didi kept on her sanitary belt, but a guard walked up to her and snapped, *"Alles aus!"* Everything had to come off.

They were then forced to walk past a dozen sneering male guards— some of whom ogled the women while others shouted insults—to the showers. The water was freezing cold and they were given tiny shreds of soap and dirty, threadbare washcloths. After that, they were subjected to yet another humiliation: the lice check. If any trace of lice was suspected, the woman's head and pubic area were immediately shaved.

Didi mercifully escaped this indignity. Naked and shivering, she was told to stand in line for a medical examination. After what seemed like hours, a man in a white coat shoved an icy metal clamp into her privates. He barked something and Didi was pushed off the table. The man then inserted the clamp into the next girl without cleaning it.

Didi was given a striped dress made out of a paper-thin material. "Sew this onto your left shoulder," another prisoner said, handing her a needle, thread, and a small red triangle.

After she'd finished sewing, another male guard ran his hands all over her, searching her, as if she could have found the opportunity to steal a weapon from the infirmary and hide it underneath her ragged dress.

The same guard escorted her to one of the long wooden huts where hundreds of women were packed into bunks three beds high. He led her through the maze of women until he located an empty bed. "This one's free," he said in broken French, pointing to the lower bunk. The sheets were stained—probably with bodily fluids, and, in a few spots, with what looked like blood.

As the guard walked away, Didi set her parcel down and then collapsed onto the hard bed.

The next day Didi was awoken by a blaring sound broadcasted over the loudspeaker.

"*Appell,*" one of her fellow prisoners said as she shuffled to the door. "*Vernichtung durch Arbeit.*"

"What does that mean?" another new recruit demanded.

"Extermination through work," someone else replied. "*Appell* is where they line us up to count and make sure no one has escaped."

Didi slipped her feet into her scuffed, prison-issued clogs before trailing the others to the open clearing, where thousands of women were already lined up in rows of five, standing as still as possible. Didi followed suit and forced her eyes to stay forward, even when a fat man on a bicycle rode past her. He carried a whip and occasionally lashed out at the prisoners as he shouted, *"Achtung, achtung!"* Didi had gathered enough German words by now to know that he meant 'caution' or 'be careful,' which was odd considering that the only immediate danger came from him and his whip.

A woman pushing a wheelbarrow emerged in Didi's field of view. Her stomach turned as she saw the cargo: a pile of dead bodies. They were partially covered by a blanket, but some of their lifeless eyes stared at Didi as the corpse cart passed by.

Finally Appell was finished and they were released back to their hut for breakfast: bitter acorn coffee and a piece of bread. The siren sounded again. This time when they lined up at the Appelplatz, they were given their tasks for the day. Some were commanded to go to the nearby Siemens plant, shovel sand, or build roads. A corpulent woman guard barked at Didi to report to the camp garden, and Didi understood her well enough, even down to the final, "Move it, you lazy bitch!"

It was back-breaking work, and Didi could only assume the vegetables she tended would end up on the SS guards' plates, not her own.

After a while, Didi was conscious that another woman had moved over to the spot next to hers. "How goes it, Didi?" the strangely-familiar voice asked.

Shocked to hear her name after so long, she glanced up from her work. Even though her head was shaved and her once-womanly frame had disappeared, Didi could easily recognize the woman was Yvonne Baseden, her roommate from Fawley Court. She too wore a red triangle on her left shoulder.

Didi longed to embrace her old friend, but knew that would attract the guards' attention. "How long have you been here?" she asked instead.

"Too long," Yvonne responded through a half-hearted whack of her hoe. "A week, maybe more. It's hard to keep track. You?"

"This is my first day."

"Well then, welcome to Hitler's female slave camp."

The guard shouted and waved at them, her meaning all-too clear. *"Schnell, schnell."*

Yvonne and Didi bent down and continued hoeing, this time with renewed vigor. After a few minutes, Yvonne nodded toward three women pulling weeds a few meters away. "They're SOE too. I've been with them since Saarbrücken."

"What are their names?"

"They tell everyone they're Nadine, Ambroise, and Louise," Yvonne said, nodding at each one in turn.

"That's Violette Szabo," Didi whispered, gazing at the still beautiful, dark-haired woman. "I met her in London once."

"The other prisoners call them the 'Little Paratroopers.' Brave as they may be, they've let on that they're British. I think that's a bad idea," Yvonne added and Didi nodded in agreement.

She squashed down a pang of familiarity at the sight of Violette, who seemed fervent in her duty and had a bag of weeds that was twice as full as her companions. Didi had only met her briefly in Leo Marks' office, but she had liked her immediately. She also knew that Violette must have been a favorite of even her famously aloof boss, considering Marks himself had written her poem code. But Didi vowed to keep her distance from Violette, sensing it would be dangerous for the guards to catch on to their acquaintance. If they did, she'd have to abandon her alias of Jacqueline du Tetre.

While Violette appeared in good health, it was obvious that Nadine, who was also raven-haired, but much thinner than Violette, was not doing well. She could barely walk.

"She won't eat," Yvonne whispered to Didi as she struck the earth with her hoe. "She says she doesn't like the food. Nobody does, but everyone else knows that you need to force it down anyway."

"*Halt die Gosche!*" a deep voice shouted.

Didi bit back a shriek as a stream of cold water showered her, causing her to shiver in the summer sunshine. The guard, holding a hose with one hand, gestured to the garden. Didi and Yvonne had no choice but to continue their work in silence.

CHAPTER 76

ODETTE

*I*t would be autumn now in Somerset, and mist would cover the woodland paths next to the creek. Odette pictured herself raking the leaves and dumping them into a bonfire. But the smoke wafting into her nostrils now was not the pleasant smell of burning leaves. She tightened her eyes against the darkness, knowing the acrid odor was coming from the ovens in the crematorium.

She focused her mind once again on the house in Somerset and her daughters playing underneath the willow tree. They were wearing the dresses Odette had made them in her imagination the day before. She had spent a long time carefully picking out the fabrics for each girl, and then mentally made her own patterns, cut the fabric, and sewed them. She had spent hours envisioning each step, even down to threading the machine needle.

"Did you wash your hands for tea?" she asked her girls.

Marianne shook her head.

"It's no matter," Odette replied with a smile. "As long as you are good girls and behave yourselves, you can have your tea. I'll even give you a biscuit."

"Oh, thank you, Mummy!" Lily exclaimed.

Odette smiled to herself in the darkness, but her revelry was interrupted by a flood of artificial light as her cell door banged against the wall.

A female voice commanded her to stand.

"I cannot," Odette replied, indicating her skeletal legs.

She was hoisted to her feet by two pairs of strong hands and hauled out of her cell. As they reached the outside door of the Bunker, Odette shielded her eyes from the sun, which stabbed at her swollen pupils. The fresh air felt like icicles puncturing her lungs. She felt herself drop to the ground.

She had the sensation of floating as her eyes tried to adjust. She peeked once at the retreating ground—someone was carrying her. She was deposited in a room, where everything was a metallic gray. She was plopped onto a soft bed, and then there was the pinch of an injection and then nothingness.

CHAPTER 77

DIDI

here were only two ways to leave Ravensbrück. One was "through the chimney," a camp euphemism for the gas ovens. The other was by going to forced labor camps. Most of the women at Ravensbrück were made to work on site, or at the nearby Siemens plant, but the slave-labor also extended to other locations throughout Germany.

The F Section women—Didi, Yvonne, Violette, Nadine, and Ambroise—were moved to the work camp at a munitions factory in Torgau. It took them three days to get there, packed in cattle wagons, but it was still a sight better than the Appelplatz at Ravensbrück.

During the march to the subcamp, Nadine, the raven-haired SOE woman, seemed likely to fall over. Jeannie, another Frenchwoman who had joined them on their journey from Ravensbrück, took Nadine's arm to guide her.

As they walked past a long iron fence, they were surprised to see healthy, strong-looking men lined up against it. "It won't be much longer," one of them shouted in English. "The Allies are approaching Germany and they'll be here before you know it! Keep strong!"

Yvonne waved and called out *Allo* to them as she passed. "POWs," she told Didi.

Didi's face relaxed and she also waved to the men, hoping that one day soon Hitler would give up his futile fight and they could all go home.

The factory campus seemed clean enough. Each woman was given their own mattress and a blanket, and they had running water in their barracks. For dinner, they were provided a whole piece of sausage in addition to sauerkraut and fresh bread.

"I think I'm going to like it here," Yvonne commented.

"You can't be serious," Violette fixed her with a hard stare. "This is a munitions factory. They are going to force us to build weapons that will be used against our boys."

Yvonne stopped chewing, the bread dropping out of her mouth. She picked it up and finished it before replying, "Not even the Nazis can do that."

"If you refuse, you might get sent back to Ravensbrück," Didi said aloud, weighing the choice in her mind.

"The war is nearly over. What would it matter if we help make guns that won't be used?" another woman asked.

"I think they're bombs," Jeannie, the Frenchwoman who'd helped Nadine, stated.

"Still, Ravensbrück will be the death of you if you go back," the other woman refuted.

The rest of the women remained silent as they finished their ample dinner and contemplated their options.

At Appell the next morning, Jeannie announced that she would not work in the munitions sector.

"What was that?" the commandant demanded, looking confused.

Jeannie spoke slowly so her comrades could work out what she was saying. "I've heard about your V2 bomb—I worked as an interpreter for your generals in France. I've been through a lot, and I'm not going to create weapons that will cause our people to suffer anymore."

He nodded at the other women, who, with his permission, had brought blankets to wrap around them. "Haven't I treated you well enough?"

"Better than what many of us have experienced thus far, but our treatment should be that according to the Geneva Convention. We are political prisoners." Jeannie pointed to the red triangle on her shoulder. "We will pick your potatoes, not make your bombs."

He seemed aghast and cast his eyes among the line of women. "Do you all feel this way?"

"No," murmured someone nearby.

"I do," Didi said, stepping forward.

"Me too." Yvonne did the same, Violette, Ambroise, and Nadine, her legs looking about to crumple beneath her, followed suit.

His face turned red with anger. "You," he said, pointing to Jeannie. "Come with me."

Some of the women were marched off to the factory, while the rest of the SOE women, excluding Nadine, were sent to the vegetable fields. Jeannie had disappeared and Nadine had been taken to the infirmary. Didi worried for both of them, assuming Jeannie would be punished for her outburst. As for Nadine, it was no secret in the slave camps that if you couldn't work for the Germans, your life was forfeit.

The SOE women spent most of the morning and afternoon picking vegetables and clearing weeds. While Didi was still apprehensive over the fate of her friends, she had to admit it felt good to be out in the fresh fall air—especially since they hadn't been forced to toil in the ammunition warehouse.

Violette approached Didi mid-afternoon. "Do you remember me?" Violette asked in her cockney accent.

"Of course," Didi replied. She leaned in to whisper the opening lines of the poem Marks had written for her code:

> *The life that I have*
> *Is all that I have*
> *And the life that I have*
> *Is yours.*

"That's right," Violette's face softened. "How is Leo doing?"

"I'm not sure," Didi replied. "I haven't seen him since I left for training at The Drokes."

"What's your story?"

Didi looked around, but the attention of the sole guard had been drawn by a female dressed in a skirted SS uniform. Didi gave Violette a quick rundown of all that had happened to her, including the water torture at rue de Saussaies. "I've maintained the cover Buckmaster gave me: Jacqueline du Tetre, the clueless Frenchwoman."

"I think you should tell them you're an English spy. I've never been mistreated and neither have Nadine or Ambroise," Violette insisted. "I think they're afraid Britain will avenge us when the war is over."

Didi, remembering her previous conversation with Yvonne, voiced her disagreement. "I'm going to stick to my cover story of being French. It's worked for me so far."

Violette gave her a searching look. "I suppose only one of us has the right idea." The tone of her voice made it clear she thought it was herself. "Still, if you find a way to escape, will you let me know?"

"Of course," Didi promised.

About a week after they arrived, Violette arranged to dig alongside Didi during garden work. "I have access to a key for one of the gates," Violette whispered.

Didi looked around. It was true Torgau was less guarded then Ravensbrück, but it was still risky and one false move could get them all shot. "We should go as soon as possible," Didi told her.

"No," Violette replied. "We shouldn't rush into anything. We have to make sure it's the right time and that everything is in place."

Didi nodded, slightly reluctant, but all the same feeling buoyant over the new plan.

A few days later, Violette contacted Didi again. "Is it time?" Didi asked eagerly.

"No," Violette said sadly. "Someone overheard me telling Ambroise of our planned escape and informed the guards. Yvonne was in earshot when the guards were discussing it, and knew we'd been given up. I had to throw the key in the creek."

"The key?" Didi gasped. Both of their gazes landed on the creek, which was swollen with fall rain. "It's gone?"

Violette held out her hands. "It was the only thing I could think of.

They searched me, and then my quarters. When they didn't find anything, they left. It saved my life."

"But the key is gone," Didi repeated, deflated.

"I'm sorry." The defeat was equally obvious in Violette's voice.

CHAPTER 78

ODETTE

Odette awoke to see a line of women waiting across the infirmary room from her. Most of them were naked, with bloated stomachs and withered breasts, their knees sticking out from their stick legs like turtles on a log. Their gazes were infused with dread; they knew that one casual judgment deeming them unfit for work meant their lives would be in even greater peril.

They X-rayed Odette's lungs and put drops in her eyes. She was diagnosed with both dysentery, as she had suspected, and scurvy. A nurse gave her a bottle of brown liquid before nodding to a guard, who led Odette out into the sunshine.

On the way back to the Bunker, Odette paused to consider a leaf, its green form lying against the sand. It wavered in the breeze, threatening to blow away. She bent over, seemingly to cough, and picked it up by its fragile stem.

This time when she was shoved back into the black hole that was her cell, she was no longer alone. She had found a friend in her leaf and spent the night pondering all that it had been through. Maybe it had blown all the way from France, moving through the electrified fence with ease, bringing the promise of freedom with it.

. . .

When Sühren paid his monthly visit, he informed Odette that her X-ray from the infirmary showed she had tuberculosis.

Odette took a painful breath, guessing such a diagnosis usually resulted in the murder of the inmate. "Can I see these X-rays?"

He frowned, as if actually considering her request. "You are not a doctor. You will not understand what they show."

Odette kept the plea for her life simple. "Please."

Sühren was back the next day, a shadow in the bright light of the hall. "You do not, in fact, have tuberculosis. But if your condition does not improve, you will surely die." Though Odette's hand was shielding her eyes, she could sense him shift his posture. "You will be moved upstairs as soon as a cell becomes available. There you will have access to sunlight, better food, and exercise."

"Thank you."

"That is all." He saluted her before he left.

Odette went back to contemplating her leaf.

Though she remained in her accustomed crypt for three more weeks, the quantity of her food improved slightly. When she was finally moved to Cell 32, she tried not to think of the previous occupant who—willingly or, most likely, unwillingly—had given up their accommodations for her.

It was indeed better lit upstairs, and, after her eyes stopped burning, she discovered her new lodgings had a window. Upon opening it, she saw she faced the crematorium. *Ahh,* she thought. That explained the black dust covering the windowsill. A dark cloud of smoke billowed from the chimney across from her, and again Odette's thoughts went to the former inhabitant of her cell.

When Sühren came next, he didn't stand in the doorway this time, but took a few steps into the room, holding out his hand in what could almost have been perceived as a conciliatory gesture. "Is everything all right?"

"Yes."

"Do you wish for anything?"

"No, thank you."

· · ·

Odette hadn't been in her new room for more than a few days when she was awoken by the sound of shouting. She rushed to the window. Though it must have been past midnight, an electric street-light blazed below and she could see three women kneeling in the alleyway outside the crematorium. Odette couldn't help but think there was something familiar about the way they carried themselves. Sühren stood a few feet away, appearing to read something from a piece of paper. She watched as he dropped the paper, and nodded to a uniformed guard holding a gun. The crack of a shotgun reverberated through the alleyway before it repeated twice more. Though Odette was no longer looking, she surmised the women had been shot in the back of their heads.

After she'd recovered from her shock, she forced herself back to her post at the window, but the only sight was the gray smoke curling from the chimney of the crematorium.

CHAPTER 79

DIDI

*N*ot less than a week after their failed escape attempt, Didi was transferred to Abteroda, a subcamp of Buchenwald. She'd heard a rumor that the other girls from F Section were sent back to Ravensbrück. She had always been considered a loner, but, nonetheless, Didi felt remorse at their disappearance, especially Yvonne and Violette.

In Abertoda, Didi was forced to make parts for BMW's Messerschmitt airplanes. As her commandant told her, females were preferred as workers because their tinier fingers were more deft at putting together the miniscule engine components.

The food was much worse at Abteroda, and the combination of focusing on her work and having little nourishment to sustain her 12-hour shifts gave Didi a constant headache. Through the blurry haze of staring at the tiny parts, she tried to make yet another escape plan, but the plant and her hut were always surrounded by armed guards.

As she manipulated a screwdriver into an almost-microscopic screw, Didi recalled what Jeannie had said about making German bombs at Torgau. Jeannie, she was sure, had been punished heavily, and the other SOE girls had supposedly been sent off for their protest. This must have been Didi's penalty for her part—to do exactly what she had refused to: help make planes to drop more bombs on the Allies. Her screwdriver fell to the ground.

"You there, lazy cow!" one of the guards called. "Pick that up."

"No," Didi replied.

"No?" He seemed at a loss for words. "Why not?"

"I'm tired. And I no longer want to assist Hitler's army in its injuries against France."

It was probably the longest sentence she'd spoken in German so far. But the guard was not going to congratulate her. "If you refuse, then we will shave your head and not give you any food."

Didi shrugged. "I could use a haircut, and I suppose I could forgo a day or two without your watery soup."

It was clear the guard had expected her to go back to work. His eyes wide, he stared her down, but Didi refused to be intimidated. The guard motioned for another man. After a few heated words in German, the other man clasped his hand around Didi's arm and dragged her away.

Half an hour later, Didi was shoved back to her bench, her hair shorn to her scalp. The original guard approached and told her to get back to work.

"No," she replied.

This time the man shouldered his rifle. "Get back to work or I'll shoot you."

His voice was hesitant and Didi wasn't completely sure he would go through with his threats, but she also wasn't certain she wanted to test him. It seemed ridiculously fruitless to have survived all that she had, only to die by this anxious imbecile.

She held out her arms as she bent down, her eyes on the man with the rifle. Slowly she reached for the dropped screwdriver and picked it up.

"That's better," the guard said, lowering the rifle. "Don't try that again."

She stabbed at the screw as he walked away, noting with a slight sense of satisfaction that she'd stripped the metal off of it. *If I can't outright refuse, at least I can sabotage them.* She poked the screw into the part without securing it, hoping it was a vital piece of the plane and would give way at the slightest gust of wind.

. . .

She carried on this way for the next few days, doing everything she could to hinder the German war effort. Occasionally she was rebuked for her slowness, but she apologized, saying her eyes hurt and that she wasn't used to such intense work.

"You're going to be transferred," the insecure guard with the rifle told her, a hint of satisfaction in his voice.

Didi's hand stumbled for real. *Had they figured her out?* Though it had given her a sense of accomplishment that she hadn't felt in a long time, she knew her game had put her at risk. Still, it might have been worth it.

CHAPTER 80

ODETTE

*S*ometimes, when her wardess bothered to remember, Odette was actually allowed to exercise. One day in mid-December, Odette was in the yard outside the Bunker when a woman approached. She was terribly thin and wore no coat, although it was freezing.

Her slight form shoved into Odette as she passed and thrust something into her hand "*Chocolat,*" she said. "*Joyeux Noël.*"

"*Merci,*" Odette replied. The chocolate was no bigger than the tip of her finger, but her heart warmed anyway.

"*Nein!*" the wardess exclaimed, approaching the prisoners with her whip. "Not on my watch!"

The bearer of chocolate tried to walk away as fast as her gaunt legs would let her. The whip met the woman's back and she fell to the ground before the wardess turned on Odette.

"Give it to me," the wardess demanded, but Odette had already shoved the chocolate into her mouth, relishing the hint of taste the miniscule morsel produced on her tongue.

The wardess raised her whip and Odette's first reaction was to cower but she steeled her spine. A masculine voice shouted and both of them looked over to see Sühren standing nearby.

"No exercise for three days," the wardess stated, reluctantly lowering her arm.

. . .

That Christmas Eve, Odette could hear the celebrations of the guards, who got rip-roaringly drunk, singing Christmas songs in German until near daylight.

On New Year's Day, they celebrated by shooting the woman who had given Odette the chocolate. They made sure to do it in the little alleyway directly below Odette's window, this time in broad daylight. Odette, who had mostly grown immune to trauma in the past year, still jumped at the sound of the shotgun.

CHAPTER 81

MATHILDE

*I*n December, 1944, despite a slight setback with the Nazis' offensive at the Battle of the Bulge, the Allies were making headway across Europe and planning to invade Germany. The British were convinced the war could not last much longer, and the prisoners at Holloway received a special gift basket that year, which included fresh linen for their beds, honey from California for their bread, soap from Virginia, and even a chocolate bar wrapped in gold foil. The female guard who delivered the goods informed Mathilde that the chocolate had come from liberated Paris.

Mathilde broke the chocolate bar in half. "If you wouldn't mind, I'd appreciate it if you would deliver this to Stella Lonsdale."

The guard shook her head. "First of all, every prisoner is getting the same basket. And secondly, Mrs. Lonsdale has been released."

"Released? Where to?"

The guard shrugged. "Now that the war is sure to end in our favor, our government is not so concerned about espionage. I expect you to be gone too, before this new year is out," she added before closing the cell door.

Mathilde felt numb at the announcement. She'd finished her memoirs and had them sent to Buckmaster at the SOE, but had heard nothing in months.

Normally she didn't like to think about what would happen in the next few hours, let alone the next few days, but this time she pondered her future, after the war was over and she was released. Obviously they'd send her back to France, to pick up the pieces of what was left of her life. Even though they'd imprisoned her, Mathilde couldn't help admiring the English for their aloof politeness and calm discretion, which contrasted greatly with the excitability of the French. Would her countrymen and women resent her for the fall of Interallié, or would they come to their senses and respect that she did what she had to do during war-time? *Only time will tell*, she supposed.

CHAPTER 82

DIDI

*I*n February 1945, Didi was transferred yet again, to a camp outside Leipzig. She had become seriously emaciated and was probably suffering from malnutrition and exhaustion, among a host of other things. Her chest ached so badly she couldn't take in any more than the shallowest of breaths.

Almost all the women in the new camp wore the familiar red triangle on their uniforms—political prisoners—and the majority of them were also French. Their uniforms were baggy dark-gray overalls and the winter wind constantly swept through the thin material. They were forced to build roads, but they made little headway with the ice-hardened earth.

One day the woman working alongside Didi collapsed.

Didi tried rousing her, to no avail, before a guard shouted at her to get back to digging.

At the end of the day, the woman's body had frozen to the ground. Didi watched as another prisoner chipped away at it with a shovel before loading it onto the corpse cart. After the macabre job was finished, the woman said to Didi, "The most important thing is maintaining the will to carry on. Don't let them see that they are winning. It will be over soon, you'll see."

"Let's hope so," Didi replied.

·   ·   ·

Slowly the signs of spring appeared. Crocuses, seemingly immune to the suffering around them, sprouted through the warming soil. Though she had now developed a hacking cough, Didi decided to revisit her escape plans. The guards whispered that the Americans were approaching from the west while the Russians were moving east.

One morning in early April, the prisoners had just lined up for Appell when a siren sounded and the loudspeaker crackled to life. "We have just received orders from Berlin to evacuate the camp," the commandant's voice squawked. "We are leaving in twenty minutes."

"You heard him, you filthy bitch." A guard shoved Didi. "Get moving."

A few feet away, a woman fainted. "Fetch a cart," the guard shouted. "Anyone who can't walk will be carried."

The sick and dying prisoners, some of them walking, some of them pushed in wheelbarrows, must have made for a pathetic sight. They marched south all through the rest of the day and into the night. Didi overheard a guard telling someone their destination was a camp 80 kilometers away.

There's no way I can make it that far, Didi decided, trying to catch her breath.

The prisoners travelled much slower than the well-fed, well-rested guards, who marched double time up and down the line. Didi realized that she might be able to leave the procession right after one guard had passed her, while the next was still far behind. To the left of them loomed a heavily wooded forest, and she knew it represented her last chance.

She waited until night had completely fallen and then made her exodus. Luckily her adrenaline kicked in and she found her legs were able to move quickly, even run, toward the woods. She spotted a large tree and ducked behind it, her lungs burning.

She could still hear the stomping of the guards' jackboots on the road ahead, followed by the softer sound of hundreds of women's bare feet. But there was no shouting, no gunshots. No one seemed to have noticed her absence.

As her breath slowed, she became aware of a rustling in the shrubbery directly in front of her. She stifled a gasp as she saw the whites of two pairs of eyes staring at her.

"Who's there?" Didi whispered.

Slowly the forms came closer. Didi recognized one of them as the woman who'd spoken to her the other day. "I'm Suzanne," she said. "And this is Nicole."

All three of them glanced toward the road and the retreating backs of the guards.

"Are we free?" Nicole asked.

"I think so," Didi replied, choking up.

All three of them met in a silent hug before proceeding deeper into the forest.

Didi, Suzanne, and Nicole stayed for three days in the remains of a bombed-out house. They only went out at night, slipping through a tiny hole in the wall no bigger than a dog-door, to forage for food. The girls were too worried that they had been discovered missing to venture very far and made due with dandelion leaves washed down with hand-fuls of melting snow. The lack of food did little to heal Didi's ailments; her chest still ached and now she had developed a hacking cough. Still, she was no longer a prisoner and no longer being punished at the will of vengeful guards.

Didi's mental state wasn't the greatest—she jumped at every little sound, thinking that the guards had sent out a search party. The nights were the worst, but Suzanne tried to soothe the other two's nerves by telling jokes and stories. She had been in the French Air Force, but, after the Occupation, had joined the Resistance with the Free French. She, too, had been taken to Fresnes but left for Ravensbrück on November 11, 1943.

"November 11th," Didi repeated. She sat up. "Did you keep a calendar on the wall in your cell?"

"Yes," Suzanne replied.

"I think we had the same cell at Fresnes. Someone named Lise had done the same thing, but she left in May 1944, a few months before I arrived."

"Probably another woman agent of the SOE."

Didi voiced the thought that had been bothering her since Torgau.

"Do you know what happened to the British women they called, the 'Little Paratroopers?' Specifically Violette Szabo?"

"I heard they were taken back to Ravensbrück and killed," Nicole said softly.

Suzanne reached out to squeeze Didi's hand. "Someday soon the Allies will win the war and the sacrifice of the Little Paratrooper's—and that of all the people who supported the Resistance for that matter—will not have been in vain."

Didi wiped away an errant tear before nodding.

The next morning, Didi was startled awake by the sounds of gunfire. She imagined that the search party had finally found them. *I won't go back to the camps. They'll have to kill me first.* The decision made, Didi rolled over and fell back asleep.

The next time Didi was awakened, it was by the marching of many soldiers. Their uniforms were a darker green than that of the Germans and they spoke English with unfamiliar accents. With a start, Didi realized the Americans had arrived.

They entered their little house, guns pointed. Didi put her arms up. "I am English." She gestured toward Suzanne and Nicole, who were cowering in the corner. "And they are French."

The lead soldier lowered his gun. "Come with us," he told them.

CHAPTER 83

ODETTE

*T*he smoke from the crematorium became a constant presence. It was rumored that the Allies were advancing from all sides and Odette figured that the Germans were trying to destroy the proof of their misdeeds by incinerating both paperwork and dead bodies.

Remnants of the charred evidence swept through Odette's open window, cinders of skin, bone, and the occasional singed hair. Sometimes she heard screaming, which meant they were burning live souls instead of the remains of those shot in the alleyway or hanged on the gallows.

There was increased commotion around her cell as well, and Odette assumed they were cleaning out the Bunker. She could only predict her own death was approaching as quickly as the Allies.

On the eve of her 33rd birthday, Sühren appeared in the doorway of her cell. "You will be leaving tomorrow morning at six."

"Leaving how?"

He lifted one of his manicured fingers and drew it across his throat.

She spent the night preparing herself, mentally saying farewell to her girls, kissing each in turn. In her imagination, there was someone else waiting for a goodbye: Peter. She embraced his imaginary form, pouring kisses all over his face.

"Be well, my love," she said aloud.

The sun was high in the sky by the time Sühren sauntered into her cell. He was late.

"Pack your things," he told her. "Time is short. *Schnell, schnell.*"

"Why should I bother to pack?" She figured he was taking her out to the woods to shoot her, so that he would leave no trace back at camp. The beasts that haunted her nightmares would finally be able to feed upon her, though she hoped Sühren would have finished the job by the time the wolves got to her.

"I am bringing you to the Americans," Sühren stated.

Odette didn't reply—she wouldn't allow herself hope after all these months in hell.

She followed him outside the Bunker to find chaos. SS guards were running every which way, some of the women dressed in the clothes of those they had murdered. With no one to police them, the prisoners wandered about aimlessly, a few attempting to scale the monstrous wall.

"Our mighty Führer, the great Adolf Hitler, is dead," Sühren declared, his voice melancholy. "He died a hero's death in battle."

"Why don't you unlock the gates, then?" Odette asked. "The war is over."

"It's not over yet." Sühren nodded to a guard, who opened the gate just enough to let them out. A prisoner rushed forward, only to be shot down.

Odette paused, wanting to say a prayer over the body, but Sühren pushed her toward an awaiting Mercedes-Benz and told her to get in the passenger's seat.

Odette had no idea why she'd been singled out, or what Sühren's destination was. He said nothing and she didn't bother asking.

They drove for hours before they came across a unit of soldiers in dark-green uniforms blockading the road. One of them shouldered his Tommy gun and waved at them to stop.

Sühren shut the car off and rolled down the window. "This Frau Churchill," he said in his halting English. "She is related to Winston Churchill, the Prime Minister of England."

So that was Sühren's ploy. He was using her as a bargaining chip, hoping the Allies would overlook his murderous record if he delivered the prime minister's supposed relative into their hands.

"I know who Winston Churchill is," the soldier replied in a strange accent.

Odette rolled down the other window and waved at another soldier. "This is Fritz Sühren, Commandant of Ravensbrück Concentration Camp. He has kept me captive against my will for many months. Now it's your turn to make him a prisoner."

She turned to see Sühren's astonished face staring at her. "Give me your pistol," she commanded. With shaking hands, he handed it to her.

Tucking the gun into her bag, Odette opened the car door and exited. "I'm going to need your help locating another one of Churchill's relatives," she told the American soldier. "His first name is Peter."

EPILOGUE

The True Fates of the Characters in *The Spark of Resistance*

*M*athilde Carré : After seven years languishing in prison, in England, and then, after the war was over, in France, Mathilde was put on trial for treason, along with Viola (Renée) Borni. Throughout the trial, Mathilde maintained what French newspapers called "an unrepentant air." One reporter went so far as to declare her mannerisms not that of a cat, but "more a serpent."

Viola, who managed to win more sympathy from the press, had become so weak from illness that she had to be brought to court on a stretcher.

Notable witnesses for the prosecution included René Aubertin, who had managed to survive Mauthausen concentration camp, Mireille Lejeune, Maître Brault, and Pierre de Vomécourt, AKA 'Lucas.'

Hugo Bleicher had been arrested by the British Army after the war and briefly imprisoned, but, seeing as no war crimes could be directly attributed to him, had been released. He had opened a tobacconist's shop in his German hometown, which he was reluctant to leave and was therefore not present at Mathilde's trail. Nor was Roman Czerniawski (Armand), though he too had survived the war. In fact, Armand had convinced the Germans to release him to London from Fresnes under the guise he would become a double-agent and went on to play an integral role in the purposeful disinformation the Allies provided to the German Army leading up to D-Day.

During his testimony, René Aubertin declared that Mathilde "preferred her own life to that of thirty-five other people." He also told the story of how Lucien de Roquigny, the Polish aristocrat who had once carried a torch for The Cat before she assisted in his arrest, had become "the whipping-boy of all the Gestapo guards and (had been) literally beaten to death."

Lucas had been arrested by Bleicher only three weeks after he returned to Paris and spent eighteen months in Fresnes Prison before he was transferred as a prisoner-of-war to Colditz Castle. While on the witness stand, Lucas maintained that Mathilde had worked faithfully for him and that she had been sincere in her desire to plot with him against the Germans to "make amends." He did point out, however, that Mathilde had not informed him of her association with Bleicher until he relayed his own suspicions over the near arrest of Maître Brault. In a letter he wrote after the war, Lucas declared that Mathilde had distinguished herself from the other Resistance members "by the whole-hearted way she sent her former comrades to death."

During the trial, it was revealed that Viola, in fact, had been responsible for Mathilde's arrest. An earlier MI6 report had stated, "It is felt that if Mme. Borni disclosed the name and address of Mme. Carré to the Germans, she did the (Allies) a disservice, the gravity of which she cannot possibly have realized at the time of the offence. It was, however, a case of consequential damage since the real trouble started only when Mme. Carré allowed herself to be turned immediately into a double agent by the Germans." The jury found that "extenuating circumstances" had dictated Viola Borni's actions; she was sentenced to two and a half years of prison and a fine roughly equivalent to $50. She bore out half of those years in a hospital, and was released early.

Though Mathilde was given the death penalty, it was commuted to life in prison in 1949. She was released in 1954 and, unlike many of her Interallié colleagues, managed to live to old age. Her memoirs were eventually turned into a book titled, *I was 'The Cat': The Truth about the Most Remarkable Woman Spy Since Mata Hari*. She died in Paris in 2007, at the age of 98.

. . .

Odette Sansom: After Fresnes, Peter Churchill had been taken to Sachsenhausen concentration camp. As the Allies approached, he was moved to different camps, first to Flossenbürg and then to Dachau. Once Odette and Peter had both returned to England, Vera Atkins was the one responsible for coordinating their reunion.

Someone in the SOE, probably Miss Atkins again, arranged for Odette's quiet divorce from Roy Sansom in 1946, and she and Peter were married shortly after. However, Odette and Peter's great love didn't last long. They divorced ten years later and Odette married Geoffrey Hallowes, another SOE agent, that same year. Peter never remarried and he and Odette remained friendly until his death in 1972, at the age of 63.

Odette's story was retold in a 1949 biography called *Odette* by Jerrard Tickell and made into a 1950 movie with the same name. She was the first—and only one still alive—of three FANYs to receive the George Cross, Britain's second highest award.[1] Of the seventeen F Section women who were arrested, only three survived. Odette was the only one who had officially been condemned to death. She passed away in 1995 at the age of 82.

Notable associates of Spindle who died in concentration camps include Paul Frager, who was executed at Buchenwald, and Adolphe Rabinovitch (Alec). Alec had been captured shortly before D-Day and, probably because he was Jewish, was gassed at the Rawicz extermination camp, located in Poland, in 1944. Frager had been betrayed by his colleague Roger Bardet—and probably also by Bardet's close associate Jean Keiffer (Kiki of Interallié fame)—and was arrested by Bleicher in 1944. Although Bardet and Kiki were both sentenced to death after the war, like Mathilde, their sentences were commuted and both were eventually released.

Eileen "Didi" Nearne: After she'd encountered the American soldiers, Didi thought her ordeal was over, but the Americans didn't believe her incredible story. Although she was clearly malnourished and still in her prison uniform, the Americans thought she was a German agent and kept her in a room with captured female SS guards. It didn't help that, in her fragile state, Didi's mind had become muddled, nor that the Americans were unaware that female British agents had been sent to France.

She was in their custody for three weeks until Vera Atkins came across a report written by the Americans and recognized that the "unbalanced" subject they described was one of their own.

When Didi finally returned to England, she moved in with her sister, Jackie. Though Didi suffered from "exhaustion,"[2] Miss Atkins tried to help her find gainful employment in London.

Though, unlike Odette, Violette, and Nora, Didi was never awarded the George Cross, she did receive the Croix de Guerre from the French government, and was appointed a Member of the Order of the British Empire (MBE) by King George VI for "services in France during the enemy occupation."

In 1993, Didi returned to Ravensbrück to attend a dedication ceremony. Odette, Yvonne Baseden, Vera Atkins, Leo Marks, Francis Cammaerts, and Violette Szabo's daughter were among those also in attendance.

After Jackie died in 1982, Didi lived alone until her death in 2010, at the age of 89. Neither sister ever married.

A note to the reader: Thanks so much for reading this book! If you have time to spare, please consider leaving a short review on Amazon. Reviews are very important to indie authors such as myself and I would greatly appreciate it!

Read on for a sample of *L'Agent Double: Spies and Martyrs in the Great War!*

---

1. The other F Section women to receive the George Cross, Violette Szabo and Noor Inayat Khan (Nora in the novel) did so posthumously. The women who were shot outside Odette's cell at Ravensbrück and then put in the crematorium were the "Little Paratroopers": Violette Szabo, Lilian Rolfe (Nadine), and Denise Bloch (Ambroise). For more information on their stories, visit www.kitsergeant.com
2. Didi probably suffered from what is now known as "Post-traumatic Stress Disorder."

SELECTED BIBLIOGRAPHY

Carré, Mathilde Lily. *I Was the Cat*. New York, Lancer, 1969.

Garby-Czerniawski, Roman. *The Big Network*. London, G. Roland, 1961.

Helm, Sarah. *Ravensbrück: Life and Death in Hitler's Concentration Camp for Women*. New York, Anchor Books, 2016.

Helm, Sarah. *A Life in Secrets: Vera Atkins and the Missing Agents of WWII*. New York, Ny Nan A. Talese, 2006.

Jerrard Tickell. *Odette*. London, Headline Review, 2008.

Loftis, Larry. *Code Name: Lise: The True Story of World War II's Most Highly Decorated Spy*. New York; London; Toronto, Gallery Books, 2019.

Marks, Leo. *Between Silk and Cyanide: A Code Makers's War, 1941-45*. Stroud, Gloucestershire, The History Press, 2013.

O'connor, Bernard. *Agent Rose: The True Spy Story of Eileen Nearne, Britain's Forgotten Wartime Heroine*. Stroud, Amberley, 2014.

Ottaway, Susan. *A Cool and Lonely Courage: The Untold Story of Sister Spies in Occupied France*. New York, Little, Brown And Company, 2014.

Paine, Lauran. *Mathilde Carré, Double Agent*. London, Hale, 1976.

Rose, Sarah. *D-Day Girls: The Spies Who Armed the Resistance, Sabotaged the NAZIS, and Helped Win World War II*. New York Crown, 2019.

Tremain, David. *Double Agent Victoire: Mathilde Carré and the Interallié Network*. Stroud, Gloucestershire, The History Press, 2018.

Young, Gordon. *The Cat with Two Faces*. London, White Lion Publishers, 1975.

L'AGENT DOUBLE PROLOGUE

OCTOBER 1917

The nun on duty woke her just before dawn. She blinked the sleep out of her eyes to see a crowd of men, including her accusers and her lawyer, standing just outside the iron bars of her cell. The only one who spoke was the chief of the Military Police, to inform her the time of her execution had come. The men then turned and walked away, leaving only the nun and the prison doctor, who kept his eyes on the dirty, straw-strewn floor as she dressed.

She chose the best outfit she had left, a bulky dove-gray skirt and jacket and scuffed ankle boots. She wound her unwashed hair in a bun and then tied the worn silk ribbons of her hat under her chin before asking the doctor, "Do I have time to write good-byes to my loved ones?"

He nodded and she hastily penned three farewell letters. She handed them to the doctor with shaking hands before lifting a dust-covered velvet cloak from a nail on the wall. "I am ready."

Seemingly out of nowhere, her lawyer reappeared. "This way," he told her as he grasped her arm.

Prison rats scurried out their way as he led her down the hall. She breathed in a heavy breath when they were outside. It had been months since she'd seen the light of day, however faint it was now.

Four black cars were waiting in the prison courtyard. A few men scattered about the lawn lifted their freezing hands to bring their cameras to life, the bulbs brightening the dim morning as her lawyer bundled her into the first car.

They drove in silence. It was unseasonably cold and the chill sent icy fingers down her spine. She stopped herself from shivering, wishing that she could experience one more warm summer day. But there would be no more warmth, no more appeals, nothing left after these last few hours.

She knew that her fate awaited her at Caponniére, the old fort just outside of Vincennes where the cavalry trained. Upon arrival, her lawyer helped her out of the car, his gnarled hands digging into her arm.

It's harder for him than it is for me. She brushed the thought away, wanting to focus on nothing but the fresh air and the way the autumn leaves of the trees next to the parade ground changed color as the sun rose. Her lawyer removed his arm from her shoulders as two Zouave escorts appeared on either side of her. Her self-imposed blinders finally dropped as she took in the twelve soldiers with guns and, several meters away, the wooden stake placed in front of a brick wall. *So that the mis-aimed bullets don't hit anything else.*

A priest approached and offered her a blindfold.

"No thank you." Her voice, which had not been used on a daily basis for months, was barely a whisper.

The priest glanced over at her lawyer, who nodded. The blindfold disappeared under his robes.

She spoke the same words to one of the escorts as he held up a rope, this time also shaking her head. She refused to be bound to the stake. He acquiesced, and walked away.

She stood as straight as she could, free of any ties, while the military chief read the following words aloud:

By decree of the Third Council of War, the woman who appears before us now has been condemned to death for espionage.

He then gave an order, and the soldiers came to attention. At the command, *"En joue!"* they hoisted their guns to rest on their shoulders. The chief raised his sword.

She took a deep breath and then lifted her chin, willing herself to die just like that: head held high, showing no fear. She watched as the chief lowered his sword and shouted *"Feu!"*

And then everything went black.

A Zouave private approached the body. He'd only been enlisted for a few weeks and had been invited to the firing squad by his commander, who told him that men of all ranks should know the pleasure of shooting a German spy.

"By blue, that lady knew how to die," another Zouave commented.

"Who was she?" the private asked. He'd been taught that everything in war was black and white: the Germans were evil, the Allies pure. But he was surprised at how gray everything was that morning: from the misty fog, to the woman's cloak and dress, and even the ashen shade of her lifeless face.

The other Zouave shrugged. "All I know is what they told me. They say she acted as a double agent and provided Germany with intelligence about our troops." He drew his revolver and bent down to place the muzzle against the woman's left temple.

"But is it necessary to kill her a helpless woman?" the private asked.

The Zouave cocked his gun for the *coup de grâce*. "If women act as men would in war and commit heinous crimes, they should be prepared to be punished as men." And he pulled the trigger, sending a final bullet into the woman's brain

L'AGENT DOUBLE CHAPTER 1

M'GREET

JULY 1914

"*H*ave you heard the latest?" M'greet's maid, Anna, asked as she secured a custom-made headpiece to her mistress's temple.

"What now?" M'greet readjusted the gold headdress to better reflect her olive skin tone.

"They are saying that your mysterious Mr. K from the newspaper article is none other than the Crown Prince himself."

M'greet smiled at herself in the mirror. "Is that so? I rather think they're referring to Lieutenant Kiepert. Just the other day he and I ran into the editor of the *Berliner Tageblatt* during our walk in the Tiergarten." Her smile faded. "But let them wonder." For the last few weeks, the papers had been filled with speculation about why the famed Mata Hari had returned to Germany, sometimes bordering on derision about her running out of money.

She leaned forward and ran her fingers over the dark circles under her eyes. "Astruc says that he might be able to negotiate a longer engagement in the fall if tonight's performance goes well."

"It will," Anna assured her as she fastened the heavy gold necklace around M'greet's neck.

The metal felt cold against her sweaty skin. She hadn't performed in months, and guessed the perspiration derived from her nervousness. Tonight was to be the largest performance she'd booked in years: Berlin's Metropol could seat 1108 people, and the tickets had sold out days ago. The building was less than a decade old, and even the dressing room's geometric wallpaper and curved furniture reflected the Art Nouveau style the theater was famous for.

"I had to have this costume refitted." M'greet pulled at the sheer yellow fabric covering her midsection. When she first began dancing, she had worn jeweled bralettes and long, sheer skirts that sat low on the hips. But her body had become much more matronly in middle age and even M'greet knew that she could no longer get away with the scandalous outfits of her youth. She added a cumbersome earring to each ear and an arm band before someone knocked on the door.

A man's voice called urgently in German, "Fräulein Mata Hari, are you ready?"

Anna shot her mistress an encouraging smile. "Your devoted admirers are waiting."

M'greet stretched out her arms and rotated her wrists, glancing with appreciation in the mirror. She still had it. She grabbed a handful of translucent scarves and draped them over her arms and head before opening the door. "All set," she said to the awaiting attendant.

M'greet waited behind a filmy curtain while the music began: low, mournful drumming accompanied by a woman's shrill tone singing in a foreign language. As the curtain rose, she hoisted her arms above her head and stuck her hips out in the manner she had seen the women do when she lived in Java.

She had no formal dance training, but it didn't matter. People came to see Mata Hari for the spectacle, not because she was an exceptionally wonderful dancer. M'greet pulled the scarf off her head and undulated her hips in time with the music. She pinched her fingers together and moved her arms as if she were a graceful bird about to take flight. The drums heightened in intensity and her gyrations became even more exaggerated. As the music came to a dramatic stop, she released the scarves covering her body to reveal her yellow dress in full.

She was accustomed to hearing astonished murmurs from the audience following her final act—she'd once proclaimed that her success rose with every veil she threw off. Tonight, however, the Berlin audience seemed to be buzzing with protest.

As the curtain fell and M'greet began to pick up the pieces of her discarded costume, she assured herself that the Berliners' vocalizations were in response to being disappointed at seeing her more covered. Or maybe she was just being paranoid and had imagined all the ruckus.

"Fabulous!" her agent, Gabriel Astruc, exclaimed when he burst into her dressing room a few minutes later.

M'greet held a powder puff to her cheek. "Did you finalize a contract for the fall?"

"I did," Astruc sat in the only other chair, which appeared too tiny to support his large frame. "They are giving us 48,000 marks."

She nodded approvingly.

"That should tide you over for a while, no?" he asked.

She placed the puff in the gold-lined powder case. "For now. But the creditors are relentless. Thankfully Lieutenant Kieper has gifted me a few hundred francs."

"As a loan?" Astruc winked. "It is said you have become mistress to the *Kronprinz*."

She rolled her eyes. "You of all people must know to never mind such rumors. I may be well familiar with men in high positions, but have not yet made the acquaintance of the Kaiser's son."

Astruc rose. "Someday you two will meet, and even the heir of the German Empire will be unable to resist the charms of the exotic Mata Hari."

M'greet unsnapped the cap of her lipstick. "We shall see, won't we?"

Now that the fall performances had been secured, M'greet decided to upgrade her lodgings to the lavish Hotel Adlon. As she entered the lobby, with its sparkling chandeliers dangling from intricately carved ceilings and exotic potted palms scattered among velvet-cushioned chairs, she nodded to herself. *This was the type of hotel a world-renowned dancer should be found in.* She booked an apartment complete with electric Tiffany lamps and a private bathroom featuring running water.

The Adlon was known not only for its famous patrons, but for the privacy it provided them. M'greet was therefore startled the next morning when someone banged on the door to her suite.

"Yes?" Anna asked as she opened it.

"Are you Mata Hari?" a gruff voice inquired.

M'greet threw on a silky robe over her nightgown before she went to the door. "You must be looking for me."

The man in the doorway appeared to be about forty, with a receding hairline and a bushy mustache that curled upward from both sides of his mouth. "I am Herr Griebel of the Berlin police."

M'greet ignored Anna's stricken expression as she motioned for her to move aside. "Please come in." She gestured toward a chair at the little serving table. "Shall I order up some tea?"

"That won't be necessary," Griebel replied as he sat. "I am here to inform you that a spectator of your performance last night has lodged a complaint."

"A complaint? Against me?" M'greet repeated as she took a seat in the chair across from him. She mouthed, "tea," at Anna, who was still standing near the door. Anna nodded and then left the room.

"Indeed," Griebel touched his mustache. "A complaint of indecency."

"I see." She leaned forward. "You are part of the *Sittenpolizei*, then." They were a department charged with enforcing the Kaiser's so-called laws of morality. M'greet had been visited a few times in the past by such men, but nothing had ever come of it. She flashed Griebel a seductive smile. "Surely your department has no issue with sacred dances?"

"Ah," Griebel fidgeted with the collar of his uniform, clearly uncomfortable.

Mirroring his movements, M'greet fingered the neckline of her low-cut gown. "After all, there are more important issues going on in the world than my little dance."

"Such as?" Griebel asked.

The door opened and Anna discreetly placed a tea set on the crisp white tablecloth. She gave her mistress a worried look but M'greet waved her off before pouring Griebel a cup of tea. "Well, I'm sure you heard about that poor man that was shot in the Balkans in June."

"Of course—it's been in all of the papers. The 'poor man,' as you call him, was Archduke Franz Ferdinand. Austria should not stand down when the heir to their throne was shot by militant Serbs."

M'greet took a sip of tea. "Are you saying they should go to war?"

"They should. And Germany, as Austria's ally, ought to accompany them."

"Over one man? You cannot be serious."

"Those Serbs need to be taught a lesson, once and for all." Upon seeing the pout on M'greet's face, Griebel waved his hand. "But you shouldn't worry your pretty little head over talk of politics."

She pursed her lips. "You're right. It's not something that a woman like me should be discussing."

"No." He set down his tea cup and pulled something out of his pocket. "As I was saying when I first came in, about the complaint—"

"As *I* was saying..." she faked a yawn, stretching her arms out while sticking out her bosom. The stocky, balding Griebel was not nearly as handsome as some of the men she'd met over the years, but M'greet knew that she needed to become better acquainted with him in order to get the charges dropped. Besides, she'd always had a weakness for men in uniform. "My routine is adopted from Hindu religious dances and should not be misconstrued as immoral." She placed a hand over Griebel's thick fingers, causing the paper to fall to the floor. "I think, if the two of us put our heads together, we can definitely find a mutual agreement."

He pulled his hand away to wipe his forehead with a handkerchief. "I don't know if that's possible."

M'greet got up from her chair to spread herself on the bed, displaying her body to its advantage as a chef would his best dish.

"Perhaps we could work out an arrangement that would benefit us both," Griebel agreed as he walked over to her.

Griebel's mustache tickled her face, but she forced herself to think about other things as he kissed her. Her thoughts at such moments often traveled to her daughter, Non, but today she focused on the other night's performance. M'greet always did what it took to survive, and right now she needed the money that her contract with the Berlin Metropol would provide, and nothing could get in the way of that.

M'greet was glad to count Herr Griebel as her new lover as the tensions between the advocates of the Kaiser—who wanted to "finish with the Serbs quickly"—and the pacifists determined to keep Germany out of war heightened throughout Berlin at the end of July.

Although Griebel was on the side of the war-mongers, M'greet felt secure traveling on his arm every night on their way to Berlin's most popular venues.

It was in the back room at one such establishment, the Borchardt, that she met some of Griebel's cronies. They had gathered to talk about the recent developments—Austria-Hungary had officially declared war on Serbia. M'greet knew her place was to look pretty and say nothing, but at the same time she couldn't help but listen to what they were discussing.

"I've heard that Russia has mobilized her troops," a heavyset, balding man stated. M'greet recalled that his name was Müller.

"Ah," Griebel sat back in the plush leather booth. "That's the rub, now isn't it?"

Herr Vogel, Griebel's closest compatriot, shook his head. "I'd hoped Russia would stay out of it." He flicked ash from his cigar into a nearby tray. "After all, the Kaiser and the Tsar are cousins."

"No," Müller replied. "Those Serbs went crying to Mother Russia, and she responded." He nodded to himself. "Now it's only a matter of time before we jump in to protect Austria."

As if on cue, the sound of breaking glass was heard.

M'greet ended her silence. "What was that?"

Griebel put a protective hand on her arm. "I'm not sure." He used his other arm to flag down a passing waiter. "What is going on?"

The young man looked panic-stricken. "There is a demonstration on the streets. Someone threw a brick through the front window and our owner is asking all of the patrons to leave."

"Has war broken out?" M'greet inquired of Griebel as she pulled her arm away. His grip had left white marks.

"I'm not sure." He picked up her fur shawl and headed to the main room of the restaurant. Pandemonium reigned as Berlin's elite rushed toward the doors. Discarded feathers from fashionable ladies' hats and boas floated through the air and littered the ground before stamping feet stirred them up again. M'greet wished she hadn't shaken off Griebel's arm as now she was being shoved this way and that. Someone trampled over her dress and she heard the sound of ripping lace.

She nearly tripped before a strong hand landed on her elbow. "This way," the young waiter told her. He led her through the kitchen and out the back door, where Griebel's Benz was waiting. Griebel appeared a few minutes later and the driver told him there was a massive protest outside the Kaiser's palace.

"Let's go there," Griebel instructed.

"No." M'greet wrapped the fur shawl around her shoulders. "Take me home first."

"Don't you want to find out what's happening?" Griebel demanded, waving his hand as a crowd of people thronged the streets. "This could be the beginning of a war the likes of which no one has ever seen."

"No," she repeated. It seemed to her that the Great Powers of Europe: Germany, Russia, France, and possibly England, were entering into a scrap they had no business getting involved with. "I don't care about any war and I've had enough tonight. I want to go home."

Griebel gave her a strange look but motioned for the driver to do as she said.

They were forced to drive slowly, as the streets had become jammed with motor cars, horse carts, and people rushing about on foot. M'greet caught what they were chanting as the crowd marched past. She repeated the words aloud: *"Deutschland über alles."*

"Germany over all," Griebel supplied.

The war came quickly. Germany first officially declared war on Russia to the east and two days later did the same to France in the west. In Berlin, so-called bank riots occurred as people rushed to their financial institutions and emptied their savings accounts, trading paper money for gold and silver coins. Prices for food and other necessities soared as people stocked up on goods while they could still afford them.

Worried about her own fate, M'greet placed several calls to her agent, Astruc, wanting to know if the war meant her fall performances would be cancelled. After leaving many messages, she eventually got word that Astruc had fled town, presumably with the money the Metropol had paid her in advance.

She decided to brave the confusion at the bank in order to withdraw what little funds she had left.

"I'm sorry," the teller informed M'greet when she finally made it to the counter. "It looks as though your account has been blocked."

"How can you say that?" she demanded. "There should be plenty of money in my account." The plenty part might not have been strictly true, but there was no way it was empty.

"The address you gave when you opened the account was in Paris. We cannot give funds to any foreigner at this time."

M'greet put both fists on the counter. "I wish to speak with your manager."

The teller gestured behind her. M'greet glanced back to see a long line of people, their exhausted, bewildered faces beginning to glower. "I'm sorry, fräulein, I can do nothing more."

She opened her mouth to let him have the worst of her fury, but a man in a police uniform appeared beside her. "A foreigner you say?" He pulled M'greet out of the bank line, and roughly turned her to face him. "What are you, a Russian?"

M'greet knew her dark hair and coloring was not typical of someone with Dutch heritage, but this was a new accusation. "I am no such thing."

"Russian, for sure," a man standing in line agreed.

"Her address was in France," the teller called before accepting a bank card from the next person.

"Well, Miss Russian Francophile, you are coming with me." For the second time in a week, a strange man put his hand on M'greet's elbow and led her away.

M'greet fumed all the way to the police station. She'd had enough of Berlin: due to this infernal war, she was now void of funds and it looked as though her engagements were to be cancelled. She figured her best course of action would be to return to Paris and use her connections to try to get some work there.

When they arrived at the police station, M'greet immediately asked for Herr Griebel. He appeared a few minutes later, a wry smile on his face. "You've been arrested under suspicion of being a troublesome alien."

M'greet waved off that comment with a brush of her hand. "We both know that's ridiculous. Can you secure my release as soon as possible? I must get back to Paris before my possessions there are seized."

Griebel's amused smile faded as his lip curled into a sneer. "You cannot travel to an enemy country in the middle of a war."

"Why not?"

The sneer deepened. "Because…" His narrowed eyes suddenly softened. "Come with me. There is someone I want you to meet." He led her to an office that occupied the end of a narrow hallway and knocked on the closed door labeled, *Traugott von Jagow, Berliner Polizei.*

"Come in," a voice growled.

Griebel entered and then saluted.

The man behind the desk had a thin face and heavy mustache which drooped downward. "What is it, Herr Griebel? You must know I am extremely busy." He dipped a pen in ink and began writing.

Griebel lowered his arm. "Indeed, sir, but I wanted you to meet the acclaimed Mata Hari."

Von Jagow paused his scribbling and looked up. His eyes traveled down from the feather atop M'greet's hat and stopped at her chest. "Wasn't there a morality complaint filed against you?"

M'greet stepped forward, but before she could protest, Griebel cleared his throat. "We are here because she wants to return to Paris."

Von Jagow gave a loud "harrumph," and then continued his writing. "You are not the first person to ask such a question, but we can't let anyone cross the border into enemy territory at this time. People would think you were a spy." He abruptly stopped writing and set his pen down. "A courtesan with a flair for seducing powerful men…" He shot a meaningful look at Griebel, who stared at the floor. "And a long-term resident of Paris with admittedly low morals." He finally met M'greet's eyes. "We could use a woman like you. I'm forming a network of agents who can provide us information about the goings-on in France."

M'greet tried to keep the horror from showing on her face. Was this man asking her to be a spy for Germany? "No thank you," she replied. "As I told Herr Griebel, I have no interest in the war. I just want to get back to Paris."

Von Jagow crossed his arms and sat back. "And I can help you with that, provided that you agree to work for me."

She shook her head and spoke in a soft voice. "Thank you, sir, but it seems I'll have to find a way back on my own."

"Very well, then." Von Jagow picked up his pen again. "Good luck." His voice implied that he wished her just the opposite.

L'AGENT DOUBLE CHAPTER 2

MARTHE

AUGUST 1914

𝓜arthe Cnockaert didn't think anything could spoil this year's Kermis. People had been arriving in Westrozebeke for days from all over Belgium. She herself had just returned home from her medical studies at Ghent University on holiday and had nearly been overcome by the tediousness of living in her small village again. She gazed around the garland-bedecked Grand Place lined with colorful vendor booths in satisfaction. The rest of Europe may have plunged into war, but Belgium had vowed to remain neutral, and the mayor declared that the annual Kermis would be celebrated just as it had been since the middle ages.

The smell of pie wafted from a booth as Marthe passed by and the bright notes of a hurdy-gurdy were audible over the noise of the crowd. She had just entered the queue for the carousel when she heard someone call, "Marthe!"

She turned at the sound of her name to see Valerie, a girl she had known since primary school. "Marthe, how are you? How is Max?" As usual, Valerie was breathless, as though she had recently run a marathon, but it appeared she'd only just gotten off the carousel.

Marthe refrained from rolling her eyes. "Max is still in Ghent, finishing up his studies." Valerie had never hidden the fact she'd always had a crush on Marthe's older brother, even after she'd become betrothed to Nicholas Hoot.

Valerie sighed as she looked around. "There's nobody here but women, children, and old men. All the boys our age have gone off to war and now there's no one left to flirt with."

"Where is Nicholas?"

"He was called to Liége. I suppose you've heard that Germany is demanding safe passage through Belgium in order to get to Paris."

"No."

Valerie shrugged. "They are saying we might have to join the war if Germany decides to invade. But the good news is some treaty states that England would have to enter on our side if that happened."

"Join the war?" Marthe was shocked at both the information and the fact that Valerie seemed so nonchalant about it. There were a few beats of silence, broken only by the endless tune from the carousel's music box, as Marthe pondered this.

"Ah, Marthe, I see you have returned from university." Meneer Hoot, an old friend of her father's, and Valerie's future father-in-law, was nearly shouting, both because he was hard of hearing and because the carousel had started spinning.

"Yes, indeed. I am home for a few weeks before I finish my last year of nursing school," Marthe answered loudly. "Glad to see you are doing well. How is your wife?"

"Oh, you know. Terrified at the prospect of a German invasion, but aren't we all?"

Marthe gave him and Valerie a tentative smile as the church bell rang the hour. "I must be getting home to help Mother with dinner."

Marthe knew something was wrong as soon as she entered the kitchen. "What is it?" she asked, glancing at her father's somber face.

"It's the Germans. They have invaded Belgium."

Marthe fell into her chair. Mother stood in the corner of the room, ironing a cap.

"Belgium has ordered our troops to Liége." Father sank his head into his hands. "But we could never defend ourselves against those bloody Boches."

Mother set her iron down and then took a seat at the kitchen table. "What about Max? Will he come home from Ghent?"

Father took his hands away from his face. "I don't know. I don't know anything now."

"I suppose we should send for him," Marthe said.

Mother cast a worried glance at Father before nodding at her daughter.

For the first time Marthe could remember, Kermis ended before the typical eight days. That didn't stop the endless train of people coming into Westrozebeke, however. The newcomers were refugees from villages near Liége and were headed to Ypres, 15 kilometers southwest, where they had been told they could find food and shelter.

Max sent word that he would be traveling in the opposite direction. He was going to Liége, a town on the Belgian/German border that was protected by a series of concrete fortifications. The Germans were supposedly en route there as well. Both Father and Mother were saddened by Max's decision to enlist in the army, but Marthe understood the circumstances: Belgium must be defended at all costs. She wrote her brother a letter stating the same and urged him to be careful.

As Westrozebeke became a temporary camp, Marthe's family's house and barn, like many of the other houses in the village, were quickly packed with the unfortunate evacuees. Soon the news that Liége had fallen came, and not long after, the first of the soldiers who had been cut off from the main Belgian army arrived.

Marthe stood on the porch and watched a few of them straggle through town. Their frayed uniforms were covered in dark splotches, some of it dirt, some of it blood. Their faces were unshaven, their skin filthy, but the worst part was that none of them were Max.

Upon spotting Nicholas Hoot's downtrodden form, Marthe rushed into the street. "Have you heard from Max?" she asked.

Nicholas met her eyes. His were wide and terrified, holding a record of past horrors, as though he had seen the devil himself. "No."

"C'mon," Marthe put his heavy arm over her shoulders. "Let's get you home."

· · ·

Mevrouw Hoot greeted them at the door. "Nicholas, my son." She hugged his gaunt body before leading him inside.

After his second cup of tea, Nicholas could croak out a few sentences. After a third cup and some biscuits, he was able to relay the horrific conditions the Belgian soldiers had experienced at Liége, especially the burning inferno of Fort de Loncin, which had been hit by a shell from one of the German's enormous guns, known as Big Bertha. De Loncin had been the last of the twelve forts around Liége to yield to the Boches.

"Do you know what happened to Max?" Marthe asked.

Nicholas shook his head. "I never saw him. But it was a very confusing time." His cracked lips formed into something that resembled his old smile. "The Germans are terrified of *francs-tireurs* and think every Belgian civilian is a secret sniper out to get them." The smile quickly faded. "The Fritzes dragged old men and teenagers into the square, accusing them of shooting at their troops. It was mostly their own men mistakenly firing upon each other, but no matter. They killed the innocent villagers anyway." He set his tea cup down. "The Huns are blood-thirsty and vicious, and they are headed this way. We should flee further west as soon as possible."

Mevrouw Hoot met Marthe's eyes. "I'll tell Father," Marthe stated before taking her leave.

Mother was ready to depart, but Father was reluctant, stating that if Max did come home, he would find his family gone. Marthe agreed and disagreed with both sides. On the one hand, she wanted to wait for her brother, and judge for herself if the Germans were as terrible as Nicholas had said. On the other hand, if he was indeed correct, they should go as far west as possible.

The argument became moot when Marthe was awakened the next morning by an unearthly piercing noise overhead. The shrieks grew louder until the entire house shook with the crescendo, and then there was an even more disturbing silence.

Marthe tossed on her robe and then rushed downstairs. No one was in the kitchen, so she pulled Max's old boots over her bare feet and ran the few blocks to the Grand Place. She could see the mushroom cloud of black smoke was just beginning to clear.

She nearly tripped in her oversized boots when she saw someone lying in the roadway. It was Mevrouw Visser, one of her elderly neighbors. She bent over the bloodied body, but the woman had already passed.

The sound of horse hooves caused Marthe to look up. She froze as she saw the men atop were soldiers in unfamiliar khaki uniforms.

"Hallo," called a man with a thin mustache and a flat red cap. He stopped his horse short of Mevrouw Visser. "Met her maker, has she?" The way he ended the sentence with a question that didn't expect an answer made Marthe realize the British had arrived. The men paused at similarly lying bodies, giving food and water to those who still clung to life, but after an hour or so, they rode off.

Marthe went home, her robe now tattered and soiled, her feet sweaty in her boots. "What now?" she asked her father, who was seated at the kitchen table, also covered in perspiration, dirt, and blood.

"Now we wait for Max."

A knock sounded on the front door and Marthe went to answer it, fearing that she would greet a Hun in a spiked helmet. But the soldier outside was in a blue uniform. "The bloody Boches are on their way," he stated in a French accent. "You must flee the village, mademoiselle."

She glanced at Father, who was still sitting at the kitchen table. "I cannot."

The French soldier took a few steps backward to peer at the second floor before returning his gaze back to her. "Our guns will arrive soon, but we are only a small portion of our squadron, and cannot possibly hope to hold them for long. We are asking the villagers to allow us access to their homes in order to take aim."

She nodded and opened the door. He marched into the kitchen and spoke to her father.

Marthe went outside, and looked up and down the street, which was now dotted with soldiers in the blue uniforms of the French. The sound of hammering permeated the air. The soldier she had spoken to went upstairs to pound small viewing holes into the wood of the rooms facing the street. She helped Father barricade the windows and front door with furniture.

Marthe and her parents sequestered themselves in her bedroom, which faced the back of the house. Although half of her was frightened, the other was intensely curious as to what would happen. She used her father's telescope to peer through a loophole in the wood-barricaded window.

"I see them!" she shouted as a gray mass came into view.

"Marthe, get down!" her father returned.

She reluctantly retired the telescope, but not before she peered outside again. The masses had become individual men topped by repulsive-looking spiked helmets. There were hundreds of them and they were headed straight for the Grand Place.

The windows rattled as the hooves of an army of horses came closer. Marthe knew that many of those carts were filled with the Boches' giant guns.

The French machine guns, known as *mitrailleuse,* began an incessant rattling. *Rat-a-tat-tat:* ad infinitum. Marthe couldn't help herself and peeped through the hole again, watching as the gray mob started running, men falling from the fire of the *mitrailleuse.*

Mother's face was stricken as a bullet tore through the wood inches above her daughter's head. Wordlessly Father grabbed both of their hands to bring them downstairs. At the foot of the stairs was a French soldier rocking back and forth, clutching his stomach. Father tried to pull Marthe toward the cellar, but she paused when she saw the blood spurting from the soldier's stomach. All of her university training thus far had not prepared her for this horrific sight, his entrails beginning to spill out of the wound, but she reached out with trembling fingers to prop him against the wall. "You must keep still."

His distraught eyes met hers as he managed to croak out one word. "Water."

Marthe knew that water would only add to his suffering. The sound of gunfire grew closer, and Father yanked her away.

They had just reached the cellar when a shell sounded and a piece of plaster from the wall landed near Father. He struck a match and lit his pipe. "Courage," he said. "The French will beat them back," but the defeated tone of his voice told Marthe that he did not believe it to be so. Nothing could stay that rushing deluge of gray regiments she had spotted from the window.

When the *mitrailleuse* finally ceased its firing, Marthe crept upstairs to retrieve water. The man at the stairs had succumbed to death, and there seemed no sign of any live blue-clad soldiers anywhere in the house. The hallway glistened with blood and there were a few spots where bullets had broken through the exterior wall. An occasional shot could still be heard outside, but it sounded much more distant now. Marthe glanced at her watch. It was only two o'clock in the afternoon.

The front door burst open and she turned to see a bedraggled young man standing in the doorway with his eyes narrowed. Something in the distance caught the sunlight and she glimpsed many men on the lawn, their bayonets gleaming. Marthe marveled that the sun had the audacity to shine on such a day.

The soldier before her holstered his revolver and spoke in broken French. "*Qui d'autre est dans cette maison avec vous?*" He marched into the room, a band of his comrades behind him. Marthe assumed he was the captain, or *hauptmann*. The men outside sat down and lit cigarettes.

She felt no fear at the arrival of the disheveled German and his troops, only an unfamiliar numbness. She replied in German that her parents were downstairs.

"There are loopholes in the walls of this house," the captain stated. "Your father is a *franc-tireur.*"

Marthe recalled what Nicholas had said about the Hun's irrational fear of civilian sharpshooters. "My father is an old man and has never fired a shot at anyone, and especially not today. The French soldiers who were here were the ones shooting but they have gone."

"I have heard that story many times before. Yours is not the first village we have entered."

You mean demolished, Marthe corrected him silently.

"Fourteen of my men were shot, and the gunfire from this house was responsible. If those men who were with him have run, then your father alone will suffer."

"No, please, Hauptmann." But the captain was already on his way to the cellar. Two other burly men stalked after him. Marthe was about to pursue them when the first man appeared on the steps, dragging her mother. The other soldier, a sergeant judging by the gold braid on his uniform, followed with her father, who held his still smoldering pipe.

The soldiers shoved her parents against the wall of the hallway. Marthe bit her lip to keep herself from crying out in indignation, knowing that it couldn't possibly help the situation they were in. She cursed herself for her earlier curiosity and then cursed fate for the circumstances of having these enemy men standing in her kitchen, wishing to do harm to her family. If only they had left when Nicholas gave her that warning!

"Take that damned pipe out of your mouth," the sergeant commanded Father.

The soldier who had manhandled Mother grabbed it from him,

knocking the ash out on Father's boot before he pocketed the pipe with a chuckle.

"Old man, you are a *franc-tireur*," the captain declared.

Father shook his head while Mother sobbed quietly.

"Be merciful," Marthe begged the captain. "You have no proof."

"You dare to argue with me, fräulein? This place has been a hornet's nest of sharpshooters." He turned to one of the men. "Feldwebel, see that this house is burned down immediately."

The sergeant left out the door, motioning to some of the smoking men to follow him to the storage shelter in the back of the house, where the household oil was kept.

"Hauptmann—" Father began, but the captain silenced him by holding up his hand. "As for you, old man, you can bake in your own oven!" He dropped his arm. "Gefreiter, lock him in the cellar."

The corporal seized Father and kicked him down the steps, sending a load of spit after him.

"Filthy *franc-tireur*, he will get what he deserves," the corporal stated as he slammed the door to the cellar.

Mother collapsed and Marthe rushed to her. "You infernal butchers," she hissed at the men.

"Quiet, fräulein," the captain responded, taking out a packet of cigarettes. "Our job is to end this war quickly, and rid the countryside of any threats to our army, especially from civilians who take it upon themselves to shoot our soldiers."

The feldwebel and two other men entered the house carrying drums of oil. Mother gave a strangled cry as they marched into the living room and began to pour oil over the fine furniture.

The captain nodded approvingly before casting his eyes back to Marthe and her mother. "You women are free to go. I will grant you five minutes to collect any personal belongings, but you are not permitted to enter the cellar. Do not leave the village or there will be trouble." He lit his cigarette before dropping the match on the dry kitchen floor. It went out, but Marthe knew it was only a matter of time before he did the same in the living room where the oil had been spilled.

Marthe ran upstairs, casting her eyes helplessly around when she reached the landing. *What should she take?* She threw together a bundle of clothes for her and Mother, and, at the last second, took her father's best suit off the hanger. She shouldered the bundle and then went back downstairs, grabbing Mother's hand. They went outside to the street to gaze dazedly at their home where Father lay prisoner in the cellar.

The German soldiers walked quickly out of the house, carrying some of the Cnockaert's food. Gray smoke started coming from the living room. Soon reddish-orange flames rose up, the tongues easily destroying the barricaded windows. Marthe put her hands on the collar of her jacket and began to shed it.

"What are you doing?" Mother asked, her voice unnaturally shrill.

"Father's in there. I have to try to save him."

Mother tugged Marthe's jacket back over her shoulders. "No," was all she said. Marthe lowered her shoulders in defeat. As she stared at the conflagration, trying not to picture her poor father's body burning alive, she made a vow to herself that she wouldn't let the Germans get the best of her, no matter what other horrors they tried to commit.

Eventually Mother led Marthe away from the sight of their burning home and down the street to the Grand Place. The café adjacent to the square was filled with gray-uniformed men who sang obscene songs in coarse voices. A hiccupping private staggered in the direction of Marthe and Mother as the men in the café jeered at him. Marthe pulled her mother into the square to avoid the drunken soldier.

The abandoned Kermis booths had now become makeshift hospital beds for wounded Germans. The paving stones were soaked in blood and perspiring doctors rushed around, pausing to bend over men writhing in pain. In the corner was a crowd of soldiers in bloodied French uniforms. Marthe headed over, noticing another, smaller group of women and children she recognized as fellow villagers. She had just put her hand on a girl's forehead when a German barked at her to move on.

"Where should we go?" Mother asked in a small voice.

Marthe shook her head helplessly, catching her eye on Meneer Hoot's large home on the other side of the square. They walked quickly toward it, noting the absence of smoke in the vicinity. Marthe reached her fist out to knock when the door was swung open.

Marthe's heart rose at seeing the man behind the door. "Father!"

"Shh," he said, ushering them into the house.

"How on earth—" Marthe began when they were safely ensconced in the entryway of the Hoot home.

"I took apart the bricks from the air vent. Luckily the hauptmann and his men were watching the inferno on the other side of the house."

Mother hugged him tightly, looking for all the world like she would never let him go. Father brought them into the kitchen, where Meneer and Mevrouw Hoot greeted them. Several other neighbors, including Valerie, were also gathered in the kitchen, and they waited in a bewildered silence until darkness fell.

Meneer Hoot finally rose out of his chair. Taking the pipe from his mouth, he stated, "We have had no food this morning, and I'm sure it is the same for you all. Unfortunately," he swung his arms around, "the bloody Boches ransacked our house and there is nothing to eat here." He put the pipe in his mouth and gave it a puff before continuing, "I am going to get food somehow."

Mevrouw Hoot clutched his arm. "No, David, you cannot go out there."

Father also rose. "I will join you."

Meneer Hoot shook his head. "No, it is safer for me to go alone."

Mother gave a sigh of relief while Mevrouw Hoot appeared as though she would burst into tears. Meneer Hoot slipped a dark overcoat on and left through the back door.

An eternity seemed to pass as they sat in the dark kitchen, illuminated only by the sliver of moon that had replaced the sun. The silence was occasionally broken by Mevrouw Hoot's sobbing.

Marthe was nodding off when she heard the back door slam. Someone lit a candle, and Marthe saw the normally composed Meneer Hoot hold up a bulky object wrapped in blood-stained newspaper. His rumpled trousers were covered in burrs and his eyes were wild-eyed. He tossed the bulk and it landed on the kitchen table with a thud.

Mevrouw Hoot unwrapped the package to reveal a grayish sort of meat from an unfamiliar animal.

"I cut it from one of the Boches' dead horses," Meneer Hoot told them in a triumphant whisper. He lit a fire and put the horsemeat on a spit. Marthe wasn't sure if she could eat a dead horse but soon changed her mind as the room filled with the smell of cooking meat. Her stomach grumbled in anticipation.

Just then the kitchen window shattered. Marthe looked up to see a rifle butt nudging the curtain aside. The spikes of German helmets shone in the moonlight beyond the window. The Hoots' entire backyard teemed with them.

"We must get downstairs, now!" Meneer Hoot shouted. He grabbed his wife and rushed her into the hallway. Father did the same with Mother, and Marthe followed, stumbling down the steps to the Hoots' cellar.

To Marthe's amazement, she saw the large room was already nearly filled with other refugees—men, women, and children of all ages— with dirty, tear-stained faces.

The sound of many boots thundered overhead and it wasn't long before the Germans once again stood among them. One of them pointed his rifle at the opposite wall and shot off a clip, the bullets ricocheting around the room, followed by wild screaming. Somebody had been hit, a child Marthe guessed sorrowfully by the tone of its wail.

She wanted to go aid the poor creature, but she felt the sharp point of a bayonet at her chest. "Get upstairs," the bayonet wielder sneered.

The soldiers lined up the cellar's occupants outside, and separated out the men. Without allowing a word of parting, the Germans led the men of the village down the hill, and Marthe watched Father's lank form until she could no longer see him. The remaining soldiers shepherded the women and children back down into the Hoot's now blood-covered cellar.

~

Enjoyed the preview? Purchase *L'Agent Double: Spies and Martyrs in WWI now!* Thank you for your support!

Books in the Women Spies Series:
    355: The Women of Washington's Spy Ring
    Underground: Traitors and Spies in Lincoln's War
    L'Agent Double: Spies and Martyrs in the Great War

Now available: Books 1-3 in one ebook bundle !

Sign up for my mailing list at kitsergeant.com to be the first to learn of new releases!

ACKNOWLEDGMENTS

Thank you to my critique partners. Ute Carbone, Theresa Munroe, and Karen Cino for their comments and suggestions. Also thank you to my Advanced Review team, especially Jackie Cavalla for her eagle eyes, as well as Matthew Baylis for his excellent editing skills and Hannah Linder for the wonderful cover.

And as always, thanks to my loving family, especially Tommy, Belle, and Thompson, for their unconditional love and support.